THE MARCH

E. L. DOCTOROW

THE MARCH

A Novel

RANDOM HOUSE
LARGE PRINT

This is a work of historical fiction.
Apart from the well-known actual people,
events, and locales that figure in the narrative,
all names, characters, places, and incidents
are the products of the author's imagination
or are used fictitiously. Any resemblance
to current events or locales, or to living
persons, is entirely coincidental.

Copyright © 2005 by E. L. Doctorow

All rights reserved.
Published in the United States of America
by Random House Large Print
in association with Random House, New York.
Distributed by Random House, Inc., New York.

The Library of Congress has established a Cata-
loging-in-Publication record for this title.
ISBN-13: 978-0-375-72848-8
ISBN-10: 0-375-72848-1

www.randomlargeprint.com

FIRST LARGE PRINT EDITION

10 9 8 7 6 5 4 3 2 1

This Large Print edition published in accord
with the standards of the N.A.V.H.

HELEN

CONTENTS

—

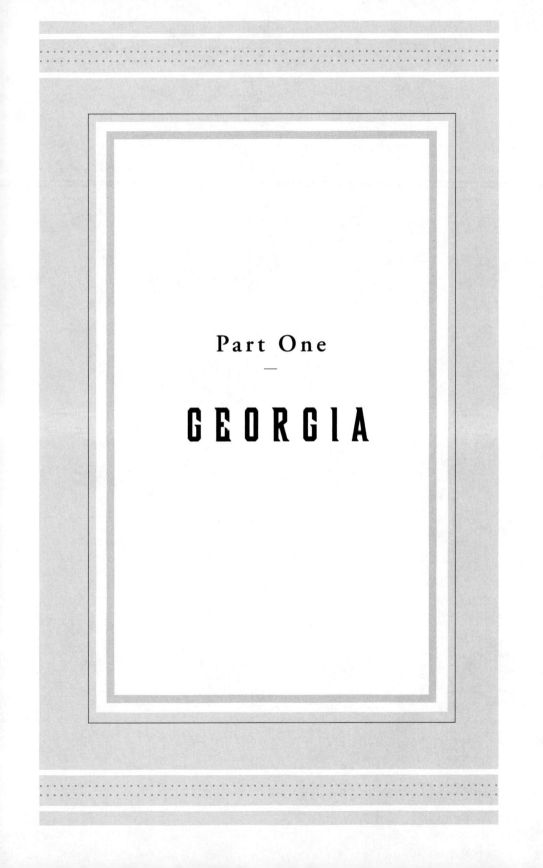

Part One

—

GEORGIA

I

AT FIVE IN THE MORNING SOMEONE BANGING on the door and shouting, her husband, John, leaping out of bed, grabbing his rifle, and Roscoe at the same time roused from the backhouse, his bare feet pounding: Mattie hurriedly pulled on her robe, her mind prepared for the alarm of war, but the heart stricken that it would finally have come, and down the stairs she flew to see through the open door in the lamplight, at the steps of the portico, the two horses, steam rising from their flanks, their heads lifting, their eyes wild, the driver a young darkie with rounded shoulders, showing stolid patience even in this, and the woman standing in her carriage no one but her aunt Letitia Pettibone of McDonough, her elderly face drawn in anguish, her hair a straggled mess, this woman of such fine grooming, this dowager who practically ruled the season in Atlanta standing up in the equipage like some hag of doom, which indeed she would prove to be. The carriage was piled with luggage and tied bundles, and as she stood some silver fell to the ground, knives and forks and a silver candelabra, catching in the clatter the few gleams of light from the torch that Roscoe held. Mattie, still tying her robe, ran down the steps thinking stupidly, as she later reflected, only of the embarrassment to this woman, whom to tell the truth she had respected more than loved, and picking up and pressing back upon her the heavy silver, as if this was not something Roscoe should be doing, nor her husband, John Jameson, neither.

Letitia would not come down from her carriage, there was no time, she said. She was a badly frightened woman with no concern for her horses, as John saw and quickly ordered buckets to be brought around, as the woman cried, Get out, get out, take what you can and leave, and seemed to be roused to anger as they only stood listening, with some of the field hands appearing now around the side of the house with the first light, as if drawn into existence by it. And I know him! she cried. He has dined in my home. He has lived among us. He burns where he has ridden to lunch, he fires the city in whose clubs he once gave toasts, oh yes, someone of the educated class, or so we thought, though I never was impressed! No, I was never impressed, he was too spidery, too weak in his conversation, and badly composed in his dress, careless of his appearance, but for all that I thought quite civilized in having so little gift to dissemble or pretend what he did not feel. And what a bitter gall is in my throat for what I believed was a domesticated man with a clear love for wife and children, who is no more than a savage with not a drop of mercy in his cold heart.

It was difficult to get the information from her, she ranted so. John did not try to, he began giving orders and ran back in the house. It was she, Mattie, who listened. Her aunt's hysteria, formulated oddly in terms of the drawing room, moved her to her own urgent attention. She had for the moment even forgotten her boys upstairs.

They are coming, Mattie, they are marching. It is an army of wild dogs led by this apostate, this hideous wretch, this devil who will drink your tea and bow before he takes everything from you.

And now, her message delivered, her aunt slumped back in her seat, and gave her order to be off. Where Letitia Pettibone was going Mattie could not get the answer. Nor how much time there was, in fact, before the scourge arrived at her own door. Not that she doubted the woman. She looked into the sky slowly lightening to its gray beginnings of the day. She heard nothing but the cock crowing and, as she turned, suddenly angry, the whisperings of the slaves gathered now at the corner of the house. And then with the team away, the carriage rolling down the gravel path, Mattie turned, lifting the hem of her robe, and mounted the steps only to see that horrible child Pearl, insolent as ever, standing, arms folded, against the pillar as if the plantation was her own.

JOHN JAMESON was not unprepared. As far back as September, when the news had come that Hood had pulled out and the Union armies had Atlanta, he sat Mattie down and told her what had to be done. The rugs were rolled, the art was taken down from the walls, her needlepoint chairs—whatever she valued, he told her—her English fabrics, the china, even her family Bible: it was all to be packed up and carted to Milledgeville and thence put on the train to Savannah, where John's cotton broker had agreed to store their things in his warehouse. Not my piano, she'd said, that will stay. It would rot in the dampness of that place. As you wish, John had said, having no feeling for music in any case.

Mattie was dismayed to see her home so depleted. Through the bare windows the sun shone, lighting up the floors as if her life were going backward and she was again a young bride in a new-built unfurnished manse and with a somewhat frightening husband twice her age. She wondered how John knew the war would touch them directly. In fact he didn't, but he was a man whose success gave him reason to suppose he was smarter than most people. He had a presence, with his voluminous chest and large head of wild white hair. Don't argue with me, Mattie. They lost twenty or thirty thousand men taking that city. There's hell to pay. You're a general, with a President who's a madman. Would you just sit there? So where? To Augusta? To Macon? And how will he ride, if not through these hills? And don't expect that poor excuse for a Rebel army to do anything about it. But if I'm wrong, and I pray God I am, what will I have lost, tell me?

Mattie was not allowed to disagree in such matters. She felt even more dismayed and said not a thing when, with the crops in, John arranged to sell away his dozen prime field hands. They were bound, all of them, to a dealer in Columbia, South Carolina. When the day came and they were put in shackles into the wagon, she had to run upstairs and cover her ears so as not to hear the families wailing down in the shacks. All John had said was No buck nigger of mine will wear a Federal uniform, I'll promise you that.

But for all his warning and preparation she could not believe the moment had come to leave Fieldstone. The fear made her legs weak. She could not imagine how to live except in her own home, with her own things, and the Georgian world arranged to provide her and her family what their station demanded. And though Aunt Letitia was gone, she had infected them with her panic. For all his foresight, John was running around this way and that, red-faced, shouting and giving orders. The boys, roused out of bed and still only half dressed, came down the stairs with their rifles and ran out through the back.

Mattie went to her bedroom and stood not knowing where to start. She heard herself whimpering. Somehow she dressed and grabbed whatever she could from her armoire and bath and threw everything into two portmanteaus. She heard a gunshot and, looking out the back window, saw one of the mules go down on its knees. Roscoe was leading another from the stable, while her older boy, John Junior, primed his rifle. It seemed only minutes later, with the sun barely on the treetops, that the carriages were waiting out front. Where were they to seat themselves? Both carriages were loaded with luggage and food hampers and sacks of sugar and flour. And now the morning breeze brought the smoke around from the stacks where John had set the fodder alight. And Mattie felt it was her own sooty life drifting away in the sky.

WHEN THE JAMESONS were gone, Pearl stood in the gravel path still holding her satchel. The Massah had only glanced at her before laying his whip on the horses. Roscoe, driving the second carriage, had come past her and, without looking, dropped at her feet something knotted in a handkerchief. She made no move to retrieve it. She waited in the peace and silence of their having gone. She felt the cool breeze on her legs. Then the air grew still and warm and, after a moment in which the earth seemed to draw its breath, the morning sun spread in a rush over the plantation.

Only then did she pick up what Roscoe had dropped. She knew immediately what it was through the cloth: the same two gold coins he had showed her once when she was little. His life savings. Dey real, Miss Porhl, he had said. You putem 'tween yer teeth you taste how real dey is. You see dem eagles? You git a passel of dese an you c'n fly lak de eagles high, high ober de eart—das what de eagles mean on dese monies.

Pearl felt the hot tears in her throat. She went around the big house, past the outbuildings and the smoking fodder and the dead mules, and past the slave quarters where they were busy singing and putting their things together, and down along the trail through the woods to where the Massah had given leave to lay out a graveyard.

There were by now six graves in this damp clearing, each marked by a wood shingle with the person's name scratched in. The older grave mounds, like her mother's, were covered with moss. Pearl squatted and read the name aloud: Nancy Wilkins. Mama, she said. I free. You tole me, Mah chile, my darlin Porhl, you will be free. So dey gone and I is. I free, I free like no one else in de whole worl but me. Das how free. Did Massah have on his face any look for his true-made chile? Uh-uh. Lak I hant his marigol eyes an high cheeks an more his likeness dan de runts what his wife ma'm made with the brudders one and two. I, with skin white as a cahnation flow'r.

Pearl fell forward to her knees and clasped her hands. Dear God Jesus, she whispered, make a place fer dis good woman beside you. An me, yore Porhl, teach me to be free.

—

SLOWLY, THE SLAVES, with their belongings
wrapped in bundles or carried in old carpetbags,
walked up to the main house and distributed
themselves out front under the cypresses. They
looked into the sky as if whatever it was they
were told was coming would be from that direction. They wore their Sunday clothes. There
were seven adults—two men, the elder Jake
Early and Jubal Samuels, who had but one eye,
and five women, including the old granny who
could not walk very well—and three small children. The children were unusually quiet. They
stayed close by and made bouquets of weeds or
pressed round stones and pebbles in the earth.

Jake Early did not have to counsel patience.
The fear they had all seen in the eyes of the fleeing Massah and Mistress told them that deliver-
ance had come. But the sky was cloudless, and
as the sun rose everyone settled down and some
even nodded off, which Jake Early regretted,
feeling that when the Union soldiers came they
should find black folk not at their ease but
smartly arrayed as a welcoming company of free
men and women.

He himself stood in the middle of the road
with his staff and did not move. He listened.
For the longest while there was nothing but the

mild stirring of the air, like a whispering in his ear or the rustle of woodland. But then he did hear something. Or did he? It wasn't exactly a sound, it was more like a sense of something transformed in his own expectation. And then, almost as if what he held was a divining rod, the staff in his hand pointed to the sky westerly. At this, all the others stood up and came away from the trees: what they saw in the distance was smoke spouting from different points in the landscape, first here, then there. But in the middle of all this was a change in the sky color itself that gradually clarified as an upward-streaming brown cloud risen from the earth, as if the world was turned upside down.

And, as they watched, the brown cloud took on a reddish cast. It moved forward, thin as a hatchet blade in front and then widening like the furrow from the plow. It was moving across the sky to the south of them. When the sound of this cloud reached them, it was like nothing they had ever heard in their lives. It was not fearsomely heaven-made, like thunder or lightning or howling wind, but something felt through their feet, a resonance, as if the earth was humming. Then, carried on a gust of wind, the sound became for moments a rhythmic tromp that relieved them as the human reason for the great cloud of dust. And then, at the edges of this sound of a trompled-upon earth, they heard the voices of living men shouting, finally. And the lowing of cattle. And the creaking of wheels. But they saw nothing. Involuntarily, they walked down toward the road but still saw nothing. The symphonious clamor was everywhere, filling the sky like the cloud of red dust that arrowed past them to the south and left the sky dim, it was the great processional of the Union armies, but of no more substance than an army of ghosts.

CLARKE HAD IN his foraging party a two-wagon train, a string of three extra mules, and twenty men mounted. General orders specified no fewer than fifty men. He was several miles off the column, and so, coming upon the plantation, he resolved to make quick work of it.

As they rode onto the grounds he immediately saw, and ignored, the slaves standing there. He shook his head. They had their old cracked drummers' cases and cotton sacks tied up with their things on the ground beside them. He posted his pickets and set the men to work. In the yard behind the outbuildings, the fodder stack was a smoking pile, flakes of black ash blowing off in the breeze. There were three mules with their heads blown all to hell. His orders were to respond to acts of defiance commensurately. Nor was he less determined when the men marched out of the dairy with sacks of sugar, cornmeal, flour, and rice on their shoulders. In the smokehouse, the shelves sagged with crocks of honey and sorghum. Hanging from hooks were the sides of bacon and cured hams the Massah didn't have time for the taking. And one of the bins was filled with a good two hundred pounds of sweet potatoes.

The men worked with a will. They slaughtered the sows, but somehow, from someone's incompetence, the chickens flew the coop. There commenced a holy racket—enough to bring the Negro children running. They laughed and giggled and leapt around happily as the soldiers dived for shrieking hens and struggled to tie squawking geese by their legs. Everyone is having a good time, Clarke thought. It's a happy war, this.

He was one of the few Easterners in the Army of the Tennessee. As such, he was not as easygoing and, to his mind, provincial, as most of the men. Even the junior officers were scarcely literate. Clarke, on duty at the White House, had carried a letter from the President to General Sherman's headquarters in Allatoona. He arrived in the midst of battle. Afterward, the General had simply told him to stay on. Presumably, a wire had been sent to Washington, but still, it was all very casual, and quite humiliating to Clarke that his service could be determined in such an offhand manner.

Now something else was troubling him. Where was the stock? He went around to the front of the manse and spoke to the tall gray-haired Negro who said his name was Jacob Early. Early led him beyond the slave quarters into a woods and past a little graveyard, and then downhill, where the ground became soggy. Behind a stand of bamboo was a swamp where the Massah had thought to drown his cows. Five cows were still standing in scum up to their withers, impassive, uncomplaining. A calf had succumbed and was half floating, only its rump out of the water. It took several of the men hauling on ropes to get them out of there. And it took time. They butchered the calf. The cows were brought to the wagons and tied to clop along behind.

The takings were a good day's work, but the hour was well past the meridian. The men now took it upon themselves to explore the house and see what they could find for their amusement. Impatient as he was to get moving, Clarke knew better than not to go along. This was an example of orders issued unspoken from the rank and file. It was not something for which he could give a coherent explanation in a letter home. In the great mass of men that was an army, strange currents of willfulness and self-expression flowed within the structure of military discipline. The best officers knew when to look aside. Even the generals issued orders for the sake of the record only. For Clarke, all of this was unsettling. He liked order. Discipline. He kept his own person neat and clean-shaven. His uniform brushed. His knapsack packed correctly. His writing paper secured in oilskin. But foraging was daring duty, and attracted free sprits. His bummers liked their independence. They liked to benefit themselves, and they could do so with impunity, because their takings were crucial to the success of an army designed by General Sherman to live, unencumbered, off the land.

A domed skylight lit the honey-colored hardwood floors of the front hall. A rather elegant curved staircase with trumpet balusters led to the second-floor landing. A window halfway up was stained glass. As a Bostonian, Clarke was continually shocked by the grandeur of these mansions risen up from the fields in the rural South. There was such wealth to be got from slave labor, it was no wonder these people were fighting to the death.

In the dining room, Privates Henry and Gullison had found in the sideboard a tray with cut-glass decanters of bourbon. They joined the others around the piano in the parlor, and when Clarke heard the first chords struck he considered what tactics he might employ to move his men out. The pianist was Private Toller. His plump hands ran over the keyboard with surprising authority. Clarke had not attributed to Pudge Toller any skills whatsoever beyond eating and drinking.

Sergeant Malone offered cigars from a humidor. The men sang:

Just before the battle, Mother
I was drinking mountain dew.
When I saw the Rebels marching,
To the rear I quickly flew!

Clarke accepted a cigar and let Sergeant Malone hold a match to it. Then he mounted the grand staircase, and in one room after another he gutted the upholstery and the mattresses and used the butt of his sword to smash the windows and the mirrors. All this was heard to effect, for in a few minutes several of the men were upstairs with him, taking axes to the furniture, tearing the curtains down, and soaking everything with kerosene.

There was an attic floor, and when Clarke went up there he was stunned to find a child—a girl, bare-legged—standing in front of a mirror and wrapping around her shoulders a beautiful red shawl with threads of gold as calmly as if the house weren't being destroyed under her. Only when she raised her eyes and stared back at him in the mirror did he realize she was a white Negro, white like white chocolate. Her chin lifted, she regarded him as if she were the mistress of the house. She couldn't have been more than twelve or thirteen, barefoot, in a plain frock to her knees, but caped by the shawl into a shockingly regal young woman. Before he could say anything, she darted past him and down the stairs. He caught a glimpse of smooth white calves, the shawl flying behind her.

THERE WAS NOTHING else for it but to let the darkies find places for themselves and their belongings in the wagons, sitting amid the plunder or up beside the teamsters. They had come up with a pony cart for the old granny. Clarke was made somber by their joy. They could not be usefully conscripted. They were a hindrance. There would be no food for them, and no shelter. About a thousand blacks were following the army now. They would have to be sent back, but where? We do not leave a new civil government behind us. We burn the country and go

on. They are as likely to be recaptured as not—
or worse, with guerrillas riding in our wake.

The men had thrown their torches through
the windows, and now the first smoke rose from
the roof and licks of fire began to flash out of
the siding. Clarke thought, We are burning the
darkies' livelihood. But everyone was merry,
chattering and laughing. Sergeant Malone wore
the Massah's top hat and cutaways over his uniform. They had found some old colonial militia
hats for the slave children. Private Toller had
donned a flouncy dress, and each and every man,
including the two old Negroes, was smoking a
cigar. Christ, what am I leading here? Clarke said
to no one in particular. He gave the signal to
move out. The whips cracked, the wheels rolled,
the horses were urged to a trot. Clarke, riding
on, saw from the corner of his eye the white nigger girl. She had stood apart, not having joined
the others aboard the train, and there she was
now, in her bare feet with her grand red-and-
gold shawl tied around her, watching them go.
Later, Clarke would wonder why he didn't think
it ridiculous that she required a special invitation. He swung his mount around, cantered
back, leaned over, and grabbed her hand. You'll
ride with me, missy, he said, and in a moment
she was behind him in the saddle, with her arms

wound tightly around his waist. He didn't understand his feelings at this moment, except that the heavy responsibilities of his command had suddenly lifted from him. He felt the warmth of her arms and their tight grip. She rested her cheek on his shoulder, and after a while her tears came through his tunic.

And in this way, in the late afternoon of a still warm November, they moved out, whites and blacks, toward the column of sunlit dust pushing southeast in the Georgia sky.

II

At first the boy, will, wouldn't eat anything. he had been brought in thin as a rail, no flesh on his bony face, a pair of eyes on a stick as he held on to the bars and stared across the corridor. Arly, in the cell opposite, said, You got to eat, boy. They're intending to kill you doesn't mean you have to do it for 'em.

Arly kept up his chatter, conceiving it as a tonic. Supposing it happens we are reprieved? he said. Won't do you no good if you're too weak to march out the door. Me, I will eat their maggoty salt pork and beans and politely thank Prison Sergeant Baumgartner down the corridor there for the fine vittles, though in fact he is as deaf as a doorpost. What was your affront, young Will? Say what?

Deserting, the boy whispered. I just needed to go home.

Now, I didn't know that is become a capital offense. So many of the boys are quitting this war I guess the C.S.A. needs to set an example. Me, I was found for sleeping on picket duty. But it could be worse. Raper John, who was up here until just last week? He got hisself hanged, but that was for affronting the civil law. You and I, as soldiers coming afoul of military legalisms of one sort or another, will only be put in front of a firing squad.

The boy didn't smile but went to his pallet and lay on his back with his hands behind his head.

But don't you worry, Arly continued, because General Hood, he likes to march a company in front and a company behind, and stand everyone out in their raiment with the flags flying and the drummers drumming and whoever is to be killed sitting on the edge of their coffins so as to drop right in them when the firing squad squeezes the trigger. But since every mother's son was dispatched to the redoubts in Atlanta, there isn't enough troops in Milledgeville to mount a fitting execution. There is caydets from the Military Institute up the street, but wiser heads must have thought as their being small boys it was no proper job for them. Are you for religion, young Will?

I never did countenance it.

Well, I look at it this way. God has raised his hand to give us respite. It could be he has something more in mind for us. With this time on our hands, we should try to figure what it is. Because he don't do pointless acts of charity.

THE WARMTH OF early November dropped off suddenly, and the two men wore their blankets around themselves day and night. The cell windows were without sashes. When it rained the walls turned damp, and then when it cleared and grew colder the stone coated up with ice. The bars were too cold to touch. The Milledgeville penitentiary was as moldy and cold as a crypt.

Sergeant Baumgartner, sir, you have that little fire pail at your feet, Arly shouted. Why don't you move it up here, along with yourself, so as we don't freeze to death before you shoot us.

The prison guard said nothing. He was a fat man who could be heard drawing every breath.

Sergeant Baumgartner, Arly shouted, I do prophesy the day is coming when you will unlock these doors and set us free.

Baumgartner sighed. I am too old to fight, he said, and so my service is to sit here with the likes of you. If that don't deserve a medal I surely don't know what does.

—

THEY WERE UP before dawn, as usual, jumping up and down to get the blood moving, and lifting their knees high in a stationary walk. Will had watched Arly do this, and it became his own regimen. But on this morning at first light there was something else besides the chill in their bones and the sight of their expelled breaths. They heard the agitation of raised voices and the rattle of carriage wheels. Will went to his window and stood on tiptoe to look through the bars. He had a view down the hill.

What is it? Arly said.

One carriage after another. Like a parade, Will said. They are whipping their horses.

By God, then, it's come!

Above all this clamor Will heard something from the sky—not so much a wind as like a pressure of the air, as if the sky was being pushed in on itself, and it had a murmur to it, or maybe a scent, like what you sometimes smelled after a bolt of lightning. He sensed the heaviness of a storm approaching, though as the sun rose the sky turned a cold blue and there was no approaching storm that he could see.

There was now a commotion inside the penitentiary. They were on the top floor and they could hear shouting on the floors below. The convicts had begun to rap their tin cups against the bars. Whistles blew.

Arly had a big grin on his face: You had best gather your belongings, young Will. We are leaving our dear home.

Sergeant Baumgartner, alarmed by the ruckus, had roused himself and stood facing the oaken door, his musket at the ready.

Oh now, Mr. Baumgartner, sir, Arly called, be careful with that thing lest you hurt yourself.

As if agreeing, the poor man sat back down to catch his breath.

They heard footsteps on the stone floors, the clanging of cell gates. For a moment, Will worried that in their little aerie, too far away from everything, they would be overlooked. But then came a pounding on the door. Baumgartner, startled out of his wits, had all he could do to find the right latchkey.

Arly and Will met outside their cells and shook hands for the first time in their friendship. They joined the procession of convicts down the iron flights and came out into the prison yard in the cold sun, amid maybe a hundred and fifty others also in their shoes without laces and their blankets wrapped around them.

They stood there shivering. This ain't the prettiest picture in the world, Arly said, looking around at the weathered bearded faces and the hunched shoulders in their blankets and the guards and gray stone walls and the packed, hard earth under their feet. But it's God-created, Will my man, it is his mysterious work, all right.

A lieutenant and four enlisted men with rifles escorted a senior officer in handsome gray attire into the yard. He was clearly important, with a plume in his hat and a maroon sash around his belly. They helped him to stand on a box. The convicts murmured among themselves when they saw his epaulets. He waited until they were quiet, then he cupped his hands around his mouth. I am Major General Nathaniel Wayne, he said. With the full agreement of Governor Brown, I am authorized to declare your sentence served, every damn one of you, providing you accept induction into the militia and swear to defend our great state of Georgia under my command!

Behind him, guards had brought out a table and a chair.

You have three minutes. I'll give you three minutes to raise your right hand to be sworn and signed up, with all the rights and privileges of this service. If not, back to your cage you go, and may you sit there until Hell freezes over.

Everyone was astir at that. Some of the convicts were for it, and some, who were close to parole, against. Arly shook his head. It was a debate as if by a legislature in session. A felon shouted, I'd rather rot here than have my balls shot off!

Everyone was talking at once. These men ain't no fools, Arly said. Atlanta is burned and the war is coming in this direction. If the militia is so shorthanded as to put guns in the hands of common criminals, you know what the odds are for any one of us coming out alive?

Piss poor? Will said.

That's about right. I don't know about you, Willie boy, said Arly, raising his hand high. But it's all the same to me how I am to be killed.

HOURS LATER, AS militiamen, they found themselves in the contingent deployed to defend a wooden trestle across the Oconee River about fifteen miles south of the city. They were hunkered down in the swamp mud under hanging moss on the east bank. They had muskets and cartridge boxes, hardtack in their pockets, shoes with no socks, and worn, blood-rusted tunics buttoned over their prison pajamas. They wore their blankets as capes. It was cold enough so that when they stepped in the mud their shoes left a broken imprint in a thin pane of ice.

The train that had brought them here sat on the tracks behind them, with a fieldpiece mounted on a flatbed. On the west bank, the boys from the Georgia Military Institute who had been given the honor of bearing the brunt of an attack were entrenched behind works improvised from the forest floor.

Arly said, I would have thought to make our stand back in the city to protect the women and children there, but seemingly they are of no military importance. He looked over at Will. Even chewing his hardtack the boy was given to a mournful facial expression.

You are not one to kick your heels up about anything, are you, young Will?

What does that mean?

It means we're out of those cells. It means you are a gloomy son of a bitch, for a man just removed from the valley of the shadow of death.

Sitting here under this tree, with ice water dripping down my neck and I'm waiting to be stomped on by an army? It's not much different that I can see.

Well, you might find some satisfaction at least in taking a Yank or two with you as you go. Besides which I been thinking. The paper we signed said our sentences were declared served. How can you have already served a death sentence? One way is by being executed and coming back from the dead.

I don't remember doing that.

I neither. The other way to have served a death sentence is by dispensation from God. I mean, no general can decide that. Not even the Governor has the authority to do that. The inspiration for it has to come from God, because it is such a serious supernatural matter, turning death into life. Do you agree?

I suppose.

And so why would God reprieve us from the firing squad if he only intended for us to die in the muck by a railroad trestle? And the answer is, He wouldn't. So try to put a proper face on things.

At that moment they caught their first sight of the enemy, a cluster of blue cavalry through the trees beyond the opposite bank, pulling up their reins as their horses reared in the cracking of gunfire. Will found himself relieved to see they were just human beings. But after that his mind was stripped of thought, as if thinking was an indulgence. He would later reflect that although a deserter he had proved himself no coward, but at the moment he was simply assistant to a musket. He knelt and fired and reloaded and fired again. He was no longer cold. It was as if the air had heated up from the friction of shot and shell. The cannonade behind them was deafening. As the fieldpiece fired, his ears felt the concussion, and everything for seconds afterward was silence. Treetops across the river fell away in the silence, convicts on his line clutched their chests and fell, in silence. Then, all at once, the racket returned. Beside him Arly was coolly blowing the smoke off his musket barrel. Shatterings of tree ice collapsed on their heads. The bullets whistled. They got them new repeating rifles, Arly shouted as he raised his musket for firing. One of the bluecoat riders reached the bank, where he took a ball, the force of which wrenched him half out of the saddle, overturning his steed, and they both fell into the river.

Will couldn't tell if he had shot anyone. All at once the bluecoats withdrew and faded back into the woods. An officer shouted, Hold your fire! And in the ear-ringing peace some of the men began to cheer. Arly said, The cheers'll stick in their throats come the next foray. Will was breathing as hard as if he had been running. The woods were hung with smoke.

And then the Yanks were back, but with no more tactics on their part than the first time. It was as if they had to learn that the trestle was defended. Will seemed to sink farther into the mud each time he fired. The rifles snapped and the shells exploded, and the pungency of the battle seeped into his nostrils. He heard the shouts and cries of boys, and the screams of horses, until the

Union force in its superior numbers withdrew once more. Now the silence seemed menacing. Smoke drifted through the trees.

That wasn't the full army we heard from, Arly said. That was the cavalry out to poke into places and see what happens. Now they will bring up the armaments, and while we are busy with that they will send around a flanking movement upstream, with their pontoons, and we will be overrun.

Will was sweating, his hair was damp. He made to brush the sweat from his forehead and his hand came away with blood. I'm shot, he muttered.

Well damn, so you are.

I'm bleeding.

You got a nice little furrow in your scalp, that's all, Arly said. As I told you, God has his eye out for us. But that don't mean he can't play around a little. Look.

To their right and left, the convict militia were rising from their positions, throwing their weapons down and turning tail. An officer shouted and fired his pistol into the air.

They have the right idea but the wrong direction, Arly said. Follow me. Before Will knew it, Arly had scrambled down the embankment onto the bridge. He turned and beckoned.

They ran across the bridge, which was on

fire in places. Men were throwing blankets down and stomping on the flames. Arly and Will donated their blankets and kept running. Over on the other side the terrain was less swampy, and in the mossy glades Milledgeville cadets lay dead or wounded behind their logs and mounds of earth. Boys without a scratch on them wandered in a daze. Some were crying. Cadet officers went among them, pushing them back to their positions, slapping them to make them obey.

Arly led Will forward past their lines. They stumbled on some Union dead along the railroad tracks. Also fallen mounts groaning like men, some struggling to raise their heads off the ground.

They heard voices echoing in the forest ahead, and the crashing of caissons through the brush. Hurry, Arly said. He began stripping the uniform off one of the dead Yankees.

What are you doing? Will said.

Find something that fits you, boy!

Will looked around and pulled the tunic off a fellow who, as he lay with legs splayed, seemed about his height. He'd had his eye shot out. Will tugged off the trousers and the boots. His stomach turned with the resistance he felt from the dead body. What are we doing? he muttered, availing himself of the rolled poncho and the hat in the grass, though there was blood on it.

Then he noticed that the dead man held one of the new repeating rifles, so he threw his weapon away, bent the clenched fingers back, and took up the rifle. Then the cartridge box and his tin drinking cup.

With their bundles in their arms they ran along in a crouch parallel to the river. They came upon a riderless horse, its nose in yellowing grass, and, leading it by the bridle, pressed on until they were a good mile downriver. There they halted and dressed themselves as Union soldiers.

Will shivered in the cold, damp uniform. His face was smeared with his own blood. He walked in circles, trying not to feel the tunic as it pressed across his back and dug under his arms. He tried to remember what the word was for the next thing down from a deserter.

Arly sat cross-legged, with his back against a tree. We are rich men with that horse, he said. Patting his tunic, he found a flask of bourbon in the pocket. He unscrewed the cap and took a swig. **Whooee!** Taste this, young Will. Go on. If you had any doubts God meant us to survive, just you have a taste of this.

III

EMILY THOMPSON SENT WILMA UPSTAIRS TO sit with him in his bedroom. I have the steam kettle on the hearth so the Judge will breathe easier, she said. If he wakes, call me.

Yes'm.

She'd done all she could—hidden coffee, sugar, cornmeal, lard, and two hams in the hope chest under two embroidered pillows and her mother's wedding gown. She'd left enough of the staples in the pantry so that they might not think she had hidden anything. Then she threw on a shawl and stood outside at the top of the steps, with the front door closed behind her. She was Georgia Supreme Court Justice Horace Thompson's daughter, and she posed herself with her hands clasped at her waist to indicate as much, though her heartbeat was tremulous as a rabbit's.

The street, the entire neighborhood, was unnaturally quiet as the first of them appeared. Mounted or on foot, they were not exactly shy, but they weren't arrogant, either. And they were so young. Few were the age of Foster Thompson when he fell. A lieutenant dismounted, opened the cast-iron gate, and came up the walk. Standing at the foot of the steps, he saluted her and said she had nothing to fear. General Sherman does not war against women and children, he said.

He was apparently to present these sentiments to whomever he saw still in Milledgeville. In front of each house, as he rode on, he left behind a standing guard. The private stationed out by the gate glanced back at her and smiled, and touched his forefinger to his hat brim. At that she nodded and withdrew, closing the door behind her and locking it.

By the time she got upstairs and looked out the library window, the street was filled with them. Drummer boys kept the beat, but the soldiers walked in a careless manner, chatting and laughing and looking anything but military. A deep misgiving arose in her. Sure enough, the guard so nobly assigned to her saw chums of his in the passing crowd and joined them without even looking back.

And then there were so many that they overflowed the street and spread themselves through the yards like a river widening its banks. White canvas wagons pulled by teams of mules appeared, the mule skinners with their sleeves rolled, and behind them caissons, the gun barrels catching the late-afternoon sun with sudden, sharp shards of light that suggested their propulsive murderousness. She pulled the curtains tight and stood with her back to the window and closed her eyes. She heard the lowing of cattle, shouting, the crack of whips. This was not an army, it was an infestation.

She was a churchgoer only from obligation, but she thought of praying. What should she pray for? What should she hope for? It could be no more of a practical hope than to see Foster Thompson ride up, waving his hat and with a broad smile on his face, to tell her he was no ghost.

I'm gone to fight tyranny, he had said, his last words to her as he kissed her cheek. He'd looked so gallantly cocksure in his uniform, the emblem of their way of life, their freedom, their honor.

Now, what she heard was men not in their marching but in their vacillating movement, as if they were more personally in an eddying awareness of where they were. A bugle sounded at some distance. She heard individual voices, as of visitors at the gate. She could not help herself, and looked out again. Everywhere, they were setting themselves out to make camp. In the yards, in the town square at the end of the street. And now someone pounded at the door. She went to the landing. Wilma had come out of the Judge's room, fear in her eyes. The Judge had awakened. What! What is happening? he called in his weak voice. Nothing, Father, nothing at all! And then, going downstairs, softly, angrily, she said behind her to Wilma, I don't need you to worry about—go back in there as you were told.

She unlocked the front door and stepped back as a swarm of bluecoats shouldered past her and made the house their own.

SHE WOULD NOT sleep that night. She and Wilma were remanded to the Judge's bedroom. It was all the residence allotted to her. She lay curled on the sofa. Places in the city were on fire. She saw this recorded in the looming and flickering light on the ceiling. She supposed she was fortunate that her home was the chosen bivouac for staff officers. They had advised her in a gentlemanly way to go upstairs and stay there, so that she could hope that when they left—and God let it be soon—the house would not have suffered from their presence. But she heard laughter and a coming and going all through the evening. The pitcher on the end table beside her head shook as their boots trod the floor below. There was traffic to the outbuildings. Tobacco smoke drifted under the door.

The oppressive maleness of them all unnerved her. She realized this was a familiar feeling—a revulsion for their gender, its animality, all the more offensive because they were so unconscious of it. They existed and left the sensibility of it to her. She had felt this way even when as a young girl her brother Foster brought his friends home. Even Foster, dear Foster, would somehow be shouldering her off her own life. He seemed to take up more room than he had to. His appetites were prominent, all of their appetites. It was like living with jungle creatures, the look in their eyes as they professed their gentlemanly courtesies. And it was they who made war. Women did not make war— they did not gallop off waving their swords and screaming about honor and freedom.

But she had not believed this war would destroy the life she had known and consign her to a permanent state of dereliction until, rising suddenly from the sofa, she was convinced of it. What had frightened her? It was now perhaps two or three in the morning. The hearth fire was out, there was no movement in the downstairs. Only moonlight lit the chilled room. She went over to her father's bedside. He lay quiet on his back. But his jaw was dropped and both hands were clenched into fists above his coverlet. She touched his cheek and it was dry and cold to the touch.

Wilma, Wilma, she whispered insanely, as if not wanting to disturb her father. The girl was asleep on the floor at the foot of the bed. Emily shook her. Wake up, wake up!

Emily ran down the stairs and out of the house into a city she did not recognize. Fly tents in every yard, on every green, were like a crop of teeth sprung up from the earth. The embers of cooking fires cast their red glow into the moonlight. Horses were tethered to lampposts. She heard a strange music, and coming into the Capitol Square saw there a dance going on by the light of torches. It was military bandsmen, their uniform coats unbuttoned, who supplied the merry tune, from a clarinet, a tuba, a fife. And it was slave women and children holding hands and dancing in a circle. A Yankee flag flew from the dome of the capitol. Confederate notes of tender blew in swirls and scuttled along the ground like autumn leaves. Books flew out the windows of the Georgia state library to soldiers catching them below. She heard the screams of a woman coming from the darkness at the end of an alley.

Dr. Stephens's house was dark. She rattled the doorknob, peered in the windows. She ran to the back. The stable was empty. There was no more Dr. Stephens. There was no more Milledgeville. She didn't know what to do. She ran. She saw bright light and ran toward it. Behind one of the stately city mansions, the yard was lit with torches. A line of white canvased wagons stood there, the mules with their muzzles in feedbags. She heard groans and slipped between two wagons to their rear. Nurses had lifted out a soldier on a pallet. The soldier raised himself on one elbow and grinned at her. His tunic was soaked in blood.

On the ground outside the open barn doors was something from which she couldn't in time avert her eyes. She didn't want to believe she was looking at a slimed heap of severed human arms and legs.

The light inside was as bright with many lanterns as if the barn were on fire. An army surgeon stood beside a table, his team of nurses around him. He turned to look at her, frowned, and muttered something. At this fearful moment he was recorded indelibly in Emily's mind. He was a short, neatly put-together man who seemed inviolate in the carnage around him. He wore a rubber apron over his tunic. A bloodied saw was in his hand. He had thick eyebrows, and the eyes that had peered from under them were a pale blue. It seemed to her they were filled with an anguish that reflected her own. A nurse ran toward her. You shouldn't be here, miss, he said, turning her to the door. We must have a doctor, Emily said. My father is Judge Thompson, and something is terribly wrong.

Saying this, she gasped. What was wrong, she knew, was that her father was dead.

WREDE SARTORIUS, AS a colonel, was the superior of the young officers who'd billeted themselves in the Thompson home. He ordered them out.

The old man had indeed given up the ghost. It was almost odd to see death in an old person. The face on the pillow stared blindly upward, as if the journey to Heaven had begun. With the eyes closed, the nose seemed to grow.

He could supply a coffin, Wrede told Miss Thompson. He smiled sadly. We have every-thing. We meet every need.

Emily was terribly moved by the surgeon's kindness. At the same time, it confirmed her ex-pectation of what was due her.

When Wilma was sent to summon Father

McKee, she found him almost too stunned to come back with her. St. Thomas had been vandalized, he reported to Emily. They tore out the pews for their campfires. They befouled the altar. Do they call themselves Christians who did this? the Father said to Emily. And she, the bereft, found herself comforting him.

By morning troops were on the march, moving through the town in endless procession. The penitentiary had been set afire. Muffled explosions came from the city arsenal. Milledgeville was devastated—windows broken, gardens stomped on, stores stripped of their goods.

Wrede urged an immediate burial. He supplied a mounted guard. And so a single carriage bore the casket through the traffic and up the hill to the cemetery, where the eminent Judge Thompson was laid to rest. Emily wept at the tragically brief obsequies. Her father should have been lying in state. He was a great man, she told Wrede, on the way home. She dabbed the corners of her eyes with her handkerchief. His opinions made legal history. If you all were not here the church bells would be tolling all over Georgia, and everyone in town would be lining up to pay their respects. And, yes, the Negroes too, because he was a kind man, and a generous man.

Wrede said nothing. He felt Emily Thomp-

son had known all along that her father was
going to die, another casualty of war. She had not
seen in another part of the cemetery that Union
gravediggers were busy interring those wounded
at the Oconee River whom the medical service
had not been able to save. She seemed not aware,
either, of the extended attention he was paying to
her. Wrede was a naturalized citizen, a German.
His courtliness was European. He had recognized
a kind of backwoods aristocracy in the deportment of this young woman. She was a trim little
thing, with a bosom bound tightly to her and a
prim mouth that he was sure had never been
kissed. Yet there was a fire in her eyes, a spirit not
gutted by her sorrow.

The army was on the march out of Milledgeville. Wrede took his leave. He identified his
brigade and suggested that if it happened to pass
by the house he would stop in again for a moment. He expressed his condolences and closed
the door behind him.

THE NORTH AND south wings of Sherman's army
had converged at Milledgeville. All day, troops
following those who had bivouacked in the city
moved through it and kept going. Emily stood
at the window. Endless files of them, and caissons, commissary wagon trains, ambulances,

herds of cattle. Drummer boys beating the pace with each company. She tried to make out the numbers on the regimental pennants.

Her street was lined with young shade trees. Troops and wagons made detours away through the gardens and alleys while black pioneers with two-man saws felled the trees. Other black men stripped off the branches, and still others loaded trunks and limbs aboard drays pulled by teams of six and eight mules. It was all very efficient, a matter seemingly of a few moments in which to flatten the city. Emily had loved this concourse of saplings, and stood now too stunned to feel anything except that the light in her house had changed. She heard a regimental band at some distance. It seemed to be celebrating her sorrow. She decided not to wait anymore for the reappearance of the surgeon with the impeccable manners and the strange name: Wrede Sartorius.

Wilma had removed the bedding in the Judge's room. She had opened the windows to the cold sun and swept, and dusted, and packed the Judge's medicines in a box. Only when she had put his slippers and shawl in his closet, among his suits and cutaways and his stovepipe hat, did she begin to weep. Downstairs she was like a cyclone, sweeping away the dirt and tobacco ash and general mess left by the army men. Wilma worked with a servant's possessiveness. When Emily Thompson thought to turn around, the house was as it should have been but for a few scars and broken chair legs.

The two women draped black bunting from the second-floor windows. Emily, her hair loosened and fallen about her face, sat dry-eyed in the kitchen, staring at nothing, while Wilma made tea. The tea was cold and still in her cup when Emily became aware that Wilma stood beside her, dressed for travel and with a carpetbag in her hand. Emily studied the brown face, feeling that she had never seen it before. Familiar were the dark eyes, and the slightly Oriental cornering of them. But now they stared back. The broad rounded forehead and the firm mouth and high cheekbones suggested a girl no longer but a fine-looking woman. There was nothing deferential about her. I'll be going now, Miss Emily, Wilma said. The two had grown up together, Wilma perhaps a year or two the younger. Where will you be going? Emily asked. With everyone, Wilma said. Emily ran after her. Wait, wait! she called. Wilma, please wait. Emily raced upstairs to the bedroom, where sat her mother's hope chest. She removed the burlap sack of foodstuffs she had hidden, and after withdrawing a few items for herself she retied the sack and brought it down. Please take this. Wilma shook her head. Take it, it is my last instruction to you, Emily said. For God's sake take it!

By now the last of the troops were straggling by, and behind them the parade of black folks who had chosen to follow the army. There were hundreds—men, women, and children—walking, riding in wagons, some limping along, and the sound of them was different from the sound of army men. No drumbeats here, no rumble of caissons, no military blare. It was a rhythmless festive sound that came up from them, a celebratory chatter almost like birds in a tree, from which laughter emerged or bits of song. It was the sound of a collective excitement, as if these people were on some sort of holiday and on their way to a church meeting or a picnic. Children, with their high, piping voices, were skipping along or pretending to be soldiers, or running ahead and then running back. As Emily stood at the door and watched, Wilma slipped into the crowd and, looking over her shoulder, smiled and gave a shy little wave, and was gone.

AND THEN THE town of Milledgeville, empty and quiet, sat in its dishevelment, gusts of wind flying paper and brush against the sides of buildings and the leavings of coal fires scuttering in the street. The air was acrid. When the war began, Emily had not understood what war meant. It meant the death of everyone in her family. It meant the death of the Thompsons. She felt hollowed out, as if there was nothing left of her to mourn them. The power of war and what it had done seemed to wipe away her past until this moment. She wandered through the house she had lived in all her life. One room after another seemed to confront her. She stood in the door of her father's bedroom. The historic vigorous father, the way he looked and acted, his dignity, the respect he commanded, the handsome ruddy face and the full head of thick white hair, all devolved in her mind to the pathetic sepulchral end of the man, frail and whining, and then frozen dead with his clenched fists in the air. She could not forget his face in death. She thought of him now in his coffin underground, what were called the remains. And her mother's remains. And her brother Foster's remains buried somewhere in Tennessee. She shivered and pulled her shawl about her. How awful. How hideously awful. And was she remains as well? Was this house her tomb?

In the wake of the Union armies, a squad of General Hood's cavalry now appeared. People came out in the street to greet them. The guerrillas had captured three Union stragglers, including a boy drummer. The prisoners, lassoed like cattle with their hands behind their backs, were jeered at as they stumbled along. Emily watched from the window as her neighbors, having hidden themselves like mice, came out now to cheer the troops as heroes. And so here was another parade, a scraggly one, a few citizens following a ragtag bunch on horse, looking proud and victorious in their intention to execute two men and a boy. This was the secessionist answer. She was appalled.

Emily packed some things in a portmanteau, and her small store of food in another. Putting on her winter coat, and taking with her a blanket against the cold, she went to the stable and hitched the Judge's dobbin to the buggy. It was another gift of the army surgeon Wrede Sartorius, who had seen to it that their horse was not trotted away for the Union. She did not even look back as she rode out of town. She flicked the reins. The wind blew her tears dry. She knew the direction the armies had taken. You just followed the roads that were beaten down, and before long you would hear a sound not natural to the countryside. And then you would smell them.

IV

THEY HAD TAKEN THE TROUBLE TO APPLY MUD to their unit insignia. But they needn't have. It was dark when they found themselves back in the city. Milledgeville was a big party. The Governor's Mansion was filled with Union officers. Will saw them through the windows. Officers in the legislature, too—you could hear them shouting and singing. Oh yes, there had to be considerable drinking and putting their feet up on desks. Stiff and sweating and cold at the same time in his corporal's uniform, Will worried that he would be recognized by a prison official, or one of the penitentiary guards. He imagined himself protesting—hadn't he been pardoned? But what was he thinking—there were no guards. There were no prison officials. Everyone from the Governor on down was gone. He was so tired and hungry that he wasn't thinking straight.

It was Arly's turn to be in the saddle, Will walking alongside.

Will, boy, you are too quiet. I expect whatever is in your mind right now ain't helping our cause any.

Well, it's cautionary hard being a damn turncoat.

Is that what you are? You might put a better face on things. As a loyal son of the South behind enemy lines, frinstance, you might be a spy.

Whatever I am maybe I don't even know anymore, standing in for a dead man.

Well, you know you're hungry and that's a start. Here, down this street looks about right. You smell that? Come on.

He had seen a campfire in the front yard of a house where they had piled up the picket fence for a nice blaze. An old man and his woman were standing on their porch. Troopers marched past them going in, and others were coming out with their arms full. The woman cursed while the man patted her hand.

Just march right in like that, Arly said from the side of his mouth. Like you belong.

And what about dobbin here?

We'll tend to her feed later. Right now we want a good, safe tether so someone don't steal her away.

At that, Arly rode the horse up the porch

steps and through the front door into the entry hall and hitched her to the newel post at the foot of the stairs. This was just the thing to get the Union boys laughing and the old woman shrieking.

And so Arly and Will were in the game, rummaging in the pantry and then the root cellar, where they found sacks of sweet potatoes. Will was wary that they wouldn't have a Christian welcome from this victory party of revelers all from the same company, but when he and Arly came out and dumped their contribution by the fire that was entry enough, given that most of the men were half drunk anyways.

Tears came to Will's eyes. There were chickens on spits and potatoes on the coals and pans frying with bacon and cabbages. There were jars of put-up summer fruits and vegetables, and loaves of real bread. A sergeant poured generously from his bottle into Will's tin cup. Will sat down cross-legged in the grass and set about the best meal he had had since leaving home. His mouth full, his chin dripping with grease, he considered the possibility that all men are brothers.

Later, as the moon came up, Arly smoked a cigar, and recounted with some modesty his heroism at the Oconee River, for which he was attended with respect by his listeners, though his lieutenant's cockade might have had something to do with it.

But Arly didn't just talk, he listened, too. After he and Will said good night and they had found fodder and a stall for the horse in a barn behind an abandoned house, and they were getting comfortable in the house, up on the second floor, in a sitting room, Arly told Will that the army was moving out at dawn. The cavalry will feint to Augusta, but it is to Savannah the army will go, he said.

Does Gen'ral Sherman know that? Maybe you ought to tell him.

Son, this general he's almost too smart to be a general, and if there is a force waiting in Augusta, as is the impression of everone I talked to, why go there? Besides which there is a Union navy, as I understan it, and in those ships waiting off Savannah, as they are sure to, will be the mail and ordnance and new shoes and soldier's pay we ain't had since Hector was a pup.

We? We ain't had? I thought we was Reb spies.

Well, so what? Their money is good. In fact a damn sight better than the paper Jeff Davis thrown at us.

They broke up some chairs and desk drawers and made a nice, warm fire in the hearth.

Arly took the sofa and Will the floor, with the cushion from an upholstered chair for a pillow. For blankets they sliced up some rugs with their bayonets.

Outside, some Union men were singing:

The years creep slowly by, Lorena,
The snow is on the grass again;
The sun's low down the sky, Lorena,
The frost gleams where the flowers have
    been . . .

There was still occasional shouting in the streets as indication the troops were settling in for the night. Will thought what a strange thing it was, an army, making its camp always the same whether in some woods by a stream or amidst homes and public buildings. The rifles are stacked, the pickets are sent out, and the bugler plays taps no matter if you are in a forest grove or a metropolis of civilization.

No need to get up with them at dawn, Arly said. We'll wait for the commissary wagons and the ambulances and such. That'll be a while. You want to hang back where the army is comprised of doctors and cooks and clerks who know no more of soldiering than ladies in a tea room. They won't take roll calls back there.

—

WILL STARTED AWAKE long after he had heard reveille. He roused himself up on his elbows to listen for the rattle of the wagon trains or the brigade drums as the long end of the Twentieth Corps trailed after the regiments. He heard nothing. The sun shone all over the floor. It was like high noon in this place. He crawled to the window. The street was empty.

The army was gone.

He woke Arly, and moments later they were rushing down the stairs and out the back door to the barn.

Someone was leading their horse by the bridle. A Johnny Reb in his grays. Will's heart leapt up. He might in that instant of his confusion have hailed the boy. But Arly rushed to the attack. As the two of them went down, the Reb didn't let go of the bridle and the horse, twisted down by the head, planted her forelegs to keep from going over. But she was screaming.

Will slowly realized there was more of a racket than there should be if Hood's men were in town on the heels of the Union army. He looked down at his uniform.

Now the Reb had let go of dobbin so as to have both hands available for fighting. He was a heavier boy than Arly, if not as fit, and so they went rolling over each other, rolling, punching, and grunting, as the dust rose. Will! Arly shouted. Will! He meant the horse, who nearly knocked Will over as she reared and cantered away around the side of the house to the street.

Will, off in pursuit, noticed the bed of chrysanthemums planted along the side of the house, a society of modest yellow and white blooms crowned with ash and shuddering in the breeze. He thought what blessedness there was in the immobility and unthinkingness of plant life, that there might be something to say for it, as in the street now, beyond the front yard, two Rebel cavalry were a-gallop after the free running creature and another three horsemen had turned their mounts toward him, one with his sword drawn, another with his pistol cocked, and a third with a big smile and a couple of front teeth missing on his unshaven face.

Will stopped in his tracks. He held out his arms in what he might have thought of as a welcoming recognition, a kind of embrace in the air, but which these guerrillas preferred to take as surrender. They laughed, and the wielder of the pistol joyfully shot a ball into the ground at his feet.

People came into the street from the homes where they had been hiding. They were ecstatic to see their own troops arrived to save them. Will stood immobilized, his gesture frozen. The wind pasted a newspaper sheet to his legs. Ash settled in his open mouth. Up in the blue sky, the smoke from the smoldering ruins of the penitentiary scurried off like the departing army that he had been depending on. One of the riders trotted past him back to the barn. Will prayed that Arly would have lost his encounter. For if he had not, if he'd killed the Reb, then they would be executed, after all, here in Milledgeville, though perhaps with less ceremony than he'd expected as a deserter. But he didn't want Arly to have perished, either, Arly being the flickering if not entirely gutted hope Will had for his unhappy life other than his wish, in this latest wretched moment of his nineteen years, to have it end entirely.

A FEW MINUTES later Will, Arly, and some straggling drummer boy the Rebs had found were being marched through the street with their arms roped to their bodies. A growing crowd followed them. Every once in a while one of the horse soldiers looked down from his saddle and spit. Someone threw a rock, and it hit the drummer boy in the back. The boy stumbled along, tears streaming down his face.

Arly said something and had to repeat it, because Will couldn't understand the words. Arly's cheek was puffed out, an eye was half closed, his lower lip was swollen, and he'd lost a few teeth. Also, he was limping because, as he had gotten up off his opponent with his hands raised, he'd received a kick in the ribs. Your own kind, is what Will made out.

My own kind? Is that what you're saying?

Arly nodded. He gestured with his head to people running alongside, laughing and jeering. Folks you come fum, he said.

V

CLARKE KNEW THAT HIS ATTENTIONS TO PEARL were a source of cynical amusement to the men. Pearl wasn't the first freed black girl to get special treatment. The lighter-colored, especially, were being picked up all along the march and ensconced in the wagons. They were given choice edibles and clothes pillaged from the plantations. This was a different situation entirely, but he knew better than to try to explain. He couldn't even make sense of it himself. He was terribly moved by this child in a way that took him completely by surprise. He wanted to do things for her. He wanted to take care of her. Yet, at the same time, he knew he was attracted inappropriately. He noticed the way she carried herself, with a kind of head-high grace that was unlearned and entirely natural. He found himself comparing her to women of his generation back in Boston. Everything they did and said

was learned comportment. They were unorigi-
nal girls, argued by propriety out of whatever
genius they might have had. They practiced the
arts as inducements to marriage.

He thought that perhaps Pearl had some
royal African blood, or else how would that
angry intelligence, so commanding, have come
to her. She missed nothing with those cat-pale
eyes of hers. She was suspicious of him. She
was critical of the men. She thought they were
filthy and told him so: You white mens smell
like de cow barn back at Massah's. No worse,
dat how bad.

That, he said.

That how bad, she said. Lord! Even stinky
brudders one an two back home more tolable
dan dis.

Than this, he said.

Than this. Dese mens doan never wash off
demselves in no netherpart, jus shit in de groun
and move on like dumb animal do.

Animals. Dumb animals, he said.

Thas right. An de gun grease gone sour in
dere hair, and God know what else grown fum
dere hide and dere feet dat stink so. **Phewy!**
Dint dey hab mothers to teach'm?

Didn't, he said.

I 'spect not.

Pearl bathed herself with hard soap and a

basin of cold water every evening in Clarke's tent while he stood guard outside. Then she went to sleep in a fly tent he'd put up next to his own. He wanted the men to know that she was under his protection but that his behavior was honorable. After the first few days of snickering and talking among themselves, they seemed to understand and accept the situation at face value. They, too, became protective. It was Sergeant Malone who came up with a drummer-boy uniform for her. At first she was pleased. They were camped in a pine grove at the time, and she came out of her tent, having wriggled into the tunic and trousers, and stood for all of them to admire her, though everything was just a mite too big. There was a hat too, and silver buttons that she rubbed to a shine. But then she grew thoughtful.

I ain't never played no drum, she said.

Nothing to it, Malone said. We'll show you how.

Sompun wrong bein a white drum boy, she said to Clarke.

What?

I too pretty fer a drum boy. I not white, neither, if white I be.

Clarke said, By and by, Pearl, the black folks will have to go back. Those are the standing orders of General Sherman. You don't want to go back, do you?

You burned de house, took de vittles. Back to what?

Exactly. When the war is won, the authorities will work out the legalities for freed slaves to own their own land. But now if they trail along they are too many mouths to feed. The young men we can enlist, but the women and children and old men, they will fall by the wayside and then where will they be? So it's best this way.

Well, a gul chile not much good fer shootin neither.

Clarke was astonished at the aplomb with which he was subverting orders. You can beat the drum when we're marching, he said. And you can ride in the wagons when we're foraging.

Pearl was not persuaded. She began to feel that staying with Jake Early and the others was what she should do. The prospect was unsettling, and she didn't know why she felt that way. They had never been kind to her, but there was something wrong in their being sent back while she went on. She enjoyed having a fuss made over her. She had never had that—it came of being free—but she thought now of the plantation, where she loved the fields and the stands of trees. She knew every inch of that place she had lived on all her life. She knew every stream, every rock, every shrub. But, most of all, she worried that if she was not there her mother's grave would be forgotten, with nobody to care about it or tend to it. The slave quarters were still standing. And if she was free, wasn't she free to go back if that's what she wanted? To starve, if she wanted to? To be John Jameson's slave chile again, if she wanted to?

In this state of mind Pearl sat down near the fire in her new uniform and joined the men for supper. She was given a tin plate with a roasted chicken leg and sweet potatoes and corn bread with sorghum. This in itself might have been persuasive, but at that moment Jake Early appeared out of the darkness along with Jubal Samuels, he of the one eye. They were under escort, two privates with rifles at the ready.

Sergeant Malone said, Jesus! What's this?

Should be plain we ain't Johnnies, Jubal Samuels said.

We been lookin fer dat chile, Jake Early said, pointing at Pearl.

Here she be, Pearl said.

Ifn you know yo Bible, Miss Porhl, you 'member 'bout dat Jez'bel. You bes cum wiv us, Jake Early said.

I ain't no Jez'bel.

I see you wiv dese soljer. You got a white pap like to put you sinnin in a white skin. You bes come wiv yo gibn folks now, lest you be some Jez'bel fer de army like your mam been to der Mass' Jameson.

Pearl put her plate down and got to her feet. My mama she a po slave lak you, Jacob Early. But wiv a warm, sweet soul, not de cold ice you got in yo heart. You never take no heed of Porhl, you Jacob, nor you, Jubal Samuels—no, non of youn. All dat time only dat Roscoe a frien to me. Lak he my pap. Gib me from de kitchen when I hongry. Watch out fer me. But you ain never be gibn folks to Porhl, no sir, not den and not now.

Clarke stood and addressed the two privates. Get these men back where they belong, he said.

Nobody doan never have touch Porhl! When I little, de brudder try. Oh yeah. I raise up dis bony knee hard in his what he got dere, and dat were dat and nobody since! You hear dis gul, Mr. free man Jacob Early? And nobody since! An I ain't no Jez'bel, she screamed.

In this way was Pearl's decision made, and by the time they were on the march through Milledgeville she was drummer for Clarke's company. She just hit the drum once every other step and they kept the pace, some with smiles on their faces. She looked straight ahead and kept her shoulders squared against the shoulder straps, but she could tell that white folks watched from the windows. And none of them knew she wasn't but the drummer boy they saw.

EAST OF MILLEDGEVILLE the weather changed and the terrain grew swampy. A hard rain spattered on the palmettos and snapped in the muck. Pioneers had corduroyed the road with fence rails and saplings. Clarke, in the vanguard with his foragers, was the first to lead his wagons across the pontoon bridge at the Oconee. Thereafter the land rose and hardened, the rain slacked off, and they left the army behind as they rode toward Sandersonville. Clarke wanted to pick the town clean and wait there. He had thirty men mounted, six wagons, and as many pack mules.

Clarke knew from maps that the country played out east of Sandersonville and from then on, as far as Savannah, it would be progressively poorer takings, with the lowlands good only for growing rice. And how in God's name would the army hull rice? His foraging detail had got much praise from the regiment, and he'd been running a kind of competition with Lieutenant Henley's squad.

At a bend in the road a quarter mile west of the town, he called a halt. Sergeant Malone rode up to confer. This was more formidable than a plantation. They could see over the treetops a church steeple and the roof of a public building, probably a courthouse.

Evening was coming on. Clarke smelled no chimney smoke and saw no lights.

Sergeant, take two men with you. On foot and off the road. Tell me what's going on there.

The patrol moved off, and Clarke waited. Behind him, softly in the dusk, the leather traces creaked, the animals breathed and snorted. Clarke rode back to the wagons and found Pearl the last in line, sitting up beside the driver. Her eyes gleamed out at him from the darkness, as if they had drunk up what light there was, invisible to him but imperially available to her.

He rode ahead to meet the patrol. Malone reported that the town was quiet, the streets empty, but there were lights in the houses. He did not look at Clarke as he spoke but at the ground, which meant, in Clarke's interpretation, that he, Clarke, was acting as was only expected of a prissy New England Brahmin.

If that's what Malone thought, so would the others. A fog was rolling in. Clarke ordered the men to unsheathe their rifles, and the company rode on into Sandersonville.

WHEN THE FIRING started, the driver of the last wagon was in a crossroads at the town's edge, so that, shouting and cursing, he was able to turn the panicked team around. Pearl left the box and clambered into the wagon and looked out the rear. Nobody was following. She heard screams. She saw men falling off their horses in the instant flashes of musket fire. The driver was whipping the mules and the wagon was rolling. Pearl jumped, landing on her hands and knees. She limped into the brush and cowered there.

Moments later two riderless horses galloped past. A minute later three or four of the Union men, and then two of them on one horse. She couldn't count how many after that. She prayed that the Lieutenant would not leave her.

Clarke couldn't have retreated even if he'd thought of it. He was not thinking, just trying to rein in his panicked rearing mount with one hand while, with his Enfield musketoon wedged in the crook of his arm, firing at every looming shape and shadow. The Rebs had ridden out of the side streets and come together as one charging line. In an instant, it seemed, they were riding past on both flanks. Sergeant Malone, standing in his stirrups to aim, was hacked by a passing sword. He looked at Clarke, his neck bleeding like a mouth widening in astonishment, as he toppled to the ground. The Rebel yells made of them screeching phantoms in the fog, unholy apparitions appearing and disappearing. Clarke was screaming as well. He felt no fear until his rifle stopped working. At that, he put his head down and bent over his horse like a jockey and tried to urge her forward—in what direction he had no idea. But his mount was stepping on bodies and then a wall of mounts and riders rose around him. As he straightened up he felt a pistol at the back of his head and heard the cock of the hammer. He sat quite still and it was as if he had given an order, as gradually the tumult subsided, and all he heard was the heavy breathing of horses and men.

PRIVATE TOLLER, PUDGE TOLLER, the pianist, helped him out of his tunic and tore out the sleeve of his long john to make a tourniquet. That he was bleeding from a bullet wound in his arm he was hardly aware.

A dozen of Clarke's men were in the jail cell with him. He didn't know how many others had gotten away or how many were dead. He believed Pearl was dead. He had put her in harm's way from the most selfish, immoral impulses. His throat filled with an anguish of self-castigation. He'd always believed in reason, that it was the controlling force in his life, and confident in that belief he had slipped into such an unnatural state of bewitchment that he hardly knew himself. And now she was dead.

Private Gullis every few minutes grabbed the window bars and chinned himself up. There were two guards outside, he reported. But now some men were standing around talking in groups. He couldn't tell if they were Reb soldiers or not.

Toller said, Sir, what will they do with us?

We're prisoners of war, Clarke said. They'll ship us to one of their damn holding pens.

Clarke wanted to put the best face on things. We have word there's one such in Millen, he said. That'll be on the march. We'll be sent to Millen and in a few days the armies will overrun it and we'll be back on duty.

There are more of 'em now, Gullis said. They got rifles.

With difficulty, Clarke stood up. He realized that all the men in the cell were on their feet and listening. Them guards? Gullis said. I can't see them no more. Something of a crowd out there now.

Clarke withdrew writing paper and a carbon pencil from his oilskin packet and, using the stone wall in lieu of a writing box, he spent the next few minutes composing a letter. He could hardly see what he was writing. He had just sealed the letter and addressed the envelope

when the first battering jolt shuddered the jailhouse doors.

PEARL DIDN'T KNOW what to do other than go
on. She wanted to find the Lieutenant Clarke.
She felt he couldn't have been one of those
who'd run away. But if he hadn't where was he?
If he had driven off the Rebels, why didn't he
come find her? She had watched the road, and
once everything was quiet nobody had come by.

She kept to the woods except where the fog
was gathered black and thick like smoke in the
kitchens when wind blew down the draft. Then
she followed the road. As she approached the
outskirts of the village she heard a volley of rifle
fire and darted behind a tree. She stood quite
still while the sound echoed off into the woods.
She waited for something else to happen, but
nothing did. Still, she waited.

Underneath her uniform Pearl wore her
frock tied around her waist. She removed her
tunic and shook the frock down to her ankles,
then rolled up her hat and tunic and hid them
at the foot of the tree. When she entered the village, it was as a white Negro girl.

The fog had lifted and the sky was beginning to clear. She saw a few stars. She stepped in
something wet and slippery. Blood was all over

the road and it was like a trail, as blots and spots and strings of it led her to the street where the jailhouse was, and right up to the jailhouse doors. The doors were open. It was too dark to see inside, but she smelled the blood and sensed the emptiness.

Past the jail was an open field and as the clouds cleared there was moonlight to see by, and so she came upon the men's bodies. Dear God Jesus that you made me see this, she said to herself. Ain't I seen enough of this since I been born? She found Clarke in a twisted position on his side, one leg flung over the other. His left arm had a big bandage. She pressed his shoulder till he was faceup. He looked about to say something to her. His teeth shone. His eyes were far away. In his hand was a letter and he seemed to clutch it as she pulled it from his fingers.

VI

SOPHIE PACKED A HAMPER WITH CORN BREAD, salt pork, boiled potatoes, sugar, and tea leaves. She put in candles, and soap, silver and table linens, his tobacco and a box of matches. His flask he could stash in his pocket. She packed his valise and then put some of her own things in a shawl, which she tied in a knot and slung from her elbow. She walked behind him through the village, the valise in one hand, the hamper in the other.

Come along, come along, he growled. He leaned on his cane and hopped right along for a lame old man. With her weight and all she was carrying, she found herself breathless.

The train was waiting at the station. She helped him up the steps. The car was empty. Nobody but Mr. Marcus Aurelius Thompson wanted to get in the way of this war.

The train lurched and tilted and stopped,

jerked forward and crept along. After several miles the countryside looked flattened hard and scorched, as if a hot clothes iron had been taken to it. It was no longer the natural world God had made. Where houses had been were chimneys standing up from blackened mounds like gravestones.

In the next village they were told that was the terminus. He was outraged. He would not get off the train. The conductor came in and said, Mr. Thompson, sir, you're welcome to stay aboard. Sit here ifn you like—we'll be going back by and by.

They stood on the station platform, their luggage beside them. They were out in the open, under a clear sky. The depot had been burned to the ground. The village behind it was destroyed, houses and stores collapsed into piles of smoking rubbish. Tufts of cotton were stuck in the bushes. Up ahead, the rails had been torn up and put to fire and twisted around trees.

Sophie shook her head and sat herself down on a chunk of wall. The old man stood leaning on his cane, his shoulders hunched, and he kept turning his head this way and that in little jerking movements, like some perching bird. I s'pose you want to go back, don't you? he said.

No, suh.

Well, you're coming with me no matter if

it's to Hell. I have a few things to say to my brother afore he dies.

The sun was up toward noon before they saw a farmer in his wagon. He was looking at the ground on either side as his mule pulled along. The old man waggled his cane in the air.

You'll take us to Milledgeville, he said. How much?

A thousand of Jeff Davis's dollars, the man said. He laughed. He was sun-darkened and all hunched up in a gray army coat.

I'll do better'n that, Mr. Thompson said. I'll give you a two-dollar gold piece of the U.S. Treasury. How you going to get me up in the wagon is for you to decide.

The farmer rode off around the village and came back with a wing chair. Its upholstery was bulged out. Its skirt looked dipped in blood. He and Sophie lifted the old man up by the elbows and stood him in the wagon bed and he sat down in the chair. Sophie, after putting up the luggage, climbed laboriously aboard and sat on the side bench.

We never did get along, Mr. famous Chief Judge Thompson and I, the old man said. I could tell you things.

I s'pose.

No supposing. The man was an atheist—you know what that is?

Don't believe in the hereafter.

That's right. A blasphemer against the Lord God Jesus Christ.

The stench from the dead cattle lying beside the road was intolerable. The sun had caused their bellies to burst open. Sophie caught some cotton batting out of the air, and took a vial of cologne from her satchel and soaked the cotton and handed it over to him.

Where'd you get that? he said.

Fum the Mistress bureau.

You stole it?

She sighed. I keep her room like it was. Everything in its place, just like she still there. You want to keep breavin the stink it's all the same to me.

All right, all right, he said, his face muffled in the cotton.

You ought to know better'n to say that.

All right, he said.

The dogged mule, head down, trotted on. What homes were still standing had been stripped bare, the windows shattered, the doors hanging by hinges. Outbuildings fallen in on themselves like playing cards. Corncribs bare, fodder blowing loose in the fields. By and by they were passing soldiers just sitting there beside the road and not even bothering to look up. Then one man staggering after them, begging for something to eat. Away, sir, said Mr. Thompson, waving his cane in the air. Away with you! Out in the fields people were on their knees culling. But what was there to cull? And the wagon bumping over dead dogs—every hound to be seen was shot through the head.

She saw one soldier picking oat grains from a pile of horse manure.

The bridge over the Oconee was down, and they took their place in the line waiting for the ferry. Behind them were the tramped-upon fields where the bluecoats had camped. Down below, across the river, was the destroyed state capital. Corkscrews of smoke arose from the burned buildings.

What's taking so long! Old Thompson stood up from his chair and addressed the wagons in front of theirs: What is your business here? He could not bear the wait. He had things to say to Horace before the Devil took him.

You best not tire yourself with all this frettin, Sophie said.

She was right. He sat back down, closed his eyes, and said a prayer to calm himself. With his eyes closed, he smelled a dead country.

Sophie, he said, am I the Pharaoh?

She shook her head. She never knew what would come out of that mouth. You jes yerself, she said.

Because if I'm the Pharaoh I'm convinced. I don't need no frogs, nor no locusts, I'm letting you go. You want your freedom, I grant it to you. And this, he said, waving his hand about, is what goes along with it. This is what you get with your nigger freedom.

Tears came to his eyes. The wretched war had destroyed not only their country but all their presumptions of human self-regard. What a scant, foolish pretense was a family, a culture, a place in history, when it was all so easily defamed. And God was behind this. It was God who did this, with the Union as his instrument.

In fact, he loved and admired his brother as much as he hated him. He saw them together as young men in their competition and he dreaded how old and suffering he might find Horace now at the end of life. And as long as he dreaded what he might find, there was resistance in that, resistance to the God who had taken every presumption from them. Even love aghast was love, and God could not destroy that.

VII

Wrede's surgery wagons were with the division sent up the road to Waynesboro to rescue the embattled cavalry of General Kilpatrick. Sherman had deployed the cavalry as a feint, and the Rebels, thinking he was preparing to move on Augusta, put up a stiff resistance. The strategy worked, but the losses were heavy. With Waynesboro finally secured, Wrede established his field hospital in the railroad depot. There were so many wounded in the hand-to-hand fighting that orderlies had to leave them on canvas stretchers outside on the station platform. They lay there moaning, calling for water. Emily Thompson moved among them with soft words to ease their suffering if she could. She'd discovered, and Wrede had concurred, that a woman's nursing meant something more to the men in the way of reassurance. His army nurses, too, had noticed the quieting balm of her presence. And she had learned quickly. You did not give men with stomach or chest wounds more than a sip of water. For those whose pain was unendurable, she gently held her hand under their heads and put tincture of opium to their lips. To others she dispensed cups of brandy. The men made weak self-deprecating jokes, or thanked her for her ministrations with tears in their eyes. For some, she wrote their letters as they lay dying.

Emily was astonished at herself. That she had like a brazen hussy found Wrede Sartorius on the march and joined him. That she had proved able to look upon hideous sights. That she could live in the open as men did, with none of the soft fluff and appurtenances of grooming that women were supposed to find essential to living.

She felt no pangs of guilt for betraying her Southern loyalties. It all had to do with this Union doctor. She was absolved by his transcendent attentions to the war wounded. North or South, military or civilian—he made no distinctions. Even now, some gray uniforms were among the bluecoats lying on their pallets. He seemed above the warring factions, Wrede Sartorius. He was like some god trying to staunch the flow of human disaster. She had lost her entire family in this war, yet she felt that his comprehension of its tragedy was beyond her own. It was characteristic of him to have come to her home to see about her poor father. She felt privileged when he talked to her or inquired after her comfort. He spoke with something not quite like a foreign accent, it was more an intonation that might have come of his formal way of talking. She did not detect in him any of the signs she had been getting from men since she was a child. Of course his responsibilities were enormous but she felt that even in ordinary social circumstances he would not be given to social stratagems. There would be none of the practiced gallantry of Southern boys who at the same time, she knew, would not think twice if given the opportunity to take advantage of her.

Yet she received from him a manly acknowledgment of her person, some subtle acceptance of her presence that was not entirely official.

It was late into the night by the time the work was done. Emily stood in the door of the railroad station watching as, by torchlight, nurses loaded the amputees into ambulances. A few yards into the woods, men dug the pit for the severed limbs. A burial squad arrived with their wagon of coffins to remove the dead to a graveyard. Corpses were searched for personal items—the letters, rings, diaries, and enlistment papers that would identify them. Company

commanders were required to write official condolences to the families of the dead men.

Emily was exhausted. She had as yet no indication of where she was supposed to sleep this
night. Inside the depot, nurses were scrubbing
the floor and operating tables with sand. Sartorius sat at the stationmaster's desk writing his
notes in the light of a kerosene lamp. For this
task he wore wire-rim spectacles that she found
charming. He was rendered boyish by them, a
student at his studies. And he had the most
beautiful hands, squared and strong but with
long, slender white fingers. How skillful those
hands were. One of the nurses told her, because
she still couldn't manage to watch the surgical
procedures, that the doctor was renowned in the
corps for removing a leg in twelve seconds. An
arm took only nine. The field hospitals always
ran short of soporifics. There was never enough
chloroform to go around, and so given only a
slug of brandy a soldier would have reason to
bless the doctor who did the job as quickly as
possible.

WREDE'S MEN FOUND billets for them—a house
on the main street that was still reasonably intact, though windows were shattered and
grapeshot had pocked and splintered the siding.

The owner, an elderly widow woman, met them at the door weeping. I've nothing left, she cried, I'm plumb cleaned out. What more do you want of me? She was a wailing supplicant, clasping her hands over her heart. But when she saw Emily she squared her shoulders, threw her head back, and assumed an imperious expression. You run my slaves off, stole my provisions. I thought there was no more you could do to befoul this house, she said to Wrede. Emily looked away, too embarrassed to say anything. But Wrede didn't seem to be listening. He ordered a private to bring the woman some rations and escorted Emily upstairs.

They stood for a moment on the landing.

We return-march to the corps before dawn, Wrede said. He looked at his pocket watch. I'm sorry, I should have released you hours ago.

I've done nothing to compare with what has been required of you this day.

He smiled and shook his head. We know so little. Our medical service is no less barbarous than the war that requires it. Someday we will have other means. We will have found botanical molds to reverse infection. We will replace lost blood. We will photograph through the body to the bones. And so on.

Wrede chose a room, nodded, and closed the door behind him.

Emily stood thinking of what he had said. She didn't know if she had heard him correctly.

She went to her room, closed the door, undressed, and lay down in a soft bed for the first time in many nights. Yet she was far from sleep. She had never before known a man whose thoughts could startle her so. She was an educated woman. She had taken first prizes in Essays and French at St. Mary's Junior College for Episcopal Young Women. After her mother's death she sat as hostess at her father's dinners. Distinguished jurists dined at their table. She'd always acquitted herself well in the conversation which was often philosophical. Yet it was as if this doctor put into her mind images of another world, one she could see only from afar, appearing and disappearing as through drifting clouds.

She lay staring into the darkness. The bed was cold. She shivered under the blankets. She did not like their smell. In time of war men in uniform could occupy a home with impunity. She herself had suffered such an invasion, had she not? But for a woman it was different. The old lady had simply assumed I was a trollop, Emily thought. I would have made the same assumption in her place. I have compromised myself. Never before in my life have I given anyone reason to question my respectability.

She sat up in bed. What would Father say? A

wave of cold fear, like nausea, passed through her. What could have been in her mind, what had possessed her? To have chosen this vagabondage! She was truly frightened now, shaking and on the verge of tears. She lay back down and pulled the covers to her chin. In the morning, she must somehow find a way to get back home. Yes, that is exactly what she must do. She belonged nowhere else but home.

Her resolution had the effect of calming her. She thought of the man in the next room. She listened for any sound that might have suggested Wrede Sartorius was awake. She could believe of him that he did not require sleep. But she heard nothing. Nor was any light coming from his room or she would have seen it through her window, where she saw only the shadow of a large tree.

WREDE HAD PROCURED a mount for her, and on the march she rode beside him. The sun rose as they were passing through a forest of towering pines, straight as a rule and greened out only at the tops. Emily felt herself in a hallowed place, the footfalls of the horses and mules and even the creak of the rolling wagons hushed by the thick bed of brown pine needles covering the forest floor. As the day came on she could see, on either side of them off in the woods, the covering infantry drifting among the trees, disappearing and reappearing as if with discretion.

She found in the steady peaceful march through the pine forest a reason to admire men. As Northerners these soldiers were far from their homes and families. Yet they persisted and walked the earth as if the earth were their home. She became aware that Wrede was speaking and didn't know if she had transferred his words into her own thoughts or if he had been reading her mind.

I confess I no longer find it strange to have no habitation, to wake up each morning in a different place, he said. To march and camp and march again. To meet resistance at a river or a hamlet and engage in combat. And then to bury our dead and resume the march.

You carry your world with you, Emily said.

Yes, we have everything that defines a civilization, Wrede said. We have engineers, quartermaster, commissary, cooks, musicians, doctors, carpenters, servants, and guns. You are impressed?

I don't know what to think. I've lost everything to this war. And I see steadfastness not in the rooted mansions of a city but in what has no roots, what is itinerant. A floating world.

It dominates, Wrede said.

Yes.

And in its midst you are secure.

Yes, Emily whispered, feeling at this moment that she had revealed something terribly intimate about herself.

But supposing we are more a nonhuman form of life. Imagine a great segmented body moving in contractions and dilations at a rate of twelve or fifteen miles a day, a creature of a hundred thousand feet. It is tubular in its being and tentacled to the roads and bridges over which it travels. It sends out as antennae its men on horses. It consumes everything in its path. It is an immense organism, this army, with a small brain. That would be General Sherman, whom I have never seen.

I am not sure the General would be pleased to hear himself described so, Emily said in all solemnity. And then she laughed.

But Wrede clearly liked this train of thought. All the orders for our vast movements issue forth from that brain, he said. They are carried via the generals and colonels and field officers for distribution to the body of us. This is the creature's nervous system. And any one of the sixty thousand of us has no identity but as a cell in the body of this giant creature's function, which is to move forward and consume all before it.

Then how do you explain the surgeons, whose job it is to heal and to save lives?

That the creature is self-healing. And where the healing fails, the deaths are of no more consequence than the death of cells in any organism, always to be replaced by new cells.

Again that word **cells.** She looked over at him, her expression an inquiry.

Wrede guided his mount alongside hers. That is what our bodies are composed of, he said. Cells. They are the elemental composition, to be seen only under a microscope. Different cells with different functions comprise tissues, or organs, or bone, or skin. When one cell dies, a new cell grows in its place. He took her hand in his and studied it. Even the integument of Miss Thompson's hand has a cellular structure, he said.

He glanced at her with those alarmingly ice-blue eyes, as if to see that she understood. Emily blushed and, after a moment, withdrew her hand.

They rode on. She was extraordinarily happy.

VIII

THEY STOOD IN THE STOCKADE TOWER, WET and miserable as the cold rain pelted their shoulders and dripped off their caps and down their necks.

Will said, I was ready to tell them who I was.

Yes, Arly said, that we was hiding out in disguise just waitin for 'em. Sure, that would've been the thing, all right.

Well, look where you have got us? Can you say we are more better off than these poor Yankees here we are supposed to be guarding? We eat the same slop they get. We stand without a roof over our heads in this damn rain just like them. So where is anything different?

Will, son, you just don't think.

And then to have a pistol put to my head till I swear an oath of allegiance to my own side! Like I wasn't who I am! No wonder they couldn't trust us no more than to send us up here to this miserable duty. What would you do in their place? Because you can't ever trust no man who swears the oath because you put a pistol to his head.

Well, you are back on your own side even so. That was what you wanted—you never did cotton to the blue coat you was wearing.

Captain, I should have said, I am as much secesh as you. I am Private Will B. Kirkland from the Twenty-ninth Infantry Regiment out of North Carolina. I don't need no pistol to my head.

And that would have been that.

That's right. And a grand welcome and good duty.

He wouldn't have asked any questions such as traced you right into the Milledgeville prison for deserting your Twenty-ninth Regiment. Or that found me for sleeping on guard duty in a combat situation.

We was pardoned by that general.

Sure, and you had the papers to prove it. Can you hear me in this rain, God? I am standing with this boy here who thinks an army at war is a reasonable thing. He thinks a soldier is something more than the uniform he is wearing. He thinks we live in a sane life and time, which you know as well as I is not what you designed for us sinners.

Well, anyways, you said God had his intentions for us, and it don't seem like this is what they were.

We are alive, Will my boy. And why? Because we didn't claim to be but what we appeared to be. We didn't stretch some dumb Reb captain's brain all out of shape. We didn't tell no story to get him so fussed he would shoot us for lyin dogs. We looked like Union, and that's what he understood. And that's what we were. And what we ain't anymore.

I'll vouch for that.

Yes, we are wet and cold and hungry on this dark November night, but alive, which is a sight better than the dead falling to the ground every minute in every state of the Confederacy. And that we are alive by shifting our way about from one side t'other as the situation demands shows we already have something gifted about us. I feel the intention, all right, and I am sorry you don't. And I will pray He don't task you for being ungrateful. Or take it out on me.

THEIR DUTY WAS two on and four off, but with the first paling of the sky they still hadn't been relieved. The rain let up and the wind blew as if that was what was bringing up the light. Below them the camp appeared, sodden and bare of any vegetation, and with rivulets of swamp water trickling through the stockade walls. Prisoners who had no huts for their shelter stood up from the watery holes in the ground where they had slept. With the first rays of a cold sun, everyone was up and out on the grounds, hunched over shivering, or dancing up and down. The hacks and coughs crackling from this mass of men sounded to Will like rifle fire. Everyone turned toward the kitchen sheds, but there was no smoke from the chimneys.

Beyond the far walls of the stockade and through the pine trees, he could see the river flowing high and fast from the heavy rains.

The smell was particularly bad this morning, the open latrines brackish and the burial trench just under their guard post having lost topsoil in the rains. Here and there, a body had emerged. Will turned his back on the sight and tried to draw in some scent of the surrounding pine forest. It was then that he saw the guards running along with their bloodhounds and torches.

Not long after that, the Union prisoners—wet, bedraggled, skeletal—were being herded down the road through the village of Millen to the railroad yard. There were more than a thousand of them still, and few had the spirit or the strength to question why they were leaving the pens at Millen. Every twenty yards on either side of the prisoner column, guards with rifles at the ready, and some with guard dogs, policed the march. Arly drifted back till he was abreast of Will. We will not be riding any damn railroad, he said. Can you hear me?

I hear you.

There's even less grub where they're going. Watch me and do what I do, Arly said.

I should have known, Will said.

At the depot a long train of boxcars was attached to two engines, smokestacks chuffing black, boilers hissing. As each car was filled, the door was slid shut and bolted. Some of the prisoners, who could no longer walk, were carried on the backs of their companions. Arly, with Will following, walked backward as if to double the guard at each car as it was loaded. Will noticed how conscientious Arly looked, his rifle at the ready, his eyes alert to any escape attempt. In this manner, they reached the last car, and at the moment when nearby officers had dismounted and were conferring over their maps, Arly and Will slipped around the last car and took cover behind the depot.

Here they had another view of the Ogeechee

River. On the far banks a line of Union cavalry watched helplessly as the whistles blew and the train jerked into motion.

Someday, Will said, I am going to see one of them head doctors—what d'ye call them?

Phreenologists, Arly said.

That's it. And I will ask him—I mean, if by some strange chance I am still alive—what was wrong with my head that I went along no matter what misery you thought up for us.

Nothing wrong with your head, Arly said. You recognize good sense and artful cunning when it is explained properly to you.

They were back in the pens, empty now but for a few dying prisoners in the stocks and several more who had died during the night. Arly stripped, tied the wet Confederate uniform into a ball and threw it in the latrine trench. In a kind of instructional performance for Will, he rolled his naked body in the mud and slopped handfuls of mud in his hair. Then he dressed himself in the rags he had taken from one of the corpses. Then he jumped up and down, and raced around whooping and hollering.

What's that for? Will said.

I'm cold, you damned idiot! Arly shouted.

An hour later Union infantry were everywhere in Millen. In the stockade, a detachment of black pioneers set about burying the dead and shoveling mounds of earth into the open burial trench. Officers inspected the kitchen and hospital sheds, and the wooden stocks. Peering from the back of an ambulance wagon, Will saw how angry these Union men were. They made fists and cursed and swore. They walked around shaking their heads. He shivered under the thick wool blanket given to him. Arly's teeth were chattering, but the expression on his face was one of serene satisfaction.

Preparations were made to burn everything in sight. Men ran along the stockade walls putting them to the torch. Soon the sheds were burning with a heavy black smoke and fitful licks of flame. As the ambulance rode off and came up over a knoll, Will and Arly looked back and saw smoke rising from the village, too. The Yankees were burning down everything with the name of Millen.

As they rode along at a good mule trot, Arly noted how soft the ride was. These ambulance wagons are fitted with springs, he said. Damn, we got to get us one of these. They were taken to a hospital tent in the pine grove where the army camped. They lay on cots under wool blankets and with real pillows under their heads. After a while the flap lifted and Will was stunned to see a woman in a white frock coat. She wore a Union cap pinned to her hair. Good morning, gentlemen, she said, and at that moment the tent walls lit up with the rising sun. She knelt beside Will's cot and lifted his head and held a cup of broth to his lips. He looked into her blue eyes and she smiled at him. He had never seen a more beautiful girl in his entire life. He felt her warm hand on the back of his neck. Tears of gratitude brimmed in his eyes just as if he had really been a prisoner at the infamous camp.

On the adjoining cot, Arly leaned on his elbow to observe the scene, a big grin on his face.

IX

WILMA JONES WAS SO USED TO TAKING CARE of people that even on the march to freedom she found herself being useful. The old man who called her Daughter was stone deaf and shouted everything at her. A cane held him up on his right side, and she propped him up on his left. He had on a threadbare coat with no sleeves, and his skinny old arm was all muscle, long and stringy. His hand clutched hers with the strength of ten. He limped badly, this old slave, but there was no getting away from him. He was bald, all skull under his wool cap, and toothless, and with an ancient brand burned into his cheek. But he was going! He would not falter! And like so many old people he would not care who saw him do his business. She had to shake her head and smile. Old Uncle here reminded her of the Judge. He'd been just as demanding, expecting everything of her as if she had no life of her own. Only Judge Thompson never called her Daughter, having Miss Emily for that.

The people had stopped singing and the women held the children to them tightly. The causeway was narrow and on both sides swamp water lay thick and still, with trees poking up every which way from the muck. The air was fetid, and wisps of fog blew across their path.

When they came to the creek they were ordered to move aside along the bank while the soldiers trotted past them and crossed over on the pontoon bridge. Wilma looked around: more and more of the freed slaves were arriving to be kept waiting while the army moved through. From the far side, several officers on horses watched the maneuver. They sat astride their horses, unmoving. There was a general among them, because he wore a lot of gold braid such as the high and mighty affect. Wilma had a premonition. She had heard the stories. The Rebs were always behind them. They overran Negro stragglers and shot them or took them back into slavery.

The creek was at high water and running fast. It was a whole army going across. Division after division ran and rode past them, pulling their gun carriages and whipping their mules.

Daughter, the old man shouted, why ain't we crossing! Wilma ran to the side of the causeway and stopped an officer. Mammy, he said, we are fighting a damn war for you. Alls we ask is you don't get in the way.

Some of the women and children were crying now. It was clear something had changed, as if with the sky, which had gotten darker. Fewer and fewer soldiers were coming along now, and finally the last of them were on the bridge. Wilma took the old man's arm as the crowd surged forward. And then she couldn't see over their heads, but a great wail went up among them: the ropes had been cut and the pontoon bridge swung away from the bank. Soldiers across the river were pulling it up behind them.

People didn't know what to do. Someone shouted that the Rebs were coming. Wilma tried to hold her ground but the old man was pulling her down the bank. Ise a free man! he shouted. Ise a free man! And then she couldn't hold him any longer and he jumped into the stream. Around her people were screaming, praying, importuning God. They slid into the water and started swimming across. She saw on the other bank that some black pioneer soldiers were throwing logs and brush into the water for people to hold on to. But the old man couldn't swim. He was waving his cane in the air and twisting around in the current and going under and coming up with the cane waving in the air.

Women holding their babies over their heads tried to breast the current. Somehow the men tied a raft together out of some logs and strips of tarpaulin, and women's skirts and blankets. The pioneers threw a line over, and a semblance of order set in as people were pulled across four and five at a time on the raft. But those huddled on the bank looked behind them with fear. They thought they heard Rebs coming down the causeway and couldn't wait their turn. Holding their bundles and satchels, they jumped into the river.

Wilma found herself on the raft. Almost across, it dipped under the current and capsized. She came up sputtering and felt a hand holding her by the arm. She was lifted onto the bank, water streaming from her. A strong black man had lifted her entirely out of the water with one hand. She sat on the ground shivering. Those who had gotten across were running after the army. And, back on the other shore, there were maybe a hundred or more folks still crowding the bank, afraid to move. Women and crying children. She heard gunshots and thought she saw some men on horses coming down the causeway.

Here, missy, the man who had rescued her said. He put a blanket around her. Best not to linger. God will give those folks their freedom, jes not now is all. Come on. He was tall and wore a uniform tunic unbuttoned and ragged trousers and he was shoeless. He took Wilma's hand and got her standing, and led her down the road. She kept turning, looking back, until she couldn't see the creek anymore. But the cries came across the water and seemed to float above her in the trees.

X

PEARL COULD NOT FORGET THAT NIGHT OF the murdered soldiers. They lay about on the hard ground lit blue by the moonlight. Twelve of them like fallen statues. And Lieutenant Clarke staring up at nothing and so surprised, so surprised. She hid at the edge of the field and watched townsfolk come out with their wagon. Some white men, and two Negroes to do the work. They slung the bodies onto the wagon as if they were handling sides of beef. She followed them to the cemetery and watched from the underbrush as they took up their spades. Often they looked up to see if they were being observed. It was near dawn before they got them all buried.

Pearl couldn't stop her shivering. Her teeth chattered. She looked at her hand and saw that she was holding his letter. It was now that first light had dimmed the moon and shown its own gray self up over the field, and she knew she'd better get away from there. She skirted the town, going through the woods to the road they came on and to the tree beside the road where she had hidden her tunic and cap. And so, once again, she hiked her frock up and tucked it under the waist of her trousers and put her drummer-boy uniform back on. And then she had a pocket in which to keep his letter.

Not knowing what else to do, Pearl slid down with her back against the tree and waited.

She awakened to the lowing of cows. It was broad daylight and the army was going by, men driving cattle and goats, teamsters crying out to their mule teams, soldiers with rifles on their shoulders marching in file along the side of the road, and a great rising of dust from all the clamor.

She stood up and made herself visible. Sometimes they grinned and said something as they went by, the men, or occasionally an officer on his horse would glance down at her, but nobody seemed inclined to stop. She kept looking for the wagon driver from her company who had turned back when the shooting started. Two bummers all decked out in claw-hammer coats and stovepipe hats came along in a four-wheeler filled with their pillage. But they were not any-one she recognized. They were laughing. They saw her, and one of them reached into a sack and tossed her a sweet potato.

She knew the Lieutenant Clarke and the others had not fallen in battle. If they had fallen in battle, why were the townsfolk in such a hurry to hide their bodies. No, she had heard that volley of rifle fire, clear in the silence. She had seen the blood going right up to the jailhouse doors, and she had seen the men lying in the field where they had been shot down in a row. They were unarmed.

She had to tell someone. But she was still unsure of her white talk, and if she spoke naturally they would hear she weren't no white drummer boy. Where was her teacher the Lieutenant now she needed him? At the moment she decided she dasn't say a thing she bolted into the road in front of an officer with gold shoulder straps and saluted. His big bay horse snorted, tossing its head and rearing and turning in circles. What in hell! the officer shouted while Pearl stood there with her hand at her cap.

His horse quieted, the officer looked down at Pearl. Don't you know better'n that, boy? Why are you not with your company?

Dead.

Say what?

Dey . . . is. I means . . . they . . . is.

Speak up, lad!

They is. I means they . . . are.

Are what?

Dead.

Don't you know how to address an officer?

I do.

I do, SIR!

Yes, me too, sir.

Put your hand down and stand at attention! Goddamn it, the officer said to one of the men who had stopped beside him. Now he's crying! Is this what we're fighting a war with?

At this moment another officer came along on a mount not much taller than a pony, so that his feet practically touched the ground. He was not at all military-looking, with his tunic covered with dust and half unbuttoned, and a handkerchief tied at his neck, an old beaten-up cap, and a cigar stub in his mouth, and a red beard with streaks of gray. Pearl would remember that first impression she had of General Sherman, that he wasn't an officer in deportment or dress, and she wouldn't have thought of him as such except for the deference paid him by the high and mighty fellow who towered over him on his fine bay mount.

The General on his little horse was practically at her eye level. Well, here's a handsome young Union man, he said. Are you a good drummer, son?

Pearl nodded.

A fellow has to be brave to join the army and fight for his country. Drummer boys come under fire like the rest of us, don't they?

Yessir.

Sometimes I want to cry, too.

Yessir.

And what seems to be the problem? he said to the officer on the bay horse.

General, he says he's lost his company. He believes they are casualties.

Were they in the vanguard, son? They came through last night?

Yes sir, Gen'ral.

That would be Wheeler again, the General said to the officer. I imagine we took some losses.

No, Gen'ral sir, Pearl said. It were no battle when they murdered my Lieutenant Clarke.

Pearl couldn't help herself. She wept copiously, the tears streaming down her face as she held the reins of the General's little horse, and led him and his staff through the town to the cemetery and pointed to the fresh-dug trench.

XI

SHERMAN AFFECTED THE SLOPPY UNIFORM, and shared the hardships, of the enlisted man. He slept in a fly tent, when he slept at all. Only one servant attended him and his string of mounts consisted of exactly one, and that one plug hardly befitting a man of his rank. Of course, having issued orders for an army stripped down to essentials, it was right that he should serve as an example. But to Morrison, a West Pointer on the General's staff, it was all somehow unseemly. Morrison saw no reason why a general officer, especially one not holding a political appointment but a true West Point professional like Sherman, should not distinguish himself from the men under his command. Perhaps some smartness of attire and a measure of remoteness would put some starch into the army he led. The men could fight, all right, they had proved that, but a firm and formal observance of rank and its attendant privileges engendered respect. Respect, not affection, was what a commanding officer depended on— it was a surer thing and lasted longer, and through such ordeals of the march that affection might not survive.

Besides all that, Morrison felt demeaned. He was a loyal aide-de-camp and did his job as signal officer impeccably, with not so much as the expression on his face to indicate anything but his complete devotion to duty. But he liked his comforts and privileges. Sherman had made a point of depriving his staff of their wall tents and all but two mounts per man. Morrison had to leave behind his trunk, his books, and his cook. He had only his body servant. He said nothing, of course, but could not help feeling that the General secretly took a malicious glee in imposing hardships that he by nature was disposed to, knowing full well that others were not.

Stiff and proper though he was, a burly red-faced young man already balding, Morrison was a good student of human nature, first of all his own. He could perceive his taste for field luxuries as a kind of weakness, or lack of assurance that his own person imprinted on the world. In fact, he tended to be self-effacing and believed Sherman tolerated him without liking him very much. They were too different as men. But Morrison knew of himself that he would not pretend to a style of leadership that was so cynical as to greet and talk like a comrade with enlisted men on the march but feel nothing when twenty-five hundred of them were lost at Kennesaw Mountain. He had seen the General's reaction then—a moment's disappointment in the outcome and a consideration of the next stratagem.

After Atlanta was theirs the General pretended not to take seriously the mail that came in, the plaudits, the expressions of gratitude akin to worship. His correspondence, which Morrison took down, displayed a calm rectitude, a modesty that was in direct contrast to the joy of triumphal vindication in his soul and his obvious feelings of superiority to all those, including the President, who had sent their congratulations. How did Morrison know this except by the tone of the dictating voice, the sly self-satisfied laughter after a particularly elegant self-deprecating phrase, or the impatient pacing of a general so happy to be who he was that he could not contain himself for the tremors of excitement that ran through him before he assumed his sober mien and went from his study to receive the latest politician come to praise him.

And now here, this latest example of a general's prerogative—that he would simply by whim attach this drummer boy to his staff, and a strange child, too, who did not speak very much or do very much but sit by his side and listen in on the most confidential military discussions. It was unfortunate that Lieutenant Clarke had been killed, but did that mean his company drummer could not be reassigned?

Morrison confided his feelings to Colonel Teack, who had been with Sherman since Shiloh.

Well, you see, Morrison, Teack said, drawing on his meerschaum, the General wouldn't permit himself a leave two summers ago, and so his family came down from Ohio for a visit. Miz Sherman and the children, including his son Willie, Teack said, as if this explained everything.

Morrison was immediately sorry he had begun the conversation.

At the time we were in Vicksburg, Teack said. There is no worse place to suffer the heat of summer than Vicksburg.

Morrison waited.

And the son Willie, a Northern boy, he succumbed to it, Teack said. It was very sad, because he was not a party to the war.

What, he died?

Like that, from the typhoid, Teack said. Now, this drummer boy—something is not right. He's a strange one, I grant you. But if he does nothing else he is good for the solace of a grieving father. You don't have to go to Harvard to see he is standing in for the poor dead son in General Sherman's mind. And we want that mind to be sound, don't we, Morrison?

Of course.

Because it hasn't always been, Teack said, and turned away.

IT WAS COLONEL Teack, though, who quietly made some inquiries. No drummer boy was assigned to the late Lieutenant Clarke's foraging company. His regiment had lost one around Milledgeville, but in that case the boy was attached to an infantry company. Perhaps Teack would have attempted to find and speak to one of the survivors of the skirmish at Sandersonville, but he thought he saw the answer to the mystery in Pearl's hazel eyes, which, when he caught their attention, flashed with a defiance not at all typical of the humblest of all the enlisted.

In any event, Pearl could not keep her secret very long, conditions in the field being what they were. Soon enough Teack and the other members of Sherman's staff had reason to be satisfied that this strange boy of few words and moody disposition was, in fact, a girl. And circumstances being what they were in this war, they knew that, white as she was, she had to be Negro. At this point their protective feelings for General Sherman prevailed. With scant discussion, hardly more than an exchange of looks, the officers came to the consensus that kept Pearl's secret from their commander. Sherman's manservant, Sergeant Moses Brown, was delegated to see to it that neither the General nor anybody else in the army would know the truth, and he did his job well. He made sure the girl's privacy was maintained when she saw to herself. In camp one day he built a sort of shebang from the underbrush beside a brook so that Pearl could bathe without being seen.

In all of this, Pearl accepted the arrangement as her due. Moses Brown was very formal, and gave no indication that he had any opinions about her or the orders he had to look after her. He was good at his work, protective and forbearing. For this she was grateful. She came to have for him some of the same regard she had had for Roscoe back home. But she felt no particular gratitude to these officers that had conspired to protect her. She was still grieving for Lieutenant Clarke. She kept the letter he had written in her breast pocket. She kept the two gold coins Roscoe had given her in her trouser pocket. She wore her red shawl with the gold thread under her tunic. These items were her estate. As for the

General, she quickly learned that she had less to fear from him than from any of the others. He enjoyed seeing her eat well and supposed she didn't speak much as a result of the terrible sights she had seen in the engagement at Sandersonville. Won't you tell me your name, son? he would say. And she would shake her head. At night she lay in her fly tent and heard him walking about the grounds, unable to sleep. She smelled his cigar smoke and listened to his back-and-forth patrol among the tents. She surmised that he did his thinking at night. And in the daytime, when it was possible, she listened to his conversation with his men and mouthed the words silently as she strove to train herself to speak white speech. On the march, the General liked to ride forward of his headquarters wagon, then back again toward the rear of the march. Everywhere, the men knew him and called out to him as he waved. They called him Uncle Billy, and she delighted him one morning when he asked how she was feeling and she said, Thank you, Uncle Billy, I are quite well.

XII

A DAY'S MARCH OUT OF SAVANNAH, THE FIF-
teenth Corps found themselves on a road
that the Rebels had mined. There were two or
three muffled explosions that were unlike anything the men had ever heard. Infantrymen
took cover. Everything halted. A rider came at a
gallop to bring Wrede's hospital unit forward.

It was a warm day for December. Arly and
Will followed the Colonel in Ambulance Two.
The going was slow, the wagon train slow to
move aside, the teamsters reluctant to take their
wheels onto the soft ground off the road.

At the head of the column the road was
cratered. Men and horses had been blown into
the fields. Wrede's nurses brought out the stretchers and went about collecting those who were still
alive. Emily Thompson tended a boy whose leg
was gone at the knee. She applied a tourniquet at
the thigh. Just over the fence rail lay a decapitated

body. It was an awful carnage here on this warm December day.

Wrede had to ask an officer who was comforting one of the wounded to step aside. Please, he said. The officer stepped back, saying to Wrede, Now we see these Rebels for the murderers they are. They are not soldiers. Soldiers stand and fight, they don't do this. He turned and shouted, Provost guard! Bring me prisoners, get some damn prisoners up here! Emily realized, as Wrede had not, that this was General Sherman.

About a half mile away off to the left was a woods before which stood a house and barn. That will be our hospital, Wrede said.

Several prisoners were brought forward. They were given picks and spades and commanded to march in close order down the road. You will find every mine planted there, Sherman said, or be blown up in the process. Jesus! General, have mercy, one of them said, it wasn't us did this. Forward march! Sherman said, and gave the man a kick. He then raised his arms and pushed the air to indicate that everyone was to move back.

Whimpering and trembling with fear, the prisoners after a few stumbling steps abandoned their tools, dropped to their knees, and with their fingers began to search for the land mines.

They crawled forward, feeling with their out-stretched hands like blind men. Each time they uncovered something they cried out. Sherman's engineers studied the first device, figured out how it was constructed, and disabled it. Six mines were found, all of the same design. They were pressure-sensitive via friction matches, housed in copper cylinders, and with the deto-nating power of a howitzer shell.

Arly and Will loaded their ambulance with groaning, bleeding men. Two tiers of racks ran lengthwise under the tarpaulin. They saw a drummer boy standing in the middle of the road looking down at his bare foot, which had blood on it. You don't look too bad, sonny, Arly said, but we'll fix you up anyways. Get away! the boy shouted. Arly took him by the shoulders and Will by the knees, and they brought the screaming, squirming boy to the wagon.

Only when he saw Emily looking down at him from the rear of the ambulance did the drummer boy go quiet and consent to be put aboard. But tears brimmed in his eyes and Emily thought how oddly beautiful his face was.

Will, for his part, stood a moment gazing up at Nurse Thompson while Arly, waiting not one moment, took his place on the box and got the mules moving. Will had to hurry forward and leap on at a run. To a chorus of moans and curses and cries, the mules trotted down the road toward the house by the woods. Mounted troops cantered past them in the same direction and Emily saw Wrede, too, riding past.

Each rut or ravel in the road brought forth screams. Up front Will, his shoulders hunched, said, One man's suffering is pitiable. But when it's a howling chorus it can only be you're in Hell.

Why, Will, son, I only got us this amblance duty so as you could moon over that Miz Thompson.

Never mind that. I could never aspire to a woman of her degree.

How can you know a woman's degree till you put it to the test?

She just don't see me now that I am a recovered Union on his feet again.

Well, then, think on Savannah. We will have Christmas in Savannah. The ladies there will see you. They will pucker up under the mistletoe. We will have ourselves Christmas goose and figgy puddin. And when we're through with all that we'll get back on the march.

I ain't getting back. This is not me wearing this blue. To where? Will said after a moment.

To all the way to Richmond, maybe, and I wouldn't mind if to the North Pole. On the march is the new way to live. Well, it ain't exactly that new. You take what you need from where you happen to be, like a lion on the plains, like a hawk in the mountains, who are also creatures of God's making, you do remember. We may have dominion over them, but it don't hurt to pick up a pointer or two. I never was much good for settling down with the same view out the window every morning and the same woman in bed every night. It is only the dead in their graves who should live like that, Arly said to the gasps and urgent prayers and implorings for water rising into the warm December morning.

THE SMALL HOUSE Wrede had chosen for his field hospital was unoccupied. The front door swung on its hinges. The glass panes were shattered. It was just two rooms on the ground floor, a parlor and a kitchen. The two upstairs bedrooms were small, with little headroom under the slanting roof, and they were baked hot from the sun.

Wrede indicated the parlor for his surgery. His nurses carried the furniture outside and within minutes they had set up the two tables, brought out the sheets, drawn water from the well, opened the medicinal case, and laid out the surgical instruments.

Outside, the ambulances were unburdened of their riders. The wounded were arranged on pallets outside the front door, in the shade of an oak tree. The dozen or so cavalry rode about to check the surroundings, especially the woods behind the house, and set themselves out as pickets.

Emily stayed outside with the wounded, trying to keep them comfortable until they were brought in for surgery. When it was the drummer boy's turn, she went with him, walking beside the stretcher and holding his hand. It was a soft, small hand. He was quiet enough, though his eyes showed fear, but when he was placed on a table and Wrede's nurses took a pair of shears to the bottom of his trousers he hollered, struggling to raise himself, squirming and shouting, twisting like a bronco, as one of the men said with a laugh.

Emily at this moment understood the boy's reaction as the same she would have had under the circumstance. Soldiers about to undergo surgery often struggled, but for some reason it was the fact of the nurses intending to enforce their will that was to her the essential meaning of what was happening here. Was it only a matter of the boy's age? The nurses were doing their duty, but, without knowing why, she felt that she had to stop them. And then all at once, as she read the look of anguish the child flashed at her, her intuition named itself. No no, wait, stop, she said, and moved to stand between the nurses and the table.

On the other side of the room Wrede, doing a procedure, and his attendants waiting upon him, were in such poses of intense concentration as to release her to her own authority. She had by now a respect from the medical detachment that was only partly due to her serious accommodation to the work. It was Wrede's attentions to her that gave her the credential she assumed this moment as she ordered the men to carry the patient upstairs. And bring me towels and a basin of water, she said.

Alone with Pearl, Emily Thompson removed her trousers and washed the blood from her leg.

You know what this is?

Yes'm.

Is it the first time?

Uh-huh.

Are you hurting?

Naw.

It's nothing to be scared of, is it?

Take more'n this put a scare into Pearl.

I do believe that, Emily said, looking into her eyes.

And the two women smiled at each other.

XIII

SHERMAN'S GLASSES WERE TURNED ON FORT McAllister, which guarded Savannah from the south, a formidably risen, parapeted earthwork with a ravine before it and obstructions of abatis made of felled oak trees, and chevaux-de-frise whose stripped branches had been honed into sharp spikes. It was late in the afternoon. He stood with Morrison, his signal officer, atop a mill roof on the left bank of the Ogeechee a mile or two distant. Above them on a crow's nest hurriedly constructed by the engineers was Morrison's signalman, who was in communication with one of Admiral Dahlgren's squadron laying at anchor in Ossabaw Sound. So the navy was there with the clothing and shoes, provisions, and mail that the men had been yearning for these many weeks. But it could not come in up the river till the fort was taken.

Entrenched in a great arc of siege in the

swampland south and west of the city, Sherman's Fourteenth, Twentieth, Seventeenth, and Fifteenth Corps were hunkered down in the pooling sumps of canal water and sand. His men were cold and miserable and hungry, having marched through a barren sandy territory that devolved into waterlogged rice plantations where there was no forage to be had. They could not light fires to warm themselves lest they invite grapeshot from the Rebel guns. Miles behind them was the wagon train with its hardtack and coffee and its beef on the hoof, but nothing could move forward into this chilled watery lowland until the city was taken.

Your division will storm Fort McAllister, Sherman had told General Hazen. I won't fuddle about. I've come this far and my army wants its prize. We take Fort McAllister and we'll have Savannah.

Now, he saw Hazen's regiments moving into position through a woods and halting at its edge. Signal Admiral Dahlgren the assault is about to begin, Sherman said. Then order Hazen to begin. Yes, let it begin, let it begin, Sherman said.

Within moments the blue lines appeared in parade at the edge of the open land and began their advance—a quick trot, arms at the ready, through the fields in the late-afternoon sun toward the fort some eight hundred yards away. Rebel Napoleons immediately boomed forth their round shot. The lines, he saw now, were converging from three directions—north, south, and along the capital—colors flying. My God, they are magnificent, Sherman cried. Within moments the smoke of the big guns enveloped the scene like fog drift, and the wind brought to Sherman the pungency of blown powder. And now only the caprices of the wind would let him see discrete moments of the action, tantalizing glimpses as if, he thought, the smoke were the diaphanous dance veil of the war goddess. And I'm seduced, Sherman said, aloud, to a startled Morrison.

Yet even from these glimpses Sherman saw things that assured him the assault would succeed. The Rebels had left fallen trees in the field where his men could take cover and return fire. And the big guns were without embrasures: his sharpshooters would kill the artillerists. And as he listened the tempo of shot and shell seemed to slow. The white smoke of the battle began to lift, and now he could see his men clambering up the glacis from the ravine, some of them blown into the air by torpedo mines embanked there. But the blue lines came on, more and more of them, and the parapet was gained. He could see the fighting hand to hand. Sherman had to lower his glass, too overcome to watch. He loved a brave man. Regiments of them brought sobs of joy.

How many minutes later was it when Captain Morrison called out, It's ours, sir, I see the colors! And it was true. All at once the firing ceased, and they heard a great shout over the field. And through his glass Sherman saw his men waving their fists, and firing their muskets into the sky.

IT WAS DARK when Sherman arrived at the fort. He made his inspection and complimented the defending commander, a young major who admitted that he had not expected an attack so late in the day.

The moon had risen, throwing a chill white light over the dead, who lay where they had fallen. But among them lay his own sleeping soldiers. Sherman's men had found foodstuffs and wine in the cellars, and now they slept.

Sitting with crossed legs on a barrel, a cigar in one hand and a cup of wine in the other, Sherman contemplated how matter-of-factly his men accepted the dead that they could lie down, so casually, beside them. All of them asleep, though some forever. He barely noticed the coat thrown around his shoulders by his servant, Moses Brown. His thoughts ran this way: What if the dead man dreams as the sleeper dreams? How do we know there is not a posthumous mind? Or that death is not a dream state from which the dead can't awaken? And so they are trapped in the hideous universe of such looming terrors as I have known in my nightmares.

The only reason to fear death is that it is not a true, insensible end of consciousness. That is the only reason I fear death. In fact, we don't know what it is other than a profound humiliation. We are not made to appreciate it. As a general officer I consider the death of one of my soldiers, first and foremost, a numerical disadvantage, an entry in the liability column. That is all my description of it. It is a utilitarian idea of death—that I am reduced by one in my ability to fight a war. When we lost so many men in the first years of the war, the President simply called for the recruitment of three hundred thousand more. So how could he, the President, understand death, truly?

Each man has a life and a spirit and the habits of thought and person that define him, but en masse he is uniformed over. And whatever he may think of himself, I think of him as a weapon. And perhaps we call a private a private, for whatever he is to himself it is private to him and of no use to the General. And so a generalship diminishes the imagination of the General.

But these troops, too, who have battled and eaten and drunk and fallen asleep with some justifiable self-satisfaction: what is their imagination of death who can lie down with it? They are no more appreciative of its meaning than I.

AND SO WHO is left but the ladies? Perhaps they know. They bring life into being, perhaps they know what it is as afterlife. But often they talk of Heaven or Hell. I take no stock in such ideas as Heaven or Hell. And fate? In war a fate is altogether incidental. In fact, it is nothing as awesome as fate if you happen to raise your head in the path of a cannonball. That nigger who was killed the other day by the railroad track not ten yards from me—I saw the ball coming, a thirty-two-pound round shot, and I shouted, but as he turned it bounced up from the ground and took off his head. That was not fate. There are too many missiles in the air for it to be your fate to be killed by one of them. Just as the number of men set to fighting deem any of their deaths of no great moment.

In this war among the states, why should the reason for the fighting count for anything?

For if death doesn't matter, why should life matter?

But of course I can't believe this or I will lose my mind. Willie, my son Willie, oh my son, my son, shall I say his life didn't matter to me? And the thought of his body lying in its grave terrifies me no less to think he is not imprisoned in his dreams as he is in his coffin. It is insupportable, in any event.

It is in fear of my own death, whatever it is, that I would wrest immortality from the killing war I wage. I would live forever down the generations.

And so the world in its beliefs snaps back into place. Yes. There is now Savannah to see to. I will invest it and call for its surrender. I have a cause. I have a command. And what I do I do well. And, God help me, but I am thrilled to be praised by my peers and revered by my countrymen. There are men and nations, there is right and wrong. There is this Union. And it must not fall.

Sherman drank off his wine and flung the cup over the entrenchment. He lurched to his feet and peered every which way in the moonlight. But where is my drummer boy? he said.

XIV

PEARL'S FIRST CITY SHE HAD EVER SEEN WAS Milledgeville, but it was not a city so grand as this Savannah, with its little parks everywhere with fountains and iron railings and the big old live oaks dripping with moss, and with the grand courthouse and customshouse and the ships in the harbor. And it's true that some of the cobblestoned streets had been dug up and the stones piled at the corners for the Confederate soldiers to stand behind, but that didn't happen. They had fled across the Savannah River to fight another day. Along the waterfront were shops and open warehouses where the Union troops were unloading comestibles. The sun was out, and she was riding in a carriage just like the Jamesons', with Miz Emily and those two ambulance drivers up front escorting them for their tour. Every day it seemed there was another parade, and now they were held at the corner while one went by.

She stood up to see it, and grabbed Miz Emily's hand till she got to her feet to see it too. What mighty music this was, the drums spattering better than she could ever manage with her one-two thump, and the brass horns shooting out the rays of the sun like to their blare, and flutes and piccolos peeping from the top of the music like birds lighting on it, and the big tubas pumping away under it, and at the very back the two big bass drums announcing the appearance of the blocks of bluecoats in dress parade behind them. And all their Union flags!

She heard below the music the sound of the soldiers' footsteps all in rhythm, a soft sound, and after the band had gone down the street and the bluecoat companies kept coming all she heard now was the soft-shoe whisper of their footsteps marching, it was almost a hush, and if not for the cries of the sergeants at the side, and their pennants in the air to remind her, she would think it was so sad, these men with their rifles on their shoulders making a show of their victory but looking to her eyes like they was indentured as she once was, though maybe not born into it.

CROWDS HAD GATHERED on both sides of the thoroughfare to watch the parade. Across the street, Wilma pulled Coalhouse Walker by the hand back through a wrought-iron gate and into the front yard of a house with a mansard roof and stood with him behind the hedges.

What is it, Miss Wilma, he said in his deep voice.

She could not answer but stood with her eyes closed, shaking her head and holding her fist to her mouth.

Tell me, he said.

It's Miz Emily, she said finally. Judge Thompson's who I was bound to. Look, but don't let her see. She's in a carriage driven by army men, and with another white girl. You see her?

He peered over the top of the hedge. No, ma'm. Parade's over, he said, everyone's moving on. He turned and smiled at her. 'Sides which, he said, you free, you disremember that?

Wilma burst into tears. He took her in his arms. Now, now. We come this far. You a fine strong woman that marched in the rain and cold and nothing to eat some days, and I never seen a tear in your eye. An here, with the worst behind us, in this free city with the sun shinin, ain't you jes like a ordinary woman cries at the leastmost thing. He laughed.

I'm sorry, Wilma said, and she laughed, though the tears were still brimming.

At this moment a woman with a hound on

the leash came out on the porch and stared at them.

They left, closing the gate behind them, and walked on hand in hand.

He was right, of course, this good man. He had lifted her out of the river and taken her for his responsibility. She had never seen a man as strong as this. He was enlisted as a pioneer, as the army moved forward he cut down trees and laid the logs across the road when it rained. She had seen him pry railroad track up from its ties, she had seen the fine, beautiful skin of his chest glistening with his effort under the sun, the muscle moving in his arms and shoulders—and then his back was turned and she saw the thick scars there and gasped, though it was as nothing to him. He was a beautiful man, his blackness of a rich purpled hue in the sunlight.

By the grace of God they had met and all through the march he had managed to acquit himself at his duties and see after her as well, finding dry clothes for her and an army coat against the cold, sharing his rations when he had them, keeping her with him when that was possible and, if not, seeing that she was safe among the black folks. They were the same age, twenty-two, but he was inclined to make the best of things and with all sorts of grand ideas for their future together, and so she felt older by comparison but instructed by him, too, in the ways of hope.

Yet the city that made him so cheerful filled her with misgiving. They were still black in a white world. Coalhouse had drawn his few dollars of army pay, but the merchants in the stores put out prices as if it was Confederate tender. He wanted to buy some sweet potatoes. Don't buy, she urged him, I'd rather go without. And another thing was she knew Coalhouse's company was camped outside the city in a rice plantation, but here he was roaming the streets with her like a man free of everything, including the army, and without the pass he was supposed to have from the officers. So there was something reckless about him too, and all that good cheer had a wild edge to it that caused her to look behind them where they walked and up ahead to see where the danger might lay.

And now what was he up to as he took up an empty bushel basket from an alley behind a shop and led her to the river? Miss Wilma, he said, we are going to have a fine lunch. But what was he doing, getting out of his shoes and jacket and rolling up his trousers to his knees and walking onto the flat rocks and hunkering down there? And then before she knew it he had eased himself into that cold river water.

And so this was how Wilma Jones, who

grew up in the hills, learned about oysters. Coalhouse Walker came back with almost a bushel of them. He was sopping wet, and shivering and smiling broadly. They sat there in the sun on a flat rock and he shucked the oysters with his knife and swallowed them down raw, with his head thrown back. But she had no taste for any of that, and so they moved on in the lanes between the houses and the stables and found a kitchen with some black folks there, where she was welcome to use the stove.

Wilma was now in a role that was familiar to her. She pan-fried the oysters with a bit of cornmeal and in their own juices, and it turned from a day full of worry for her to a good time with people she wouldn't have known but for the holiday season and the freeing of Savannah. Everyone ate what she cooked, and there was real bread to go with it.

Coalhouse surprised her, picking up a banjo and strumming it and singing some old song in his deep voice. She hadn't known he could do that. People clapped in time, and a boy stood up and danced. She was among these new friends whose names she barely knew and would probably never see again, some still working where they'd been slaves, but they had a way about them now, and she supposed she was getting to it too, of celebrating off to the side just beyond the ken of the white folks. And somehow in her mind it all came from the spirit of Coalhouse Walker, like he had this way of making the people around him glad to be alive.

> **Say, Miz Mary, what that on the pillow**
>   **where my head orter be**
> **For sakes, it jes a mush melon, can't you**
>   **plainly see**
> **A mush melon on de pillow, oh yes I do**
>   **agree**
> **But why it got a mustache an two eyes**
>   **a-lookin at me**

There were young girls there from the kitchen and she could see what they were thinking, so she didn't let him from her sight. And maybe from her serious mien, and her upbringing in the Judge's house that taught her how to do most anything that needed to be done, Wilma knew that she was good-looking enough but that what made Coalhouse Walker take to her was just that soundness of her—that and because she knew how to read and write and would not lie down with him until they were properly wed. He honored that, and in her heart she knew she had nothing to worry about because she was the one he'd been looking for.

They slept in a hayloft that night after some

kisses and hugs that were not entirely pious, and in the morning she told him her idea. He went down to the river and by noon, in one of the town squares, with the troops everywhere and the sky bright with sun, she stood behind a makeshift stand and pan-fried oysters over a fire Coalhouse had built in a steel drum. Coalhouse made newspaper sheets into cones, and kept up a smart patter. Miz Wilma's very best fresh roasted oysters! he called, and they sold the catch to folks by the paper cone—soldiers and even officers, and finally some of the secesh townspeople themselves, who couldn't abide the fate of their city but found the oysters as she roasted them too good not to partake of. And in this way she and Coalhouse sold off three bushels and found themselves at the end of the afternoon with thirteen real Union dollars.

I will hold these, Wilma said, and turning her back, she lifted the hem of her skirt and tucked the folded bills under the waistband of her pantaloons.

ARLY AND WILL had no trouble getting their new shoes—they just stood a while on a line, and when they got to the quartermaster they had only to show their feet. But drawing pay was different, it was done by name and regiment.

You were checked off against the paymaster's book.

Well, what does God say to do now? Will said, looking down at his stiff shoes. They felt tight against his toes and the backs were already rubbing up into his ankles.

He's telling me to be patient and it will come to me, Arly said.

They had leave from Colonel Sartorius only to get themselves outfitted, but they were in no hurry to return to the Savannah military hospital where his surgery was. The city having fallen without a fight, there was not much call for ambulance driving now, so they had been made over into nurses there in the army sick ward, emptying bedpans and doing other lovely chores.

Clumping along in their unaccustomed footwear they had reason to feel sorry for themselves. Every bluecoat but them, it seemed like, had a day pass and money in his pocket. And then there was that great to-do about the mail. Tons of it came off the ships, and for one whole day everyone sat around reading letters from home. Arly said it was a pathetic sight to see grown men carrying on so. But Will thought he wouldn't mind a letter from someone. That he and Arly had no letters was because who they were, or where they were, was now a matter of total indifference to the universe.

They were almost swept off the sidewalk by a throng of grizzled troops, some of them happily drunk, chattering away and half running, half walking, in a great hurry to get where they were going. Hey! Will shouted. But Arly was curious. He motioned to Will and they tagged along. They followed the soldiers to the waterfront, where, on Charleston Street, in a row of connected two-story redbrick houses, a woman stood smiling in each window.

Armed soldiers stood guard at the doors. But the men ignored them and they had the good sense to stand aside as the troops poured through the several doors. Looking at one another, and then carefully up and down the street, the guards themselves stepped inside and the doors closed behind them.

As Arly and Will watched, the women, one by one, disappeared from the windows. This is cruelty beyond name, Arly said. A particularly fair maid in a second-floor window looked down into his eyes and motioned invitingly with her head before she, too, disappeared. And, sadly for that poor girl, she's fallen in love with me, Arly said.

The two men stood in the empty street as the sounds of revelry rose in volume through the brickwork.

Will was secretly relieved to have no money.

Seeing the women in the windows he had felt uneasy, as if just standing there and thinking what he was thinking was to sully the shining image in his mind of Nurse Thompson. It didn't matter that she had no idea who he was, let alone what his feelings were, he felt that just looking at those whores was to betray her. Well, that's that, he said. Let's go.

Arly took a stogy out of his pocket and lit it. God gave me something else beside my natural abilities, Will my boy. He gave me spirit. He gave me the juices of a man. He made me someone who rises to a challenge, be it a firing squad or a army that divests me of my natural rights of personal expression.

They walked back through the city. I am a champion of survival, Arly said. It won't take but a drop of my talent for surviving an entire war to come up with a Federal dollar or two.

It's just a damn whore, Will said.

No, sir, you are wrong. When I was in the field with the grapeshot whizzing past my head I thought of nothing but staying alive. I was consumed, I had a survival compunction and it brought me through. And now I am consumed with this. You put me in a trench, that's one thing, you put me in a city with women everywhere you look and that's another. But the powerful need to satisfy a life instinct is the same. They are both a matter of survival.

With a whore it's less likely, Will said. I seen in the ward just today some of what a whore can do. You seen it, too, where the mercury has ate away half that poor man's face.

You ain't never been with a woman, have you?

Will was silent.

Come on, it ain't no shame—you're but a boy yet, though I have to admit I was not thirteen years when a kind lady took me out to the barn. And how old are you now? But that's all right, I don't need to ask where you was raised or how you live. It is clear enough you was over-protected and pro'ly some preacher messed with your mind and it's because you been held back and ain't been with a woman that you speak in ignorance of the soft, sacred vessel they carry 'tween their legs. My God, just thinking of it— let us sit down on this bench a moment.

Will watched the setting sun glimmer through the moss hanging off an oak tree. Arly said: If there is any good reason for war, it ain't to save Unions, and it certainly ain't to free niggers, it ain't to do anything but to have you a woman of your own, or even of another's, in a bed with you at your behest. You are talking the highest kind of survival, young Will, the survival you achieve after you are gone to your God that by the issue of your loins has created them that look like you and sound like you and think like you and are you through the generations of descendants. And you know how He fixed it: so that we turn our swords into plowshares and at the end of a day go into our houses and after a good, hot dinner we take them upstairs, these blessed creatures of God who are given to us, and pull off their dresses and their shifts and their corsets and whatever damn else they use to cover themselves till just the legs and breasts and bellies and behinds of them are in presentation to our wonderment . . . oh Lord. And when we go inside them, plum into their beings, and they cry out in our ear and we feel there is nothing softer, warmer, or more honeyed up in God's world than what embraces our stiff tool, and we are made by God to shiver into them the issue of our loins, well, boy, don't talk to me about what you don't know. And if the bordello ladies you slander are not half of what I am telling you, please to remember they are as much our glorious Southern womanhood as whatever you been dreaming about that Miz Nurse Thompson, who, I can promise you, would taste no sweeter when put to the test than the uglymost whore in those houses by the waterfront.

AS HE SAT there in contemplation of his slander of Southern womanhood, Will became aware of the unmistakable sound of hymn singing. Arly heard it, too. He leapt up: God said it would come to me. It has!

Grabbing Will by the elbow, Arly hurried them through the streets till they found the church. It was a First Baptist, towering in lordly granite over a town square. The front doors were open and the hymn poured forth so as to seem to fill the live oaks abounding in the park. They climbed the steps and found themselves in the overflow of soldiers standing just inside. Pardon me, Arly said, pushing his way forward. Pardon, 'scuse me, pardon. I hope we're not too late, he said to Will, who was pushing along right behind him, though not knowing why. Maybe halfway down the aisle, Arly saw some small space in the middle of a pew. Pardon us, brother, 'scuse us, I do beg pardon, he murmured, flashing hallowed smiles at the men whose toes he was stepping on with his new shoes.

And then they were standing in place like everyone else, and with hymnals in their hands. The congregation was in color a uniform blue, though some civilians could be seen here and there. But the rich chorale was of soldierly voices, strong and not entirely on key but powerfully fervent in calling upon one another to go down to the river to pray.

Churches had always made Will nervous, perhaps beginning when he was just a tad and saw his mama and papa become completely different people in church from the drunk and the shrew they were the rest of the week. He didn't know what churchgoing was for except for people to pretend to be better than they were, and it was that pretense that frightened him. From this his idea grew along with him and now, looking around, he saw the same open mouths and glazed eyes of singers but knew they not only pretended but wanted to be better people than they were. But this was a no more comforting insight, given the war that was going on which meant no matter what people wanted, or thought they wanted, they would still go and do what they had always done, finding different ways to sin against their Lord and then going to church to buy some repentance that would clear them for a while and then building up the sin again and coming back for another installment of repentance, and so on. By that measure, Will thought, there ought to be their own church for this Yankee army to take along on their backs, for how does anyone know when they're supposed to burn one to the ground or pray in it?

God help me, Will thought, with no sense of the contradiction in him, because I can't give myself to the nigger-keeping side I was born to neither. I don't know nothing or no one to give myself to with my whole heart except maybe Miss Emily Thompson.

When the hymn singing was done a pipe organ murmured softly as the basket was sent around. Will worried that he hadn't even a penny to offer so as not to look bad. But glancing over to where the usher was handing the basket to the first man on the aisle, and then watching as the coins and even Federal dollars dropped into it, and the basket advanced toward him, he turned his mind to the fact that not he but Arly had put them in the middle of this pew, and in the very moment the basket was placed on his fingertips he knew it would happen that Arly would punch it up from the bottom and it and the money would fly into the air, and they would be on their hands and knees, banging their heads on the back of the pew in front of them while picking up the coins and bills and putting almost all the money back where it belonged and then risen to their feet— the usher glowering down at the end of the aisle, the soldiers on either side shaking their heads—the bumbling oafs smiling sheepishly, which was true in his case, and plain cunning in Arly's, and with the sacrament of giving now running smoothly again, and the organ playing softly its deferential piping to the hallowed name, their standing and facing forward, just two red faced with embarrassment worshipers hardly able to wait on the end of the service before taking themselves with someone else's pay in their pockets back to the whores on Charleston Street.

WREDE SARTORIUS WAS given the ground-floor ward and operating room of the Military Hospital, a luxury that he relished after all this time in the field. But Emily couldn't see it that way. Of the twenty beds on the ward, half were filled with soldiers of the Confederate army. They were men dying of their wounds or wasting away with disease. The smell was awful even after she had the windows opened to air the place out. And because of the Union blockade, the hospital lacked even such things as rolled bandages. There was no calomel, no chloroform. There were no emetics, rubefacients, or narcotics. So it was a matter of supplying the hospital from the surgical field cases. Besides that, the army at rest in Savannah hardly meant a falling off of patients. Men were reporting with fevers and bronchial congestions acquired during the siege of the city: sitting out in the swampy terrain around Savannah, living in wet clothes, hungry and unable to light fires, they were coming in sick and hardly able to stand. And now that there was a general relaxation of military discipline the enlisted men were on the town drinking and fighting and knocking one another about and showing up, the worse for wear, in the early hours of the morning. This hospital in the genteel city of Savannah was more like a madhouse. To make matters worse, they were understaffed. Sartorius was without an assistant surgeon. Three of the regimental nurses were down—two with pneumonia, the other with a recurrence of swamp fever. So not only Emily and the pair from Millen were doing hospital duty but also little Pearl, who was stationed in the supply room folding towels and rolling bandages.

But where were those two men now? They had a way of not being there when you needed them.

Wrede had told her that the moment he examined them back at Millen he knew they were not what they said they were. They could not have spent any time at all in that mud hole. They were not starved. Their eyes were clear. Their skin was healthy, their fingernails were pink, and their beards were not long.

I suspect they are spies, Wrede had said.

Spies? She was shocked. She thought one of them, Will, was rather a sweet boy. How could someone like that be a spy?

Such scoundrels abound in the chaos of war. I don't know if the regimental affiliations they professed are real or not, and I don't care. If they decided to attach themselves to my medical company because it was less apt to follow military protocol, they reasoned correctly. Whatever they might be after—perhaps my procedures for resections?—they are welcome to. He laughed. In the meantime, they will scrub the floors and clean up after the dysentery patients.

Wrede Sartorius didn't usually speak of his past, so she was surprised when he said that as a boy he'd been sent by his father to a military academy in Göttingen. The experience had taught him to detest drilling and saluting and all the other hierarchical warrior nonsense. That was the phrase he used—she smiled—**hierarchical warrior nonsense.**

A CIVILIAN WAS brought in, a man with a depressed skull fracture. He arrived in the arms of a Negro. He did not belong in a military hospital, as one of the guards had insisted, but the victim's wife said, The likes of you did this to him, and we are not leaving. On Wrede's orders the man was brought to the surgery. His head was shaved. Emily came in with a cloth moistened with bromine and washed the bare skull. Gently, she patted the skin dry. The patient was perhaps sixty. He was muscular and deep-chested, but his chest hairs were gray. The face was ashen. The eyes were closed. The jaw was slack and the breathing barely perceptible. The skull was caved in an ellipse on the right side just above the forehead. She stepped back, her eyes fixed on the operating table. She would not flinch.

Wrede made an incision front to back through the length of the injury and two lateral incisions at either end of that, and folded the flaps back to reveal the damaged skull. A male nurse sponged the area. The loose fragments and splinters Wrede removed one by one with a forceps. The depressed bone was four centimeters in length. Taking up a trephine, he locked its perforator pin into the fracture line. This is to prevent cutting into the membrane under the bone, the dura mater, he said to Emily. He had lately found himself instructing her as if she were a medical student. Emily was no less aware of this. She'd discovered that his medical terminology, and the Apollonian calm with which he attended to the most awful matters, enabled her to find her courage. She looked on and learned.

He tightened the pin with a screw positioned halfway up the shaft of the trephine. Like that, he said. Emily nodded, though Wrede, bent over the patient, could not see her. Now he rotated the handle of the trephine and the circular cutting head ground into the bony plate until the disk of bone was all but cut through. He loosened the perforator pin, retracted it, and locked it and passed the trephine off. Then he inserted a flattened blade under the bone and slowly levered the disk away from the skull.

Under the cerebral membrane was an enormous blood blister purple in color. To Emily, it looked like the head of a toadstool. Hematoma, Wrede said. He chose a small scalpel with a curved blade and incised the membrane to set the hematoma draining. Linen dressings were applied to take up the blood. There should be no pressure now, he said. Until the discharge ended, the wound would be lightly covered with linen dressings and lint. If he survives, Wrede said, he will wear a lead plaster until eventually something like bone will grow back.

The patient was moved to the ward. They had not yet taken the trouble to know his name. Emily was prepared to sit by the bed and attend to the dressings. No, Wrede said, we will have the widow sit by him. You will come out with me and comfort her.

Emily said, The widow?

Wrede washed his hands in a basin of water. He looked at her and smiled. It was a sorrowful smile, with those ice-blue eyes of his suggesting the pain of his own limitations. We will find out how much time passed before I attended him. You cannot remove the pressure too soon. He is not a young man. The concussive shock is severe. He may never awaken. Even if he does, there is almost always infection. There is not much to be done with an infected brain. Come, Wrede said, you will help me not to leave the woman hopeless.

As they walked to the anteroom, Wrede asked Emily if she'd remembered that tonight was Christmas Eve. She hadn't. It surprised her that the holidays of life were still applicable. He took her arm. We will dine this evening with the officers at the Pulaski Hotel. And then would you like to see the Negroes dancing?

When they came into the anteroom, Mattie Jameson stood and, seeing Emily, blurted out the first thought that flashed through her mind. Aren't you Judge Thompson's daughter from over in Milledgeville? she said.

FROM THE DAY they arrived in Savannah, Mattie did not recall a moment in which John was not enraged, shouting at everybody, cursing the powers that be. In the first place the army would not have him. They enlisted the boys readily enough, and now where were they? Gone to God knows where, to South Carolina, her sons, her babies, fifteen and fourteen years old, gone for soldiers. But not their father. John had actually accosted General Hardee, who had looked at him and said he was too old to march as an enlisted man and could not be commissioned an officer unless he brought in a regiment of his own. I'll do that then, by God, Hardee, John had said, and reported that the General had smiled, as of course he would, the entire state having been scraped bare of able-bodied men and his so-called army a hapless assemblage of militias and cadets.

And then John had found it intolerable that, there being no decent houses available in Savannah, they had to board on Green Street with her older sister Cissie, whom he had never liked for her officiousness. And it was true that Cissie had a way about her of knowing better than anyone else, in any given situation, what must be done and how it should be done and giving orders accordingly. That was surely the reason she never found a husband. She had been that way even as a child, as Mattie well knew— the games they played always Cissie's games,

with Cissie's rules—and even though there was
but a year and a half separating them, she
seemed to have been born knowing everything
and pronouncing errorless judgments so that
Mattie had always to give in, to revise her opinions, to gainsay her own judgments, just as she
did living with John Jameson who had not a little of the same overbearing nature, which is why
he probably found his sister-in-law so intolerable. They were two peas in a pod. Cissie wore a
perpetual frown—it had been grooved into her
face from so many years of it and now, with her
lips pressed together and her eyes narrowed,
her simplest remark, however well meant, had a
knife edge to it. The meals in her dining room
were cold and silent. Her menus reflected the
wartime shortages and the darkies were somewhat slower in serving than they should have
been, as if, in anticipation of Sherman's advancing armies, they were practicing their independence. And she, Mattie, was strung taut between
her sister and her husband, deferential to one
and placatory of the other. Cissie had inherited
the family manse, and above all, without her saying a thing, like a miasma in the house, was the
fact of their imposition. It had been not even a
month, but it seemed like forever.

Of course John was out of the house as
much as possible, God knows what he was

doing all day in the streets of Savannah, with the army stationed behind entrenchments everywhere you looked. But removed from his land he was a lost soul. And one day, without her knowledge, he went out with our Roscoe and when he came back he was alone and dear Roscoe was gone, as if he'd never existed after all those years with them and never a bit of trouble. But all John would say was he'd got the best out of Roscoe and what was left wasn't worth providing for.

Mattie didn't know how, when they got back to Fieldstone, the place would get up and running again, John having sold off all the working hands. She knew, of course, that there might never again be slaves but she couldn't quite see how anything could be done without them. And so when she imagined the war over and a return to their home, as often as not in her imagination the slaves would still be there. She would read in the papers the bad tidings for the Confederacy but somehow she couldn't connect it to a whole change of Southern life. She would, for a moment, and then the connection would dissolve and the war would seem to her, however horrible, a temporary thing, an interruption only, without any great consequences. She worried about her sons going off to battle, but at the same time she couldn't imagine them not coming back or, when they did come back, being any older or different from when they went away.

And then it pained her terribly when she one day expressed hope for the future and John called her an idiot. It was hard to forget that, such a cruel thing it was to say. She was no idiot. She was a very capable person, a loyal wife, and a smart and insightful mother, she was good with accounts and knew how to run a household. It was her educated taste in fabrics and furnishings that created their beautiful home. He had been too strict with their sons when they were but little boys, and she had explained to him why that was wrong and he had listened. He had come to her for advice on many an occasion, and she had given good advice. And, finally, she was bearing up under these circumstances with more grace and dignity than he was. It was not she who was running around madly all over Savannah and telling the military what they were doing wrong. The boys had confided in her—he had done that to the point of embarrassing them when he followed them to their picket-duty posts and had to be shooed away by their officers.

But she didn't begin to think that perhaps John had gone mad and that everything he'd done, selling off his good working slaves, rushing

the family to Savannah to live like indigents—
for even if he and the boys rode off she could
have remained and not come to harm, just as she
saw now in Savannah how women kept their
homes whose husbands and sons were fighting
for the South, and the Union army might have
passed through and left them without food or
stock, but she would still be mistress of Fieldstone in their own home among their own
things, and making do until their return—she
didn't begin to ask herself if everything John had
done, and that she had deferred to, was in fact
the judgment of an unstable mind until the
night of the retreat, when General Hardee's
troops fell back and made their way across the
Savannah River to South Carolina. John had
stood there on Broad Street as the soldiers waited
in formation to cross the pontoon bridge, and he
called them cowards. These poor boys—I saw
them myself—looking cold and miserable standing there in the street and waiting for their turn
across. It was after midnight and so windy and
cold—why, some of them were barefoot and
some had their feet in women's shoes, that's how
ill equipped these soldiers were. And I looked for
John Junior and little Jamie, and walked up and
down the ranks trying to find them, but to no
avail, while in the meantime John stood there
shouting, with his hair sticking up and his face

red and the veins in his neck popping out, he
was ordering them all to turn back and man the
trenches and act like men and not miserable
damn cowards—till an officer rode up and said,
Sir, I'll thank you to remove yourself from sight
or I'll have you shot for treason.

It was such a windy night, and in fact the
retreat was well managed, and spared the city
the destruction it would have suffered if we had
fought, as I heard people say who might have
been just as fearful of losing our troops as anyone. The big fires were kept up as if the army
was still in place, and all night the cannon fired
toward the Union lines outside of town just to
fool them into thinking they dare not attack
while in fact the troops and their wagons and
supplies, and my two sons, were spiriting themselves away, thank God, instead of lying dead
like so many others under the boots of General
Sherman.

And from that night—when was it, just a
few nights ago—he, John, did not talk, he did
not say a word, this man of such rage, such fist-
shaking rage, he became so calm, so silent, that
that was even more frightening to me, the way
he stared at whoever spoke to him and didn't
reply: my husband. Can a man age so in just a
few days? Or was it that he was always this old
but that his vigor had suddenly deserted him

that hid just how old he was? And why did he
have to go to the warehouse where our things
were, where our furniture and art and our rugs
were stored for safekeeping? Perhaps to talk
with his friend the cotton broker, Mr. Feinstein, who had been so kind as to accommodate
us and who was always so patient listening to
John. It was more than just a business connection, such an odd friendship for my husband to
have, Mr. Feinstein being a Jewish gentleman,
but maybe John had to talk to someone if not
to me. I followed him. I was so frightened for
his state of mind, I didn't know what he might
do. Two Union soldiers stood guard at the
warehouse doors with their rifles held in front
of them. And there out in the street was Mr.
Feinstein with one of his workers, and he was
locked out of his own building. John, he said,
my business has been taken from me. I have
this piece of paper with the order signed by
General Sherman. He says my warehouse and
all the cotton it holds is the property of the
Union army. And Mr. Feinstein held his hands
up to Heaven.

And of course John Jameson being who
he is, he could not abide this. A more reasonable
man might have gone to see the General or
someone on his staff to explain the situation, just
to explain that our personal things were stored in

there with the cotton bales and, granted, cotton was a prized spoil of war, but of what use, for instance, would my needlepoint chairs or my English fabrics be to the Union army? Or my Persian rugs? Or my white leather-bound family Bible, with its steel-engraved illustrations and its own claw-foot oak stand? But John was now beyond reason. He argued with the soldiers to let him in—why? Was he going to carry off our things by himself? He became bellicose and threatened them, and he took up a paving stone from the pile in the street and came back to where the soldiers stood. Oh, I tried to hold him but his arm tore out of my grip, and Mr. Feinstein shouted, Wait, Jameson! One of the soldiers raised his rifle and I screamed. What was so hateful is that he said nothing in warning he did not say anything, this soldier—and I never want to hear such a sound again—when he brought the rifle butt down upon John Jameson's head. And I watched my husband of nineteen years, who married me when I was a girl and took me to live on his plantation, drop like a tree felled, all the sense blown from him on the blood sprung from his poor head.

WHEN PEARL CAME into the ward a woman was sitting by one of the beds, and from the back she looked like the wife ma'm. Pearl didn't want to believe it. She moved closer, sidling, ready to run. And then over the woman's head she saw the patient with the bandage on his head, and it was her pap.

At this moment Mattie Jameson turned and found herself looking up at the child who had haunted her life. Pearl wore the sky-blue Union trousers under her skirt and a uniform sash around her waist, and held a stack of white towels in her arms. Her hair had grown longer and she wore it pulled back and tied in a bun. Mattie had not shed a tear, sitting beside her unconscious husband. Now the tears filled her eyes.

Her life had collapsed, come to pieces, and here stood this child of her husband's sin to announce to her such upheavals of fortune as only God in his vengeance could design.

How many times during the years did she want to touch this beautiful child, how many times she had wanted to make her life easier. But John wanted nothing to do with her and it was easy enough to comply. When Nancy Wilkins died, Mattie was relieved. She thought that would be the end of the shadow that lay daily upon her own life in the form of such an extremely beautiful slave woman as Nancy

Wilkins. She thought that would be the end of the humiliation of an entire plantation of slaves knowing that her own bed was not sufficient for the Massah. But there was still Pearl. And if she, Mattie, had any instinct of kindness, or made any gesture of conciliation, it was Pearl herself who discouraged her, making it easy to dislike her by the insolence of her manner and the glances of contempt that flashed from her. And the older she grew the worse she became. It was Pearl's own fault that she found no place for herself at Fieldstone, accepted neither in the house nor in the quarters, too sassy for one and disdainful of the other, with only old Roscoe to guide her, putting her to work in the kitchen and the laundry, or sending her out to the field when she was needed there. But Mattie, knowing herself a good Christian woman, saw herself now as something else as she remembered her last glimpse of Pearl standing with her satchel and waiting for John to tell her to get up in the carriage and come with them, and how glad Mattie was that he didn't, thinking good riddance, and that maybe there was something to be said for this war after all. And all these thoughts overwhelmed Mattie now as the tears burst from her and she sat bowed and sobbing beside her comatose husband.

Pearl, disdainful of the woman's tears, turned her attention to her pap. How peaceful and handsome he looked with his eyes closed, as if thinking worthy thoughts in the calmness of his being. But this ain't like you, she said, hardly aware that she was speaking. I never remember you layin abed, Pap. Always up and about ridin down the field hands, shoutin an stompin ever'where, I could hear your footsteps all through the house. Won't you open your eyes, Pap? This is Pearl, your own born chile here. Never christened 'cept by my mama. She name me Pearl for my white skin. Your skin, Massah Jameson my pap. Your fine white skin. What happened that you layin here? I never seen you so quiet. I wish you was to wake up so I could tell you I am free. And by the laws of the Bible that you can't do nothin about I carry your name. This is Pearl Wilkins Jameson speakin in your ear, Pap. Your Pearl, as I hope you will rise up and live long to remember. Come, Pap, open your eyes and look on the daughter of your flesh and blood. Your eyes is closed, but I know you listenin. I know you hear me. And if you worryin about me I can promise no man will ever treat me like you did my mama, nosir. So you needn't worry 'bout your Pearl. She here in Savannah

now an thas just to begin. She goin far, your
Pearl. She will take your name to glory. Scrub
it up of the shame and shit you put upon it.
Make it nice and clean again for peoples to remember.

XV

IN THE FIRST TRIUMPHANT DAYS OF THE OCCU-
pation, Sherman had sent a telegram to the
President: I beg to present to you as a Christmas
gift the city of Savannah, with one hundred and
fifty heavy guns and plenty of ammunition. Also
about twenty-five thousand bales of cotton.

He held in his hands Lincoln's letter of
humble thanks. An adoring note from Grant. A
copy of the congressional resolution in his
honor. Editorials fulsome in their acclaim.

The country had gone wild. The General
whom nobody had heard from in months had
buried an ax in the Southern heart.

Sherman's billet was the mansion of a cotton broker. Its many rooms were hushed by
thick rugs and heavy draperies. There were pot-
ted palms and busts of Roman senators on
pedestals. The walls were hung with paintings of
pink-nippled harem women lolling under the

eyes of Negro eunuchs. He slept little. In his apartments upstairs he sat in his bath and smoked his cigar and read of his greatness. Letters of adulation were coming in by the bundle. He called for Moses Brown to add to the hot water, for that was the only thing that could calm him now, national recognition working in him as a nervous excitement. Also, the steam eased his breathing—his asthma was acting up. Not only the rain but the sea wind was having its effect. Sherman came from Ohio. Even to be near the sea unsettled him, and whenever he had to be on it all he could think of was the perversity of God in composing something that only heaved and wallowed and slopped about.

He wrote to his wife: I will not trust this acclaim to last. Are these not the newspapers that, after Shiloh, announced to the world that I was crazy? It is the verso of the same coin. Yet, day and night, crowds of blacks stood outside the house waiting for a glimpse of him. By eight every morning petitioners were lined up in the parlor. Periodically he went downstairs to receive them. Among his visitors were the wives of Confederate generals. They brought letters from their husbands asking that they be given safe passage. He readily complied. He affected gallantry. He wanted the people of Savannah to know that he was, despite all reports, human.

The women were the hardest to convince. The older they were, the more likely they were to let him know what they thought of him. In a way, he found this salutary. A Mrs. Letitia Pettibone appeared whom he vaguely remembered from his days as a young officer stationed in Atlanta. What she said he couldn't later recall, for she carried a beaded purse looped to her wrist, and when she swung it at him, had he not with his quick reflexes stepped back he was a certain casualty of war. After the woman was escorted from the room, he took a puff of his cigar and said to his adjutant, A new Field Order, Morrison: Ladies will please check their handbags at the door.

Christmas morning the rain poured from a black sky. Sherman had called for a review of the troops. His remarks for the occasion were written out for company commanders to read to their men. While they stood on parade the troops heard that they would be remembered in the military history of the world. Sherman, on a reviewing platform, listened to his words coming dis-synchronously from all directions and as if through water. The tarpaulin roof over his head billowed and snapped in the wind. Two regimental bands combined played a march. It sounded as if every note was played twice.

Sherman considered again the measures

he had taken: The Ogeechee and the Sound
cleared of mines, secesh coastal guns dismounted. Slocum's corps deployed from the Savannah River to the seven-mile post on the
canal, Howard's to the sea, Kilpatrick's cavalry
by the King's Bridge and the roads leading
north and west. Shops open, streets cleared, fire
companies intact. All public buildings, abandoned plantations, etc., the property of the
Federal government.

He'd missed nothing. Then what was
wrong? The national praise heaped on him in
the past several days seemed as cold and wet as
the rain on his face. Is that all it is, this damn
weather in my lungs? He left the platform and
was ridden to his rooms.

Sitting facing a warm hearth, his feet in
their damp socks held before the fire, Sherman
began to work it out: None of this of Savannah
was war. It was governance. Warring in the field
was pure, clear of purpose, it had a form. But
governance was conferring with civil authorities,
it was dealing with Northern recruiting agents
who wanted to conscript blacks as army substi-
tutes. It was dodging ladies' handbags. The local
population was swollen with whites who'd fled
here along with the freed slaves who had trailed
after the columns. He was feeding them all,
white and black. The port was thick with pack-

ets and steamers and cutters. The city was rife with unattached and bereft women of childbearing age. His soldiers were gambling, and those who were not in the whorehouses were filling the churches. He'd ordered drills and installed curfews, but none of it could staunch the drip by drip depletion of their war blood. It was as if his fighting force had melted and spread over Savannah like some viscid pool of humanity. Somewhere in all this there must still be an army, Sherman said to himself. Where are they when I need them? Until I get out of here I'm a sitting duck for Washington.

At this moment Major Morrison entered the room with the message that Secretary of War Edwin Stanton was arrived in port on a revenue cutter.

SO DOES THE LAUREL wither, Sherman thought. What will Stanton say: that I let a Confederate force of ten thousand men slip away into South Carolina? The human capacity for gratitude is limited. Inside the gratitude is envy. Inside the envy is the indifference of a heedless world. The Secretary's carriage rolling to a stop under the porte cochere, the honor guard presented arms. Stanton was second only to the President

in authority, but in Sherman's eyes the man stepping down was a portly figure whose soft face,
with its plump cheeks, bespoke a constitution
that would not survive a day's march.

General, he said, and gave Sherman a limp
hand. That concluded the amenities. Stanton
began speaking even before they were in the
door. He had a lot on his mind. His stiff forked
beard rose and fell with his words. Sherman, en-
tranced by the brandished beard, missed a good
deal. Something about how the blacks had been
treated. So that was it.

I would meet with your general officers,
Stanton said. At dinner Sherman produced his
wing and corps commanders. They were an imposing sight, decked out in their ceremonial
swords, gauntlets, and sash. But they sat as
stiffly as schoolchildren while Stanton walked
around the table as if conducting a lesson. I am
not sure, gentlemen, of your armies' appropriate
conduct regarding the freed slaves, he said. My
understanding is that they were discouraged
from accompanying the forces, that they were
sent back to their masters, or left as prey to
guerrillas. The men looked at Sherman slouched
in his chair with a severe frown on his brow. Mr.
Secretary, Sherman said, how do you expect me
to march sixty thousand fighting men through

enemy country with the weight of the entire slave population of Georgia on their backs? As it is, the darkies seem to be here, as you will see if you look out the window.

You have refused to enlist them in your army except as menial laborers.

As laborers is the way they are best used.

There is one report of an incident at Ebeneezer Creek, was it? Your General Davis, who pulled up the bridge and left hundreds behind to die. Some of them drowned, some of them were slaughtered by guerrillas. Where is he? Why is he not here?

He is on duty. I will have him summoned.

I will hear from him his explanation.

And you will be satisfied of the military necessity of his action.

In the morning the cavalry had to be brought in for parade. The Secretary stood with his belly pressed against the cast-iron railing of the balcony outside Sherman's apartments and watched, unsmiling, as the horsemen passed in the street below him. Kil Kilpatrick rode at their head, a Beau Brummel in his gold sash and braid, peeking from under his plumed hat with a sly smile, his slight figure seeming to post with some insolence, Sherman thought—or was it his bobbing hunchback that conveyed his attitude? Kil is a reckless fool, he enjoys war too much, he makes camp in women's bedrooms, but I wouldn't trade him for anything.

By the third day of the visit Sherman wondered how much longer he would be able to hold his temper. The Secretary didn't talk, he fulminated. He was like a spoiled child, and was always in need of something—a drink, a hot water bottle, a telegrapher. Behind everything the Secretary said or did was a desire for attention. Sherman had wanted the captured cotton for the army exchequer. Stanton countermanded it for the Treasury. He had strong views on who should garrison the city. He presumed to advise Sherman on strictly military matters.

And then came his demand to meet with some Negro elders. He was impatient until they were rounded up from the black churches. When they were gathered in the parlor he asked them what they understood by slavery.

The black men looked at one another and smiled. Slavery is receiving by irresistible power the work of another man and not by his consent, one of them said. The others nodded their agreement.

And what, said Stanton, do you understand of the freedom that was to be given by the proclamation of President Lincoln?

The freedom promised by the proclamation

is taking us from under the yoke of bondage and placing us where we can reap the fruits of our own labor and take care of ourselves and assist the government in maintaining our freedom.

Sherman hid his astonishment at how well spoken these blacks were. At that moment Stanton turned to him. General, he said, I will now confer with these freedmen regarding the colored people's feelings toward yourself. Would you mind leaving the room for a moment?

Sherman was livid. He paced the hallway, muttering to himself. To catechize these blacks regarding my character! How would any of them be here if not for me? Ten thousand are free and fed and clothed by my orders! That they are not fighting is my best military judgment. Nor have I had the leisure to train them. I have marched an army intact for four hundred miles. I have gutted Johnny Reb's railroads. I have burned his cities, his forges, his armories, his machine shops, his cotton gins. I have eaten out his crops, I have consumed his livestock and appropriated ten thousand of his horses and mules. He is left ravaged and destitute, and even if not another battle is fought his forces must wither and die of attrition. And that is not enough for the Secretary of War. I must abase myself to the slaves. Damn this Stanton—I am sworn to destroy the treasonous insurrection and preserve the Union. That is all. And that is everything.

Sherman was hardly mollified to hear that he was held in high favor by the black elders. Late that night he called in Morrison. The fellow had been sleeping.

Your pen, Major. Get this down. Field Order whatever it is.

It would be Number 15, sir.

Number 15, he said. The Sea Islands from Charleston south, and all the abandoned plantation acreage along the rivers for thirty miles inland in South Carolina, and I'll throw in parts of Georgia, and the country bordering on the St. John's River in Florida, are reserved for black resettlement. Have you got that? Black resettlement. Every free Negro head of family is to be given title to forty acres of tillable ground. Yes, and the seed and equipment to farm them. All boundaries to be determined and possessory titles issued by a general officer of the U.S. Army as—call him—Inspector of Settlements and Plantations. And tidy it up for my signature, with a copy for Mr. Stanton.

I am no abolitionist, Sherman thought. But with this enticement I both shut up Edwin Stanton and disengage the niggers, who will stay here to plant their forty acres, and God help them.

———

TO CELEBRATE THE Secretary's departure, Sherman had a dinner for his generals. It was as if they all needed to regain their dignity. Everyone was jolly. They were themselves again. Sherman sat at the head of a long table while the black waiters marched in with the pillage of the city: platters of oysters, roasted turkeys, baked hams, steaming mounds of seasoned rice, platters of sweet potatoes, loaves of warm bread and salvers of real butter, hampers of red wine. Sherman ate and drank and offered toasts. But he wanted to be on the march again where nobody could tell him what to do. He wanted to be back in the field. What could be better than lying on the hard ground each night and gazing up at the stars? What could be better than setting out each morning to run your war the way it ought to be run? The issues were unambiguous. The demands were clear. He had had enough of Savannah and its glory. The real glory was in the uncommunicable joy of doing well what God had deemed for you. There was no envy there, no praise to explode in your face.

Gentlemen, Sherman announced, we have had enough of these fleshpots. Tomorrow we begin preparations for the new campaign. You all know what it is. We have Grant's leave to take the Carolinas. It will be hard, no mistake. Georgia was no more than a hayride. We must divest ourselves of surplus horses, mules, and Negroes. We must pare ourselves down to our fighting essence. The terrain is forbidding, the march will be arduous. But I assure you the infamous state of South Carolina, as instigator of our war, will have never known the meaning of devastation until it feels the terrible swift sword of this army.

Hear! Hear! The generals raised their glasses.

At the end of the evening Sherman went to his rooms mellow with wine and feeling more relaxed than he had in days. He was humming "The Ride of the Valkyries." Some newspapers were newly arrived from Ohio. He lit a cigar and, expecting to amuse himself with the local gossip, sat back and read in the Columbus, Ohio, **Times** that Charles Sherman, the six-month-old son of General and Mrs. William Tecumseh Sherman, had died of the croup.

His hands dropped to his sides. Oh Lord, he cried, is the envy yours as well?

XVI

ON THIS COLD, DARK DAY, WITH THE CLOUDS sailing in low from the Sound, Savannah was alive with the movement of men and animals, so that it seemed as if the streets themselves were moving, that the city in its dimensions had come apart from the land and was fluttering loose in the blow. The wind piped its music to the rattle of the wagons on the cobblestone and the cries of the teamsters and the cadence calls of the platoon sergeants. Columns of troops were marching to the bridge over the Savannah River, and others stood in their mass along the docks waiting to board the fleet of navy gunships, cutters, and packets while seamen stood in the yardarms looking down on the scene like roosting birds. Among civilians, too, a sense of urgency was attached to their comings and goings, as if the departure of the army was in its way as frightening as its arrival had been.

Only the soldiers who were to garrison the city were unmoving at their posts. All else was hectic intention, with the wind blowing tufts of cotton through the alleys and even the live oaks in the squares bending and swaying to the wind.

In all of this Wilma Jones felt the smallness and insignificance of her own purposes on this morning. But that is the slave still in me, she thought. I must watch my own thinking—I must be as free in my soul as I am by law. She glanced at Coalhouse Walker who clearly had no such problems standing beside her with his shoulders squared and a kind of solemn joy on his face. He held her hand. Slowly the line moved forward and they came around the corner. Some of the people ahead of them were singing. Not loudly—they were singing for themselves, a prayerful hymn, so that this blessed thing that was happening would continue to happen. Up ahead, in front of the steps to the city hall, a table had been set up right there on the sidewalk, and a Union officer sat behind it with two enlisted men standing with their rifles at the ready on either side. Because of the wind they had put big stones over the sheaves of paper on the table. Wilma didn't know why the whole business couldn't have been right there up the steps inside of the city hall.

It was a very slow process. Some of the black folks thought they would be given a deed right then and there along with a map to get to their property. But these were applications only, and that had to be explained over and over again, apparently. And then of course most of the men couldn't write and the officer had to write their names in for them and let them sign with a mark and then the mark had to be attested to by the officer. And then, every once in a while, the officer got up and went into the building for one reason or another while everyone stood there waiting and singing and the wind blew wet along the ground, darkening the hem of Wilma's skirt and chilling her ankles.

When it was finally their turn, Wilma read the application and explained it to Coalhouse. He nodded and looked at the officer and smiled. But there was a problem. Resettlement deeds were exclusively for the heads of families. Is this Mrs. Walker? the officer asked, indicating Wilma. Coalhouse, frowning, shook his head no. Is there a Mrs. Walker even so? the officer said with a sly smile.

Coalhouse grew deadly still and stared at the man. Wilma grabbed his forearm, feeling the muscles tense. Give me that paper, she said. We'll bring it back to you and everything that we require we will have.

Whatever you say, Auntie, the officer said.

I expect you will recognize us, Wilma said. We will come directly to the front here, you will not have us start tomorrow at the end of the line, as we have done that today.

In a nearby town square they found a bench sheltered from the weather by a weeping willow. Yet it was chilly here too, and dark. Coalhouse put his arm around Wilma's shoulders. She leaned away from him, sitting hunched over with her hands in her lap. Let's talk about this again, she said.

I know to farm the land, Miss Wilma. That's what I know.

You saw that man's mind. Whoever they are, these are white folks first and foremost.

For forty acres around, we won't have to see a white face.

What they give they can take away.

That the Lord you talking about who can do that. No man will take what is mine.

Wilma shook her head.

Aw now, Coalhouse said, where is that spirit? It was there telling that officer man what would be. You will see us tomorrow right here! Yes! That was my Wilma. But where is it now, the spirit? Don't see it anywhere, Coalhouse said, looking into her eyes.

For a while they were silent. They listened to

the city astir. On the street behind them a procession of mule-drawn field guns clattered by.

My Judge Thompson? Wilma said. He used
to go up to New York or to St. Louis or
Chicago. Went to all those places. Take the
trains hither and yon. And he'd come back and
have his dinner and talk about it. I made sure to
stand behind the door and listen to him tell Miz
Emily about these big cities up North. How fine
they were. Each of them a whole world, with all
kinds of wonders that you wouldn't expect in
your lifetime. Of course, he was there to talk to
other judges and such, and staying in the fancy
hotels as a man of the world. But it made me
think. I would like to live in a big city. I could
do that. Nobody bother you there, everyone too
busy with theirselves to bother with you. And
you make your life. You're free.

The only way north in this war is walking
with the army. Is that what you mean?

Yes. Like before. If we are going, we ought
to go.

Live in the swamps, snakes bite you, guerrillas chase you. Shoot at your head.

You got us this far.

Oh, lady, don't tell me you know what's
coming. Six, eight hundred mile before you
even see your city.

He had stood and was pacing now, disturbed, agitated. So you heard your damn judge. A course. The fine things of the big city is made for the likes of the Judge. Is that the same city you expect, woman? Make your life? How? What can you do?

I can work at something. In cities they have jobs.

Yes, slaving. Wash the Judge's underwear, wash the underwear of ten judges, a hundred judges.

I can read and write.

Well, damn it, I can't. You understand, Miss Wilma? I can't. What job do you think to be givin me to do in your fine city?

You know music. You play music. Got a fine voice. I heard you. You made those people happy, picking on that banjo.

Oh Lord, oh Lord. Coalhouse paced back and forth, wringing his hands. I thought she had more sense than Coalhouse, this good woman. But her mind is afflicted. Listen, he said, and got down on his knees before the bench. I am a loving man, Miss Wilma. I have no bitterness in my heart for what has been done to me all my life until now. I have the whip marks of that life forever after across my back to testify that I have endured. I am strong. But I can only give you what I have in me, and what I have is I know how to work the land.

This paper in your hand is Mr. Lincoln present-
ing me with what I am owed—forty acres of
good loam and a plow and a mule and some
seed. And with that I will make a life for us. A
man who owns his own land is a free man.
Works for himself, not for nobody else. Sings
and dances for himself, not nobody else. Puts
the food on his table that he has brought from
the earth. And you tell me what is better than
that? At night, we will sit by the fire and you can
teach me to read and write. Then we will go to
sleep and wake up when the cock crows and do
the very same thing tomorrow we did yesterday,
under God's warm sun. And if you don't see the
blessedness of that then I will go down to the
river right now and drown myself.

You won't.

I swear.

Wilma leaned forward, put her hand to his
neck, and pulled him to her and kissed him. You
very handsome, she said.

I know.

Shame to put an end to all those good
looks.

He shrugged.

How about instead we find us a preacher,
she said. You know any?

He raised his head and smiled. Can't turn a
corner and not meet one.

Come get up from there and sit beside me,
Wilma said. Now, look here, you see on this
paper there's two lines to write in our names—
one for you as head of family and one for me as
real head of family.

Oh, how they laughed!

And so their course was chosen. They left
the park square and hurried toward one of the
black encampments. They were startled anew by
the military movement through the city. Streets
were clotted with wagon trains and marching
troops. They waited at a corner.

What about your service? Wilma said.

When I threw off the tunic it was over,
Coalhouse said. White officer can't tell who's
gone when we all look alike, can he?

This is my man, she thought. He is brave
and smart. And he's right-thinking. Staking a
claim, you stake out your freedom. After all,
how had the whites lorded over everything all
these years but by owning the land?

There was no doubt in her mind that he
would give his life for her. But, Lord, what if it
came to that? She knew what happened to stub-
born, strong-willed slaves. But then, foolish
Wilma girl, we are not slaves anymore, are we?
Coalhouse is younger than me, but stronger in
his convictions. He doesn't think about things
till he don't know what to think. I will simply

stop troubling myself. We have made our decision and I will stand by it.

But at the same time she knew that living
the rest of her life in Georgia she would never be
without misgivings.

After the parade had passed they continued
on their way. How you want to be called?
Wilma said. On the application I will have to
write it in for you.

Say Coalhouse Walker, Sr.

Oh? She looked right and left. I don't see no
Junior hereabouts.

Miss Wilma ma'am, Coalhouse said with a
big, wide smile. Just come along to the preacher,
if you please, and I promise you before you
know it there will be a Coalhouse Walker, Jr.

XVII

ARLY AND WILL HAD NOT BEEN OUTDOORS for several days. They stood on Waterfront Street blinking in the gloom of the dark, cloudy afternoon as if the sun were shining in their eyes.

This is a strangely quiet city all of a sudden, Arly said.

Will ran to the end of the street. They're gone, he said.

Who?

The ships.

Savannah was ghostly in the grayness of the day. They hurried along through streets that had not been swept. Many of the houses and shops were dark. The city looked devastated, though there was no visible damage. This town's like a dog with its tail between its legs, Arly said.

Sherman was here, Will said.

Appears so.

At one point, a patrol appearing up the

street, they hid in a park square behind some bushes. A few woeful stragglers were being marched along under guard.

The hospital gates were open. The court-yard was empty but for a Rucker ambulance wagon, its trace poles angled to the ground. The ward where they had worked was almost empty. A few of the hopelessly wounded were still there, gazing at them with the eyes of the dying, but the only doctor to be seen was a civilian.

Colonel Sartorius's surgery was bare.

Now we're in for it, Will said. While we been debauching ourselves the whole damn army has gone.

Don't speak ill of debauching, Arly said. It is no mean feat to make camp for a whole week running in a whorehouse.

I told you yesterday something was going on when we were the only ones left with those women.

You did. But I was too happy being like the last man on earth to worry about it. Arly sat himself on the operating table. I don't think you 'preciate that when we walked in there we had just enough for one tipple each until I discovered the poker game in the back parlor.

Well, you have the black eye for a medal.

He caught me one on the side of the nose, too. Some folks don't understand pure luck. It is a endowment, and those not blessed with it think something untoward is going on. But for that fellow, the Union boys was mostly good sports about it.

Why not? You had that Ruby feed them liquor till they was cross-eyed.

Ah, yes, Ruby, speaking of endowments.

I didn't like her laugh.

Her laugh, her laugh? Arly said, staring at Will in disbelief. I think I have wasted my time with you. You did understand what we were about in that house?

Of course. I went with that Lucille. She told me all about herself.

The skinny one with the buck teeth?

Well, I didn't mind. She was a nice girl. She liked to cuddle.

Arly saw come over Will's face a beatific gaze of recollection directed at the ground and, for once, he was at a loss for words. He found himself looking out the window at the ambulance in the courtyard. Hold on, he said. Just wait a minute. God has given me the answer, he said, and got down from the table.

What?

That hospital wagon out there. Go on and find us a mule and we will hightail it after the army.

How'm I to do that?

Jesus, man. Just find one and take it. This is a captured city. Are you not of the military authority that is running things?

And what do you do in the meantime?

I'm to think further on this plan. Arly looked back into the ward. We will need some wounded to take along for appearances.

IN THE COURTYARD Will buttoned his tunic, brushed himself off, and set his hat on straight. At the gate he looked both ways down the street. I could just walk around till they pick me up, he thought. Maybe even turn myself in. What if I'm made for a straggler. I don't care. Let them hang me, even. I'm owed that anyways. At least I won't have Arly Wilcox telling me what to do day and night. But there were no patrols to be seen. He came upon a livery stable just a few blocks away. In the dimness it smelled used enough, but all the stalls were empty. Then he heard a nicker. Down at the end of the row was a small bay mare with a braided mane. She looked him in the eye. A sudden rush of happiness came upon Will. Hey, pretty one, he said. However did the troops miss you?

He led the creature out of its stall. The tail was braided as well. He took a harness down from the wall and, talking to her in a soft croon, put the collar on, the belly band, the crupper, the bridle. Draping the traces over her back, he led her out the stable doors. Confronting him there with a cocked pistol was an old man with a wrinkled face and sparse gray hairs poking out of his chin in the name of a beard.

You'll have to get by me, son, he said.

This horse is now military property, Will said. Stand aside.

You're just a thief far as I can see. That's the Miz Lily Gaylord's carriage mare, given a by from your Gen'ral Sherman hisself, which she has placed in my charge until she returns.

Well, the Gen'ral has countermanded that order, Will said. Now get out of the way or you will be put on trial for disputing the Federal gov'ment.

The old man raised his pistol. It was one of those old long-barreled pieces with a curved wooden grip and a tinderbox. He could hardly hold it still. Will laughed and moved forward. There was a sizzling sound and then a loud report. Will's ears rang, and in the next moment he was trying to control a rearing horse and did not realize he'd been hit until, raising his arm to grab hold of the bridle, he noticed the hole in his sleeve. In the next moment his own bright blood pulsed forth with what he thought was something like a greeting.

The old man seemed surprised by what he had done. Will did not feel any pain, but a nausea rose in him and his legs threatened to buckle. It seemed to him absolutely necessary to show no alarm. All right, he said, you've shot at a Union soldier after the city has surrendered. That's treason, old man, that's a hanging offense.

The mare, skittish now, snorting and pawing the ground, Will led her by the throatlatch as he walked up to the old man and took the pistol out of his hand. It was a heavy piece, and he examined it as one would any antique. In the next moment the pain of his wound tore through his arm and, feeling a rage so great that he almost choked on it, he drew back and with all his might felled the old man with a blow of the pistol barrel to the head. He stood there a moment looking at the still form. Stupid old man, he said, dying for Miz Lily Gaylord.

A WHILE LATER Arly was driving them across the bridge over the Savannah River. Will, lying on his back in the wagon, strained to hear him over the clatter of the wheels. His arm hurt terrible. Arly had said they shouldn't linger.

We'll find a surgeon on the march, Arly shouted as he snapped the reins across the mare's back. Maybe even our own man. You'll be fine.

Will was cold. His teeth were chattering. He couldn't tell if he was shivering or accounting the ripples in the road. His sleeve was soaked. He held the arm upright as he lay on the side bench, and with his other hand pressed a finger into the wound to try to hold the blood in.

The shanks on this little horse is like toothpicks, Arly shouted. She ain't made to pull four wheels. You would of done better to get us a mule, like I asked you. On the other hand, it makes things easier with you laying back there considering the trouble I ran into intending to load up a couple of those dying Rebs. Where would I be taking them, and for what? So you're more like what someone would expect, Willie. And what with one thing and another we have to take the bad with the good and trust the Lord to guide us as he has done so far, even if he had to bleed you a little to get us past the guard posts.

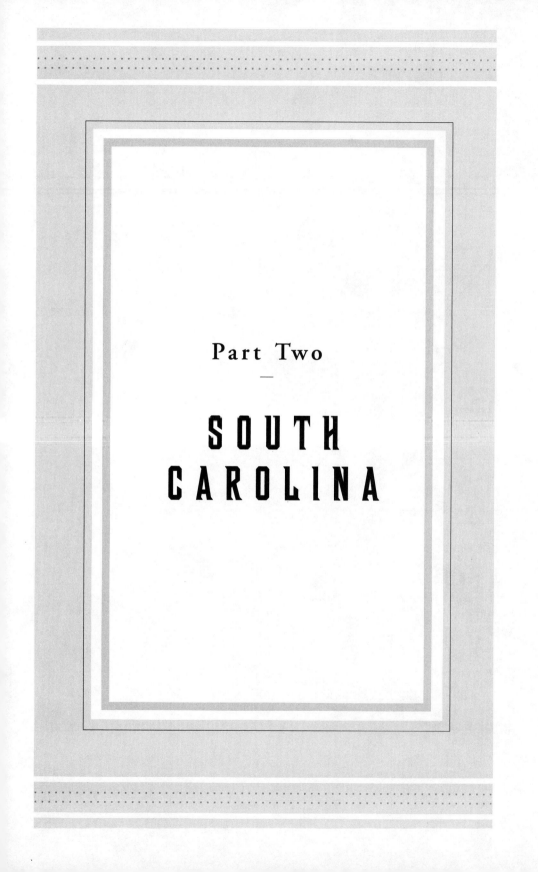

Part Two

—

SOUTH CAROLINA

I

THE RIGHT WING OF SHERMAN'S ARMY, GEN-
eral Howard's Fifteenth and Seventeenth
Corps, marching west from their landing at
Beaufort, and the left wing, Slocum's Fourteenth and Twentieth Corps, following the Savannah River in a northwesterly direction, the
secesh generals would not know if it was Augusta they were to defend or Charleston. In fact,
Sherman's target was Columbia, and despite
Morrison's personal resentment of the man, he
could not gainsay the genius of his strategy. It
was a double-pronged feint, and though by now
the secesh knew Sherman for the trickster he
was, they could not amass their forces until he
declared himself.

But what the Confederacy had by way of
recompense was this hellish Carolina swampland and the weather to go with it. The rain
poured off Morrison's hat brim, a curtain of

water through which the lighted pine knots
men carried to see their way through the bogs
were like glimmering stars. Up and down the
half-submerged road were the shouts and curses
of teamsters, and officers giving commands,
and though he was a major with the cockade
visible on his bedraggled shoulders, there was
no deference to his rank on this night, everyone, enlisted man and officer, too engaged in
the struggle to move forward to give a damn for
him or his orders.

Morrison led his horse by the reins. Even
where the road had been corduroyed, the weight
of the wagons pressed the logs into the muck
and another layer of rails had to be put down.
And more than once he passed teams, one of
whose mules had a hoof stuck between the logs,
a poor braying creature ready to pull his own leg
off. Where a wagon foundered, the entire train
was halted and dozens of men were rallied to
unhitch the team and empty the wagon of its
cargo before they could lift the wheels out of the
muck. Morrison found it preferable to wade off-
road through the swamp and enjoy the cold
mud seeping into his boots. He had letters from
Sherman and General Howard to General Joe
Mower, who commanded the vanguard division
of the wing. But he couldn't find Mower's headquarters.

Bearing right, Morrison moved laterally in hopes of reaching another, possibly more navigable road. But swamp turned to stream and stream to brush-clogged marsh, and in the darkness he could not be sure he was moving in a straight line. He could feel brambles tearing at his legs as he waded on through the slop, his horse balking behind him. The brush gave way to cypresses, a thick stand of them, whose snaking roots he could feel, slippery and treacherous, under his feet. I will drown now, he said, but stumbled forward eventually to find footing on the narrow bank of a high-running stream, a flood channel of the Salkehatchie, where he pulled himself up and then his mount after him, the creature shivering and shaking, its legs bleeding from the scratches on its shanks.

Following the bank for some hundred yards, he came upon a company of engineers laying a pontoon bridge across the channel. The engineers had anchored their platform boats and were bridging the boats with cut lumber, and at the near end were laying planks crosswise for footing that still had the house paint on them. This would be another road for the corps when the river was taken. The engineers' hammering and shouting were lost in the clamor of the rainfall and the unmistakable sound in the distance not of thunder but of field cannon, nighttime in this fourth year of the war no longer an agreed upon intermission between engagements. Morrison looked beyond the stream and saw only more swamp. So up ahead, how far?—a half mile, a mile?—the skirmishers were advanced to the Salkehatchie proper, where on the far shore Reb brigades were lodged behind their earthworks.

Not many more minutes of his search had to pass before Morrison was as weary and miserable as he had ever been. He wondered with some bitterness why he, a major, had been made to serve as courier, except that Sherman had it out for him. When, back in Savannah, he had told the General that Secretary Stanton had arrived, Sherman had said, You're better at sending than receiving, Morrison, and gave a kind of laugh to go with it. But Morrison had not liked it that even in jest he was being blamed for the news he had brought. He had served honorably and well, and was now paid for it with this wet, cold hell that could kill a man only more slowly than a bullet.

Someone was calling him, but as he looked around he saw no one. Then a chunk of tree limb landed at his feet with a splash and bounced as if it had not fallen but been thrown. He looked up and there, in the branches of a giant elm, he was able gradually to discern several men, some wrapped in blankets. One of them was smoking a pipe with the bowl inverted and the embers, as they glowed, brought the boughs and trunk into dim illumination. Morrison identified himself, shouting up through the rain, and understood that he had found the headquarters staff he had been searching for. In the highest crotch of the tree, standing like a sailor on the prow of a ship, and looking through the night toward the sound of battle, was General Mower, the man whom Sherman's letters were urging to turn the Salkehatchie resistance without delay. Sherman had planned for a smooth juncture with Slocum's wing on the high ground at the South Carolina Railroad, near the town of Blackville, and time was of the essence.

Morrison handed the dispatches up to the officer on the lowest limb and was invited to climb up and find a perch. Overweight and not terribly agile, Morrison didn't even want to try. He slumped down with his back against the tree, his rear end going numb with the cold.

II

RAIN HAVING MADE THE ROAD IMPASSABLE, the entire train was halted. Wrede lit a lamp and, setting his instrument case across his knees, used the time to write letters. To whom? He had mentioned a brother, also a doctor, back in Germany. Emily was uneasy. The rain against the tarpaulin was a loud roar. Through the open flap she could see the mules standing heads bowed in dumb submission. The wagon was atilt to the right, where the wheels had sunk in the wet sand. She could not get comfortable except by lying down on the pile of quilts and duvets accumulated for the use of the wounded. She lay on her side, her legs drawn up, her hands beneath her head so as not to actually have her face touching the rank quilts, some of which were stiff with dried blood.

The time was past when she felt the exhilaration of her adventure. She watched Wrede, who was hunched over his letter oblivious of the world, of the war, and of her. His powers of concentration were unnatural. At such times as this he was established in her mind as a total stranger to whom she was enslaved. How desolate, how lonely she felt. In the excitements of her boldly chosen vagrancy she had not thought about the future. Now it loomed ahead of her as a darkness, as a night of unceasing rain. Dr. Wrede Sartorius was not a normal man. She could not imagine him domiciled. He lived in the present as if there were no future, or in such a state of resolution that when the future came it would find him as he was now, as finished in his soul as he was at this very moment. Nothing fazed him—he had a preternatural calm. He was constantly sending to the Army Department of Medicine papers on surgical procedures he had devised, or improved courses of postoperative treatment he had discovered. He regarded the thick manuals of army medicine as virtually useless, and had a regal disregard of any and all advisories that came down from Corps. He was, finally, a man who needed no one other than himself, either professionally or, God help her, in his personal life. She could not imagine his becoming melancholic or nostalgic or unhappy, or giddy or foolish or anything temporary like that. He was an isolated, self-sufficient being who lived in his own mind, unneedful of anyone else. And, while he had shown her affection and had brought her like a teacher into his interests, she seriously wondered if she were to die in some attack, would he gaze upon her lifeless body as a bereaved lover or would he do an autopsy to see the effect on her tissues and organs of the grape or minié balls that had killed her?

Why am I so resentful? she wondered. But she knew the answer. It came to her as a moment's internal cringing sensation that made her press her thighs together. It was not as if in her girlhood she'd been a fantasy-ridden romantic destined to be shocked by the reality. She was an educated woman and had read enough to know of the reality that there was a bodily mechanics to love. But she had given herself in devotion. And she had felt only that she had been inhabited.

Yet beforehand he had not been without concern for her. As she lay there undressed, her eyes closed, she felt the weight gone from beside her on the bed. He had made a determination. She heard him open his instrument case. To spare you pain, he said, standing above her, I will do this small procedure. You will feel only a slight sting. And she felt his fingers dilating her, and then it was just as he said and there was no blood to speak of. And of course it was a solici-

tous and commonsense thing to do, but so of
his medical mind as to make her feel more like a
patient than a loved one. But then the inhabita-
tion. And at the moment of his crisis she made
the mistake of opening her eyes, and in the light
of the hearth fire his face was hideous, contorted
by a stunned and mindless expression, the eyes
frozen in a blind stare that seemed to her an
agony of perception as if into a godless universe.
And when he made his guttural, choking groan
she held him to her, feeling him shudder into
her, and holding him not in passion but in concern for him, that he should suffer so, though of
course it was not suffering, was it, but only
something in contrast to what she felt, which
was . . . inhabited.

And since then—was it just a few nights
ago?—he had been somewhat remote, seemingly glad to be occupied with preparations for
the renewed march, giving his quiet instructions
to everyone, including her. And now she felt
surely there was no future with this man. She
was an encumbrance, a Southern refugee whose
only justification was as fill-in nurse for the ab-
sent staff he would have preferred. And she had
never felt so desolate, not even when her father
had died, for it was in her own home, with familiar things around her, and she had not yet realized that the life she had known was over and

that in no time at all she would find herself a ruined woman in an army wagon, with the rain like gunfire against the canvas, somewhere in the God-soaked floodplains of South Carolina.

IN THE NEXT wagon back, Pearl studied the sealed letter she had removed from Lieutenant Clarke's dead hand in Sandersonville. Making up her mind that the letter was addressed to his family with the same last name, she was then able to work out the sound of the letters, except that the "C" at the beginning and the "k" seemed to have the same sound and she didn't know why there would be two different letters for it. The "e" at the end gave her trouble, too, she couldn't imagine what that was for. But anyways, she thought, I can read most of the letters in this name, so I can read them if I sees them elsewheres. But even though she held the letter at several different angles in the light of the kerosene lamp, try as she would she could not will herself to understand the rest of the words, there were three more lines of them, and she could not work out what they meant to say.

Mattie Jameson was asleep on the stack of folded stretchers. She was all curled up, with her hands under her chin, she was like a child in the womb. More than once Pearl had seen miscarried children, and that is the posture they all had, the way she was lying now, the wife ma'm. And in all the hard traveling with this army it was as if she was riding on a cloud, sleeping her life away most of the time, even now with the rain making a roar so that you could hardly hear yourself think. And when she was awake and Pearl tried to give her something to eat she wouldn't do more than bite into a biscuit or take a sip of coffee. And she did not talk, not a word, and looked at Pearl sometimes as if trying to re-member her name.

It seemed to Pearl, though she wasn't sure, not having the opportunity to study the wife ma'm's face that closely at the plantation, that her hair was grayed at the temples where it was all wheat before. She had it pulled back and string-tied behind the neck, and it made her look like an older woman, though Pearl knew for a fact that she was years younger than the pap. But her face was weary and soft, and there was no light in the skin. The pap was an old man when he passed on, sixty years on him if a day, and the wife ma'm couldn't be anywheres near that, though she was trying, wordless and grieving as she was, like she had died too and was sleeping all the time to prove it.

When, after he died, Pearl had told her in case she was thinking of going home that Fieldstone was burnt to the ground, that's when the wife ma'm had gone so quiet, staring into her own self.

Pearl looked around—it seemed too close in the wagon in this moment. She pulled off her tunic and immediately felt the wet wind coming in under the tarpaulin. She thought of the plantation where she had been born and had lived all her life till now, and thought of the sun on her head and the fields she loved. And then she was angry at herself. Thinkin that is not bein wholly free, girl. Not that I be free tendin to this wife ma'm who never paid me no mind, like I am her slave still. Hey, Miz Jameson wife ma'm, she shouted, wake up, wake up! And she leaned over and shook Mattie by the shoulder.

Awake, Mattie blinked, sat up slowly, and held her hands over her throat. She heard the drumming of the rain and felt the chill of her awakening. She pulled her shawl about her shoulders and only then was aware of the child Pearl staring at her.

You up now? Pearl said.

She nodded.

All right then, put you in mind of where you are. You see the cases here, these bottles an such? You are in this medicine wagon here with Porhl, your massah's natural chile. An if you can't speak, tell me you know that with a nod of your pore head.

Mattie nodded.

Thas right. An we are with Gen'ral Sherman, an his army gonna do in what's left of slavholdin. Say you know that.

Mattie nodded.

An it the goodness of some people that they took you along just as you ast 'em. You 'member?

Mattie nodded.

Right. An I know why. You lookin for brudder one and brudder two. Ain't it so you follow this army to hope it comes on these boys a yourn? Speak up, lady. Ain't it so?

Yes, Mattie whispered.

Yes. An you will run wif your arms in the sky 'tween the armies an stop the shootin an pluck those boys away an save their skins, ain't that right?

Yes. Mattie squared her shoulders and folded her hands on her lap. Yes.

Well, you a crazy woman to think so, but you are a mother an thas de way mothers think. It a mother's craziness, an I s'pose there is worse kinds. But now you must stay awake and be goin to sleep only when it is the time for sleepin. You know why?

Mattie shook her head.

You see my uniform tunic? I am doin nursin for the Colonel-surgeon who tried to save Massah's life. I can roll bandage, I can give 'em water when they thirsty, the mens, and so on. I am useful to this army that feeds me and takes me along 'cause I got no other home in this world right now. You hear me?

Mattie nodded.

Well, so in the same way you see, wife ma'm, you will make yourself useful to them, it bein a matter of your duty since you are taggin along, 'cause they need every kind woman they can find to tend to these broken mens.

What can I do? Mattie asked, almost in a whisper.

You will ask Miz Thompson next time we make camp an she will have enough for you, you needn't worry 'bout that. Whatever Porhl can do you can surely do. But there's one more matter, since I am lookin after you in your weak state and sorrow, an you know what that is?

No.

Well, it's what you wouldn't think of for all the time I was a chile in your house. You can teach Porhl to read. Startin here, Pearl said, holding out Clarke's letter.

Mattie reached for the envelope, and Pearl put it in her hand. Their eyes met.

Now don't you go cryin on me, Pearl called

out, but to no avail. The tears flowed down Mattie Jameson's cheeks. She was shaking her head and biting her lip, and Pearl, not knowing whether to comfort her or shout at her, was suddenly overtaken by the surge of feeling in herself as, unsummoned, and unwanted, the tears welled from her eyes as well.

III

JOHN JUNIOR AND HIS BROTHER JAMIE COULD see in the openings between the logs the first of the moving shadows far off amid the swamp trees. Then there were more and more after that, and soon in the mist of the first light it was an army of them slogging forward with the water to their armpits and their rifles held high and their shoes and cartridge boxes hung from the tips of their bayonets. Hold your fire, the Lieutenant said, running up and down the line. Hold your fire, he said in a hoarse whisper, as though the Unions, though too far off to shoot at, could hear his every word.

Cavalry had been drawn off to cover the flanks, but there were so many Yanks and only a thousand and a half Rebs to stop them. Oh Lord, Jamie said. He was cold and shivering, his lips were blue, and he was like as not to piss his pants. The brothers had not slept much in the night for the skirmishing going on up and down the river. They were hungry too, having eaten the last of their hardtack the previous day. John Junior, who was a year older, took on the role of military expert for Jamie's scared sake. Don't you worry none, he said, these works as good as a fort. They'll never get up here—we man the bluff, and we got artillery and they ain't. Can't set a fieldpiece in swamp.

Moments later John Junior was able to poke his brother in the ribs, for the guns had opened up, the shells whistling overhead and crashing out there in the water, bringing trees down and blowing men into the air. But still they came, some behind floating logs, which they used to steady their rifles as they fired to keep the cannoneers' heads down. They got their sharpshooters out front, John Junior said.

We're gon die. I don't want to die, Jamie said.

Shush, s'posin Daddy was to hear you talk like this.

Well, he ain't here, is he, so I can say what I please.

Think of somethin that's pleasurin so's you don't act such a coward.

Like what?

I dunno. Somethin. Like back home how we spied on the slavey women when they washin theirsels in the creek.

Yeah.

See 'em naked and they none the wiser.

Yeah.

That Pearl, that white one. I will have to fuck her 'fore some nigger gets to it.

Yeah.

She the prettiest a them.

Yeah.

Little tittles jes a comin out. Not big baloozas like them mammies. Lord, I never seen such big ones as some of 'em have, not even on our momma.

You spied on our momma?

Naw, I jes sayin from outward appearances an all.

You spied on our momma! I'm gon tell her.

Tell her what?

You peeked at our momma naked, John Junior. Oh, boy.

Shut your mouth or I'll do you in 'fore the Yanks get to it. You can die sooner easily as later.

Jamie thought about this and was quiet. You said they wouldn't, John Junior.

I was lyin, you snivelin little bastard.

You said—

You ain't no Jameson, nosir. Lookit them tears—Jesus, he turnin into a girl 'fore my eyes. You is goin to die, you little runt, and me too, so shut your face and be a man about it. Or after you dead the Yanks will fuck your ass.

You lyin!

Nosir. That's what they do to crybaby boys. You want that, why you jes go on bawlin. Yessir. That's jes what they'll do.

THE MAN DOWNSTREAM of Stephen Walsh took a bullet, seemed to throw his rifle away, and lay for a moment floating on his back, his hands clutching at the shoes strung around his neck. Then he was gone. Who was it? Wading to the spot, Walsh felt around, bending his knees and searching in the water with his free hand. Nothing. In this flood-tide swamp in the dim light of the early morning the only sign of the dead man was the reddish water, an oily patch of it slowly eddying and thinning away with the current.

All right, soldier, someone behind him said. Keep moving.

The ranks of men pushed forward through the chest-high swamp. It was a resistant thing with a life of its own, and in Walsh's mind it was not Union or Confederate but its own nameless kingdom and, as far as he could see as he pressed forward in the kind of plod it demanded, it went on forever. He felt no fear, only the grim despair

that had filled his breast from the day he took the
three hundred dollars to lay his life on the line. As
he had marched across Georgia, burning houses
and tearing up railroad tracks, it seemed to him
he was fighting an insane war. To see the smiles
on the faces of freed slaves coming out to meet
the troops was no recompense. He had read in
their eyes the angry moral knowledge that cannot
be consoled. He did not know if he could have
stood the burden of their life. To be lost on earth
so, as on an island of godless predation.

Around him the water burst in small vicious
snaps. They had artillery, too, the balls coming
over with an eerie shriek. He could not help
himself—when he heard this sound he turned
his back and flinched. But around him men did
the same. And then the trees would crack and
fall into the water behind them. He heard over
the water a round cursing of General Mower as
the designer of this fool advance. Goddamn
you, Mower, I'm a sitting duck out here! Goddamn you too, Sherman, and goddamn this
whole goddamn war! But Walsh knew it was not
like the generals to invest in heavy losses. He assumed that this frontal assault was the diversion,
and the flanking movement downriver or upriver was the effective action. So that when the
secesh position was turned they would abandon

their lodgment. I am to trust in God that it will be soon, Walsh thought, and laughed at himself for this uncharacteristic surge of piety. Because the swamp was filling with dead men, some floating by entangled in tree limbs.

As the light filtered through the cypresses, Walsh saw the men as boats. All together, advancing through fire and water and visible only from the waist up, they were an armada gliding forward with a side to side head-dipping motion as they held their rifles aloft. Here and there one would be stopped, like a ship shelled, its rigging a shambles. Walsh was not tall, at a sturdy five seven, and most of the time was concerned to keep his torso above water. But when he waded into a downward slope he was grateful for the increased depth, with only his head and raised arms available for a bullet. When he rose up again, the water pouring from his tunic, he felt he was there for a sharpshooter's bullet.

Feeling something bumping into his side, he turned and found a detached head, bearded and blue-eyed, its expression one of wounded dignity, and with strings of integument and vein trailing from its neck. For a hideous moment, before he could push it away, Walsh felt it was appealing to him as if, given even this experience, life could seem still to be desirable.

IV

T HEY WERE A DAY AND A HALF IN THE HIGH
ground between the Salkehatchie and
Edisto rivers while the army moved on. Wrede's
surgery was one of three set up in the field. Hospital tents held forty of the wounded, but there
were nearer eighty needing treatment. Wrede
was the only surgeon in the corps who did resections in the field. He was doing one now, a suppurating fractured long leg bone. The accepted
view was that resections usually led to postoperative complications. Amputation was a cleaner
and more successful procedure with a higher
survival percentage. The soldier might lose a
limb, but he had his life. Wrede knew this was
nonsense—he had seen too many amputees die
at the hands of his colleagues. Now, as Emily attended, she became aware of the audience of
other surgeons, assistant surgeons, and army
nurses who had gathered around the open-air

operating table. It was early morning. The sky was a bright blue, the sun glimmered through the treetops and the air was fresh and bracing, but the scene was otherwise grim, with men lying about on their litters calling for water, cursing God, screaming in pain. Yet the doctors had left their patients to observe Wrede Sartorius at work.

He'd incised the leg in two places and tied retractors above and below the infected bone. He applied forceps to the major arteries. Passing the threaded needle under the bone, he brought it around and attached it to a flexible chain handsaw. The marvel was how quickly and decisively he worked. Emily, at the head of the table, watched his hands. They seemed to her creatures with their own intelligence. In only moments, it seemed, Wrede displayed the offending bone section aloft in forceps. The rejoinment and closure were effected to the murmurs of the onlookers, and the leg was lightly bandaged and placed in a box splint. Emily had been holding the chloroform bag over the patient's nose and mouth. She was now instructed to remove it. Wrede was asked questions. He quietly answered them, though she could tell that he felt it was a waste of his time. They are still using collodion dressings on wounds, he had said to her one day, which almost assures inflammation. I have written papers arguing for light and air as the healing agents, but they do not listen. They do things the way they've always done them, because that's the way they've always done them.

Soon enough he was on to the next procedure, and the other surgeons had returned to their work. Emily only then became aware that as many glances had been directed at her as at the operating table. Had she caught one of the doctors with a knowing smile on his face? Or was it more like a smirk? How intolerable this all was.

In the meantime, the service companies had arrived and coffins were unloaded from the quartermaster wagons. The corpses were laid out at the edge of the field in the shade of the trees.

Pearl held Mattie Jameson tightly by the elbow as she led her along the rows of bodies. There were Southern boys there in their tattered grays and Union in their torn and bloody blues. Mattie considered each one, it didn't matter what the uniform. She looked on them in solemn study. It was as if she were trying to understand death. She would frown and shake her head. Some of the faces were swollen and broken and bloodied beyond all recognition. Others were clear and unmarked and frozen, their teeth bared, as if they had died trying to bite someone. Why should they look like that? Mattie thought. As if death puts us back to animals. Yet my John with his eyes closed died like a human at peace, almost as if he was glad to be dead, his hand folded on his breast and only his nose grown a little longer.

When the two women reached the last body, Mattie began to cry. Pearl didn't understand. It was a Union dead. Now, wife ma'm, she said. You can see for yourself the brudders ain't wif these fallen mens. So why are you weepin like some pore mama of a dead boy? You ought to be thankin God your babies an their little army are high-tailin it fast as they can to get outen the way of Gen'ral Sherman.

V

R IGHT IN THE DAMN MIDDLE OF THE BRIDGE the mare stopped. Arly threw the reins across her back. Gitup, he shouted, move, goddamn you! She did not respond. Arly stood up to see her better in the darkness. The left front hoof was lifted, she would not put it down.

Behind them the wagon train was halted. He heard the protests going back along the whole bridge and beyond the bank into the forest. The shouting echoed through the cypress trees, and suddenly the air over his head was filled with screechy bats. If there was anything Arly hated, it was bats. Get away, get away, he said, waving his arms wildly and hopping around, his feet drumming on the boards.

Cavalry splashed by on both sides of the bridge. An officer reined up.

What's the trouble, soldier?

Arly knelt by the mare. 'Pears her leg's busted, sir.

What're you carrying? the officer said, pointing to the wagon.

One wounded.

Get him out.

By now teamsters from the wagons just behind had come up to see what the trouble was. Arly lifted the back flap and said, Will, we got to move you. Can you get up? Don't lift him by the arm, Arly said to the men. That's what's the matter with him.

Will could hardly stand. He was holding his bad arm, which seemed to have stopped bleeding. But the whole front of his tunic was wet with his blood.

The mare was unhitched and steadied on the downriver edge of the bridge. The officer tied his mount's reins to a stanchion, jumped onto the pontoon, jammed his pistol into the mare's ear, and fired. Her good leg buckled and as she went down she toppled into the water.

Arly put his shoulder under Will's good arm and held him up that way. Will smelled of his sweat, he was bathed in it.

A good dozen teamsters rocked the ambulance side to side, and with a mighty heave they shoved it into the river as well.

All right, said the officer, let's get moving.

—

ARLY AND WILL rode now in a commissary wagon filled with sacks of flour. Can't get more comfortable than with your back against this, Arly said, punching a sack into shape to suit him like it was a pillow. A whitish haze filled the air.

Where is this, where we going? Will said.

Well, we're back with Gen'ral Sherman, Arly said. You knew that.

It's dark, Will said after a moment.

Well sure, it's nighttime.

I b'lieve I'm dying, Will said.

Aw now, that's the way you talk with the least little hurt.

No, it don't hurt no more, Will said, so it must be so.

Arly could hear him breathe.

I'm thirsty.

Shit, Arly said. He crawled to the front of the wagon and negotiated a canteen from the driver.

The water made Will perkier. At least they can't execute a dead man, he said, and gave a weak chuckle that ended in a cough.

That's so, Arly said. He was beginning to wonder if Will truly was dying. The boy seemed so much older all of a sudden. Like he had managed to bypass Arly in age and get on to where men were old and wise and giving instructions.

Can you remember Coley's Mill? Will said.

Say what?

Where I'm from. Coley's Mill, up by Asheville.

Is that right? You know, I'm from over the Smokies there in Gatlinburg.

More'n a few Kirklands in town, Will said. But ours is the biggest place. You tell them, O.K.?

Who?

My momma and daddy. Be best if you catch Daddy sober. Tell 'em Will fought an died for the C.S. of A. Can you do that for me?

Well, sure, if it comes to that, but it won't, you know. Besides, if you die how you going to see your sweetheart Miz Thompson and make your case. I mean, when we find them she will be the one to nurse you along, won't she? So it wouldn't pay you to die just now and miss her smiling at you and putting her soft hand behind your neck and lifting your head for a drink of good brandy, or, even better, some laudanum or other sop'rific to ease your mind. See as how even I have picked up on the nomenclature? I should consider after all of this to try medical college for myself. I mean, I have always been good with my hands. Except it is prob'ly not

God's plan because it is not a secure enough thought in my mind to be his thought. And it sure ain't God putting your dying thoughts into your mind. It is some Devil pretender just to make your ride in the wagon a little bumpier. Hell, there ain't nothing wrong with you that Miz Thompson can't fix up with a smile.

Will was silent.

I didn't tell you before, son Will, but though God has given me his signs, he's always meant 'em for the both of us, as we have been together since the morning they put you into the penitentiary across from me. That was God's doing too, as you must know. And I swear to you I feel the mystery of his ways beginning to come clearer. Any day now, I b'lieve we will hear what God has meant for you and me to do in this sad war and what his reason was to take us out of Milledgeville and set us to traveling with the wrong army. There is a mighty purpose that we are meant to fulfill. And if you think I am being too high and mighty—I mean, I know yo're inclined to the skeptical—need I remind you that God's messengers in the Bible tended not to be of the upper classes, and Moses hisself had even killed a man. So if God now chooses us poor excuses for soldiers, well that's his way, maybe he thinks if he can redeem us he can re-

deem everyone. I mean, even you would agree
the human race is something of a disappointment to him, 'cepting, of course, such angels as
your Miz Thompson and perhaps that buck-
tooth whore you cuddled with in Savannah. But
for the most part God had so much expectations
for us and we have not turned out right. We are
his chief blunder. I mean, bats are his blunder,
and ticks and horseflies and leeches and moles
and cottonmouths—they are all his blunders,
but the greatest of those is us. So when I tell you
that I feel the moment is almost upon us when
his intention for us is revealed, I want you to believe me. In fact, I already have some idea of the
kind of thing he is thinking. You want to know
what it is? Willie? You want to know finally
what we may be called upon to do?

When Will didn't answer, Arly said, You fall
asleep, son?

Arly went up front to the driver's box, where
a kerosene lamp was strung from the center tarpaulin pole. I'll unhook this fer a moment, he
said. Just to check on my patient back there.

And it was as he had thought: in the light of
the lamp Will's eyes were closed and his eyelids
and cheeks were white from the flour dust sift-
ing through the air, and with that clear, untrou-
bled boyish look on him, almost a smile on his

whitened lips, he had to be having some sweet dream, perhaps of Miz Thompson, and of course, being Will, not of loving her up but maybe standing with her in a church before the preacher. And with me, Arly thought, the best man beside him ready with the ring.

VI

As vanguard for general slocum's left wing Kil Kilpatrick's riders, composed of cavalry and mounted infantry, some five thousand of them, crossed the Savannah River and made their way north, torching villages as they went. In most places the resistance was minimal. Kilpatrick accumulated treasures on the march until he had his own personal train of wagons filled with booty—silver services, fine bed linens, glassware, bottles of liquor, hampers of wine, as well as baked goods, cured meats, eggs, jams, dried fruits and roasted nuts, coffee beans, and other delicacies for the palate.

Cantering into the village of Allendale one afternoon, he smelled something delicious and raised his hand to halt the column behind him. An aroma of cooking meat seemed to be coming from a house set back from the street in a park of live oaks. The house was empty, but he found in the outhouse kitchens a half-darkie in a chef's hat preparing dinner for some slaves. The slaves, sitting at table when he strode in, jumped up in alarm. What is this? Kilpatrick said, peering into a great pot where there simmered a stew with chunks of meat hanging off the bone, greens and turnips, cloves of garlic, and spices of such subtlety as to propose to him the civilized joys he had forfeited by coming to the defense of his country. **Le lapin,** said the chef, a French Creole who gave his name as Jean-Pierre. Goddamn, Kilpatrick said, slurping some of the stew from a ladle. You all, he said, turning to the frightened slaves, you all are free. You, he said to the chef, raise your right hand. And right then and there he inducted the bewildered Jean-Pierre into the army, conferring upon him the rank of Sergeant of the Mess. With all the rights and privileges thereof, Kilpatrick said. I'll have a plate of that now, Pierre, and then we'll be on our way.

The owners having fled, Kilpatrick commandeered a handsome landau from their stable and the bay stallions that went with it.

FROM TOWN TO town it was a new young black woman Kilpatrick took to ride with him each morning and share his bed at night. He liked the best house in town for his billet, and in the house the best bedroom with the softest mattress, and the downiest pillows and warmest blankets, some of which he would take with him upon breaking camp. In his entourage also was a nephew of his, Buster, an obnoxious ten-year-old towhead despised by the staff officers. The boy lorded it over everyone, a fact that Kilpatrick tolerated with amusement. He doted on the boy and gave him reading lessons when he had a spare moment. .

At the Little Salkehatchie River crossing at Morris Ford, two miles from the town of Barnwell, Kilpatrick's column ran into a force of three hundred Reb cavalry. Kilpatrick ordered up a battery of light guns. Under cover of the barrage his mounted infantry waded the boggy river, shooting straight ahead with their repeater rifles. The secesh troops held their works until their flanks were turned, whereupon they vanished into the woods.

When the Union riders reached Barnwell, they found it undefended. Only women and children were in residence, and they were advised by the kinder officers to leave town as fast as they could. The troops were turned loose. Ragingly hungry, they ransacked homes, riding down fences, pillaging what they could find, looting the pantries, sitting themselves down in the kitchens and demanding dinner from black folks, some of whom were delighted to oblige, while others were frightened into obedience. Kilpatrick chose for his headquarters Barnwell's one hotel. Hands behind his hunched back, he gazed from a window as plumes of smoke began to appear over the town. Watch what happens, Buster, he said to his nephew. Not many boys will ever see a sight like this—it's better than a July 4th. Sure enough, flames were soon rising over the town as the volcanic hearts of black smoke. Thin tongues of fire shot skyward as the lovely late afternoon turned to dusk. Buster was so enthralled that, while Uncle was enjoying the spectacle, he got up on a chair, took a candle from its sconce, and went about setting fire to the window draperies. One of the officers shouted, and in another minute Kilpatrick's staff were cursing and stomping out the flames as the General stood there laughing. Not just yet, Busterino, he said, we've got some celebrating to do first.

While the town burned around them, Kilpatrick ordered up some musicians and black dancing partners and gave his staff a Jean-Pierre–catered dinner that went on into the night. Buster was sent off to bed but at one point in the early morning he was roused from his sleep by the shrieks of a woman. All he could see by the firelight coming through the

window was the rising and falling white back-
side of his uncle Kil in the next bed. Uncle
grunting and the spurs on his boots jingling
and the bed creaking and the woman, whoever
she was, yelping—all of it together was like a
horse and rider at the gallop, and Buster, wide
awake now, knew this was the getting-women-
naked part of the evening that always happened
after he was put to bed. But he had never seen
it this up close before.

Then after a while everything stopped and
it was as quiet as it had been noisy and Uncle
Kil jumped up from the bed and pulled up his
trousers by the galluses. Seeing the boy awake he
grinned, his teeth ashine in the flickering light.
That, Buster, was nothing but your uncle Kil
showing you what it means to be a man. And
soon as that pecker of yours puts out some hair,
he'll see to it you learn the lesson for yourself.

At dawn Kilpatrick emerged from the hotel
to gaze over a gutted village. The streets were
razed, only smoking piles of lumber and standing chimney stacks to indicate the Barnwell that
was. His troops, though clearly worse for wear,
rode at a slow gait past him, their brigade commanders saluting him as he stood half dressed
on the hotel porch. Kilpatrick yawned. He
called over his adjutant and, using the man's
back as a desk, wrote a quick note to Sherman,

who was riding with General Howard's right wing not a half day's march to the east. I have renamed Barnwell Burnwell, Kilpatrick wrote, and sent the note off by courier.

Unlike the majority of Sherman's troops and officers, Kilpatrick did not have a particular animus for the state of South Carolina. He fought with a hellish impunity wherever he was. He was a reckless tactician and had from the beginning of the war gained a reputation as a dangerous fool, with a death rate in his commands far above that of other generals. Behind his back they called him Kil-Cavalry. Yet there was about this short, somewhat malformed officer the charismatic audacity of a classic warrior. Men followed him almost in spite of themselves, and women found him irresistible. A few inches shorter and he would have been dwarfish in his proportions, with his wide-shouldered torso and his rounded back. When he rode, he gave the illusion of being top-heavy and about to slip out of his saddle. He was something of a dandy even in the field, perhaps to make up for his ungainly shape and his facial features, which were rude and emblematic of his combative nature. His wide-set eyes gave no indication of a thoughtful sensibility, his nose, hooked and fleshy, pointed to the wide mouth of a sensualist, and everything was framed in scraggly red burnsides that disappeared under a broad-brimmed hat worn at a rakish tilt.

He was far from the kind of officer Major Morrison would respect, who rode into his rest camp that afternoon with a summons from General Sherman. Without ceremony Kilpatrick grabbed the note from Morrison's hand, and in short order he and his personal guard of six horse soldiers were off at a canter.

Ordinarily in this situation Morrison would have expected a call to ride with them. But he was too tired to take umbrage. In fact he felt ill. When he'd dismounted to report, his legs had nearly gone out from under him. In any event he knew what Kilpatrick would be told: Sherman was marching north with the joined wings to Columbia. Kilpatrick would demonstrate south, toward Augusta, in the manner of a vanguard.

Kilpatrick's forces were arrayed on a road that ran beside the tracks of the Charleston & Augusta line. As far as Morrison could see in either direction, details were at work prying up the rails and laying them in bonfires made from the ties. He thought of this as an inverse industrial process. The rails, when red-hot, were removed from the fire and bowed and twisted. It was a relaxing duty for the cavalry, and the men's voices came through to him as burble of camaraderie. This put him in uncomfortable mind of his self-knowledge. Morrison had never had comrades. Even at the Point he had never been able to establish himself as one of a band of men. He was always off at the edge of things, tolerated, perhaps, but not included. There was something about him that he'd long ago re-signed himself to—an inwardness that had left him lonely throughout his life and, at his worst moments, petulant.

Pillars of smoke rose in a line above the track, smaller and smaller into the distance—al-most, he thought, like the puffs of a working lo-comotive. On the other side of the track was an open field of some two hundred yards, and then a forest of scrub oak and pine. To his back, a rolling farmland with dried-out, yellowed corn-husks lying withered in the winter sun. In either direction, Morrison knew, pickets were posted for any signs of Reb movement.

He had started out in the morning grateful for the sunny sky but as he gazed into it now it seemed to him a shimmering malevolence. He found a field chair before headquarters tent and, still holding his mount's reins, sat down heavily. He didn't know what was wrong but he felt awful. He unbuttoned his tunic, which seemed to him too tight. There was some sort of repeti-tive rasping in his ears, which he slowly realized was the sound of his own breathing. Feverish, he dozed, with the sounds and sights of the camp transmuted into the voices of his parents and the room he had lived in as a child. He awoke and almost instantly closed his eyes again. This happened over and over. He would awake with a start, look around with a high degree of clarity, seeing his horse nibbling the grass, the officers' black servants going about their tasks, everything quite sanely observed, and in another moment he was back in the fantasia of feverish illusions—people barking at him in a language he couldn't understand, rearing horses with the horns of unicorns, and that awful buzzing sound of a sawmill that was his own breath. I am fully aware of what is going on, he said to himself, I am ill with a fever. At the same time, he couldn't seem to shake himself awake.

YOU'LL COME WITH US! These were the words that resounded within Morrison as an order given over and over again. **You'll come with us!** Who had said that? He was aware of riding close quarters in a phalanx of horsemen, his feet in the stirrups pressed momentarily into the flanks of other mounts. He couldn't see clearly—the morning sun was directly in his eyes. Yet he had unsheathed his officer's sword and held it low along his leg, and with the reins wound twice in his left hand. He was not a natural horseman and rode bent low over the pommel. The road was sodden, and gobs of mud flew onto his face and affixed themselves like leeches. But then, unaccountably, the terrain went dry and the dust from the riders ahead rose as a cloud and he felt his mouth coated with dust, he was breathing through his mouth, spitting and wheezing and tasting the grit of the land. Yet the effect was to darken the sunlight, and he could see up ahead the roofs of a town.

And then they were riding down a street and all at once the purposive charge was in disarray, with horses rearing and men shouting and horses and riders going down around him. Morrison could not ride forward or turn. The hideous Rebel shriek was in his ears. In this roiling entanglement of blue and gray, men were pulling one another from their mounts. His eyes closed, Morrison raised his saber and swung it at what or who he didn't know. He felt it cleave flesh and bone. Why didn't these people understand he was not well? Someone had an arm around his neck. Morrison held tightly to the reins and felt himself going down backward. As he tried, fitfully, to wield his saber in a chopping motion over his shoulder, it flew out of his hands. His eyes opened and he was transfixed by the hoofs of his horse flailing the air. Then its head filled his vision, terror in its rolling eyes, a scream issuing from its open jaws. He caught a glimpse of the sun in the moment before he hit the ground. He felt his leg crack, and was gasping in pain at the moment his spine snapped under the weight of his screaming horse and the breath was pounded out of him.

VII

WHEN THEY CAME OVER THE BRIDGE AND into the village, Arly got down from the wagon and pulled Will out by the arms and ducked under him and stood up slowly till he had the boy slung over one shoulder.

The smoke from the burned houses and barns hung ghostly low over the road. Hell, Willie, Arly said, you wouldn't want to breathe this air, it ain't nothing but smoke and cinder. Like to burn your throat away.

Arly stepped to the side of the road and let the wagon go on.

Whatever was left of the town was dimmed in a blue haze on this cold dry morning. Women, some with babies in arms, watched in silence as the wagons passed. A dreariness of creaking wheels and the stolidness of a rolling army fol-lowing its fighting troops was all there was to see. The train was like the back end of a parade, the band long passed. The lowing of the cattle as the army drovers led them across the bridge and through the town was the music now.

Arly turned in a circle until he saw it well enough through the haze. It was at the east end of the town, past some razed houses to where the land rose. It was a low hump of land with the stones poking up any ways but plumb. There's nothing to burn in a graveyard, is there, Will? he said. You can knock down a few stones is about the worst you can do.

He set off with his burden, oblivious to the stares of the people he passed. He wore the hated uniform, but they were too stunned to do much of anything besides stare. Some didn't even do that, just glancing up as he passed and going back to their thoughts as they kicked through their rubble.

Will was thin enough in his life, but a set of dead bones was another matter when folded over your back. And he was beginning to put out a smell. Arly didn't know what he would do about a burial. He had no spade, he was tired and hungrier than he could remember, and he shouldn't let the army get too far ahead of him. But if he didn't bury Will, who would?

Arly's mind was secured with a feeling of sorrowful righteousness. I won't deny I took you outen that hospital right there in Savannah where a doctor might have kept you from bleeding to death, he said to the dead boy slung over his shoulder. But how likely was it we wouldn't shortly be back in two cells awaiting only for the coffins to arrive before they shot us for spies or some other damn thing?

A house gutted but for the sagging porch attracted his eye for the divan out in the front yard. Arly kicked open the wrought-iron gate, stumbled forward, and dropped the body on the divan. He propped it into a sitting position and sat down beside it, taking some moments to recover his breath. He found the stub of a cigar in his breast pocket and put a match to it.

I made a calculated wartime decision, Will, he said. But who can know for sure that God wasn't behind it? We are his instruments, alive or dead, and I expect your risen spirit is listening to me now up by his side there and knows better than I what will be.

As if in answer, the body toppled sideways against Arly and the head settled in his neck. Sighing, Arly put his arm around it. And the two of them sat that way in the quiet of the burned air under the blackened trees, neither the dead man nor the living inclined to move. Arly didn't doze, exactly, but his eyes did glaze over, and the cigar dropped out of his fingers onto the grass. It was in this somnambulist state that he observed a wagon drawn by one mule pull up and a man in a brown coat and derby, and a nigger to help him, establish themselves right there outside the gate in the business of photography. Out from their wagon they pulled a big wooden tripod and set that up. Then they dragged a camera box out and affixed that to the tripod. And then, while the man in the derby busied himself picking out a lens and screwing it onto the front of the box and aiming the camera and looking at the sky and aiming the camera again and looking at the sky again, the nigger was running back and forth to the wagon and bringing out boxes with stacks of metal plates. Oh yes, they were getting ready to make a photograph, they were. Arly had come awake, but he didn't move or open his eyes wider than he needed to see what was going on. The wagon had a black tent mounted on the bed and steps leading up the back, and the sideboard had printed on it Josiah Culp, U.S. Photographer. In smaller letters it said Carte de Visites. Stereographs.

Arly waited till this Josiah Culp put his head into the black hood behind the camera, and then he waved.

Don't move! came the muffled shout, so Arly got to his feet and allowed Will's trunk to drop sideways to the divan.

Josiah Culp came out of his black shroud, his arms raised in despair. I had it, I had it! Why did you move? Sit back down there, if you please, it is perfect, it's the image I've been looking for.

How do you know what you been looking for if you only just seen it? Arly said.

You know it when you see it. It leaps out at you. It speaks to you. Please, he said, pointing to the divan.

He was a portly man in a regular suit and vest and topcoat thrown open over his belly. He was so fussed about his missed photograph that he only now noticed Will's odd folded position on the divan, with his feet still on the ground. What is the matter with your comrade?

Nothing he frets over, being dead.

He's dead? You hear that, Calvin? The other one is dead. Yes, I see the stains on his tunic. Of course. That's even better. Sit back down there with your dead comrade, sir, and put your arm around him as before and look at the camera. The light this morning is not as good as I'd like it, but if you will hold still for a few moments I am going to make you famous.

I don't suppose you can keep a black man, mule, and equipage like this without you sell your wares, Arly said, walking out to the street.

Here, what are you doing? Josiah Culp said.

Arly was peering into the back of the wagon. It looked something like an army-hospital wagon in there, with its cabinets and boxes of supplies. Cooking utensils were hanging from a length of twine strung widthwise. And did he smell provisions? He climbed inside and lifted a tarpaulin and found a peck of sweet potatoes and bags of sugar and coffee and a dead chicken plucked of its feathers.

Get down from there, sir!

All sorts of things. He found a folded tent and a pick and shovel and a pile of uniform tunics, both blue and gray. He found rolled-up shades with backgrounds painted on them. He unrolled one: it showed a painted pond with ducks and painted trees such as had never been seen on the face of the earth.

But what came to Arly as a revelation was a photo—the top one in a stack of glass photos in a crate. It was mounted on black cloth and framed in silver. It showed Union army officers posing in front of their headquarters tent. He took it to the light. The caption read: General Sherman and His Staff, Georgia 1864. Sherman had to be the one who was seated. He was staring straight ahead at the camera.

Yes, Lord, Arly whispered. It has come to me now.

He replaced the picture, rummaged around

another minute, stuffed each of his pockets with a sweet potato, and jumped to the ground. He was encouraged to see Calvin, the young black man, smiling appreciatively.

You a freed slave, Calvin? You sure got yourself a nice suit and hat.

Yessuh. I am learning the photography trade from Mr. Culp.

I suppose he profits handsome from the generals wanting photos of theirselves.

Not just the officers, Culp said. I photograph enlisted men as well. Every man wants his picture taken. It ameliorates the pain of separation for the families, for the loved ones, when they have a portrait of their soldier.

Well, you got a good thing going, all right, Arly said. 'Meliorating.

A carte de visite is most reasonable. But profit is only the means to an end. I am a photographer licensed by the United States Army, Culp said. Why do you suppose that is? Because the government recognizes that for the first time in history war will be recorded for posterity. I am making a pictorial record of this terrible conflict, sir. That is why I am here. That is my contribution. I portray the great march of General Sherman for future generations.

If the money don't mean that much to you,

why not pay me if a photo of me is what you want?

Culp laughed, showing a mouth of chipped teeth. Now I've heard everything!

Leastwise you won't have to pay him, Arly said, gesturing to the divan.

You are fortunate that I'm willing to make your picture without remuneration. I agree to give you a copy. I will agree to that, but the rights in the photo will be mine. Now, please, while the light holds sit yourself down as before, with your arm around the dead man.

Arly withdrew from inside his tunic the loaded pistol he had found in the photographer's wagon. He held it out at arm's length, as if to feel its heft, and looked down the barrel at Josiah Culp. I am in mind of a different picture, he said.

VIII

S HERMAN SAT ON A LOG, WAITING FOR MEN
from Howard's Fifteenth Corps to lay a
pontoon bridge across the Broad River. It was a
clear cold bright morning, somewhat breezy.
Not a mile to the north lay his prize, Columbia,
the capital of the secessionist treason spread out
on the plains like a plum cake ready to be eaten,
a woman ready to be taken. Oh Lord, he did remember Columbia, where, as a young officer,
he'd known several families. Some lovely ladies
lived there. And one in particular, years younger,
not much more than a child, a lithe little bean-
pole but with a glance that made his knees
tremble. Would she be here still? Ellen, that was
her name—the same as my dear Mrs. Sherman.
Ellen Taylor. A married woman by now, a widow
perhaps, no longer lithe and with a bevy of children pulling at her skirts.

He could see the grand statehouse the city

fathers had been intending, a handsome half-finished classical structure in granite. Very appropriate to a community that thought so well of itself. With what a sense of security they must have kept abreast of the war up North. To be the author of it and yet safe from it. He could see the ruins of the railroad depot from which the smoke still rose. The streets were abustle with a population only too aware of the blue army gathering in its immensity to the south. The streets were crawling.

Taking up his binoculars, he saw Confederate riders on the roads going north out of town. Negroes were clustered at the depot, plundering the cars of sacks of grain and God knows what else he could use. Calling over his adjutant, he ordered a section of Howard's twenty-pounders to lob a few shells to disperse the looters. And a few over there for good measure, he said, looking again at the statehouse, which flew the Confederate flag.

An hour later he was marching with his staff at the head of the corps on the road to the city. The wind had picked up and some of the mounts were skittish with it, losing their gait, lifting their nostrils to the air. And then, all at once, it seemed he was in the city's market square, the elderly mayor coming out of the crowd on foot to greet him and assure him that there would be no acts of resistance from the citizens of Columbia. Sherman, seeing the quiet crowd of onlookers, raised his voice in answer. And for our part, Mr. Mayor, he said, looking out at them all, let me assure you that we intend no injury to your citizens or their property. We will linger here only to relieve you of those matériels and facilities of which you no longer have need.

At that moment Sherman smelled smoke and, standing in his stirrups and looking out over the heads of the people, saw down a side street of commercial buildings that a stacked row of cotton bales was on fire. One of his generals quickly gave orders and a company of troops was dispatched to put out the flames. In an unexpected and touching amity, they were soon working side by side with members of the city's fire brigade.

Later, as Sherman had found a house to his liking several squares from the statehouse and set himself a headquarters there, he dictated orders for the destruction of the arsenal and all other military, railroad, and manufacturing facilities, as well as those public buildings not of municipal but Confederate government. He then readied himself graciously to receive the inevitable petitioners. But the first applicant at his door, a nun in a flowing black habit,

aroused in him an uncharacteristic defensive-
ness. She was Sister Ann Marie, the abbess of a
convent school for girls, and she wanted his authorization for a guard. You needn't worry, he
said. You'll be quite all right. If that is so, the
abbess said, then you can have no objection to
putting it in writing. The Army of the United
States does not war on convents, Sherman
replied, and made to escort the Sister to the
door. She did not move. In exasperation, Sherman dashed off a note of authorization and
thrust it into her hands. With her departure he
found himself once again in the state of unease
that he had come to feel in cities. But he felt a
misgiving now that was quite specific. What
was it? Something in the room was whistling,
and he realized it was the wind blowing in
through the old, ill-fitting windows. It sounded
to him something like the keenings of women.
He stared at the sheer curtains curling upon
themselves in their fluting, and twisting to and
fro like a dance of dervishes.

STEPHEN WALSH HAD seen the burning bales of
cotton, stacks of them bound for shipment and
extending the length of a block. His company,
marching on an adjoining street, fell out to spell
the troops on fire brigade, manning the hoses

and the hand pumps under the direction of the local fire captain.

After thirty minutes the fire was under control, and soon there was no sign of it but for the blackened humps of the ruined bales and spirals of smoke blowing away in the breeze. Fires die, like living things, Stephen thought. The animation is fervent and the death dramatic. I am done, defeated, you are looking at my death, the smoke seemed to say.

The troops resumed their march, striding off to the applause of the townspeople.

But it had smoldered in the heart of the bales, that fire, keeping to itself till the night came down and the wind came up. It had kept its own counsel, biding its time, and when the propitious moment came, out it flamed, spewing into the night sky and tossing its tufted torches into the pollinating wind.

Who had first lit a match to those bales? Walsh thought most likely the retreating Rebs. If they could not have their cotton, neither would Sherman. So it had always been the cotton, the cotton to build the South and now, given the stupidity of these people, the cotton to burn it down.

For Columbia was an inferno, whole streets aflame, home after home collapsing thunderously into itself, its wood sap hissing and cracking like rifle fire. The sky, too, seemed to have caught fire.

Walsh, assigned to guard the gates of a convent school, realized the blaze was advancing. Flaming clods of cotton had lodged in the garden trees. It was no longer safe here. He threw open the doors. Hurry, Sister, he shouted. The girls were in chapel, kneeling at their rosary. Up up, Walsh said, we've got to get them out of here. The abbess's name was Sister Ann Marie. She glared at him and, after what he thought was an unnecessary moment of deliberation, clapped her hands and got the students lined up in the front hall, each beside a satchel on the floor. So she had known, and had prepared.

Come along, come along, Walsh shouted.

Somehow, despite the infernal roar of the blazing city, the Sister's unforced voice was clearly heard: We will not run but walk in place behind this good soldier. We will not cry. We will look only at the ground as we walk. And the Lord God will protect us.

And so Walsh led them out of the convent, the attending nuns on either side of the column and Sister Ann Marie bringing up the rear. They were a procession of incongruous order, twenty-five or thirty children hemmed in by their teachers and seeming, in their silent humility, as if on an ordinary school excursion.

—

WALSH WAS ANTICLERICAL and a resolute skeptic, but that was of no matter to his lieutenant. I want a couple of Papists, the Lieutenant had said when the order came down. Walsh, you and Brasil, step out.

Brasil, a cheerful gawky fellow with a receding chin and a perpetual glint in his eyes, was delighted. They've called me a Papist since the day I joined the damned 102nd, so who in the name of sweet Jesus is deservin of a night on the town if not Bobby Brasil. And after five minutes at the gate he wished Walsh a good evening and was gone.

The convent girls had been at their evensong, but outside only drifts of it could be heard for the wind blowing through the trees. It seemed to Stephen Walsh, too, that the wind was rushing the darkness along, so quickly was the light going. He had thought he smelled smoke, and looking up he saw a moment's red flash in the sky. This will be a night, Walsh said to himself.

But it had come on as he would not have dreamed, and as he led his charges through the streets he realized he held his rifle at the ready. The world was remade, everything become something else—the sky a shimmering bronze vault, billows of thick black smoke the clouds. He turned a corner and found the street blocked by flaming timbers. The Sister came to his side. Do you know where you are taking us? she said. I was told, if it came to that, to the buildings out there on the hill, Walsh said, pointing. Yes, the South Carolina College, she said. We will go around this way.

And for a few moments all was composure again as they detoured along a clear street, until two of Walsh's compatriots appeared out of a door, jugs of whiskey in their hands. Seeing the procession and finding it to their liking, they staggered alongside, loudly considering the possible merits of the taller girls. The Sister's glare escaped them, and as the students quickened their pace so did they, laughing and suggesting their own merits. Wearers of his own uniform, they did not in the first moments appear as more than an embarrassment to Walsh. But some of the girls were crying and pushing up against one another in their haste to get away, and Walsh, turning, saw that one of the drunks had opened his trousers and exposed himself. Didn't your Jesus have one of these? the drunk shouted. Walsh stood aside and urged the nuns to move along past him as he stepped into the path of the two men. Sister Ann Marie loomed up, her face an imperious demand for action.

Do not watch this, Sister, Walsh muttered. Move on, move on. The two men were laughing and swaying in front of Walsh, one of them holding out a jug and swinging it, either as an offering or as a threat, Walsh didn't take the time to consider. He kicked out at the man's parts and, as the other came at him, managed a sideswiping bayonet slash to his hand. In a moment the two of them were on the ground, howling, and the jugs were smashed and the liquor splashing down a trough in the cobblestone had caught fire and ran like a fuse in the direction of the fleeing women.

It was the trailing edge of Sister's habit that Walsh saw alit. She was turning in circles, trying to see behind her. He ran to her, knelt, and clapped at the cloth and crumpled it in his hands. But it was difficult, she had panicked, not wanting to be touched. You're making it worse, Walsh shouted. Finally she stood still and closed her eyes and held her crucifix tightly so as to endure a man's hands on her person. He was allowed to smother the flames, which had gone up above her ankles. He rubbed the charred cloth between his hands till every spark was gone.

Are you all right, Sister?

I am, thank you, she said, not looking at him, and as the students arranged themselves in their column she placed herself amid them. Please, let us go on.

Rounding a corner moments later, they all had to stop and cower on the sidewalk as cavalry rode by. But the troopers, their faces coppered in the light of the flames, were joyous. They controlled their panicked mounts with whoops and hollers. Some carried torches, the flames blown back by the wind, and as they rode down the street Walsh saw one torch fly up and crash through a window.

At this moment Walsh realized he could not comfortably hold his rifle.

THE MAGNITUDE OF the fire had caught General Sherman by surprise. He rushed half dressed out of his chosen headquarters, a manse on the suburban edge of the city, and several minutes later his aide, Colonel Teack, found him some blocks away, where he had joined a group of firefighters and was not giving orders but taking them like any enlisted man. Sir, this is not proper duty for the General of the Armies, Teack shouted, and actually touched Sherman's arm. Sherman was breathing heavily, and there was clearly on his soot-covered face a moment in which he did not recognize Teack. Then he nodded and allowed himself to be led back from the fire. A canteen was brought to him, and he bent over and poured the water over his head. A towel was proffered by his man, Moses Brown, and after he dried his face and dropped the towel to the ground, but still hatless and in his shirtsleeves, he said, Teack, can you tell me what in hell is going on? And he wandered off, Teack following.

It was hazardous going. Flaming walls fell flat across the roadways. Unidentifiable, seemingly immaterial pieces of cotton fire floated in the heated air. His troops were everywhere drunk. Some stood in front of burning houses cheering, others lurched along, arms linked, looking to Sherman like a mockery of the soldierly bond. It was all in hideous accord, the urban inferno and the moral dismantlement of his army. These veterans of so many campaigns, who had marched with him hundreds of miles, fought stoutly with nothing less than honor, overcoming every conceivable obstacle that nature and the Rebs could put in their way—they were not soldiers now, they were demons laughing at the sight of entire families standing stunned in the street while their houses burned.

In a park square under flaming trees, Sherman gazed on a grand dreamlike ball, soldiers and nigger women dancing to the music of a regimental band, or at least the members of it who were still capable of playing an instrument. Some old darkie was up in the band shell leading them. The General was speechless. He became aware of his own bedraggled costume and could think only of brushing himself off, tucking in his shirt, squaring his shoulders.

Down another street he was for the moment relieved to see soldiers working to put out a fire, but turning the corner he found some troops using their bayonets to puncture the fire hoses and drive off the firemen. They were not besotted, either, these men.

Nobody recognized Sherman, nor did he interfere with anything he saw, possibly under standing that, in this state of anarchy, challenges to his authority might arise. He looked at Teack and Teack nodded, knowing, as all officers did, that rank must not be invoked when it is not likely to be heeded.

Where is Major Morrison? Sherman said, looking around.

Sir, you remember. He was killed at Aiken.

Oh yes, right, right.

Teack, at six and a half feet, towered over Sherman, and when he stood in attendance tended to stoop, as a parent to a child. He had twice turned down a brigade command and the promotion that went with it, such a proprietary responsibility did he feel to protect Sherman and ensure his renown. His self-assigned guardian-ship he had assumed back in the bad days of Sherman's bouts of irresolution and hysteria after Bull Run. Teack had seen him at his worst, curled up on the ground in his tent, his knuckles in his teeth and terrible whimpering sounds coming from him. The General had asked to be relieved of command and withdrew from the field for a period of rest and recuperation at home in Ohio.

Teack was a laconic Westerner, and where Sherman was careless of his dress, he, by con-trast, and as if to counterbalance him, was something of a stickler for deportment. On the march he wore the cavalryman's gloves and boots, a blocked hat and a saber. He tended daily to his long drooping mustaches, a man who believed his vanity was a strength. In truth, while he admired Sherman for his grand strate-gies and tactical brilliance, he was secretly scorn-ful of the Shermanic temperament he had undertaken to protect from itself. He felt there was something of a woman in the General's volatile moods. You never knew what to expect from an ego that could preen with self-satisfaction or slink like a whipped dog accord-ing to its own internal weather. Teack was sure that William Tecumseh Sherman was something of a genius and he derived a pleasurable energy in close company with that quality of mind. But as a steadfast professional soldier who had seen everything and was surprised by nothing, he also felt superior to Sherman. Now, for instance, the General mumbled, Christ, what are we doing in this war but consuming ourselves, and Teack was embarrassed for the man.

They were standing in front of a stone mansion that seemed oddly indifferent to the yellow light in its windows and the flames leaping out of its chimneys. Well, Sherman said, I suppose I will need a brigade of Slocum's to come in from bivouac and bring this city under control. These drunken troops he waved his arm vaguely. They have to be punished. I will know which units they are from and who their commanders are.

Was that an order, or was the man just thinking out loud? Teack couldn't tell.

They stood looking at the burning mansion. You know, Colonel, Sherman said, when I was posted here maybe twenty years ago, I fell in love with a girl who lived in this very house. Of course it was not to be, but hers were the softest lips I have ever kissed.

In another moment Sherman was wandering off the way he had come, his hands held behind his back.

Teack let him go.

—

AFTER THE GENERAL had turned a corner, Colonel Teack withdrew a flask from his tunic and took a long swig. The heat of the burning house was like the summer sun on his face. It felt good.

It seemed to him an exemplary justice come to this state that had led the South to war. Earlier in the day he had seen a company of Union soldiers who had been among the hundreds imprisoned right here in the city's insane asylum. The condition they were in appalled him. Filthy, foul-smelling, their skin scabrous, they were hollow-eyed creatures shambling to parade in a pathetic imitation of soldiering. You saw the structures of them through the skin, the bony residue of their half-human life, and you didn't want to look at them. The capital city of the Confederacy had treated these soldiers not as prisoners of war but as dogs in a cage. General Sherman had seen these men and had wept and now all he could think of was the Southern belles he had kissed.

He had sworn to wreak terror, hadn't he? His orders were being followed. All these riotous, drunken arsonists, these rapers and looters— here were some, coming out of this fine house now, their arms filled with sacks of silver plate, loops of pearl and watches on fobs hanging from their hands—what were they but men who needed a night of freedom from this South-made war that had disrupted their lives and threatened still to take them? Now they stopped a moment to throw some torches in the windows. A soldier glanced at Teack to see his reaction and, when none was forthcoming, smiled and snapped a salute.

If these acts of vandalism are performed as vengeance, Teack thought, why, that is an efficiency of which an army should be proud.

What had brought on the almost universal drunkenness was the pillaging of a distillery on River Street. The Colonel found this out by following the trail back as men staggered by him with buckets of whiskey in their arms. It was a large brick building with loading platforms on which soldiers lay passed out. Inside was a bit livelier. The men had a nigger girl down on the floor and were taking their turns on her. They were pulling another one down from a ladder that she was trying to climb, kicking and screaming. Teack refilled his flask from a butt of bourbon and went on his way.

AT THE MAIN building of South Carolina College, three regimental surgeons had set up their dispensaries. Had they been ten they could not have met the demand. It was difficult keeping order in the entrance hall as civilians pushed against one another and cried out for help. These were whites from the city, people with burns or sprained or broken limbs. But several Union soldiers had been killed, and many more wounded, in an explosion. Sherman had ordered Columbia's store of powder and shells to be thrown into the river, and something had gone wrong. The wounds of these men were horrible and occupied the surgeons for much of the afternoon.

Two nurses, army sergeants from the Medical Department, were newly assigned to Wrede Sartorius and they had taken over in the surgery, leaving Emily Thompson and Pearl to mop the bloodied floors, sack and remove the medical detritus, wash the towels, and carry in the bandages and splints and dispense the medicines. Emily thought it better that Mattie Jameson be stationed in the supply room where she could be spared the worst.

After the emergency had been dealt with, civilian patients were led into Wrede Sartorius's examining room. The injuries he tended were of no great interest to him. For the most part the townsfolk were in states of shock and confusion. He prescribed cups of brandy, or laudanum in weak solution. He was made irritable by this seemingly endless procession of frightened people. It was left to Pearl and Emily to wrap them in army blankets, administer their dosages, and escort them to an upstairs floor where they could rest on cots set up in the classrooms.

AS THE FIRES raged through the evening, more and more people arrived at the gates. Blacks and whites were at first put in separate rooms to await a doctor. But the college was refuge, and by midnight both blacks and whites were camping out in the hallways.

Additional buildings had to be commandeered for the emergency, and more medical units set up there. Stephen Walsh could see from a hall window that two of the college buildings had caught fire. There were figures on the roofs beating at the flames with blankets. He saw them silhouetted against the red sky. What hell was this? Surely not the composed Hell of the priests and nuns. Their Hell was comforting. It meant there was a Heaven. This hell, my hell, is without ascription. It is life when it can no longer tolerate itself.

—

WALSH'S LEFT HAND was swathed in bandages. He felt that it was appended to a cocoon. Or perhaps a wasp nest. The dressing on his right hand left the fingers free. Only the palm was burned, though the hand stung as badly as the other. He felt defenseless in these bindings. He wanted to tear them off with his teeth. In the morning, no matter what, he would rid himself of them and return to his company.

He hadn't heard what she had said, that nurse, such was the bedlam of wailing and crying. But very fine-looking she was, and he had dipped his head and squinted to indicate that he was looking at her lips for no other reason than to read them.

In this gymnasium turned into a waiting area, there were more patients than there were litters for them, and people lay on the hardwood floor with folded blankets for pillows or sat, like himself, with their backs to the wall.

But she had been so gentle, leading him off to a side room as if he were her special charge. She had held his hands by the wrists in a pail of cold water and then applied the unguent. Bending to her task she invoked the power of the private act. Her light brown hair fell in ringlets on either side of her face and somehow the war was a very distant thing. Her effect on him was stunning. Marching with Sherman he had thought nothing approaching human intimacy would ever again be possible.

You got a name? she had said.

Stephen Walsh.

She looked at him. Her eyes were hazel, with lights of green. In their gaze he felt his soul was being studied. I am Nurse Jameson, she said, as if daring him to deny it.

How do you do.

Fine. But you ought to know better'n to play wiv fire, Stephen, she said. And then she had laughed.

HE WAS STILL thinking about her. The elisions of her speech, the unschooled and unselfconscious way she moved and held herself, suggested the racial truth that Nurse Jameson was a black girl, freed, and enlisted for the Union.

He was not shocked. He'd been months on the march and the fact of fair-skinned Negroes no longer surprised him. In this strange country down here, after generations of its hideous ways, slaves were no longer simply black, they were degrees of white. Yes, he thought, if the South were to prevail, theoretically there could be a time when whiteness alone would not guarantee the identity of a free man. Anyone might be indentured and shackled and sold on an auction block, the color black having been a temporary expedient, the idea of a slave class itself being the underlying premise.

But there was something more elusive about this Miss Jameson. She had been talking to him in her soft lilt of a voice, teasing him a bit, but glancing at him with eyes that for just an instant would glaze over in bewilderment. And the seriousness with which she had gone about treating his burned hands, her concentration—the slow, careful attention she brought to the problem—suggested to him a person who had only recently been given independent responsibilities.

Now he was shocked as he found himself considering if, despite her nurse's rank, this dazzling girl was not that far removed from childhood.

He wandered down the crowded hallway, hoping he might catch sight of her again.

IN THE EARLY hours of the morning, Emily Thompson was called to assist when a black woman was brought in unconscious on a stretcher. The woman's garments were half torn off and she had bruises on her chest and arms. One eye was swollen shut. Her face was battered. She was lifted to the table and what remained of her clothing was removed. After examination,

Wrede decided first to repair a vesico-vaginal fistula, and directed the nurses to position her on her knees with her head and shoulders lowered.

Emily had to both hold up a lantern and pass to Sartorius the instruments he called for. She was made queasy by the awful procedure. Wrede's hands were bloody, his eyes unblinking in their concentration. She looked for some recognizable emotion from him. Was it to be expressed only in the work of his hands? Must it be deduced? God knows what horrors this girl has endured. Emily could not bear to look. But not even the most private regions of the human body were beyond this doctor's blunt investigation. Emily supposed the modern world was fortunate in the progress of science. But she could not help but feel at this moment the impropriety of male invasiveness. She knew he was working to save this poor woman, but in her mind, too, was a sense of Wrede's science as adding to the abuse committed by his fellow soldiers. He said not a word. It was as if the girl were no more than the surgical challenge she offered.

The operation concluded, one of the sergeants said, Uh-oh. The woman was expiring. Terrible sounds came from her throat. They held her, and she stiffened and slumped in their arms.

Wrede shook his head and, with a gesture indicating that they should remove the body, threw off his apron and, with barely a glance at Emily, left the room. His departure, having given her the clear impression that death was a state that did not interest him, left her open-mouthed with shock.

Emily fled to an unoccupied alcove window on the top floor. She sat there to regain her composure. She told herself the man was overburdened, a brilliant doctor working week after week in the field. His nerves were strained—how could they not be? The responsibilities of every day on the march were bound to affect anyone. But another thought occurred to her that she would attribute to her own exhaustion, to the hours of unremitting work and the horror of a city burning. It was that Wrede Sartorius, the man to whom she had given herself, was not a doctor. He was a magus bent on tampering with the created universe.

Outside, lit by the red night sky, a crowd of the newly homeless filled the front yard. Army ambulances couldn't get through. Emily saw women in the throng who were so familiar in appearance and deportment as to make her think she knew them. The way they carried themselves, their carriage, bespoke family. They held their children pressed to their sides and stood quietly waiting amid the restiveness around them. They were women of her class, the same whom she had lived among all her life. And they had lost everything.

My God, she whispered. Why am I not out there with them?

THE STATE ASYLUM had caught fire and now some of the inmates were here in the college. They were frightened. They wandered through the halls, with their long hair and filthy clothes. They didn't know where they were. They moaned and screamed. The surgeons sedated those whom the keepers could hold down. Troops were brought in to restore order.

After the maniacs were herded into the basement, their cries could be heard on the floors above. Patients waiting for treatment looked to the army doctors and nurses for some assurance that there were still civilized controls in the world, that all was not fire and madness and death.

Mattie Jameson was folding towels in the supply room where it was relatively quiet behind a door at the end of a short corridor. In the way of someone performing a simple and repetitive task, she was thinking of something else. With her head at a slight tilt and a smile on her face, she was at Fieldstone on a winter evening early in her marriage when John had no urgent matters to keep him away and they sat in the coziness of her sewing room with the drapes pulled against the chilly night, a fire in the hearth, and each of them in a chair reading. And they didn't even have to speak, so natural was their intimacy. All at once she was still a young woman with a firmness of flesh and a secret pride in John's hunger for her body. Though she had borne the two boys, she was still almost as lissome as she had been as a bride. She wanted nothing more from life than to please this forceful man, whom she imagined in her giddier states of mind to have descended from lions.

Mattie's grief for her lost life and fears for her boys' fate had devolved into a blessed state of dreaminess, so that when, finally, the agitation in the building caught her attention, it seemed to her something she could tend to as she had tended to her babies when they cried out in their sleep.

EMILY THOMPSON, RETURNING to the main floor with her mind made up, and rehearsing what she must say to Wrede Sartorius, was immediately diverted by the sight of Mattie walking among the patients and crouching before them and touching their foreheads and speaking to them softly in a manner to soothe them. Emily stood back in some astonishment.

She had heard from Pearl something of the life on the Jameson plantation and, like Pearl, she had become accustomed to looking out for this woman, who invariably said, every time she saw Emily, Are you not Judge Thompson's daughter from over in Milledgeville? What was clear at this moment was that Mattie Jameson's mental state befitted the situation in which she found herself. The world at war had risen to her affliction and made it indistinguishable.

How fascinating this was. At one camp, Emily had asked Wrede to examine Mattie. He did, and discussed the condition afterward. This is a dementia, he had said. Yet if you were to see into her brain I am sure you would find no pathology. Some mental diseases, you do the autopsy and diagram the lesions. There are crystallized growths. Suppurating tumors. You see changes of color, soft yellow deposits, narrow canyons of eaten-away matter. But with some diseases there is no sign at all—the brain is in physical health.

Emily said, Then it's not the brain but her mind that's afflicted?

The mind is the work of the brain. It is not something in itself.

Then an affliction of the soul, perhaps.

Wrede had looked at her, regretting her re mark. The soul? A poetic fancy, it has no basis in fact, he said, as if he shouldn't have had to tell her.

As Emily watched her, Mattie, having talked and smiled her way down a corridor lined with patients, veered into a room and disappeared from sight. What was she doing? Emily, in pursuit, found her in a classroom fitted out as a studio. The gaslights here were dimmed. Patients sat disconsolately in the few chairs, their heads bowed. One wall was mirrored. An upright piano stood in a corner and that was what had caught Mattie's eye. An elderly man, seated on the piano stool and reading his Bible, sensed her standing behind him. He swiveled on the stool and found her gazing at the piano with a rapturous expression on her face. And so he rose.

Mattie sat down and stared at the keyboard in that way of pianists who see it as a universe. Then she placed her fingers on the keys and began to play. It was a Chopin waltz, and though she played it hesitantly, shyly, she did so secure in the illusion that she was home at her own Bösendorfer grand.

Emily didn't know who the composer was, but what she heard was a lilting theme of great refinement. The music evoked in her breast intimations of a civil life. It was almost a shock. Then, as Mattie Jameson grew more confident and the music became bolder and more expansive, Emily was brought back to her own resolve. She was looking at her reflection as lit in the soft light of the gas lamps. Do we have no souls? What is this I hear if not a soul given as music? I am hearing a soul, she said to herself. And immediately she ran off to gather her belongings.

OTHERS WERE DRAWN to the music as well, and when Pearl came to the door she had to stand on tiptoe to see who was playing. She said to Walsh, What do you call it when the woman wedded to your papa is not your mama?

She would be your stepmother.

So I am my pap's chile, but my step—

Mother's—

My stepmother's—

Stepchild.

Stepchild. Is that a natural thing? A step chile with a step mother?

It happens, Walsh said. It's better than nothing.

Well, that poor crazy woman in there playing her music? Can you see her? Come here to where I am. You see? Thas her, Miz Jameson, and she is my step mother, Pearl said, nodding, to affirm the relationship. My step mother, who still know to play the piano. Used to hear her all the time. It made me angry. Black folks dying back in the quarters and she playing the piano like it didn't mean nothin. Wouldn see me, look right through me, my step mother, the wife ma'm Miz Jameson.

Moving next to Pearl at her invitation, his shoulder touching hers, Stephen Walsh instinctively understood that she would have no idea of the effect on him of their closeness. He had not wanted to admit to himself how young she was, this brilliantly alive girl whose glance made him catch his breath. She had found him tagging after her and had accepted him with a smile, as a child accepts a new acquaintance immediately as a fast friend. She was confiding in him now as a grown adult would never do under the circumstances. In what terrible state of vulnerability had this war left him that he was so instantly drawn to her? So that there actually flashed through his mind the possibility that he could survive the war and have a future life as a husband to her.

In his own childhood Stephen Walsh had learned to live alone in his mind. He was the child of drunks, and had grown up learning self-sufficiency in the streets of Manhattan, working out his own rules of honor and integrity from his life as a street rat, sweeping out saloons, and delivering pails of beer. He was configured as a stoic, but it was as if from choice, as if the raging excesses of his family and the brutalities of his schooling had played no part in the formation of his character. He had come to the attention of the Jesuits, enduring their education just until he learned the titles of the books that one should read for the rest of one's life. And then he was gone into the university of the autodidact to find his own titles.

He was a sturdily built, square-shouldered nineteen-year-old with thick black hair, a heavy brow, solemn eyes, and a firm jaw. Any officer would judge Stephen Walsh a reliable soldier who would comport himself as he should. But at the moment this entire structure of character, insofar as it was self-aware, was awash in longing and loneliness. He had never paid much attention to music, even when he had to march to it. But he was listening now, and feeling this waltz as a daring summons that he must answer. Almost despising himself, he remained close to Pearl, pretending to be as unaware of their persons touching as he thought she was.

He had joined the army as a substitute for an uptowner, for which he received three hundred dollars. He thought of that money now. He had banked it with the Corn Exchange on Laight Street.

SHERMAN WAS AWAKENED by his own cry. He'd fallen asleep in an armchair. He was fully dressed. A bed had been turned back for him. A throw covered his knees. He stood abruptly, and immediately felt a chill. Where the devil was he? Wrapping the throw around his shoulders, he went to the window and flung open the drapes.

First light. He waited.

Slowly, reluctantly, Columbia composed itself from graying packets of gloom. He was looking over a garden wall to a street of standalone chimneys and charred trees. Then, in the first icy glimmerings of the new day, what he saw of the city seemed like a plan for it, as if Columbia were just going up, the streets measured out in brick footings, with the occasional risen stone wall, and heaps of ash and lumber as building materials strewn everywhere.

So is the South chastened, he said aloud. Though I didn't do this, I can't deny I am glad it is done.

He'd been up most of the night conferring with his staff and writing his orders for the campaign for North Carolina. He checked his watch. Five A.M. Rifles should be unstacked, the lead divisions fallen in, the trains assembled. At this moment he heard the distant sound of bugles. Shouts. He nodded, he had an army again.

But it was too quiet in this house. He wanted to be mounted and out of here within the hour. And he wanted this place blown up. Where in hell was Moses Brown with his breakfast?

Sherman found the stub of a cigar and lit it. Again he pondered his plan. Slocum's wing was to the west of Columbia. The wings would rejoin in Winnsboro. The combined wings to feint to Charlotte, but take Raleigh. And then it would be like a vise on Lee, Grant squeezing him from the north, and I from the south. And when he leaves his entrenchment to contest with me, as he should, Grant will have Richmond.

Puffing his cigar, Sherman raised his arms and held out the throw like the Winged Victory. He laughed and made a circle around the room.

But there were logistical problems. He'd been advised that at least a thousand blacks had assembled for the march. No sooner had he found a way to get rid of the horde in Georgia than here was another to take its place. There was no reasoning with these people. Where did they think they would live? In what promised land? And there were whites among them now, some of them Union sympathizers who could not stay here and expect to remain alive. But we are an army, not a benevolent aid society.

And it had been necessary to send off letters by courier to Secretary Seward and General Halleck, the Chief of Staff, before they heard the news from someone else. He made it clear that it was the Confederate General, Hampton, in retreat, who had ordered that cotton burned. Helped by the wind, the Rebs themselves had burned Columbia. Though of course he, Sherman, knew he would be blamed. I did not visit this Pompeii upon them, he wrote. But if I am to be the Foul Fiend I don the costume readily if it will quake them in their boots and cow their traitorous hearts. We will be finished with them presently, these secessionists, and that will be the end of them and their damned war.

But where was Moses Brown with his breakfast?

IX

CALVIN SET UP THE CAMERA TO MAKE A PHOTO-graph of the old town bell lying askew in the rubble of the spire that had held it. People had gathered to watch, so Arly had to speak out of the side of his mouth.

Why you wasting my time on this, Calvin? he said. I got an army to catch up to.

This is that famous bell, Calvin said. This is the bell they rang every time another state left the Union. He chose one of the brass lens tubes from the lens case and screwed it into the camera box.

So it gives you pleasure as a black man, don't it? Arly said while looking around at the folks and smiling. He and Calvin had worked it out that he would take the picture after Calvin had done all the work. It was Calvin who decided where to put the camera, which lens to use, and how long to expose the plate. All Arly had to do was stand beside the box and remove the lens cap and, after being told how long to hold it off, clamp it back on.

Whether it pleasures me or not, it is part of the historic record, Calvin said. This bell now fallen here in the dirt is like what has happened to the Confederacy. It is like the ruin of the old slaveholding South is laying there, so I got to photograph it, just like Mr. Culp would.

After Calvin stuck his head under the black cloth and satisfied himself that everything was ready, he stepped back, slid out the plate carrier, and nodded. Arly made a big fuss about pulling up his coat sleeves and adjusting his derby. After a solemn glance at the crowd, he stepped up beside the camera, lifted Mr. Culp's watch out of Mr. Culp's vest pocket, and held it at eye level. Wait till the sun comes out from that cloud, Calvin whispered. Expose for fifteen seconds.

Calvin had shown him how not to move his arm but just with a flex of the wrist to uncap the lens, hold steady, and then, with a reverse flex, recap it. This Arly now did, adding a little triumphant yelp of his own devising when the cap was back on, because he had noticed people wanted some indication that something had happened, whereas otherwise it was hard to tell.

Calvin joined in by applauding lightly. Sliding the wood casing back in, he removed the plate and carried it hurriedly up the back steps into the wagon.

Arly readjusted his coat and smiled again at the observers. Friends, if it seems like magic to you, you are exackly right, it is magic what my camera can make from the light of God's day. Who will step up for his portrait? Everyone needs a picture for his mantel. A portrait by Josiah Culp is a better likeness than any painter could paint. And if it is the cost that worries you, a cart dee visit is most reasonable, and you have a photo of yourself forever from these historic times.

There were no takers, the gloomy crowd slowly dispersing.

NOT A FEW minutes gone by, and still in the middle of all the ruination of Columbia, Calvin reined the mule to a stop and got down and went around the back to bring out the tripod again.

Jesus, what is it now? Arly said, putting his hand inside his vest to the pistol. You aren't wanting to try my patience, surely.

Mr. Culp has taught me to look at things, and that is what I'm doing. Most people don't really look at what they're looking at. But we have to. We have to look at things for them.

And what are we looking at now? Arly said.

Down the street? Those granite steps that don't lead to nothing. A church was there. And what's left is only that back wall with the bull's-eye window you can see the sky through.

Trouble was, Arly might have the pistol but this Calvin knew he could keep on doing what he was doing and no harm would come to him. He knew Arly needed him even if he didn't know why. He had his wits about him, this boy. He was not what you would call uppity, but he had an edge to him, all right. Without saying anything, he let Arly know how he felt about things in a quiet, cold kind of way. Not that he could say anything about it, being a nigger. But once it was over with Mr. Culp, Calvin had stopped smiling. You didn't see those white teeth no more. He was still the smooth, tan-faced nigger with a shaved head and big brown eyes, but he went about taking his pictures like the business had been willed to him.

When Calvin had gone down the street and put his camera where he wanted, some black children appeared, climbing over a pile of rubble, and they hunkered there among the rocks to watch him.

Arly sat up on the wagon and waited. He took the carte de visite out of his coat pocket. Nothing had changed since the last time he examined it. Will was still sitting in a C.S.A. tunic, ramrod straight as a proper soldier, though with that strange look in his eyes, like he had seen something alarming on the horizon. Culp had affixed a brace to the back of Will's head to keep it upright. And the chin strap on the Reb cap was what kept his lower jaw from going slack.

You wasn't this stupid-looking in your life, Arly said to the picture. You had an intelligence, though you did require instruction on a daily basis. But, anyways, I made you a promise to report on your bravery to your kinfolk, and that I will certainly do. And they will have this pictorial of you with the rifle crossways on your lap in case there was any doubts in their mind. And though you are sitting there no less dead than you are in your grave, with the earth filling your mouth, they will see you in this pose and think you were alive at this moment of the picture-taking. And even if you don't look alive to me, to them you will look alive enough given what, as you led me to understand, they thought of you in the first place.

WHAT HAD HAPPENED was that after they took that picture of the dead man in the wrong uniform, his crazy friend waved the pistol around and directed Mr. Culp and Calvin to drive up the hill to the village cemetery, where he proposed to inter the body. Calvin knew he was to do the digging and took off his coat and jacket and rolled up his sleeves. But he hadn't expected that the crazy soldier would put Mr. Culp to work. I can do this without help, Calvin had said, but it was no use. And so there was Josiah Culp, who had just about adopted Calvin Harper back in Philadelphia, when he had come out into the street where Calvin had been staring in the window of the Culp Photography Salon, and taken him in and treated him almost like a son, including him on this expedition and teaching him the trade that would secure him in a free man's self-employment for the rest of his life—well, there he was, this poor man, spading up the soil over his shoulders, doing the work of a Negro. And maybe that was the idea behind it, because Mr. Culp had strong opinions and might have seemed arrogant as a certified Union photographer with his name in gilt letters on the wagon. Given that he and the soldier had right off gotten into disputation, it could have been a kind of lesson for him, or so it seemed, because the soldier said, That's the way, that's the way, Mr. Photographer, a sly smile on his face.

It was a bitter-cold morning in that village, but Mr. Culp was drenched in sweat. It rolled out of his hair down his neck. His shirt was soaked and sticking to his back and belly. Calvin didn't like the way Mr. Culp looked. His lips were a bad bluish color, and he was heaving and panting. Calvin called up to the soldier that Mr. Culp should stop, he was not a young man, but the soldier just pointed the pistol and said, I don't mean to spend all day here. And he looked around with some apprehension, although no one else was to be seen and even if there was they wouldn't care. After Sherman's army had been through a place there was nothing strange about people digging a grave.

As Calvin feared, it was too much for Mr. Culp. Maybe the shame of it contributed something, or maybe he was in a sickly state to begin with, but four feet into the ground this funny look came over him and he clutched his chest and twirled around his shovel as if he wanted to fit himself snugly into the grave he was digging and down he went. Calvin grabbed him and held his head. Culp pointed a finger at Heaven as if he wanted to take a picture of it, and a wild look came into his eyes and he gasped for breath and tried to speak. But then his back arched and he went stiff and gurgled a bit, and right there, in the cold, damp grave, he died in Calvin's arms.

The crazy soldier just scratched his head.

He said to Calvin, Let me have his trousers. The galluses, too. You'll have to take off his boots first.

With Mr. Culp laid out in long johns in the grave he had dug, Calvin climbed up and shoveled some dirt on his corpse and said nothing aloud but just stood there. Then he and the soldier took up the dead man in the wrong uniform and laid him down in the grave over Mr. Culp.

I'm sorry you got to share these quarters, Will, the soldier had said. But in a time of war you just got to make do.

THERE WERE SEVERAL things on Calvin Harper's mind as he drove through the ruins of Columbia, stopping here and there to make a photograph. No less than Arly, who was beside him wearing Mr. Culp's coat and hat and pistol, he wanted to catch up to the Union forces. He would find a way to let the military know there was a madman loose. Maybe some army court-martial would consider the circumstances of Mr. Culp's death.

But he also felt that he must not leave Columbia before he made as many negatives of the ruined city as his supplies allowed. It was not only that pictures were the photographer's means of livelihood. Once he moved on, history would know of the city's disaster only what he had photographed. Time goes on, Mr. Culp often reminded him. Time goes on, things change from moment to moment, and a photo is all that remains of the moment past. Even now, with the air still a smoky haze two days after the fire, folks were out poking through the rubble so as to salvage what they could, load what they found into their handcarts or up on their backs, and move off in respect of their intentions. It was like the storm was over and now they were coming out into the open to size up the damage and see what could be done about it.

There were no horses left in Columbia, no mules, the army had taken everything these people owned, and Calvin was aware from the way folks looked up as he passed that it was the fact of a white man sitting beside him that kept them from appropriating Bert. Without Bert to pull the wagon, there would be no picture-taking. But a black man taking pictures would not have been tolerated in the first place. The pretense that he, Calvin, was only assisting the white man was necessary if there wasn't to be trouble where folks were already in no mood. So, endangered as he felt himself to be, he needed this madman as much as the madman sccmcd to need him, though for what mad reason it was impossible to say.

All told, though, it was a delicate matter making photographs according to his own lights with the madman unable to do anything about it except if he truly lost his patience. Who knew what would happen then? But Calvin decided he was not afraid. As with a deep breath, he drew strength from the situation. In the guise of his servitude he, Calvin Harper, was running things. And the madman pretending to be Mr. Culp, why he wasn't even as good as an assistant.

FOOD WAS HARD to find, but about two in the afternoon stores of rice and molasses and cured meat were coming in from the country where the army hadn't foraged, and while Calvin waited on the street Arly was able to get in line with Josiah Culp's Federal dollars in his pocket, at a market that had set up in a parade ground all gouged out and trodden upon and blackened with the remains of campfires. But this was one of the less devastated parts of town. The bare trees here were a natural, unburned brown. Except for a few old men it was mostly women in line, peering urgently ahead to satisfy themselves that there would still be something to buy when it was their turn. Arly, in gentlemanly fashion, endured with a smile the pushing and shoving of the ladies, while in his heart he was thinking that as a race they lacked the nobility that came so naturally to their men who were away fighting on their behalf.

It was chilly out here this afternoon though the sun shone. He was getting awfully hungry for something besides the dried-out sweet potatoes, which was all that was left in the back of the wagon. Was he in uniform he could have marched right up front there and taken what he wanted without bothering to pay for it. He was eager to load up on provisions and be on his way. The urgency was that he had the plan firmly in his mind, and with God as its deviser it would not do to linger. There is glory ahead for us, he thought, and he touched the pocket where he carried Will's photo.

In the meantime, he considered the possibilities of bedding this or that lady, though with mostly sorrowful judgments that they were an unappetizing lot, dreary and haggard, their faces swollen up from their tears, some of them with snot-nosed little creatures at their sides whining and pulling on their skirts. But still he smiled, turning this way and that as the line moved slowly forward, to see who was behind him as well as in front—maybe to spot one with a little flesh on her like it was nothing to be ashamed of, or a profusion of auburn tresses like that Ruby back in Savannah.

It was during these ruminations that he spied Emily Thompson. Hey, Will, he muttered. Look there. Is that your Nurse Thompson? Or am I seeing things?

If it was her, she wasn't a nurse in blue no more but a lady in black with no coat and her hair parted in the middle and pulled tight down over her ears. She was coming along toward him and towing a child's play wagon by its rope, leaning into the task because in the wagon, as far as he could see, was a good amount of provender: a sack or two of meal, poultry still in its feathers, foodstuffs put up in jars. When he saw two small boy helpers pushing the wagon along with their outstretched arms, he decided after all it couldn't be Nurse Thompson. But, not to take any chances, he pressed the derby firmly on his head to hide his red ringlets by which she might remember him, and pulled his coat collar up around his stubble.

She passed right by him without even a glance, the sun on her face showing how worn she looked with fine crow's-feet from the corners of her eyes and tear streaks dried black on her cheeks and her lips pressing her mouth into a thin line.

Arly had two thoughts at this point. The first was that it definitely wasn't Nurse Thompson. The second was that he never thought she was that pretty anyways.

He looked at the long line ahead of him, and back again at Emily Thompson as she left the square and crossed the street, and he made a calculation. Moments later he was up beside Calvin on the wagon.

I don't see any vittles, Calvin said.

You will, mister. Just git this dumb-ass mule and go where I tell you.

Arly had been inspired to satisfy two appetites in one fell swoop. Aloud he said, Being as bodily hungers are no concern to you anymore, you won't care if I test her out like you should have done when you had the chance.

Say what?

I'm not talking to you, Calvin. There she is, around that corner.

She had turned in to the spacious yard of a manse that had seen some fire. The front was scorched, the roof shingles half torn away, and tree vines out front hanging black and limp like dead snakes.

Calvin brought the wagon to a stop by the front gate. Emily was at the foot of the porch steps, and Arly was about to leap down and make his approach, thinking it didn't matter if she recognized him or not, since this wasn't the army no more and there was nothing she could do about it, when a black woman of some girth opened the door and was followed out by at least a half-dozen children. Then the door swung open again and even more children came out, till there must have been twenty or thirty of them crowding around and gazing at what Emily Thompson had brought from the market.

That there's a hell of a lot of children, Arly said. Damn. What am I supposed to do with such a hell of a lot of children?

He watched as some of them came down the steps, each one taking something—a chicken, a goose, a jar, a sorghum crock—and marching it into the house. The sacks of rice were carried off by the black woman.

These were awful solemn, strange children. They didn't make any noise.

Emily stood with one hand to her forehead and the other at her waist. This seemed to Arly a most attractive gesture, suggesting resignation or despair or submission to what fate had brought her, or was presently to bring her, if he could think of how to go about it. But while he was thus bemused it was Calvin who had got down from the box and dragged the big camera and tripod from the wagon. What was the damned nigger doing?

Arly watched as Calvin went up to the woman, spoke to her for a minute, and then backed away and set up the camera maybe twenty feet from where she stood. Arly thought it was time to take command. He strode into the yard with the assured gait of a master photographer, the flaps of his Josiah Culp coat floating up behind him.

What in goddamn hell are you up to, Calvin? he whispered. At the same time, he smiled at Emily Thompson and tipped his hat, though not enough to give her a good look at him.

I'm doing what I do, which is to see things, Calvin said. I see this woman and these orphan chiddren.

Is that what she said this is, a damn orphanage?

What else could it be, if you have the sense to look with your own two eyes?

You being sassy, Calvin? I won't even bother burying you like I was kind enough to bury your Mr. Culp.

You can go ahead and do what you want, Calvin said. But I judge twenty seconds in this light. And he slammed the plate carrier into the camera.

While Calvin busied himself now, arranging the subjects the way he wanted them, Arly, to maintain his dignity, put his head under the black hood and pretended to be adjusting the lens. But from there in the darkness he could study Emily Thompson in privacy. She was a figure on glass. She was looking straight at him, her arms around the children at her sides. Behind her on the porch steps rose more ranks of orphans, standing stiffly according to Calvin's instructions. You must stand perfectly still, Calvin said in a loud voice. Like soldiers at attention. And up at the back was the black woman, with one of the meal sacks on her shoulders. That, too, was Calvin's idea.

But the sight of Emily was what held Arly's attention. An unaccountable feeling rose in him that, had he been able to understand it, he would have recognized as compassion. He was disturbed to see, miniaturized on the glass, a woman looking into his eyes so as to negate all his operative calculations of self-interest. She was distraught, and for a moment, before he knew to wipe the image from his mind, she evoked in him a reflection of himself stupidly leering at her from under the black hood.

All right, Mr. Culp, Calvin called. They are ready for exposure!

And Arly felt that she was staring back at him as if she knew exactly who he was. Take your photograph, Emily seemed to be saying. Take us as we are. We are looking at you. Take it!

———

HAD HE SAID anything but what he said, had I
been given the chance to change my mind, had
he told me how much I was needed, had he
tried to convince me that there was some at-
testable humanity in all of this, I would have
stayed. I would have continued with him. Two
A.M.? Not an hour at which calm and rational
decisions are likely to be made, he said. His
watch in his hand and this—Emily in the door-
way and dressed in the black mourning she had
worn the night she rode from her home, at her
feet her portmanteau—this, like everything else
subject to diagnosis. I was overtired, possibly
hysterical, and acting rashly. What was to be
done? A sedative? Brandy? A caress? The pained,
wondering look in those widened exquisitely
ice-blue eyes. Had he neglected me? I wanted to
touch my hair, arrange my dress. I felt ugly and
grown old. On his tunic were the darker stains
of Union blood. He'd been making notes. You
must not reduce life to its sentiments, Emily. I
have just seen a man with a spike protruding
from his skull. Imagine! Propelled by a bursting
fire of some sort, an explosion, with such force
as to drive into the brain. And yet the patient
smiles, he converses, he has all his faculties. Except the one. He remembers nothing, not even

his name. You must tell me what that means. It means he is fortunate, I said. A smile. No, he is quite unfortunate. It means we know something we didn't know before. The doctor still teaching. What was the use? Dear Lord, what was the use? Independent of my state of mind, my own brain's faculty of observation judged the new beard a success: it was a strong black manly beard, very handsome. Yet when he approached me and put his hands on my arms I was repelled. Please, I said as I removed myself from his grasp. Of course, I knew I was going from something to nothing. I knew what comes of principled feeling. It is a cold, dark life, the life of principled feeling. It is my brother Foster's life in the grave. But I wanted to go home, if it was still there, and to walk the rooms and remember what the Thompsons had been, and reread the books and hold again the things I held dear, and live alone and wait there for that army of which this army on the march is just the fanfare. I had not yet seen the orphan asylum. I had not seen the children alone but for the black woman. I wanted to go home and sit and wait. I would say goodbye to dear Pearl. I would admit to Mattie Jameson for the last time that I was indeed Judge Thompson's daughter from over in Milledgeville. I do not reduce life to its sentiments, Dr. Sartorius. I enlarge life to its sentiments. I cannot stand this march any longer. I cannot forgive what has been done here in the name of warfare. I don't know how you can abide it, how you can condone it. I do not condone it, he said. Yet you are part of it, you belong to it, and so you are complicit. You are the aspect of them by which they persuade themselves they are civilized. His face flushed with anger. I knew I was saying something terribly unfair. I wanted to destroy my feelings for him. I wanted to destroy any affection or regard he might have for me so that he would not stop me from going. Yet I wanted him to stop me.

Dear God, please help me, even now, if he were to come back and seek me out, I would run to him. I would.

Part Three

—

NORTH CAROLINA

I

WHEN HUGH PRYCE, WHO HAD COME OVER for the London **Times,** applied for a correspondent's credentials with the Army of the West, he found himself interviewed by no less a figure than General William Tecumseh Sherman. Sherman hated journalists—they had the nasty habit of describing what the army was doing so that anyone, including a secesh general, could read about it in the newspaper. But most of all he hated English journalists. Your damn cotton markets have financed the South, he said to Pryce. If I hadn't taken Atlanta when I did, Parliament would have come into this thing. Never mind your letter of employment, for all I know you're a damned spy. You'll file no dispatches while this army is on the march.

Pryce was flattered by the General's distrust. He was an adventurous young fellow and got right into the campaign, wandering through the ranks and managing often to find himself on the skirmish line. He lived comfortably in the field, thinking nothing of the hardships. Of course he was no spy. He had dutifully kept his notes until Savannah was taken. There the ban on dispatches was temporarily lifted and he burned up the wires with his stories.

Now, with the army on the march northward, Pryce was reduced once more to jotting his notes and stuffing them in his pockets. Though he looked forward to the next chance to cable his accounts, he was thinking more of the book he would write when he returned home. The fact was that he loved this war in America. These provincials excited him, the sixty thousand of them swinging a thirty-mile-wide scythe of destruction across a once bountiful land. Most of the men he spoke with, even junior officers, were not terribly articulate: the South had to be punished, the niggers had to be freed was the usual level of discourse. And he found them childish in their adoration of their "Uncle Billy." (God help the poor sod of a yeoman who addressed Cromwell as Uncle Ollie.) But they were intrepid. He had seen them build bridges, dismantle railroad lines, overrun entrenchments, and maintain a pace of ten to fifteen miles a day regardless of the terrain or the weather. As men they were woefully unschooled, but as a military force they transcended their class.

What war was fought more bitterly and with more fervor and intensity than a civil war? No war between nations could match it. The generals of the North and South knew one another—they had been at West Point together or served side by side in the Mexican War. England, of course, had a great and bloody history of civil wars, but they were ancient matters to be studied in public school. This in America was to be seen with one's own eyes. And as bloody and brutal were the contests of Lancaster and York, they were hand to hand—battle-axes, pikes, maces. These chaps were industrial-age killers: they had repeating rifles that could kill at a thousand yards, grape that could decimate an advancing line, cannon, fieldpieces, munitions that could bring down entire cities. Their war was so impersonally murderous as to make quaint anything that had gone on before.

Yet some of the ancient military culture endured. The brutal romance of war was still possible in the taking of spoils. Each town the army overran was a prize. In this village was an amazing store of wine, in that a granary brimming to the rafters, a herd of beef here, an armory there, homes to loot, slaves to incorporate. There was something undeniably classical about it, for how else did the armies of Greece and Rome supply themselves? How else had Alexander's soldiers made an empire? The invading army, when it camped, sat on the land as owners, with all the elements of domesticity, including women, enlarging the purely martial function of their social order.

WITH THE VANGUARD brigades of the Twentieth Corps about to cross into North Carolina, Pryce decided that he had absolutely to ride out with the "bummers," as the foraging troops so ingloriously called themselves. He had no trouble finding an accommodating party, a detachment of General Kilpatrick's cavalry. He was a fair-haired, tall, big-boned Englishman with a ruddy open face and a quick smile, and when he identified himself as a reporter, waving his notepad about as if it were the most esoteric professional tool, a soldier was happy to give his name and spell it for him while Pryce scribbled it dutifully, though finding it of no real use.

He could sit a horse, but the mount he was given, with much laughter, was a mule so swaybacked that Pryce's feet brushed the ground. He accepted this with good humor. The party consisted of twenty or so cavalrymen casually uniformed, in a quite remarkable assemblage of styles. They were led by a sergeant, a middle-aged man with a gray stubble and an eye patch. Two of the army's ubiquitous white canvased wagons trailed along.

It was not yet dawn, and while the rest of the camp was lighting the breakfast fires the Sergeant led Pryce's party down a main road and then off through a pinewoods on a lumber trail. Here the bed of brown needles was so thick the animals' footfalls were hardly heard. Pryce wore long underwear under his thick twill trousers and sweater shirt. His half coat was lined with fleece, and he had his club scarf around his throat. Yet he found himself pounding his arms. The woods gathered the cold, as if the tall trees were a kind of vault. And the sharp redolence of pine seemed to drive the cold up behind one's eyes.

As best Pryce could determine, the party was riding ahead of the march to the northeast. They rode at the investigative pace of a patrol, with a clear purpose but no fixed destination. After a while the way ahead seemed to lighten and he could congratulate himself that they were indeed headed east, the treetops of the tall pines having turned a fiery gold. Minutes later he could feel the warmth on his thighs as he passed through patches of sunlight. Then, all at once, they were out in the morning.

—

THEY CAME TO a halt on the bank of a river. Slightly downstream was a wooden footbridge, and they went across in single file into another pine forest. Here the trees were even taller, and so abundant as to discourage the sun. The animals had to weave among the trees. In these sun-daunting woods Pryce felt in his throat the dangers of the foraging enterprise. They were, after all, a small contingent in Rebel country, with no intelligence of the enemy.

TWENTY MINUTES LATER they were on a road running alongside fallow acreage ruled off by a low stone wall. A mile or two of this and the wall was deemed an insult. At the Sergeant's direction the men dismounted and took apart a section of the piled stones wide enough to allow a wagon's passage, and in short order they were up and riding through the field at a canter, Pryce following at a trot with even the wagons pulling ahead of him. Now he saw their destination, a large white mansion with Grecian pillars for an entrance. They crossed a road onto an expanse of greensward, and then they were on a curving gravel drive that passed through formal gardens of azaleas and rosebushes and sculpted evergreens. Pryce thought he might have been in a Midlands shire.

WHEN HE CAUGHT up to the others they were deployed in two lines facing the manse. A tall elderly man stood on the porch. He was in a robe and slippers, and his silver hair was uncombed. Cassius! the old man yelled, his voice deep and hoarse. A Negro appeared. Cassius, the old man said, not lowering his voice or looking at the house slave, who stood in obeisance right next to him. Show these Union beggars what they lookin for.

Having been thus defined, the troops did not move. A slave appeared with an armchair. The old man sat. Two white women appeared, one to put a shawl about his shoulders and the other with a blanket robe for his knees. With an imperial calm, he stared at the Union troops. He said something to one of the women, who hurried back inside. He said something to the house slave, who, watching the troops all the while, went down the porch to the side steps and ran off behind the house.

Hugh Pryce could sense of the bummers' discomfort that they would have been happier to find themselves in a pitched battle. The old planter sat with his arms resting on the arms of

his chair, and from under his thick white eyebrows he was making them over into a rabble, a
thieving pack of highwaymen. Pryce recognized
the old man. The accent might be different, the
manners unrefined, but this was a lord of the
realm, one of those bred from generations of
wealth to be accorded deference from the day he
was born. Pryce's father was such a one. Pryce
had made himself a journalist and fled London
so as not to become such a one. How many of
them did not know how stupid they were beneath the manners of their class.

Shortly there emerged an entire family of
women to array themselves behind the old
planter, and they were of every age down to
three little girls—perhaps his wife among them,
but sisters and daughters and nieces, cousins
and grandchildren, all of them in familial resemblance with their gaunt faces and high
cheekbones and narrow eyes.

Just at the moment when Pryce wondered
where the slaves were, for he had never seen a
town taken or a plantation passed when scores of
Negroes did not come running out to greet their
liberators, a few appeared around the corner of
the house, and then a few more. In listless procession they came, most of them thinly dressed
for the cold, some of them barefoot, the women
with their hair in bandannas, the men many of

them bent, unshaven, elderly, and children as well, quiet and with bowed heads like the adults, until finally perhaps fifty blacks were gathered before the porch facing the old man. Pryce nudged his mule forward into the ranks. Where some of the slaves' jackets were rent he glimpsed raised scars on their backs. One man on crutches had no left foot.

All right, the old planter said, his voice deep and hoarse. Y'all see these Yankees come to free you up. Go ahead, turn around an look. There they be.

And some of the slaves did turn and look back dutifully at the troops, who were discomfited by this silent acknowledgment directed by the old planter. It was as if he had made them all, slaves and soldiers, relations of one another. The horses stirred. One of the troopers spit out a stream of tobacco juice. Another raised his rifle and took aim at an upstairs window and said, Powee! Pryce frowned. Was that all? Where was the intemperance he expected from bummers?

You been coddlin such thoughts of them Yankees, the old man said. You think I don't know that? You think I doan know ever thought goes on in them heads of yorn? I know! I know what you think, Amos, and you Sally, and you Marcus, and Joseph and Silas and Blind Henry and every one of you—yes, down to the weeist pickaninny of your wicked makin. Because, free or not free, you will never be smarter than your massah.

At this the Sergeant awoke from his trance and sent a wagon and half a dozen troops around each side of the house to the outbuildings. The rest stood with him, and at his signal they unsheathed their rifles and held them at the ready.

Well I'm tellin you now, said the planter, you thinkin to go with the Yankees, why just you do that. Out there—he pointed—is a whole army of 'em. And they is all thieves. They is all beggars. You see how these gone sniffin around back now like a pack a hound dogs? They didn't ride in here because they knowed you was here waitin, nosir, they come for my vittles and my stores, for my stock and my horses and my mules. They come for whatever their thievin souls can lay their hands on. So you go with them, go on, and good riddance if you do, 'cause they doan care one way or t'other. You be on your own and God help you, because I won't. You won't have the Massah to take care of you no more. Nor to give you a decent Christian burial when your time comes. Nosir. You'll be no better than a wanderin Jew with no place in the world to lay his head down 'cept he fall dead in a ditch somewheres for the carrion birds to peck him clean. So you just go ahead and take it, this freedom of yorn, and may the Lord have mercy on your poor nigger souls.

At this the old man rose, the blanket falling from him, and he turned and strode into the house, all his family trailing after.

AN HOUR LATER, with the sun well up in the sky, the troops were lined up on the gravel road and ready to ride back to the march. The haul was spectacular, the two wagons loaded with sacks of cornmeal and rice and flour and potatoes, turkeys and chickens, hams, sides of beef, great wheeled cheeses, barrels of nuts and dried fruits, and cases of whiskey. A dray had been commandeered to carry pillage they had discovered hidden in a hayloft: rolled Persian rugs, several paintings, cotton bags filled with blankets and pillows, a brace of pistols, an old long-barreled flintlock, and crates of china emblazoned with the planter's family crest. A string of fine mules stood patiently in tether to one of the wagons. The old man's two black stallions were harnessed to his carriage. In the carriage, uncomfortably waiting, were five Negroes—three women and two men—the entirety of those who had chosen liberation.

Yet the Sergeant did not give the signal to move out but turned his mount and sat there looking at the house. He reset his hat firmly on his head. He adjusted his eye patch. Something was still to be done, there was unfinished business.

Pryce wondered if the plantation was to be set afire. General Sherman's standing order was to burn no home where there was no resistance. Certainly there had been none here. The old planter had actually directed a slave to show them to the outbuildings. But there had been provocation in his manner. Was that it? He had refused to speak to the troops directly and had referred to them as beggars and thieves.

To the Sergeant, apparently, this was the problem. To help him think on the problem, the Sergeant now gave the order to break open a case of whiskey.

Pryce did not join the ensuing conference, although he did avail himself of a swig when the bottle came to him. The general feeling seemed to be that no soldier in Sherman's Army of the West should let a slander go unanswered. That so few of the slaves had elected to leave was another affront. Not that the men were all that anxious to have a bunch of darkies trail along. But the old planter's awful mental control of his slaves was a de facto insult to the Union liberationists come to free them. Wasn't that a form of resistance? And if it was, were they not entitled to burn his goddamn plantation?

Pryce was impressed. Feverishly he scribbled his notes. That these ordinary soldiers of a rank no higher than sergeant could, in the midst of their perilous duties, stop to concern themselves with substantive moral issues seemed to him a flash of the quintessential American genius. He could not imagine Her Majesty's rank and file in such a discussion.

By this time the troops were dismounted and walking about and talking among themselves like a peripatetic school of Aristotelian philosophers. Some of them had stripped to their shirtsleeves as if the sun were actually hot on this late February morning. There arose the question of what would happen to the slaves if the plantation was burned? Would they not bear the brunt? For, whatever the misery of their lives, the plantation was their sustenance, and of course they would suffer even worse hell when the planter turned his wrath on them as the cause of the destruction of his property.

Talking and imbibing, the men did not appear to be in any rush to rejoin the march. The black people sitting in the carriage talked worriedly to one another. Their faces full of trepidation, they were looking back at the house. It was quiet there, not a sound issued nor any sign that living people were within. And now Pryce, too, began to feel uneasy. He mounted his swaybacked mule and waited.

The door of the house flew open and a black child, a boy, came dashing down the steps. The boy saw Pryce and ran across the gravel road and raised his arms and gestured with his hands, indicating that Pryce should lift him onto the saddle. So that is what Pryce did.

At this point a soldier who had climbed onto the dray held up one of the plantation's bone-china plates and, calling for everyone's attention, scaled the plate into the air, an inspiration as far as the others were concerned, for as the plate made its parabola and fell, shattering, on the ground, they grabbed their rifles and urged him to repeat the exercise. Shortly they were having target practice with the house china, though who was hitting the flying target and who was missing was not possible to know, the shooting coming from several rifles at once.

The boy, in a fearful state, had taken the reins from Pryce and was attempting to snap them over the swayback to get it going. The mule, already frightened by the gunfire, balked and turned in a circle, whereupon Pryce saw a woman coming toward them from the house, a whip in her hand. His impression in the brief glimpse he had was that she was a younger woman in a gray dress, one of the planter's daughters, perhaps, or a niece, pale, thin-lipped, with her hair tightly pulled across her skull, and those sharp cheekbones and narrow familial plantation eyes that now intended no good. He heard from the porch another woman calling, Martha, Martha, get back inside, Martha! The whip in the woman's hand was not a horse whip, it was a shorter thong at the end of a stick, a slave whip, and she was brandishing it at the child. But somehow a soldier coming over to retrieve a plate that had not shattered got in her way, and all at once in her rage, silent and white faced, she raised her whip and struck him. And at this moment whatever minimal controls of civilized behavior still prevailed on this February morning were burst as if from a bomb.

The soldier, a bloody slash across his face, caught the whip in his hand, pulled it to him, and knocked the woman to the ground. And now he began to beat her, shouting and raising the whip high and bringing it down on her as she screamed and attempted to crawl away. You'd whip me? he shouted. You'd whip me! But as she crawled so he struck, her cries inflaming him. This seemed even more of a diversion to the others than shooting at dishes and within moments several of the troops were gathered around the action, obscuring Pryce's view. His urge was to step in and try to stop what was happening, but he knew he wouldn't. This is not your country, he told himself. This is not your war. The Sergeant had come running over, shouting, She's white, goddamnit, this is a white woman! It seemed a matter of urgency for Pryce to get the boy out of there, this awful business not for a child's eyes. The woman's screams had given way to wails. They were tearing off her clothes, and over the backs of huddled troops, hanks and shreds of the garments flew into the air.

The Sergeant, having been ignored, now made a determination that what was going on was evolved to a military event. He called to some men who were still at the wagon train and deployed them as pickets facing the house. Pryce, turning his mount to ride off, saw that the lord of the realm, having come out on the porch, stood there unmoving and impassive, as if what he was suffering at this moment must not be expressed lest it give satisfaction to the enemy. So to Pryce, riding away through the rose and azalea gardens with the pitiable shrieks and wails of the woman in his ears, the old man, too, subscribed to a war that conformed such things as this into military events.

HUGH PRYCE DIRECTED the animal down the long greensward, across the road, and over the fields to the opening in the stone wall. Some three hours had passed since he had ridden out of camp with the bummers. The line of march of a corps extending for miles, he assumed that by going back the way he had come he would find the column even if it had set off at dawn. And so he entered the woods, trusting to his sense of direction to guide him.

The boy had calmed down and, riding in front of Pryce, bent his little back and peered ahead. He was dressed in livery—tan knee pants and stockings, black buckled shoes, and a tan jacket with yellow piping. Pryce let him hold the reins, which seemed to please him. The dark woods were warm now and in their hush the mule proceeded at a leisurely pace. The boy's name was David. He said he didn't know his age. He could not remember a mother or father. He had been the household's brush-fly boy, charged with standing behind the Massah's chair and waving a big feathered fan. That was his main duty. He said sometimes he sat up in the carriage beside Cassius.

As they rode along, the mule of its own volition slackened its pace. Pryce sat back and looked right and left through the woods. The sunlight came in shafts through the tall trees, momentarily filling his eyes then leaving him in darkness. He would not need notes to remember this day. He was suddenly and uncharacteristically tired. This is not your country and not your war, he reminded himself. So what are you doing with this Negro child in your charge?

How old was David—eight, nine? The lad had made a decision that was beyond the capacity of most of the slaves on that plantation. It was true that at his age he would not think of the future or worry what fate would bring him, he would not have the thoughts that might constrain an adult, that would make an adult prefer the miseries he knew to the hazards he could not foresee. Children were of the here and now. Yet, like all of them, he had heard the lordly speech of the old man. And it hadn't worked on him, that fearsome address. With his dash from the house the child had asserted his life to be his own. It did not have to be more than a moment's impulse, but it was enough to set him free.

And now what am I going to do with you, David?

Dunno, suh.

Pryce could feel the boy's delight to be in command of this animal which, of course, would go only at its own chosen pace regardless of the instructions it received. David didn't seem to mind, languidly flipping the reins and giggling when nothing happened. And so they ambled along through the woods, Pryce with his hands on the child's thin arms.

II

CROSSING THE PEE DEE RIVER INTO NORTH Carolina, Kilpatrick's staff rode as his carriage escort. They posted with an élan despite their unshaven faces and bedraggled and battleworn attire, each of them hoping for a glance from the General's latest acquisition, the famous eighteen-year-old Southern belle Marie Boozer. And her mother, Amelia Treaster, seated on the other side of Kilpatrick, was not bad, either. The daughter was fair-complexioned, blue-eyed, and with a plump little bow mouth. Her great mass of golden curls pinned upward from her ears was crowned with a charming bonnet the size of a tea saucer. The mother was a brunette, her dark eyes alight with mischief. She was smoking a little cigar. And where Kilpatrick thought Marie's allure was in the nature of a mystery still to be plumbed, Amelia Treaster's was in the challenge of a well-loved woman. Their gowns spread out from their persons to fill the carriage like a great plume of rainbowed cloud. The two of them together were driving Judson Kilpatrick out of his mind.

He had found them in Columbia, self-attested as being Union sympathizers. And so of course they had to join the march. Nor were they without resources, the grand Victoria in which Kilpatrick now reclined being theirs, and the wagon directly behind carrying, in addition to the plunder Kilpatrick brought to them, as if the war ahead was to be an extravagant months-long picnic, their clothes and jewels, silver, china, and crystal.

While trying to maintain a conversation to keep the ladies amused—alluding portentously to General Sherman's plans for the state of North Carolina—Kilpatrick was all the while devising his own strategy for the coming night, for he wanted nothing less than a total conquest, he wanted them both. Sack duty for you, madam, he thought while smiling at the mother. And for you, dear girl, he thought while throwing her a lovesick glance, an introduction to what we in the military call horizontal drill.

What, Kilpatrick wondered, could he do to impress these women? Of course, they appeared to be duly impressed with his rank, his authority, his bodyguard of riders, but he doubted their sincerity, Marie's especially, who looked away from him every now and then to glance at one of his young officers riding escort. And both women appreciated the foolish puppy-loving competition the cavalrymen were engaged in, each man vying for the favored position at a canter alongside the carriage so as to pose straight of back, one hand loosely holding the reins, the other on his sword.

Kilpatrick was distracted, too, by his nephew, Buster, who was riding in the wagon directly behind. Damn the boy—he had found a sack of dried peas and was standing up beside the driver and blowing peas through a straw in an attempt to hit his uncle. Kilpatrick stood and motioned to the wagoner to stow the boy in the back. For his trouble, he received a pea sting on his defenselessly ample nose.

When Kilpatrick resumed his seat, the ladies were laughing. Amelia Treaster said, You've got yourself a sharpshooter, General Kilpatrick. And so he laughed, too. But he was thinking to murder the boy. Peas were all over the carriage, some distributed on the ladies' skirts. He ventured to brush the peas away. Just like the rice thrown at weddings, he said.

THE CAVALRY, RIDING vanguard for the Fifteenth Corps, was intending to secure Fayetteville, some forty miles to the northeast. There had been reports that the Rebel force under General Hardee was demonstrating in that direction. Fayetteville was a stepping-stone to Goldsboro and Raleigh, the ultimate objective of General Sherman's strategy.

Periodically scouts were reining up to Kilpatrick's carriage and leaning over to report sotto voce that Hardee's cavalry, under General Wade Hampton, was actually to Kilpatrick's rear, shadow-riding and looking for a chance to attack. Hampton had ambushed him at Aiken and was looking do so again. Over my dead body, Kilpatrick thought. But he found it hard to plan for a contest while enswathed in the perfumed presence of Marie Boozer. Again and again, as she chattered away, and gave him sidelong glances that revealed the perfect conformation of her tiny ear, he imagined her gasp of surprise when for the first time in her sheltered life of gallant Southern courtiers and elegantly phrased compliments she would find herself on her back and attaining, from one powerful thrust, revelation of the true nature of a man.

Kilpatrick halted his column at a clearing, ordered up some refreshments for the ladies, and, excusing himself, sat down among the pine trees with maps and his staff and plotted his strategy. He would lie in wait for Hampton and intercept him. If General Hardee in Fayetteville sought to make a stand, he would find himself deprived of cavalry. Kilpatrick ordered deployments of one brigade each to the two roads upon which Hampton was said to be moving, and a third brigade to a road farther north in the event Hampton chose the more roundabout route.

For his camp, Kilpatrick chose Solomon's Grove, a swamp-bordered village several miles from the road he thought Hampton was most likely to take, and after he had given orders for the troops' encampment, with genuinely sincere regrets he ordered that the ladies be taken there forthwith under escort, in command of his portly gray-haired adjutant, Brevet Colonel Melrose Mortimer, who was said to be the oldest active officer in the Army of the West.

Kilpatrick called for his horse. And, Melrose, he said, as he mounted, for he wanted personally to oversee his deployments and get a better idea of the terrain, tell Jean-Pierre I want a wham-bang dinner for three this evening. Tell him this is a Grand Cru night. Grand Cru, you hear me? This Solomon's Grove will surely be a sorry excuse for a village, but take the best house and see to the ladies' comfort. I'll be along presently. You're to keep my nephew quiet. Put him to bed. And, Melrose, this above all. If, at war's end you hope to live out your life in receipt of a full colonel's pension, do not let the women out of your sight.

Kilpatrick trotted his horse over to the carriage. Marie, Mrs. Treaster, you will forgive me if I attend for a moment to this nuisance of a war. I've arranged for your safety and will join you for dinner. And raising his cockaded hat from his head and spurring his horse, he galloped off through the woods with two dozen of his escort thunderously following.

IT WAS MIDAFTERNOON as this reconnoiter was made, but under the canopy of tall North Carolina pines it might have been evening. Kilpatrick was irritated by the gloominess. This was early March, and he thought it typical of the damn South to rush to darkness just when the days were lengthening. In New Jersey, where he was born a few miles from the ocean, there was normally brilliant sunlight and all the foul miasmas of the earth were lifted away by the ocean breezes. It was on the Jersey beaches that, as a boy, he had first discerned the natural shapes of women when they rose from their ocean baths with their skirts clinging to them.

Here it smelled of pine resin and the moldy hairless plant life of toadstool and lichen. All the more reason not to die here. The bed of pine needles was composted so thick that if you turned up a spade of it you would find moles and worms and beetles and squiggly eyeless things that had no name. Where were the birds in this forest? There were none. It was too damn quiet for his taste.

The trees now became thicker in number, and he led his men single file as they wound their way, snakelike, in a westerly direction until, according to the maps, they would come out two or three miles from the first of the roadblocks he had called for. They found a lumber trail to follow. A mist was rolling in, gauzy layers of it wrapping around the trees, and within moments Kilpatrick felt his face as wet as if he had just washed it. Drops of water landed with a thunk on his hat brim. He heard the rumble of thunder. It went on awhile and grew louder. Then, as if to assure him that his glorious plans for the night were under review by a higher authority, the forest was illuminated in a blinding blue light. There was an ominous sizzling sound of a running fuse, and a spattering crack of tree trunks splitting, and then a deafening boom, as if the whole earth were a blown munitions dump. The horses went wild, and for several moments the men had all they could do to maintain their seat. Kilpatrick, not the best of horsemen, found himself hanging by one leg from the stirrup as his mount dragged him bumping over the gnarls of tree roots. He heard himself shouting. He came loose and slammed against a tree. For some moments the air was filled with the shouts of men and the whinnies of frightened mounts, until all sound was drowned out by a torrential downpour.

Two minutes later, the rain stopped as abruptly as it had begun.

THE BREATH HAD been knocked out of General Kilpatrick. He lay at the foot of the tree, unable to control the pressed wheeze issuing from his deflated chest. His men were scattered some distance away. In the aftermath of the cloudburst, they were dismounted and wringing out their hats. Either they had not noticed him or were pretending not to have seen his fall. The horses stood by quietly, as if amnesiac. His own bay stallion came clopping back to his side, calm and self-absolved of all responsibility.

Gasping for breath, Kilpatrick lay there until suddenly, with a great wrenching roar, the air rushed back into his lungs. It was at this moment he realized that in the lightning's illumination of the forest he had seen a dead soldier tied to a tree.

THEY COUNTED ELEVEN dead besides the one strapped to the tree with the piece of paper folded in his breast pocket. The bodies were strewn about in the woods, each lying in a puddle of blood and rain. Most of them had their hands tied behind them and their throats cut. They were cavalrymen. The note said: THESE WERE THE RAPISTS.

Kilpatrick sent a rider back to the camp. A half hour later a contingent of men rode up, dismounted, and began digging by the light of torches made of cut pine saplings. Kilpatrick now went on with his escort, and when they came out of the woods they found nine more bodies at the edge of the road. These men, too, had been executed, and lay about amid other signs of the carnage—split-open sacks of flour and cornmeal, pieces of silverware, shattered whiskey bottles, a dead mule. Ordering the bodies to be carried back to the forest, Kilpatrick rode on some miles to the intersection with the Monroe Road, on which he thought Hampton's cavalry would be most likely to travel, and checking a brigade's deployment with the commanding colonel, and satisfying himself of the soundness of the position, he rode back to the forest in time to say a few words over the departed. Their pockets had been searched and emptied, letters and photographs collected, and now the twenty graves hollowed out of the soft forest floor were about to receive them. Kilpatrick checked his pocket watch, frowning at how late it was. He cleared his throat. The men removed their hats. His face glowing in the light of the pine torches, Kilpatrick said, Our foragers were murdered after they surrendered. I will inform General Wheeler and demand an investigation. And if he does not oblige I will execute one Rebel prisoner for every man lying here. So help me God. Amen.

WHEN HE REACHED the house commandeered for his use at Solomon's Grove, Kilpatrick, limping slightly and bruised and battered from his fall, was cheered by the aroma of good French cooking. He was for a moment disheartened to learn that Mrs. Treaster, whom he had regarded as a kind of first course, had departed with staff officers of one of General Slocum's infantry brigade commanders, General Ridley. Ridley had sought out the ladies to invite them for dinner at his camp. There's no trusting these infantry, Kilpatrick muttered. He wondered what reprimand he should give Melrose Mortimer, but when he realized that though Mrs. Treaster had gone off Marie herself had not, his heartbeat quickened, for it meant she preferred his company to all others'. And the mother, too, why could she not have chosen to leave as a way of—what—designating me? Entirely possible. A subtle vesting, as you'd expect from a wise and thoughtful mother.

Kilpatrick stood with his back to the hearth in the parlor of the small house and drank off a glass of port. Marie was upstairs preparing for the evening. Jean-Pierre had laid out Kilpatrick's favorite china, appropriated back in Savannah, and the little low-ceilinged dining room was aglow with candles on the table and candles in their sconces. Can there be a sweeter seduction, he thought, than the one pulled off in war? He noticed the mud dried on his tunic and trousers. His boots were caked with mud. Perhaps I should clean up. He smiled. Christ no, this is just what thrills them. Not some Southern popinjay with a handkerchief in his sleeve. They want our hero's life. That we kill and stand to be killed is what thrills them.

He felt his crotch and contemplated the night ahead. There would be a struggle, entreaties, but finally she would not be able to resist, she would be aroused to a state of ardent curiosity even if she would not admit it to herself. He knew women. They could not admit to themselves what they wanted, but there was always a moment when their emotions took them over the threshold, as it were. Miss Boozer would at last learn the consequence of her girlish flirtations. He would answer to them on behalf of all the Southern studs who had been dying to get at her.

Kilpatrick grew impatient, looking at the ceiling, listening for a footstep. He smoothed his wiry red hair. He poured himself another glass of port. He must remember to write his wife.

UPSTAIRS, MARIE WAS arranging her décolletage. She dabbed the little glass rod between her breasts, behind her ears. The things in her cosmetic case were a comfort to her, the padded case itself, with its brass snaps and the compartments lined in pink silk. So that this awful little house in this godforsaken woods was not totally disheartening. She still had her things. It was amazing how that large, expansive life of theirs was packed away now in trunks and crates and carrying cases such as this. But at least they had it with them.

She heard the General pacing. The whole wretched house shook under his boots. The man is an idiot, Mother had said. An idiot and a barbarian. But he is of the rank to ease our way north. There are no more railroads. So he is our railroad. Think of him as the track we ride on, Mother had said, and they had laughed.

The two women got along so well, they were more like sisters than mother and daughter. And they had plans. We are going to Europe, my dear. The life we knew, and what we have a right to expect, is no longer available on this continent. When the war is over it will not be over. I know these men—their war will never be over.

Mother was so wise. A year ago she had taken measures. She transferred funds to a bank in New York. She sold their farmlands and invested in Federal bonds—secretly, of course, with the help of that old lawyer Silas Fenton, who had tufts of hair growing out of his nose and who once felt her breast when Mother wasn't looking. Oh, how can you bear him, Mother, she had said. Marie, her mother said, if you keep your own counsel, if you never forget why you are doing what you're doing, nothing that they think has happened has happened. Remember that. I have had four husbands, each for a different reason. Your father was the only one I ever loved. And so the only husband who ever possessed me. This last one, Mr. Treaster, is off somewhere playing Confederate soldier. He had rather suffer a divorce than not to be thought a fervent secessionist.

There, all was ready. She would descend the narrow stairs as if it were her debutante ball at the Governor's Mansion.

He was looking up at her, this ugly man, with what could only be described as a leer. How interesting. He has no idea of the expression writ on his face. How proud he is of that laughable red scraggle on his cheeks.

And what is that smell? Good God, it is our dinner, our army dinner.

JEAN-PIERRE AROSE the next morning before dawn to attend to the kitchen. The bugle had not yet been blown, and though here and there in the surrounding camp a cooking fire had been started, the men were mostly still in their tents, and he had to pick his way carefully so as not to trip over something in the darkness.

He was shocked, on entering the little house, to see that the dinner he had spent hours preparing had hardly been touched. The candle ends were still sputtering. A layer of coagulated fat lay like a cover on the tureen. He was terribly offended. But the wine in its carafe—that, too, had hardly been touched. He sat himself down and in a self-righteous pique drank a glass and had some of the fat as well, which he scooped up with his index finger. Not for the first time was he angry with the crazy general who had kidnapped him. Not for the first time did he think about running away.

His presence aroused Brevet Colonel Melrose Mortimer, who had fallen asleep in the parlor with his head on a writing desk. Mortimer had spent the evening not listening to the sounds coming from upstairs and writing to his maiden sisters. The Mortimers were a quiet family, not terribly disposed to live life to its fullest, and since the generation of his late father and mother, no Mortimer—none of the five brothers or six sisters—had seen fit to marry. Colonel Mortimer, a stolid, unimaginative soldier, was considered the family adventurer by virtue of his long service in the military, when in fact he knew the army as an obedient child knows a parent.

It was when Jean-Pierre had begun to clear the table, and Mortimer had gone outside to relieve himself, that Rebel cavalry appeared as ghosts in the mists of first light and rode, shrieking, into the camp.

THE PICKETS WERE easily overrun, and in the first minutes the troops were helpless, their fly tents sworded into the air, horses rearing over them. Men, flinging off their blankets, ran for their rifles and were shot down, others raised their hands in surrender. But in the confusion and the white fog of the morning some resistance was organized, junior officers shouting through the gunfire. Troops ran for cover behind trees, others on one knee fired their Spencers at horses dashing by them. Cooking fires sprayed into the air as the raiders stampeded the cavalry's horses.

A bugler blowing the call to arms roused Judson Kilpatrick from the deepest, most exhausted sleep of his life. The General ran downstairs in his underwear and out to the porch, where he stumbled over the foot of the dying Melrose Mortimer, who lay upside down on the porch steps, a huge hole in his tunic gushing blood.

His cavalry's camp become a battlefield, Kilpatrick's first thought was that now he'd lost any chance for promotion. Three Rebel officers cantered out of the mist and reined in their horses. Where's General Kilpatrick? they shouted. Kilpatrick pointed the way they had come. Back there, he said, his shoulders hunched and his head bowed in what he imagined was a frightened subaltern's deference. The minute the riders were gone, the General, still in his undershirt and drawers, ran behind the house to the stable, untethered his horse, rode bareback through the melee and into the woods, and didn't stop till the sound of gunfire was a distant thing.

What was he to do? He sat astride his horse and listened to his own breathing. Goddamn, I need my clothes, it's freezing. He felt the horse's prickly hide between his knees. He felt the horse's heartbeat. They must not capture the General, he thought. I will lose some men and some horses but they won't have the General, and that's the important thing. Jesus, what a charge. I'll wait here a minute and go back quietly and retake command. In the meantime, surely we will have mounted a counterattack. Ah, I hear my battery guns, so there it's begun. We will push them into the swamp.

Almost as if he had been listening, Kilpatrick's bay stallion slowly began walking back to the camp. This is a humiliation, but that's all. The infantry will be here shortly to save my rear end, just as they did at Waynesboro. That's all right, it's my job to attract the Rebs, bring 'em out, uncover 'em. That's what I've done here.

The infantry don't like me, neither Howard nor Slocum nor their corps commanders—none of them like me, though none can tell me their columns were ever attacked while Kilpatrick rode on their flank. But Billy Sherman likes me, and he's the one that counts. I will think of something, don't worry, he said aloud to his horse, and rubbed its crest.

And as for Marie Boozer, whom he now remembered he had left in that house. . . . If the Rebs were too stupid to realize the man on the porch in his underwear had the best available quarters and therefore must be of the highest rank . . . why anyone in the house would be safe enough if they didn't show their heads. Buster would, and serve him right if he did. But she wouldn't.

Nevertheless he had run off without her. He would have some explaining to do. Damn that girl, the way she fooled me. Enough of this— will you see me to my room, General? she had said, and hardly having touched the best ragout Jean-Pierre had ever prepared, Marie Boozer had led the way upstairs, holding his hand behind her so that he could feel the sway of her skirts with every step.

In the bedroom she had slammed the door, dropped her outer garments with a swish, then the petticoats, and then the hoop, which collapsed jingling to a circle on the floor. His trembling spatulate fingers were enlisted to untie the stays of her corset. Then, pink and prominent in her undershift and stockings, Miss Boozer had pressed against him, mashing his mouth, opening his fly, and grabbing his dingus for a quick assessment. She had practically flung him onto the bed, and in the moonlight, as she dove down on him, he saw her white neck curl, like a swan's.

All but insatiable, he thought. Hips pounding like a locomotive. And yet, as she lay beside him afterward, sleeping beautifully, her face on the pillow under the mass of damp curls was the face of a virgin. Nothing can be relied on, General Kilpatrick thought. There is no morality left in this world. And damn the little whore for doing this to me, I am in love.

III

THE RESISTANCE HAVING BEEN LIGHT AT THE Cape Fear River, the Rebels firing and falling back almost immediately to turn tail and make their escape out of town, the combined corps of the Army of the West were soon across, and the city of Fayetteville was of a dark blue aspect, as if the abstract color had found an organic vestiture for itself. The streets were aswarm. Yet to someone watching the processions of men and wagons and gun carriages, broughams, buggies, and two-horse shays, it became apparent that not merely an army was on the move but an uprooted civilization, as if all humanity had taken to the road, black women and children trudging along beside their go-carts, or pulling, oxenlike, their two-wheeled tumbrels, and white citizens of the South in their fine carriages overloaded and creaking with bundles and odd pieces of furniture. The Southern population behind Sherman was refugee, having joined his march because it was the only thing left. And everyone, soldier and civilian, was damp and soggy from the recent rains. Hair lay flat upon heads, and clothes limp upon backs. The eyes of the marchers being directed at the ground, here were the generations in their trod, steam rising from them as the sun baked away one ordeal to replace it with another.

Yet Pearl smelled spring. As the Sartorius medical train rolled down the wide main street she stood up beside the wagoner to take in the breeze, to read it: a whiff of turned-over farmland, the rot of winter fields, and—was it possible?—the scent of lilac. She saw at the curbsides patches of yellow crocus just sticking their heads up, and sprigs of fox grape. In one fine yard were the greenish yellowing blossoms of forsythia. She wanted to tell Stephen to come look, but he was riding up with Dr. Sartorius. She called back to Mattie Jameson, who stuck her head out of the canvas, blinking like a groundhog coming up from the winter.

You smell the spring, stepma'm, you smell it? Pearl said.

Mattie smiled her vacant smile. But as if Pearl's announcement were the occasion for primping up, she removed the combs from her hair, let it fall, and then, after running her fingers through it, bound it back up again with the combs.

Pearl wondered if the woman understood. What spring could Pearl be talking about except the spring back in Georgia, on the plantation where until this freedom she had lived her whole life? Every spring she was to have on this earth would recall her to those first springs of her understanding, when for a few moments life shone on her with beneficence and she could see there was something else above all that that was going on, something above her fear and her pap's whip on the backs of men old enough to be her grandfathers, and her mother's misery, and the soulful singing in the white cotton, when all that whiteness seemed to bury who worked there, drown them in it, like cotton was water and they could not climb out of it—above all that, and not ruled by it, so that it was to her as a little child like the real, true Massah saying, I'm here, child, to let you know there is more than all that, as I'm showing you in these little flowers forming up everywhere for you to look at and smell and see how your pap can't do nothing about it.

But maybe Mattie Jameson did understand, as Pearl looked at her, for she was smiling and maybe thinking of Georgia and remembering that they had shared something back then, maybe without even knowing it.

THE GOOD WEATHER was a relief to Sherman, who couldn't have been happier to be out of South Carolina, a swampland, to his thinking, with its spreading rivers and miserable, seditious souls. All that moldy wetness had aggravated his asthma. His chest breathed music—for days at a time he was like a walking harmonium. But when it was really bad, drawing breath was an act of will. The terror of his life was not having enough air. It was why he hated water, it was why he couldn't sleep at night in a closed-up room as well as he could in the outdoors under a vast black sky, with the stars assuring him that there was enough volume of space and air for him to breathe.

He didn't want Fayetteville to be another Columbia. He had sent down to the brigades his order that the people of this state were to be treated with respect. The kind of thing he had tolerated to the south must not be repeated. Generally, the North Carolinians had been reluctant secessionists and he did not feel they deserved the kind of punishment he had doled out down there. But, orders or no orders, there were sixty thousand men in this army and something more than a general order was required. He chose regiments of the Fourteenth Corps to guard the city—those he thought were the most disciplined of his boys, the least raucous, hailing generally from the northern Midwestern states of pious, obedient people.

Fayetteville was a handsome city, and not that much had to be destroyed. They had found that the old U.S. Arsenal, on a plateau overlooking the city, was a hive of Confederate ordnance—rifles, fieldpieces, thousands of barrels of gunpowder. Its foundries had been producing Napoleons and nine-pounders. Its machine shops had shelves and shelves of turned rifle stocks. Sherman ordered the entire complex to be readied for demolishment when the army was about to decamp. It's a shame, really, he said to Colonel Teack. But we can't spare a garrison to guard it. Riding around town, he pointed to a manufactory here, a textile mill there, and Teack dutifully wrote them down for destruction.

And then there was the matter of the murdered soldiers. Sherman had restrained Kilpatrick, who had vowed to match every Reb murder with one of his own. But now another instance was reported—one of the advance patrol entering Fayetteville had been captured by the retreating Rebs and shot and his body hanged from a lamppost. Generals Hardee and Wheeler both had been sent messages as to what would happen if this foul murdering practice continued. Sherman ordered a public execution of a Confederate prisoner chosen by lot.

There were perhaps three hundred secesh marching under guard with the army, prisoner exchanges at this point being few and far between. They had been encamped in a field to the east of Fayetteville and were sitting on the ground in rows when a cavalry sergeant rode up, whipped a lariat in circles overhead, and hurled it as far as he could. One of the prisoners, a scrawny pimply-faced boy with a long neck and a prominent Adam's apple, who was known as his company's clown, stood up, with a grin, and caught the rope, assuming this was one of those periods of relaxed hostilities when the two sides could have some sport. A moment later the lariat was around his waist and he was lassoed out of the ranks, his arms bound tightly to his sides. Some of the prisoners stood and started shouting and raising their fists. But dozens of cavalry were on guard, each of them with a rifle in hand.

This execution was duly effected with a solemn march to a central square, the drums beating and the unlucky prisoner marched through a gantlet of soldiers at attention and officers on horseback. Such public ceremony, with a hushed, sorrowing crowd watching, Sherman thought of as the best form of communiqué to the Southern generals as to what they might expect were their men to continue murdering Federal prisoners.

It had fallen to Wrede Sartorius to certify the death of the executed man. He removed the bloodied blindfold. One bullet had gone through the left cheek. The chest was riddled, and one shot had passed through the forehead. Wrede nodded and a burial squad laid the body on a wooden gurney and wheeled it away.

THE NEXT DAY was a Sunday, with the chastened Fayettevillians marching rather righteously to their churches, to be joined, somewhat to their discomfort, by men in blue. But it was a peaceful morning, the sky clear and the weather not entirely warm but windless. With the regiments everywhere encamped in an orderly fashion, and the troops taking their ease for the first time after the long marches of the previous weeks, the army was like some great herd of ruminants quietly grazing.

Even the contingents of bummers fanning out into the countryside were soft-spoken and courteous as they trooped into homes and gathered up blankets and feather pillows, rugs for their saddle cloths and tents, and all the provender they could find.

Many of the men went down to the river to wash their clothes or hired black women to do it for them, and it was this community of the hygienists who first saw the smoke rising from the funnel of a steam tug coming upriver from the coast. The shouting and waving began even before the boat appeared around the bend, and moments later, when the steam whistle was heard across the city, it had the effect of a joyous announcement: after their long isolation in enemy territory, contact had been made with other Union forces.

Sherman was as excited as everyone else. A week before, while in the town of Laurel Hill, he had sent a courier in civilian guise down the Cape Fear River to Wilmington, informing the Union general there of the army's impending arrival in Fayetteville. Hearing the steam whistle now, Sherman knew his courier had gotten through. It told him, too, that the river was clear and that navy transports were at his disposal.

Down at the dock, troops had gathered around the boat to remark, none too kindly, on the cleanliness of the sailors' uniforms.

—

WHILE THE TUG'S captain waited in an anteroom
up at the Arsenal quarters, Sherman dictated letters as he paced back and forth, the adjutant
writing madly to keep up with him. Teack
brought in two more junior officers to secretary,
so tirelessly was Sherman's mind working. To
Grant he described his intent to join with General Schofield's Army of the Ohio at Goldsboro,
which would bring their combined forces to
ninety thousand men. He anticipated a major
battle with the regrouped Rebel forces under
General Joe Johnston, the one capable general
they had. He did not want Johnston to inter-
pose between him and Schofield, who was coming up from New Bern along the Neuse River,
so time was of the essence.

To Stanton in Washington he bragged
about the accomplishments of his army since
Savannah—the railroads destroyed, the towns
overrun, the armaments captured. Let Lee hold
on to Richmond, he wrote, and we will destroy
his country; and then of what use is Richmond?

Letters were put in the mailbag for the chief
of staff, General Halleck in Washington, General
Terry, in command of the forces in Wilmington,
and, in fact, every Union general remotely connected with the campaign in the Southeast. I am

back in the world, Sherman seemed to be saying. Perhaps my long Hegira since Shiloh will be over before summer, he wrote to his wife. Your arms, my dear Ellen, are my Medina. Back and forth he strode, scratching his head, rubbing his hands, as the pens flew to transcribe his words. To Colonel Teack, Sherman's mania could mean only one thing: the General smelled victory.

But no detail was too small to consider. When he'd finished with his letters, Sherman called Teack aside. The boat is sailing back to Wilmington at six this evening, he said. That toothsome refugee Kilpatrick took away with him in Columbia—what the devil is her name? Marie Boozer, Teack said. Yes, Marie Boozer, Sherman said. I want her on that boat. And her mother as well. And see to it that Kilpatrick doesn't swim after them.

GENERAL KILPATRICK HAD not seen Miss Boozer since the engagement with the Reb cavalry at Solomon's Grove, when he led a successful counterattack in his underwear. Afterward he had been told by one of his men that she had been seen riding off dressed only in Kilpatrick's battle flag. The loss of his personal battle flag was a general's greatest humiliation, but for Kilpatrick the loss of Marie and his colors together was a blow hardly to be endured. Where had she gone, and with whom? For it was unlikely she'd left the field of battle alone. Her bags and baggage had disappeared as well. Once in Fayetteville he had looked everywhere for her. He was a man obsessed. He thought if he found her to take her away to the South Seas and live with her on a beach. He would catch fish and shake coconut trees for their dinner. Or if she liked being a famous general's wife he would finish the war in glory and run for President. If it was money she needed, he had that—he had contrived to amass quite a bit of it on this campaign. Back in South Carolina his men had found a caravan sneaking through the woods, an entire commercial bank's treasury in two covered wagons. The safes were filled with silver bullion, gold coins, specie, bonds. Of course, most of it had been turned over to Sherman's quartermaster. But my men deserved a reward, and so did I. It is no less than on the sea that there is a law of salvage.

Kilpatrick's staff worried about him as he wandered about the camp in uncharacteristic thought, his head bowed, his hands behind his back, the rude facial features, so apt for a warrior in the field, having sagged into the mask of a dying voluptuary. He had sent several men to the city to scout about and find out what they could. Now a report came back to him: she and her mother had been seen at the riverside.

It was early evening, the sun shining coldly in a low quarter of the sky and the city blanched in a pale light. Kilpatrick galloped into town, scattering pedestrians in his path, and came up to the wharf beside the Wilmington tug, his stallion's hoofs clumping on the wooden planks. A crowd had gathered to see the boat off. The gangplank had just been pulled aboard, and sailors at the prow and stern were prepared to haul in the lines. There she was at the railing, the glorious little whore, her hand on the arm of a disgustingly handsome young officer. They looked at him. Kilpatrick, on his steed, stood in the stirrups as if he might leap from the saddle to the deck. His horse wheeling restlessly, the conversation seemed to spin around like the hands of a clock. What was that she said? This major— Kilpatrick didn't recognize him—taking dispatches to Washington, had kindly offered to escort Marie and her mother there on the ship connecting from Wilmington. The damn jittery horse would not stand still. Marie, he called, listen to me, I— But at that moment two piercing steamboat whistles blasted his ears. His mount reared. Marie laughed, and the gallant officer covered her tiny ears with his white gloved

hands. They weren't the only passengers—there
were other Southern civilians aboard. They
waved to the people on the dock, and the people
on the dock cheered and waved at them. Slowly
the boat came away from its berth. A lead of
water widened. A sailor appeared at Marie's side
and handed her something—a package, was it?
General! He heard her call, and his horse circled
once again, and when he was turned toward the
boat something flew through the air, came apart,
fluttered in the breeze, and stuck to Kilpatrick's
face and chest. He heard her laughter, and the
officer's, and when he pulled whatever it was off
his face the boat was out in the stream, white
and trim against the green far bank. And Kilpatrick was left with his battle flag and the
churned blue water where the boat had been,
and the laughter of that heartless girl blowing off
in the wind.

THE NEXT DAY gunboats and transports arrived
with coffee and sugar for the army. They were to
take back to Wilmington more of the fugitive
whites who had attached themselves to the
march. Sherman had initiated another one of
his divestitures. He wanted nothing to encum-
ber the coming campaign. The freed slaves who
had followed along since Savannah now num-

bered more than twenty-five thousand useless mouths. They were to be organized into a separate march with whatever wagons and supplies he could spare and sent off to the coast under the direction of a few officers. Let them continue their exodus, Sherman muttered, but not in the direction I am going.

The numbers of sick and wounded accumulated on the march—they, too, received their orders, and a transport came up the river to take them away. And so a slow, sad procession of ambulances was seen winding its way through the streets of Fayetteville behind a military band. The band music was intended to honor the heroic sacrifice of the men in the wagons but, more practically, to mask their cries and moans. Nevertheless the citizenry did stop and stare in stunned contemplation of the costs of war.

At the docks, regimental surgeons and their assistants and army nurses oversaw the transfer of the patients on their litters up the gangplank to their berths aboard ship. Pearl went alongside the patients, talking to them over their moans, dabbing their fevered foreheads with wet compresses, holding their hands, smiling and assuring them they were going to where the hospitals up North would heal their hurts and send them home. Working beside her, Stephen Walsh marveled at Pearl's composure. She was strong for one so young, and while he had seen his share of horrors in combat, he turned away from surgical procedures, and was demoralized to hear the sounds that pain made in the aggregate, and to see how many diseases there were to which an army of men were subject, and which rendered them pathetic and grotesque and difficult to look upon with their variety of torments—the skin lesions or deliriums or swellings or foul emanations—all of this in clear, godless mockery of the idea of human dignity. Pearl seemed to be able to see beyond the affliction to the person that had been and, with luck, might be again.

You're a feisty miss, Pearl Jameson, he said one day when they'd been attending to the detritus of one of Colonel Sartorius's field surgeries. To oblige yourself to see to these matters.

An you the big North city boy, Stephen Walsh. Else you would know what I see on this march ain't what a slave child don't see beginning wif the day she come into this world.

Stephen, as his burns healed, had applied for reassignment to the Medical Department so that he could be with her. Wrede Sartorius, always in need of help, had signed the necessary papers. Though medical duties did not usually attract volunteers and, in fact, transfers to the department were sometimes meted out as punishment, he did not question Stephen or inquire into his motives, nor did he give a moment to think what they might be. Instead, as the army left Columbia, he had Stephen sit up in the wagon beside him and drew a sketch: it was of a vertical box frame of some size, with a seat and restraining straps and a removable hand bar. The structure was to be floored and nailed to a wagon bed. Stephen did not need to be told the purpose of the rig. Wandering around the hospital that first night in Columbia, he had seen the soldier with the spike in his temple. The soldier, sitting on a table, had smiled at him and waved with a wiggle of his fingers. Later that night Colonel Sartorius had had the fellow strapped to a pallet on his back so that he could not turn in his sleep. But Stephen was surprised that, without inquiring, Sartorius assumed that he could carpenter. He could, in fact, and was handy with machine tools as well. He liked to work with his hands.

In the town of Cheraw, just shy of the border with North Carolina, the local armory included a machine shop and a lumberyard. Working from the sketch, Stephen set to his task. Outside, the town was going through the usual ordeal. He could hear the troops in their pillaging. Later they were put on parade, this happening to be the day of President Lincoln's second inauguration.

Cannon were lined up and the ground shook with a twenty-three-gun salute. Stephen measured and sawed and planed. He was as painstaking as if he were at work on the finest cabinetry. He took satisfaction in the assembly of this box that a man was to sit in. He walled in the framework only up to the waist. He used heavy woods, carefully chosen. He bolted the corners. He made the restraining straps from harness and cut the iron bar for the man to hold as the wagon swayed and lurched through the ruts and over the corduroyed roads.

How peaceful to concentrate on this specific thing. It assured you that it could be attained. It would find its form and be. In the field surgeries nothing seemed to be resolved unless by death. On the march there was no one place from which all others were measured. It was as if the earth itself rolled backward under one's feet, it was as if the armies were strung from the floating clouds.

When the box was finished he sat down in it and closed his eyes. The Colonel had trusted him to do this, and he had done it. He felt a surge of passionate loyalty to the man. And after Wrede had come around to see it and said it would do, Stephen Walsh laughed, because he felt as if he'd been awarded the Army Medal of Honor.

—

SARTORIUS AND HIS medical staff were billeted in a house at the eastern end of Fayetteville. The army had been in residence for four days, and tomorrow at dawn it would resume the march. By midnight everyone was asleep except Pearl and Stephen. They had come down from their attic billet to the kitchen because Pearl wanted a bath. They lit some candles and Stephen threw split logs and brush into the stove to get the fire up. He drew water from the well out back. One bucket he left standing, and the other he put on the stove to heat. Together they carried in the tin tub from the mudroom.

Pearl removed her clothes as Stephen filled the tub with the heated water and then put the second bucket on the stovetop. I like the water hot as hot can be, Pearl said. Ain't nothin better'n a hot-water bath. He tried not to look, but she didn't seem to mind being seen this way, though she had made sure the door was closed and the curtains drawn. Her hair had gotten long and she stood there tying it back with a ribbon. He poured in the second bucket, and she put a hand on his shoulder as she dipped a toe into the water and smiled at him. He had never known anything to render him so stupid and speechless as this slender white Negro girl standing naked in front of him.

But she sat down in the water cross-legged, like a child, and splashed water on her face and sank down to the shoulders to soak herself and sat up again with a bar of brown soap, which she ran around her neck and over her breasts, looking up at him with such pleasure in her eyes that he felt vile for the feelings going through him. Yet he could tell Pearl knew the effect she was having.

You c'n do my back, please, she said.

He pulled up a stool and sat behind her and ran the soap along her shoulders and down her back, attending glumly to each vertebra.

Now, Stephen Walsh, she said, I know what all mens have in dere minds. Don't I know? How old are you?

Nineteen.

Well, I don't know how old I am. I think thirteen—I know not much more than fourteen. I know, 'cause my stepma'm's sons, brudder one and two, they was there since I can remember and brudder two he had a birfday of fifteen this las summer. And dey both taller? So I knows that way.

You don't have to worry.

Oh I . . . I know that. I wouldn't be sittin here in the altogether if I didn't know that.

Then he nearly dropped the soap, because she said, An when the time comes when I feel it upon me, I s'pose who it is will be you, Stephen Walsh.

HE FOUND SOME towels and wrapped one around her as she stood up from the tub. She was still as he rubbed her shoulders and back and buttocks and thighs through the towel.

Wif all the soldiers writin letters for the mail boat, Pearl said, did you?

No. No one I care to write to.

No fambly?

They wouldn't read it if I did.

She turned and faced him, holding the towel around her at the throat. Sad, she said. Sad sad sad. An you from the New York City where the perfec Union is. I'm goin there, you know that?

No. Since when?

Yes, when the war is done. That poor Lieutenant Clarke's letter, 'member I tole you?

Yes?

Why give it for the mail boat if I can read the envelope now with the address? I will take that letter to his mama and papa in the New York City, so as I may tell them.

Tell them what?

How he took care of Pearl and hid her and made her a drummer boy to keep her safe. Dey will need comfort.

What is the address?

The Number 12 Washington Square, as I have read it.

Sure, and that's a neighborhood for the rich folks.

Well, some rich folks is good I 'spect, if their son joined up to free black folks.

She was smiling, with her face still dewy and her hazel eyes wide and the ribbon having fallen from her hair. There rose in Stephen Walsh's breast a feeling so painfully glorious that it was all he could do to keep from pressing her to him.

Number 12? he said, clearing his throat.

Uh-huh, and Washington Square.

I know where it is, he said. I can take you there.

PEARL WAS AWAKENED by the moonlight coming through the small attic window. The moon had arisen to shine in her eyes. She found herself with her back snuggled against Stephen. His arm lay over her shoulder. They were lying on a horsehair mattress they had pulled off the little attic bed and put on the floor. Though they were fully dressed it was a thin blanket over them, too thin for the chill of this silvery night. She lay there quite still. She was suddenly irritated by that arm around her. It was heavy, and she leaned away until it slipped to the space between them.

She closed her eyes and tried to go back to sleep. Earlier that evening their wagon had ridden past the fields where the black folk were camped. The picture of that was in her mind now. All of them sitting around their fires, and the children running here and there, and the smell of cooking, and the little tents for their sleep, and the carts for their things. And the singing, the sad hymn singing—it was like a soft murmur of the wind, it was like sound coming up from the earth. It was the sound she had been born to, the prayerful sadness of their lot on earth. And they were singing of it now, all those people like her, except she wasn't there with them, she was riding by in the army wagon with army clothes on her back and good army food in her stomach and this white boy beside her, attached to her like by a chain. But these folks had heard they were going somewhere else than on the march with General Sherman, and they didn't know where that was or what they would find or if it was possible to be free men and women without the army to protect them.

She could not get back to sleep. Why had she lied to Stephen Walsh? She knew exactly how old she was, she was fifteen, her mama had told her, and that she was born on the tenth day of June, when the air was like something sweet to drink and the leaves on the trees were still young and soft, like you could feel the sun in them. But she had told him a story so well, and with such detail, about the Jameson brothers one and two that she almost believed it herself. Why? She was attracted to Stephen, she was impressed with him and secretly flattered that he had taken to her, this grown man, to be smitten as he so clearly was by her. It made her feel good and different, so that she was encouraged to be bolder than she had ever before been in the social ways of the world. Because if he was taken with her she would see to it that he was justified.

So why did she lie? It had just come out of her mouth before she knew what she was saying. What was her purpose, because she did have feelings for him. She liked his voice and his manner, the way what he said was always a clear thought. He did not chatter about nothing. He had a silence in him that made you understand he was no fool but a deep-minded person who knew more than he spoke aloud. And that he was angry about something from his life, just as she was—he was a white man with his own troubles—that interested her, and that he didn't make himself smaller by easily talking about it. From the moment she had held his burned hands, she had felt herself different. And she loved his mouth—it was all she could do sometimes not to lean up and kiss it.

But now the thought came to her that made her sit up and nearly cry out. What had she done since leaving the plantation but attach herself to white men? From the day she was lifted up to the saddle behind Lieutenant Clarke, and then even staying with that Gen'ral Sherman hisself, who had taken to her thinking she was a drummer boy, and then even through Miz Thompson getting to nurse for the Colonel-doctor, and now Stephen, she had acted as white, and lived with the whites with a white stepma'm and dressed her blackness in a uniform given to a white Union army. Oh Lord, such a deep shame now came over her, it made her ill. Was not Jake Early a prophet when he and Jubal Samuels came by to fetch her and he called her a Jez'bel? But you got to be a whore lady to be a Jez'bel, and I ain't a whore lady. No no, dear God, but I am worse, coddling up to be like one of them, making them like me like slaves do to proteck theirselves, bowin and scrapin to the white folks and smilin like some fool, and even servin Miz Jameson an watchin out for her an takin care of her. Didn't I know she wanted my pap to sell me away when I was a little chile? Look at me—didn't nobody sell me off in the auction, I done sold myself, and what does that make me but a slave, a slave like my mama Nancy Wilkins.

This thought had brought Pearl to her feet: I am owned.

She looked down at Stephen Walsh, his face so washed in moonlight as to be spectral. Who was this white man who had felt privileged to put his arm around her? Who was she as a Negro girl that she was allowing it and pushing her body up against his for the warmth? Her mama had lain with Pap Jameson as she had this night next to Stephen Walsh and, surely that arm of Pap's was as heavy around my mama as Stephen's around me. So how is I free? Never as a black girl, and not now as a white.

MOMENTS LATER SHE was flying down the stairs in her bare feet. She let herself out the front door and headed across the road and into the pasture, where, in the distance, the blacks were camped. She could see everything clear in the moonlight, the rises and dips in the earth, the paled leaves of grass, the lean-tos and wagons up ahead, and the embers of the cook fires glowing like stars in the fields. Ten minutes later she was walking in the paths of this improvised settlement, and many people were awake, huddled in their blankets around their fires, or rocking infants in their arms, or simply standing by their rigs and wagons and staring at her as she passed by. In their eyes she was a white woman, an army woman, and if they were curious as to what she was doing among them they did not demean themselves to inquire. They were being sent off to walk by themselves in the direction prescribed for them by their hero and savior, General Sherman. All they had wanted to do was praise him, revere him, and now he was turning them away, sending them off on their own, and what their destination was or what would happen to them when they got there nobody knew. For these people staring her down, she was the General's stand-in, as if she was responsible for their wretched disillusionment solely by virtue of her color and her uniform. Pearl kept shaking her head as if in discussion with them, though they said nothing, because she knew what they were thinking. And what was she doing here, anyway? She didn't know. She was looking for someone who knew her. Maybe looking for Jake Early and one-eyed Jubal Samuels, though they would long since have fallen by the way-

side. Or Roscoe, from back at the plantation—
a good, simple, kind man like no other, who
had dropped the two gold eagles wrapped in
his kerchief at her feet. She felt now in her
pocket to make sure she still had them, something she did at least ten times a day. And for
an instant as she passed a man, a skinny bald
man with huge dark eyes who smiled a sweet,
gap-toothed smile at her, she almost called out,
Roscoe! thinking that it was him.

And now, seeing the enormous encamp-
ment this was, with no end to it in the fields, for
across the road it went on, and up to the edge of
a forest, Pearl felt as helpless as she had ever felt
on the plantation, and all the comforts and sat-
isfactions of her working life in the Union army
seemed now a terrible scandal, a way of looking
out for herself and no one else that was no better than her selfish slave-owning pap. So that
what she took from his color as a white girl was
the worst of him, and all these wretched people
around her were the people she had ignored and
left to themselves just as they said General Sherman had left them after setting them free to go
on by themselves in a land that still was not
theirs. And what had it got her except some
shelter from the storm, like she was some house
slave looking out from the window at the field
niggers and forgetting she, too, was owned.

—

EARLIER THAT NIGHT Hugh Pryce had told the boy David that he would find him a place with his own people, and the minute he said that, David, not satisfied to hold his hand, had clung to his leg, so that the Englishman limped around the black encampment as if a ball and chain were attached to him. How awkward, how embarrassing.

Pryce had got them to Fayetteville on the little mule and found himself severely tried with a child to look after. David was underdressed for the weather, and Pryce took off his pullover and belted the sweater with rope to make a coat for him. The child was constantly hungry. Pryce, with his casual British bonhomie, was usually able to cadge rations. But with a Negro boy in tow it was as if he had lost his gift—the bummers exacted money for everything.

He was by now more annoyed with himself than moved by the child's dash to freedom. It was not his responsibility to free the slaves—was it?—yet he had lifted the boy to the saddle. A rash act, in violation of the imperative to be a strictly neutral observer. Somehow, without thinking too clearly, he had assumed he would be relieved of the burden—that the authorities in Fayetteville would take David off his hands.

But what authorities? The city was in chaos. The army was everywhere, and life had become unnatural for the inhabitants. No one seemed to know anything. In London there were established asylums for orphans, a fact of which the lower classes took advantage by happily depositing their newborns on the doorstep for society to raise. Of course, these were white foundlings, but how, war or no war, was it wrong to assume that every civilized society would have homes for its unwanted children even if they were black?

Worst of all, it was impossible to be taken seriously as a professional journalist with this appendage hanging on to him. He was losing out on the stories. He had heard a rumor that the secessionists were finally gathering an army the equal of Sherman's. Where it was and how big and where it would make a stand were important questions. He had gone to Sherman's busy headquarters, and one imperious frown from Sherman's wing commander, General Howard—a sweeping glance from man to boy—was enough for an adjutant to come forward and tell Pryce he had no business being there. Yet milling about were his competition—men from the **Herald Tribune,** the London **Telegraph,** the **Baltimore Sun.** Here was the biggest story of the campaign in the making and Hugh Pryce felt it getting away from him.

But there were stories no one could deny him. This afternoon he had hurried David up the hill to the site of the Fayetteville Arsenal, where the soldiers were demolishing buildings and setting them on fire. It was weirdly festive, squads of men running battering rams into brick walls, twelve and fourteen horse and mule teams pulling away foundations. Crowds had gathered to watch, and now and then had to back away from the flames and the chunks of fire flying everywhere. David yanked Pryce's sleeve. Don't like it, he kept saying, don't like it. And then one of the buildings was detonated with a monstrous roar, collapsing in an inferno of fire and smoke, and perhaps fusing their relationship forever in the mind of this child, for from that moment David, who had been a stouthearted little fellow, became tearful and querulous and clinging. Nor was he any better in his mind this night, as Pryce brought him to the encampment of the freed slaves and told him it was time for him to find a place with his own people.

CERTAINLY THERE WERE enough of them, and a poorer, more bedraggled mass of humanity Pryce had never looked upon. A majority were women, more old than young, and there were numerous old men, but only here and there a man in his prime. Pryce, used to the outdoors himself, saw no pathos in this encampment where the sky was the only roof and the only home was the space around the fire. People had lived this way from time immemorial. But the state of these beings, so many crippled and bent, withered and worn, all of them with a history of having been kept, as horses or mules were kept, sent a fine moment's rage into his breast. Yet he needed one of them now for the service she could supply—he needed a woman with strong maternal instincts, someone still with the strength to take on a child, or another child, without thinking twice about it. He needed someone healthy, with an apron and a kerchief around her head and good, strong arms. Pryce smiled. I need a mammy.

Just hold Hugh's hand, David, he said. Don't worry, he won't let you go.

This was still fairly early in the evening, and it was difficult for him to understand the nature of the gatherings—whether people were camped according to the plantations they had come from or had simply plunked themselves down hither and yon, like bathers on a beach. He found himself at the edge of a large group listening to an elderly man who stood on a box. The man had a scraggly white beard, very biblical he looked, a distinguished ancient, though he was dressed in rags and leaned on a stick. We are the sable brethren, he said in a soft deep voice, and finer in our natures and nobler in our forbearance than these European Americans who have chained us and whipped us and sent us into the fields. For we know our God, who has made of one blood all nations of men for to dwell on all the face of the earth. And if we are freed by this General, still, is he not one of them? The worship of this Sherman is blasphemy, for he is not your God. This Sherman has his own purposes, his own reasons. The Hebrews setting forth on their exodus did not ask an Egyptian general to lead them. Those Hebrews, they followed their own, as we must do now, for we are an army in ourselves. We have no weapons—no cannon and no muskets—but are an army of the free and righteous who make their own path, and find their own way by the grace of God.

A woman called out, And who be you, old man—is you Moses? There was laughter, but the man said, No, sister. I am a poor old field slave free now to die like a man. But the Lord our God knows I speak the truth. If you long for the General to protect you, you are still unfree. Freedom should fill your heart and lift your spirit. Let you not look to white mortals for your food and shelter and salvation. Look to your own and God will provide, and God will show us the way. We have been in the wilderness far more than forty years. It is the promised land now. Be fruitful and multiply and make it your own.

Amen, came the cry from several, and some hoots of disparagement from others. Hugh Pryce foresaw himself cabling a story describing seditious sentiments among the Negroes. But first he had to deal with his problem. Wandering on, he could see no one he could reasonably approach. With David, whom he had regularly to pry from his leg, he went among the blacks until he finally saw a possibility for him—a woman and two children eating their supper by a fire. The woman had fried some cornmeal cakes, and she looked at David and then at Pryce and then at David.

You lost, son? she said.

No'm, David said, his eyes on the fritters in the frying pan.

What's your name?

This is David, Pryce said. He's an orphan. He needs someone to take him in.

Is that right? If you ain't lost, who this? the woman said to David. This your daddy talkin?

Yes'm, David said.

I am not the child's father. My name is Hugh Pryce. I'm with the London **Times**.

Not the father?

No. Surely that should be obvious.

The woman laughed. Not to me, she said. No tellin by now what color a chile will come with.

My good woman—

Vengeance is mine—ain't that what the Lord said? And she laughed again.

Do you actually think—

She appraised Pryce. Favors you. Got his mama's skin but his daddy's eyes. And lookit his hands and feet. Gonna be a tall man, like you.

That's nonsense. I'll give you money.

What money? She frowned.

Federal greenbacks.

My, my. She wrapped her hand in a cloth, lifted the frying pan off the fire, and slid a fritter onto a folded sheet of newspaper. Still hot, she said to David. Leave it cool a minute.

Well?

The woman with effort raised herself from the ground, pushing off on one knee with a groan. She brushed her skirt and put one hand to her brow and peered in several directions. I need a Union soldier, she said. I got to get someone to come an arrest you.

Arrest me?

The slave trade over and done, din't you hear? Can't buy nor sell people no more.

I'm not selling anyone. I'm giving you money to take care of this boy.

Oh, sure. He older, you would ast me to pay for 'im. He too little to be much use, so you payin. Either way is outside the law of e-mancipation, ifn you ain't heard.

I merely mean to provide means for his keep. I see you already have two of your own and I understand the responsibility this entails.

Here, David, the woman said. She bent down and made a cone out of the paper holding the fritter and handed it to the child. Take this now, and get along with your daddy before I puts him in jail. An I ain't sayin nothin 'bout a man meanin to sell off his own chile, she said to Pryce.

She folded her hands and looked up into the night sky. Dear Lord, she said, fill this white man's heart with shame. Fill him with your glory. Let him repent and give thanks to you, God, for the blessin of this fine boy David. I ask this in Jesus' name. Amen.

WHY DID YOU lie, Pryce said some minutes later, don't you know lying is wrong? Don't you know that? He was practically shouting. But David, having finished his fritter, held Pryce's hand and chose not to answer. He marched along in calm anticipation of what lay ahead. It was as if Pryce were the child and David the adult who forbore to indulge his childish outbursts. Good God, Pryce thought, whomever I approach, what's to prevent his doing it again? He'll say I'm his father and that'll be the end of it.

With the realization that he'd been outwitted, Pryce felt his face turn hot. The child had a slave's cunning. And his instinctive dash to freedom—was it really that? How foolish to think so. More likely the wretched boy was merely running from the whip. In my arms he would avoid a beating. Yes, of course, that was all it was. He probably deserved what he was about to get.

Pryce felt the child's hand in his as something glued to him. The imposition had become intolerable. But I'm bigger and older and stronger and smarter than you, my good man. Your father elect won't make the same mistake twice.

The child who is taken up, Pryce thought, is the child found alone.

AND SO IT was that later that night Pearl, wandering in her distressed state through the encampment, came upon the crowd around the boy, who had torn his clothes off. Nobody could touch him. He sat there cross-legged in the mud, beating his fists against his thighs and sobbing. If someone approached him the sobs became screeches. People, seeing Pearl in her nurse's uniform, stepped aside. She knelt in front of the child. The moonlight washed the warmth out of his color and made him a beautiful blue-black. And in the brief moment he stopped crying to study her, his expression was calm enough for her to see that he was a handsome little boy. She thought he might be six or seven years old. Pearl nodded as if to say she understood that he had every right to cry, and she smiled sympathetically. She put her hand out, and though he jerked his head back, she did touch his forehead, and he let her. She thought he felt hot. His eyes, swollen from crying, looked like sick eyes to her. How long had he been sitting here? Her own bare feet had long since gone numb from the cold, and she thought his sitting there on the wet ground for no matter how long couldn't be doing him much good. She picked up his clothing—all of it was wet and muddy.

Whose child is this? she called out. Don't nobody claim this child?

Several voices assured her that he belonged to no one that they could see.

You all standin around lookin on—this ain't a raree show, Pearl said. Somebody fetch me somethin to cover him.

Are you lost, boy? Pearl said.

He shook his head no.

You got a mama somewhere lookin for you?

He shook his head no.

Pearl accepted a blanket, and when she turned back to David he was staring at her, his sobs having gone into spasmic snuffings, and with the back of his hand he wiped his nose.

Moments later she was carrying him, all wrapped in a blanket, back through the encampment the way she had come. He was heavier than he looked, and shivering now and knuckling his teeth. Pearl was feeling defiant. I will keep this one with us on the march, she said to herself. And if Stephen Walsh means to marry me, he will understan that, white as she is, Pearl could someday bear him a tar baby for his trouble.

IV

THEY WERE UP ON THE ARSENAL PLATEAU IN front of the one building still standing amid all the rubble. It had been used as a temporary headquarters. Some of the remaining troops were loading crates and files into army wagons. Others were rolling barrels of powder up a ramp they had laid over the front steps.

If you didn't drag your feet, Arly said, I would be riding behind General Sherman, wherever he is. Now how am I to know with the columns separating down there across the river? Look from here like one blue snake breeding into two.

I needed chemicals, Calvin said. And Mr. Culp provides a list of photo salons in each city. Besides, I have the picture of General Sherman from down in Georgia, with all his lesser generals standing there.

Never you mind, we're gonna take a better one if we ever find him again.

Why?

Why? Why? You ask too many questions, Calvin. But the answer is he will have aged some. Like me, just from trying to get you a move on.

Calvin dropped the reins over Bert and they started down the winding road to the center of town.

We were talking trade, Calvin said. The people in this profession talk to one another, even if one of them is a Negro. This photographer, Swank of Fayetteville, he takes mostly women and their chiddren and young ladies in their coming-out.

Debutantees? Didn't he never hear there was a war?

Wasn't a war here until four days ago. That's why he had a good store of materials—collodion and chemical bath, and even plates fixed and ready to use in their holders, though Mr. Culp always likes to prepare his own plates. Not everybody does it right, he told me. Best if you do the work yourself.

IN TOWN THERE was a terrible smell. People in the streets had handkerchiefs wrapped around their faces. Troops were marching at the double to get to the river and across the bridge as soon as possible.

Phewee! Arly said.

They found some space in the lag of the march, and even Bert clopped along a bit faster than usual. The closer they got to the river, the worse the stench. And then finally they had to stop to accommodate the sight because horses and mules were everywhere lying dead on the grassy banks of the river. And some of them were floating in the river. It was a slow broad course, the Cape Fear, and the carcasses rolled over and stuck their legs in the air and rolled back and eddied and bumped one another in a state of hapless confusion, though they were clearly dead.

Calvin shook his head. What'd they have to do that for to all these animals?

Well, Calvin, you are clearly not a military man or you would know this is an army's night soil. An army works its animals near to death so on a re'glar basis it rids itself of its consumed-up animals and gets new ones, though I venture not a few of these dead creatures were in better shape than your Bert is. If we was more about our business, we could have made a trade and he would be one of these creatures farting their dead air into the skies of Fayetteville instead of standing here looking so pleased with himself.

Best not let him hear you when you talk like that. See him turn his head and flick his ears?

Well, if you're listening, Bert, Arly said, better get a move on lest you find yourself bumping downriver with all of them.

When Bert didn't move, Arly looked at Calvin. You dumb as he is to think he can understand me. Whop him on the ass is all he understands. Trouble with black folks, you got your stories. You got mule stories, you got whistle-pig stories, you got Yankee stories—

Yankee stories getting us freedom.

Getting you air makes you sick to breathe it. **Phew!** A good, brisk wind might have shown God's mercy in this situation. 'Course, no Southern gentleman general would leave a thousand dead carcasses to stink up a city. Nosir. He would put down his stock away in the country where nobody would suffer it. Old Sherman giving the people something to remember him by. Such manners is why we insurrected in the first place. This Yankee freedom you tell of, that's as much a tale as a mule knows the English language.

Well, we'll see, we'll see, Calvin said. He flipped the reins and Bert got them into the line of traffic to go across the river. I notice it's no Southern gentleman general we chasing after to take his picture, Calvin said.

—

ONCE WREDE SARTORIUS'S regiment was across the Cape Fear and on the march east, he hitched his mount to the wagon in which his patient rode and got up inside to ride with him. The patient was Corporal Albion Simms of the Eighty-first Ohio, the man with the spike in his skull.

It was in that freakish accident, when the powder being dumped in the Saluda River back in Columbia somehow exploded, and many men were killed, that Albion Simms, finding himself sitting on the ground, and somewhat breathless, touched the side of his head because he felt as if something had stung him.

In the aftermath, his awestruck mates had taken him to the South Carolina College hospital and there, coming under Wrede's care, he was immediately placed in restraints so as not to further injure himself. Wrede had shaved the man's head as he questioned him. Albion Simms's memory was gone. His reflexes were sound, he could see and hear normally, he could respond to questions, but he remembered nothing previous to the feeling that he had been stung. When he was told his name and the regiment of which he was a part, he heard this news with no sense of recognition.

Naturally, the appearance of this man, physically unimpaired but for an iron spike in his skull, brought the regimental surgeons running. Bored by routine amputations, and their mostly futile treatments for the miasmatic diseases, the doctors found in the case something to enliven their professional spirits. The consensus was for surgery, but Wrede, who had their jealous regard as being the best of them, said he himself would not risk such an operation.

The spike, of the common variety used in the construction of army wagons, had penetrated the cranium above the ear at an angle of 180 degrees. It was firmly lodged. It may complicate with scar tissue or inflammation, Wrede said, but surgery would without question enhance the trauma. If you look closely, you will see no impact fracture. It is a clean four-sided penetration. Some six millimeters protrude, which means seven millimeters of iron have traversed the parietal-occipital areas. And there is bone in front of it. A trepan is not possible, nor can you expect to extract the spike as you would a splinter from your finger. The damage is indisputable, but as it now stands the wound is not fatal.

During this consultation, the eyes of the unfortunate Albion, who was strapped to an examining table, darted back and forth from one doctor's face to another. The bearded and studious officers hovering over him were blocking out the world. He became agitated and began struggling against his restraining straps. Wrede Sartorius looked into his eyes and smiled, and laid a hand on his chest. Corporal Albion Simms, he said, you will not have surgery. Your survival is something of a miracle. And that miracle is precisely what invites our examination.

WREDE SARTORIUS HAD to acknowledge to himself that taking the man on the march rather than having him sent to a Northern hospital was, from a strictly medical point of view, without justification. The first ethical commandment for doctors was to do no harm. Clearly, a rough passage on weathered and rutted roads was not prescribed. Yet the possibility of learning something about the brain from the affliction of this soldier was an opportunity he was not willing to forgo. He expected the man was doomed. It was just a matter of time: more and more of the brain would respond to its insult, and the mind would recede in the manner of an outgoing tide. But that would be a process. Albion Simms would deteriorate under study.

Wrede commandeered a soft riding ambulance for Albion Simms's exclusive use, and had him strapped down for travel. In this way they rode with the army out of Columbia.

At the end of each day's march, whatever surgeries had to be tended to—the skirmishes with enemy soldiers were a daily occurrence—Wrede would find time to interview the patient and make note of the responses. After some days Albion's functional memory no longer included the moment of his injury. He saw colors when he heard sounds. He did not recognize written numbers. He sometimes complained of pain and dizziness. Through all of this his appetite was good. Though he remembered nothing of his past life, one day he suddenly remembered the words and tune of a song, which he sang for his doctor:

> **Oh the coo coo**
> **Is a pretty bird**
> **And she wobbles as she flies**
> **But she never sings her coo coo**
> **'Til the fourth day of July**

He sang in a high, reedy voice, his eyes lifted upward as if he were seeing the bird he sang about. Wrede used the song as a measure of stability, asking Albion Simms to sing it every interview thereafter. Within a week, Albion couldn't remember the words or understand that he had once sung them, and when asked what the Fourth of July meant he didn't respond. Then one day he sang the song again, and the next day it was again gone from his mind.

In the meantime, one of Wrede's colleagues—he didn't know or care who—had sent word to the Surgeon General in the capital, and he in turn had telegraphed Sherman's headquarters: a courier came down the ranks with the order that Colonel Sartorius was to have Corporal Simms transported to the Federal hospital in Washington immediately once the army reached Fayetteville. This had been delivered in the town of Cheraw.

Wrede's response was to have Stephen Walsh carpenter the box frame that now held Simms and the odd protrusion that was an integral part of him. You will not be lying down during the day, Albion, Wrede said. You will see what's going on in the world around you.

Always contemptuous of the army mind, Sartorius knew that once they were out of Fayetteville no further official thought would be given to the matter, especially if, as he believed, there was more combat in the coming days than the forces had seen in some time. But at this point his emotional estrangement from the medical community of the Army of the West was complete. Of the procedures he had invented, the treatments he had recommended to supersede the standard therapies, none had been adopted. Some were still under study. They would be under study long after the war was over. He was not looking for personal recognition. He did not need or want a higher rank. But he had become intolerant, passionately intolerant, of traditional medical thinking. It did not change, it did not advance but looked dumbly upon the disasters it devised for the poor broken and mutilated boys that were its responsibility.

Sartorius was sensitive to the issue of slavery, or he wouldn't have accepted a commission in the Union army. But as a European, with a medical degree from the University of Göttingen, he had from the beginning found himself apart. If there was any compensation for the barbarity of war, it was an enriched practice. The plethora of casualties accelerated the rate of learning. Apparently he was alone in considering this American civil war a practicum.

Though Sartorius believed himself to be fervently human, he recognized that people had not always found him so. There seemed to be a natural divide in the way he and Americans conducted themselves in social intercourse. He was a bit formal, certainly not demonstrative, by which they decided he was arrogant. He did not smile easily, by which they understood his pale-eyed attentions were something like a naturalist's looking at an insect. He was a neatly composed, self-assured man who had left a European civilization whose constraints he did not want to be part of. He had come to America, as everyone else did, to be free. But Americans lacked something—perhaps the sense of human consciousness as tragedy. It was this sense that had governed his desire to do science since he'd been a schoolboy. For if not science, then despair. But here, on this morning, as the rain began to fall, and spatter and snap against the wagon canvas, he wondered as he regarded Albion Simms, if there was a possible equivalence of their two minds, as if something had been severed as well in the Sartorian brain that impelled him now to seek knowledge with no regard for the consequences.

And what else was severed? These days he thought less often of Emily Thompson. He found that his recollection of their conversations, her quality of mind, the honest intelligence, the prim gallantry of her work for him, the soft Southern lilt of her voice, how she moved, how it felt to hold her in his arms—all of it was becoming less distinct. And his anger had diminished. Gradually, he supposed, the memory of her would fade entirely, or at least until it would no longer be painful.

THEY ARE SHOOTING at me, Albion Simms said. His eyes were wide with alarm.

No, Albion, that is the rain falling.

The rain?

Yes, it is raining very hard against our little roof. Also the canvas flaps in the wind. But it is a fearsome sound, I grant you that.

What did you call me?

Albion. That is your name.

That is my name?

Yes.

What is my name?

Albion Simms. Have you forgotten?

Yes. I have forgotten. What have I forgotten?

You knew your name yesterday.

Is this yesterday?

No.

I have forgotten yesterday. My head hurts. What is this that hurts?

Your head. You said your head hurts.

It does. I can't remember. I say a word and I can't remember it. What did I say I can't remember?

A word.

Yes. That is why my head hurts. It's always now. That's what hurts. Who did you say I was?

Albion Simms.

No, I can't remember. There is no remembering. It's always now.

Are you crying?

Yes. Because it's always now. What did I just say?

It's always now.

Yes.

Albion, in tears, held his bar and nodded. Then he rocked himself back and forth, back and forth. It's always now, he said. It's always now.

My poor fellow, it's always now for all of us, Wrede thought. But, for you, a bit more so.

Outside, the rain seemed heavier. But then he understood it was cavalry cantering past.

KILPATRICK, RIDING WITH his troops on the road to Averasboro, crossed the Cape Fear River and drew fire. He was ready for a fight. He was an angry man these days. His men were used to his relish for battle, but this was more a dark, glowering rage that some of them felt could just as easily be turned on them. The wind and rain seemed to turn him around in circles as he shouted out his orders. The orders seemed to fly up on the wind.

A regimental probe moved forward to develop the resistance. The men dismounted and spread out wide, slogging through the fields on both sides of the road. The terrain was treacherous, soft and sandy. The fire came from a woods. Lieutenant Oakey, in the lead company, lay on the ground and focused his glass. He saw a well-built works of logs and sand. Concerted volleys of spurting Enfields told him this was no mere cavalry detachment.

The men ran forward in a crouch against the wind, hampered by swampy terrain that grabbed and sucked at their shoes. A cold rain slapped at their faces. The muzzle fire of the enemy seemed to Oakey as sparklers lighting the way. They were all prone on the ground now, firing erratically into the woods. In another moment enemy artillery cut loose, twelve-pounders, with shells that whistled. He held his head and pressed himself into the mud. In the explosions behind him men were screaming. A colonel galloping along the line shouted as his steed buckled and went down. Just in time, he slid himself out of the saddle, the horse having plummeted into a pond of quicksand. He watched helplessly as the struggling animal foundered, sinking slowly, its eyes wide with terror, its poll twitching like a rabbit's ears. And then it disappeared in a sudden awful **floop** of the gulping muck.

When after twenty minutes the order came to fall back, the men found themselves tumbling over the hurried earthworks Kilpatrick had ordered. The task now was to defend a position, a formal acknowledgment of the size of the enemy force. The cavalry withdrew to a more advantageous terrain, where the orders were given to entrench, and soon hundreds of men were digging in, reinforcing their embankments with logs and brush. There was frantic effort, for soon enough enemy elements rose from their position and came forward. The firing was murderous. Inspired by their desperation, Kilpatrick's forces held. The Rebs fell back, pickets were set out, and the skirmishing went on.

Kilpatrick had dispatched couriers to Generals Sherman and Slocum. He ventured that he had happened upon one, possibly two divisions of Rebel infantry. They would be Hardee's forces. Kilpatrick asked for two infantry divisions, if not three, to bolster his lines and provide the manpower for a flanking maneuver. He wanted heavy artillery as well, pieces with greater range than the enemy's.

On the Rebels' last charge before darkness fell, the beleaguered cavalry was saved by the arrival of an infantry brigade from Slocum's Twentieth Corps. With the onset of night, the firing stopped. The two forces now hunkered down, encamped miserably in a cold and wet March night. The Union lit no fires. The men ate their hardtack, cursed the Rebs, the weather, and the war, and curled up in their wet blankets with their hats over their faces to keep the rain out of their mouths as they tried to sleep. Parties were sent out to bring in the dead and wounded, and a mile or two behind the lines the medical wagons came forward and field hospitals were set up in farmhouses taken over for the occasion.

BEFORE DAWN THE next morning, the Rebs rose up from their lines and sent waves of riflemen on the attack and everything that had gone on the day before seemed like the mildest of jabs. As the sun rose, weak and gray from the fog-ridden swampland, Slocum's infantry brigade braced for the assault and soon found itself in danger of caving in. The Rebels screamed out their fury. Another division was put in place, the flanks were reinforced, and the troops held on. The battle steadied, with the firing continuous, and then the Union artillery with its range of four hundred yards began to pummel the Rebel lines and the initiative swung to the Union side. Sherman, far back from the battle, sitting by his tent in a pine grove in which odd fragments of grape and canister occasionally dropped, contemplated his tactical options while his staff stood by ready to transmit his orders. He seemed oddly dissociated from the event, and almost lackadaisically supposed that the entire Union line should advance with a right-flanking maneuver to be undertaken by one of Slocum's infantry brigades. Colonel Teack was quick to translate this thought into an urgent order, and a courier galloped off through the trees.

PRIVATE BOBBY BRASIL, who had served a short time in the military jail back in Columbia, learned, when he was released, that the 102nd New York had moved on without him. He had thought that unfeeling, given how he exemplified the regiment's highest standards of drinking and carousing and that his achievements were acknowledged even by that other Papist in the ranks, the staid Stephen Walsh, and he so suffused with Jesuitical proprieties. Brasil's transfer to a Dutchess County, New York, regiment of dull-witted farm boys seemed especially inappropriate now as he lay among them in the swamp mud of Averasboro awaiting the order to charge that he expected would bounce him up to Heaven, where God would have a few things to say to him before another transfer took place—and that one for eternity.

And then the shout came, and the pistol shot, and up he was and running forward, screaming like the rest, leaping over bodies and keeping a wary eye out for those yellow pools of sand ready to swallow him like the morsel he was. And didn't that lovely Irish maid in Columbia tell him so, that he was delicious enough to eat? And what would I taste like? he had asked her. A pastry nut cake, she had said, with a heart of sweet cream.

Christ help him if he ever got there, never mind the Reb bullet, his chest would burst from this running, he was pulling the air into his chest in great wheezing gasps, he could feel the rain falling into his mouth and then, glory to God, up in the air he went as the boy in front of him fell dead and he tripped over him, somersaulting over the downed dead boy and smashing into the mud, gasping for air, and the rain pounding him in the face and he staring into the darkness of the day. He could feel the mud seeping onto his back and up his trouser leg and down his collar, he could feel it crawling up the back of his ears—a living, creeping thing. He would lie here like this and catch his breath but for the mud and for the boots pounding by his head, anointing him in spatters and splotches.

Judas Priest, to be stomped to death by one of these stupid Dutchess Counties! And up he staggered, spun in the right direction by the men running past him, and ahead was the earthworks, but they were behind it, they had turned it, and here he was suddenly in command, chasing after the fleeing Rebs, some of them going down on their knees with their hands in the air, and he prodding them with his bayonet like a sneering, true killer, except his bayonet accidentally went into one of them: soft it felt, no bone there at all. He would remember the look on the boy's face, but now with his foot he pushed the poor sod back off the blade and ran on, chasing after the Reb gunners who'd abandoned their pieces and were scampering back into the woods, appearing and disappearing and appearing again between the trees as he pounded after them, a screaming banshee with his wet rifle unfiring, and then his bayonet somehow stabbing into a soft pine tree so that he was trying to yank it out with the smell of resin suddenly filling his nostrils as a great cheer went up and the breastworks was theirs.

BUT THERE WAS a second line after that, and more fighting as the Rebs regrouped, and as the day darkened and the second entrenchment was taken, they fell back to a third line, this berm solidly implanted with logs and stretching across the small peninsula road to Averasboro with the Cape Fear on one flank and Black Creek on the other. So finally the position was impassable, with the Rebel flanks protected by water and Hampton's cavalry patrolling.

These people show a little more than I thought possible, Sherman said that evening. He'd studied his maps and, with General Slocum and a humbled Kilpatrick, worked through what intelligence had come in and ascertained that they were confronted with a force of about ten thousand of Hardee's troops. Sherman wondered if Hardee might not be defending against the feint to Raleigh—for that was what Slocum's wing had been demonstrating on the road to Averasboro—but simply holding the wing down until General Joe Johnston arrived with the bulk of his army. If Johnston's marching from Raleigh, he knows I'm really headed for Goldsboro. It's those damn newspapers, Sherman muttered. Joe Johnston reads 'em, everyone reads 'em, and every move I make, every time I piss against a tree, the news goes 'round the world.

Colonel Teack understood that his General, having underestimated the resistance at Averasboro, was shaken.

In the evening Sherman and his staff rode

up to the front. The rain had finally stopped, and in the cooling wet air they could hear the cries of the wounded in the fields. Litter bearers were bringing them back out of the darkness, and the ambulances dispersed them to the farms that had been commandeered for surgeries. Reb soldiers were carried in as well, and Sherman noted how young and poorly clad they were, many of them with no shoes and make-do for uniforms. He toured the farmhouses and spoke consoling words to the men awaiting surgery, and made promises to write home for the boys who knew they were dying. Teack took the names. It was very sad and Sherman was solemn riding back to his camp. In today's actions he'd sustained nearly eighty dead and four hundred seventy-seven wounded. The Rebs' third line was still to be taken. This would require a frontal assault, the upshot being more casualties. A tremor of self-doubt went through Sherman at this moment. In the next moment he roused himself: Now, Uncle Billy, what would war be without its ups and downs? Joe Johnston surely won't make the mistake of attacking you here with the Neuse River at his back. From the looks of those of his boys you've seen this evening, his battle flag is sewn from the rag bins of the South. You'll go on to Goldsboro, and if he turns up that'll be the end of him.

Sherman was unable to sleep, though. He left his tent and stood on a knoll and looked down the Averasboro road, where Rebel campfires glowed through the trees.

But the secesh had lit their fires and stolen away, and it was only in the morning, when the first skirmishers were sent out and found the breastworks abandoned, that the General allowed himself a thin smile.

MATTIE, HER HAIR now long and loose down her back, left tending the men on their pallets awaiting treatment outside the doors of the barn and walked off in the cool, damp night to look at the dead. At this farm they were laid out in the front yard of the house, where across the road the men were digging a grave for them. Pearl didn't go with her anymore when the stepma'm performed this ritual, it was something they'd all come to expect, that whenever the occasion arose Mattie Jameson would walk among the bodies awaiting burial and stop and look at each one to see if it was a son lying there. And then it wouldn't be, and she'd cry anyway and bite her hand and shake her head, maybe because their mamas were not there to cry for them.

Pearl never thought Mattie would have to see either of the brothers lying dead, because it was such a big war and, if they did get theirselves killed, the chances of her coming upon them were so small. Pearl didn't mind if the brothers fell, she just didn't want the stepma'm to find them because she was a poor shaken woman with her brains already addled. And now that this child David was riding with them, Pearl could see how a mother's love could flow from the time someone needed her who was little.

Pearl knew brother one and brother two as rotten boys, mean to the slaves for no reason, John Junior a bully and the little one, Jamie, a hanger-on and a sniveler, and she had known they spied on the women bathing in the creek and did other bad things, like stealing from the kitchen and blaming black folk. And once when Pap had whipped one of the field hands—it was Ernest Hawkins, the strongest of the men and the proudest—and the whipping was done and Ernest lay on the ground with his hands tied to the fence rail and his back sliced up, it was the boys who come running with the salt to rub into him. They were hated boys all over the plantation. Even Roscoe, so gentle and forbearing, with never a bad word—even he would go off muttering that someday he would take it into his own hands. Pearl had kept the brothers at bay without much trouble, but she remembered now the thought that crossed her mind, that when she grew up and they as well, she didn't know what she would do, especially if Pap died and the brothers became the owners of her. She had cried at that thought, and Roscoe had said, Miss Porhl, don't worry your mind, if it ever come to that, Roscoe would kill them before they raised a hand, and he would die a happy man knowin surely he was bound for Heaven.

And now, anyway, there was enough going on, there were three surgeons in the barn, and you didn't know what to do first. She and Stephen raked the bloody hay into the corners and broke fresh bales to spread round the operating platforms. There was such screaming, such moaning. Once a nurse called her and made her hold the towel with the chloroform over the soldier's face—she had never been trusted with that before. Every few minutes, when she could, she ran to the barn doors to look up to the house where she'd put that child David in the care of the white folks who lived there because he had found a window where he could look out at what he shouldn't be seeing and would probably never forget if he lived to be a hundred and ten. For the ambulances were still trotting them in, and the wounded soldiers were everywhere, sprawled on the ground, sitting with their backs against the trees, some of them pray-

ing and some of them just lying there quietly,
saying nothing while they concentrated on con-
tinuing to live. And then the boy would have to
see the body waste coming out the door and
being thrown into the big pit. She did that
along with everything else—in one instance
when the man who'd been amputated was a big
man and the leg had been removed close to the
hip, and it was so heavy that she couldn't manage it herself and Stephen had to take the upper
part while she carried the other end by the big
bare foot that was still warm.

But now Pearl and everyone else heard curling out of the night the thin thread of a howl, a
cry that stopped the chorus of the moans of the
wounded, the bustle of the medical nurses, the
gruff commands of the surgeons—all of them
shocked silent in deference to a wail so finely
drawn and appalling as to resound in every
breast as despair of the war in which they lived.
No salvo of musketry, no thunderous cannon,
could quake the military heart as this sound
did. Even Wrede Sartorius for a moment
looked up from his bloody labors, and when
he turned back to them his own science suddenly seemed futile given the monumentality
of human disaster.

Pearl knew who it was, of course, and when
she ran outside and around to the front of the

house, she came upon the stepma'm on her knees before a corpse lying calmly in the grass except that its face was shot away. There was no jaw, the hair had been burned off, and what remained was caked in black dried blood. Mattie's cries wavered and soared, dipped and rose, the sounds she made did not seem to be coming from a human throat. And now she began to pull her hair. Pearl knelt and, holding her in her arms, she said, That's not your boy, stepma'm you can hardly see who it is for the awful thing done to his face. Come away, come away now.

Two of the gravediggers had come across the road to look on the scene and shake their heads. It made no difference that the dead boy was a Reb—in their young soldiers' minds nothing was worse in war than the grief of mothers.

What Pearl hadn't seen she saw now. Mattie knew her son, and to prove it she had unbuttoned the bloodied tunic and pulled it away from the white chest, and there, just below the collar bone on the right side was the birthmark looking like a copper coin that she had loved of John Junior's endowment since the day he was born.

PEARL GOT BUSY and speaking softly to the soldiers she had them put the body on one of the two-wheeled carts that served as a bier. They pushed it across the road and packed some dirt into a sidewall at one end of the mass grave to make it look like a separate grave, and as Pearl held Mattie Jameson to her and hid her face, the body was set down and the dirt shoveled over and the men stood around with their hats off and the Sergeant in charge of the detail spoke some words as he knew how to do.

Thank you, Pearl said to them and took the stepma'm to the wagon and put her to sleep with a dose of laudanum tincture which Stephen had brought over, with his permission, from Colonel Sartorius's medicine chest.

There was still work to be done, and several hours were to pass before Pearl and Stephen had the chance to talk. The yard, still brightly lit with torches and lanterns, was empty now of traffic. The Medical Department had organized a convoy of the seriously wounded to travel with Slocum's wing in the morning. The many Rebel wounded were to be left here, with some of their own captured officers put in charge of them and a supply of rations to tide them over until the officers worked out some means of sustaining them.

Stephen, Pearl said, those two boys—you never saw one without the other.

What two boys?

The brothers one and two. The stepma'm's own real chiddren. John Junior, he was the older. And then that little runt following along? I can't think he ain't around here somewheres, that Jamie.

Why is that?

Well, if they was servin together and Junior is dead, where is Jamie? Maybe taken.

It's herself you're thinking of?

I fear stepma'm will not want to live no more.

You told me she never did much for her slaves.

Nosir, she didn't. Didn't care, didn't stop'm when he sold families apart, the pap, didn't stop'm when he took the lash to someone. She wasn't bad like him, yellin and screamin, she just didn't think about nothin. A weak thing. Liked to play her piano and let the world be.

Well, now it's come home to her.

Stephen Walsh, won't you hep me find where they keep the captured mens?

He shook his head. Oh Lord. And what will you be doing if you do find him?

Don't know.

Aren't you tired? I'm tired. Let's find somewhere to lie down. And we'll talk about it in the morning.

They held hands as they walked to the house. Pearl looked back across the road. It so witchy how all along the march she has worried the dead to find her son and now she has found him, Pearl said.

PEARL WOKE HIM before dawn and they were out on the wet road, riding one of the wagon mules bareback. She held Stephen Walsh about his waist. Only the birds were up, singing in the swampland and leaving shadows of themselves as they flew across the road so swift that their color didn't register. Pearl knew the songs back in Georgia, but these were unknown to her. They were not purely tuneful but softer, twittier songs, like the birds knew full well what a fearful war was around them.

The column stretched back forever, it seemed, the wagon trains lined up on the road and the regimental camps in the pines on either side. Pickets out on the flanks, a cooking fire here and there.

Stephen felt her arms around his waist as her trust in him. He could feel her breasts pressed to him and the beating of her heart. Or was it his own? Whole hours went by in which he accepted this state of intimacy without thinking about it, just living in it, as if Pearl had led him there by the hand. It had become so naturally assumed that the worst thing he could do, he knew, was to express his feeling for her—it would alarm her, frighten her. He wouldn't have to speak of it to make sure it was there and that she knew it. She knew it as long as it went unspoken.

He was a changed man in having forsworn his habit of melancholic reflection. Never had he opened himself to his life to this extent, living it with no questions, simply living it, though swept up in this nomadic war with its bizarre triteness of death. He had a new strong faith that he would survive and that he and Pearl Jameson would go on. How extraordinary that this girl had become the organizing principle of his life. Yet they were only keeping company. He smiled. What you did, when another person was at the center of your being, was to accommodate her wishes no matter what your own judgment might be.

As the mule clopped on, and as the darkness began to pale and the sounds drifted through the trees of men and animals beginning to stir, the pine trees themselves, as they became distinguishable, seemed to be taking the darkness out of the night and invoking it in themselves. And then, with the first touches of the sun in the treetops, the mule rounded a bend and Stephen pointed to an open field. The encampment of

Reb prisoners was unmistakable. These soldiers had no fly tents and no weapons stacked, and they lay about on the ground or sat with their arms around their knees, as dispirited an assembly of men as Stephen had ever seen. In fact, they were not wholly men—in their rags and makeshift uniforms many of them were no more than boys. He felt old looking at them. The few standing pickets at the perimeters testified to the unlikeliness of this sad host attempting to escape.

Stephen and Pearl dismounted, tied the mule to a wagon trace, and without ceremony or finding a need to explain themselves went into the field to walk among the prisoners. The guards watched them idly, yawning or nodding good morning. If there was an officer in command, he was still asleep in the sidewall tent before a stand of pines at the far end of the field.

The youth of so many of the prisoners suggested to Pearl that she might be on the right track. When questioned, the boys spoke of General Hardee, who had been skirmishing with Sherman's troops since back in Georgia. They were unfailingly polite, answering Pearl's inquiries with yes ma'ms and no ma'ms. Poor shivering things, Pearl said quietly to Stephen, skairt of their own shadows. They are well chastened for the years coming when the black mens workin their land will get wages or their neighbors are black farmers.

And then, of course, she found him, Jamie, the brother two. He was alone, huddled up with his arms folded, and he was shivering though sitting in a patch of morning sun, and the sun on his face showed his thin, hollow cheeks and skin marred with scabs and dirt under his nose, and dull eyes with pink rims and hair that had grown longer than she remembered it, and dirtier, not blond anymore, and caked with mud. Brudder two, Pearl said, you are a mess. I can hardly bear to look on you.

He gazed up at her with no recognition.

You comin with us. Come on, get up now.

It was a struggle just getting him to comprehend. Stephen yanked him to his feet, and while the other prisoners watched idly he held the boy by the arm and led him to the road. But at this point a guard stopped them and told them to wait, and back across the field an officer, mounted, was riding through the assemblage of prisoners scattering them right and left. He came up, swung off his horse, and demanded to know what was going on.

Stephen Walsh saluted. He was aware that the officer, a lieutenant, was hatless and half unbuttoned, with the galluses hanging out from under his tunic. It was not a sought-after duty, guarding prisoners. Sir, he said, we have orders from Colonel Sartorius of the Medical Department to remove diseased prisoners from your encampment.

The officer took in Stephen's lapel insignia, the Department caduceus, and looked Pearl up and down. Pearl was wearing her army nurse's cape, which Emily Thompson had given her, and a private's hat by which she proposed to further authenticate her military service. Why has the Colonel given this order?

This man is sick, Pearl said. You see his eyes, you see his skin? He's got a catching disease.

A what disease?

I ain't sick, Jamie Jameson said.

Sir, Stephen said quickly, the man has an infectious erysipelas that can lead to death. In such cases the patient is isolated lest he infect everyone around him with the fever. It has been known to ravage whole regiments.

What do I care if these Rebs catch his disease? the officer said. More power to it.

Sir, it doesn't stop at blue uniforms.

The officer jumped back, with a worried glance at the prisoner.

Nor at officers, Pearl put in.

I ain't sick, said Jamie Jameson.

The officer glanced at him with contempt.

Get him out of here, he said, as if the order was his rather than the Medical Department's.

IF HE'D THOUGHT to ask for a written order we were finished.

You do learn your words, Stephen Walsh, Pearl said. She hugged him.

I ain't sick, Jamie Jameson shouted. They were walking him behind the mule, with his wrists tied and the other end of the rope wrapped around Stephen's hand.

Pearl looked back at him. Shut your mouth, stupid brother, she said. Can't tell what's good from what's bad.

He had recognized Pearl by now. Don't need to hear fum no nigger gal.

They didn't bother to prepare him in any way, but when they were back with the medicals they located Mattie, who was in the house, and they untied the boy and sent him in there for their reunion. Not something I want to hear or see, Pearl said.

EVERYONE WAS GETTING ready to march. Everywhere in the woods and fields, bugles sounded the order. Sartorius, coming from the farmhouse, looked at the sky and pulled on his gloves. From the road came the cries of the teamsters, and the creak and rumble of wagons. The regimental medical ambulances were, one by one, leaving the yard to join the procession. Pearl had collected Mattie Jameson's few belongings in a sack and ran into the house to find her and her son sitting close together on a sofa, Mattie crying and holding his hand and staring at him, and Jamie Jameson looking uncomfortable.

Pearl took the boy aside. When we are gone, you best stay out of sight of the prisoners marching. Where the Rebel wounded have been put in the barn back here, they are free now, with your own officers to take care of them and even some little food. You and your mama stay with them apiece, and then you find a way to get yoursels back to Georgia.

Howmi gonna do that?

You get down to Columbia. Your mama knows Miz Emily Thompson there who will hep you.

Pearl took the knotted handkerchief out of her skirt pocket, untied it, and gave the boy one of her precious gold eagles. He looked at it in his hand. This is twenty dollar Fed'ral.

That's right, brudder two. It will keep you awhile. And you will have your whole life to 'member it was me, Pearl, got you your freedom to go home.

The boy turned the eagle over in his hands. That's my Roscoe's coin from a life of nigger work I given you, Pearl said. And nothin you will ever do in your life will be enough to pay us back. I jes want you to know that.

Pearl turned to Mattie and took her hand. Bye-bye, stepma'm. I thank you for the reading lessons. Your boy will take you home to Fiel'-stone. Maybe some of the slave quarters is still standin to start you out in.

On the way to the door Pearl said to the brother two, Your mama ain't always right in the head. You take care of her, hear? Or I will come back and see to you.

And out the door she ran.

V

EARLY SUNDAY MORNING HUGH PRYCE, RIDING up with General Carlin's division at the head of Slocum's left wing, knew something was wrong. It was the kind of raw spring day when the energies of rebirth seem ominous and one's own blood races nervously in its course. The sky was a quivering brilliant blue and everything of the visible earth had a preternatural color to it: woods and lowland, rocks and grass, and even the mud in the road—all in the superb self-definition of a world Pryce felt was about to explode. Of course, he had real evidence for his premonition. There had been reports the night before of heavy Rebel troop movements in the neighborhood. Though these had been discounted by Generals Sherman and Slocum—Sherman having thought so little of them as to have ridden off to join General Howard's wing a good dozen miles to the east—Brigadier General Carlin's order of march anticipated battle. And Carlin himself worriedly peered ahead even as his skirmishers were moving out against the Reb cavalry to test the position.

The advance brigades were approaching the junction of the two roads, the one leading east to Cox's Bridge and Goldsboro, the other diverging up toward Bentonville. Within the forks was a plantation the officers knew as the Cole place. A mile beyond, to the northeast, was a thick woodland of black pine. Whoever Cole was, his fields, marshes, and woods were about to be contested, not for their value, not for possession of them, but simply because two armies were met there. A barrage of artillery fire from Carlin's right flank stopped his advance brigades, and the day was announced.

ONLY WHEN THE troops had been deployed and their earthworks hastily thrown together—Carlin's division, bolstered by brigades of Brigadier General Morgan—did the Union commanders begin to suspect the true size of the Confederate force. General Slocum had come up to review the position and ordered an advance. Carlin's and Morgan's troops rose from their entrenchment, charged, and were met by blistering infantry fire, not only from their flank but on a long line stretching to the pinewoods, which seemed to light up with the explosion of musketry. The Federals fell back. Pryce stood with the two generals, who watched as an adjutant drew on a map laid out on the ground the outlines of the Rebel position deduced from the reports of field officers. The line drawn suggested to Pryce the form of the Big Dipper. Or a frying pan. And they were in it.

Pryce stood by silently scribbling his notes, secure at least that in such moments of crisis, despite his height, he had become almost invisible to the officers. Slocum, whose mustache and closely trimmed brown hair framed a face recessively chinned and clerklike, gave orders to bring up the full complement of the two corps that made up his wing. Then he beckoned to one of his staff officers and walked away with him a bit, speaking quietly with his hand on the young officer's shoulder. Pryce watched as the officer, a lieutenant, nodded, saluted, and leapt on his horse. In a moment the fellow was gone off on a great detour, back and around the Rebel line. Pryce watched until he could no longer see him, but the direction was clear: he was riding east, presumably to Cox's Bridge and Goldsboro, where General Sherman had gone to meet with the other wing of his army.

—

BY EARLY AFTERNOON the word had come miles back down the road to where the wagon train stood mired in the mud, and Sartorius, choosing only his assistant surgeon, a male nurse, and Stephen Walsh to go with him, rode forward to establish a surgery tent on the field of battle. Several of the regimental surgeons were so ordered. Sartorius and the others rode horses. Stephen drove the four-wheeled medicine-supply wagon. The going was difficult because much of the distance had to be traveled off-road. He could hear the medicine bottles clinking in their racks. The mule strained, the wheels jamming, then rolling over rocks, or tilting dangerously in mud pits, and Stephen was bumped airborne from his perch, as he raced forward. Now the sounds of a skirmish were sharp and precise. He heard shouting, the crack of rifles, and, following the Colonel into the declivitous patch in sight of the plantation house, he was, once again, introduced to combat.

They set up the field surgery at the base of a black oak perhaps two hundred yards behind an earthwork of logs and brush that the troops were still constructing. Once the battle began and the wounded arrived for treatment, so, theoretically, would brigade ambulances come up to carry them off afterward. The nurse and the assistant surgeon set the operating slab on sawhorses, and Stephen climbed to the lowest branch of the oak to tie the tent corners in lieu of poles. With that done, he took a moment to climb a bit higher for the view it afforded. Another Union line was off to the right, arrayed behind an improvised breastworks that came across the road. The positions looked shaky to him, shallow and unconnected. No artillery was in place. He wondered where the Rebels were, why they were not moving on a clearly unprepared Union force.

The gunfire tailed off and in the silence, after a moment or so, he heard birdsong.

MIDAFTERNOON THE OFFICERS at the fortifications saw their skirmishers dropping back, and then turning and running outright and clambering over the entrenchment, shouting and falling all over themselves. Here they come, boys, a sergeant said. Bobby Brasil steadied his rifle on his sighting log. He peered through the opening. Indeed they were coming and, given their intention, it was strangely beautiful to see, but their lines were straight with their mounted officers waving their sabers and their color-bearers carrying the battle flags flying, and they singing their pagan Rebel shrieksong, which was enough to make Brasil's neck hair rise. Where did they get them all, it's a whole damn army, Brasil muttered. Fire! the Sergeant shouted and so he did, and so did everyone, so that his ears went dead with the concussion. In the smoke and fire he could see men going down, but the charge did not waver, they were keeping on, and now from the corner of his eye they were coming from the flank, too, it was like one long, flowing banner of sparkling fire, the bullets cracking against the log, scutting up bark, as suddenly a Rebel officer was risen into view, his horse rearing, and he turning it and waving his men on, his broad back square in Brasil's sights, like a gift. And how sad to destroy such a great, stolid human gallant with just the slightest squeeze of the finger. But they had breached the barricade, they were coming over, and Brasil, catching one on his bayonet, couldn't shake it out of the boy, so left it and the rifle stuck there and turned and ran, finding himself not alone, the onslaught unstoppable, the shouting and scrambling screaming not from his own throat alone. And he ran and ran through the woods till he found the reserve lines, where he fell down to catch his breath, panting and gasping behind the sheer bulk of blue uniforms pressing forward to take their turn. And good luck to

them, Brasil thought, for I have not known such
terror since I was held back in the third grade
under Sister Agnes Angelica.

TWO MILES AWAY on the road, Pearl could hear
the battle, they all could, the teamsters standing
by and talking among themselves, the officers
pacing up and down, the horses nickering and
lifting their heads with each thump of the cannon. A mile behind her, the cattle drove lowing
and, in the wagon in his traveling box, Albion
Simms going boom boom boom like as if it
wasn't enough to hear the real thing. Pearl was
thinking of Stephen Walsh. He was so good at
everything he did that the Colonel-doctor relied
on him now as almost he didn't on anyone else.
For sure not on me. But it wasn't as if she worried about Stephen, just that she was frightened
to be without him in her sight. Here she was sitting in this wagon up in North Carolina, with
the cold spring breezes and the march held up
by a battle so as to give her the clear feeling of
being unattached to anywheres or anything, not
even a miserable life in the quarters. Just a girl
who is free, she thought. And there was such a
big blank empty space of life ahead of her with
nothing to fix on, nothing to take comfort in.
She could see only as far as that Number 12 and

the Washington Square in New York. And when she said goodbye to those sad people in that house and came out the door, where would her life be, in what direction would she turn, and down which street, and with whom?

In her anxiety she hadn't heard David awaken. He came out and sat himself down in her lap, still yawning and rubbing his eyes. Well, boy, she said, you sure know how to sleep, don't you? You hear that? That's a war going on.

Yes'm, I hears it.

It don't worry you none?

Naw. I hungry, he said.

She got some hardtack out of the rations box and handed it to him, and soon he was chewing away, studying the hardtack in his hand and taking a bite out of it, and studying it again as it slowly got smaller and smaller.

Pearl let herself down to the road and stood there pressing her hands in the small of her back to stretch out the stiffness. She untied the ribbon holding her hair and gathered it up again and retied it, and with her hands behind her head only now saw that two of the officers had stopped their conversation to look at her. She turned away to finish her grooming and thought, Now, Stephen Walsh, you'd best come back to me for you are not the only one and I am grown beautiful.

—

WITH CARLIN'S FORCE sent running, Morgan's flank was turned and his troops found themselves attacked from the rear while they stood off a charge from the front. Men were firing one way, wheeling around and firing the other. General Davis, of the Fourteenth Corps, ordered a reserve brigade into the breach, sending the troops on the double, and Hugh Pryce chose this moment to leave the general officers. Ignoring the shouts at his back, he made his way toward the action, hopping first on a rolling caisson, then slipping off and running forward, leaping over rocks, breasting tangled brush—at this moment almost insanely exhilarated, with his long scarf trailing from his throat as if it were his personal pennant. None of the competition would be able to report what he would see with his own eyes.

The ground became swampy. He was in a thick stand of trees. He heard gunfire now, and found a large tree and pulled himself up to the crotch of the lowest branch and swung his legs over and sat astride there peering through the smoke, hearing battle at its intimate heart: men screaming, grunting, bullets pinging off logs and rocks. And he could actually feel waves of heat coming off the mass of fired weapons. War changed the weather, it whitened the day—a pungent smoke flew past him like the souls of the dead hurrying to Heaven. It was only with a sudden rift in the thickened atmosphere that he realized he had misjudged his position and was not in relation to the action that he had supposed. The war had come to him. Lines of men were grappling hand to hand beneath him, wrestling one another to the ground, wielding knives, bayonets, swinging rifles about their heads, their desperation bringing concerted sounds from the depths of them like the chords of a church organ. He had never been closer to war than at this moment and all his reportorial powers of observation were resolved to one terrifying vision of antediluvian breakout. This was not war as adventure, nor war for a solemn cause, it was war at its purest, a mindless mass rage severed from any cause, ideal, or moral principle. It was as if God had decreed this characterless entanglement of brainless forces as his answer to the human presumption. And then all thought was impossible, for Pryce heard the hideous whistle of a cannonball, and as he clasped his hands to his ears he became aware just a moment too late of the shattering treetop that came crashing down upon him.

THE REBEL ADVANCE at one point actually flowed into the hospital area. A swarm of Union troops ran past, stopping only to fire a shot at their pursuit before running on. A minute after the bluecoats had come through, there came the grays. A Confederate officer galloped up, several of their infantry behind him. Who is in command here? he shouted.

Sartorius came out of the tent, hatless, his hands covered in blood, his apron smeared with it. What do you want? he said. On the ground about the tent lay a dozen wounded men and two who had died. Consider yourself a prisoner, the officer said. Very well, Sartorius said, and went back in the tent.

The officer frowned, clearly not knowing what else the situation called for. Some of the wounded were groaning, crying out. He turned his horse away, stationed two of his men as guards, and rode off, his men trotting off behind him.

Stephen looked out from the tent at the guards, who seemed embarrassed to be there. One of them bent down, about to give water from his canteen to one of the wounded, and Stephen had to tell him not to. When it was time to bring another man into the surgery Stephen said, Give me a hand here, and the guards seemed almost grateful to be asked.

A few minutes later the Rebel elements that had come this far were in retreat, running back through the hospital field hell-bent for their own lines. A Union company came whooping after them and the two guards who had been helping Stephen were shot down. One, with a stomach wound, could not be saved. The other was hit in the leg, which shattered badly. He lay with the Union wounded, and when it was his turn Stephen and the nurse brought him into the tent and Sartorius did a double-flap amputation just above the knee.

LIEUTENANT OAKEY HAD ridden into General Slocum's field headquarters with a message from Kilpatrick. The cavalry, camped some miles to the southwest, was ready to assist.

Slocum, at that moment deploying the Twentieth Corps to seal the breaches in the Union lines, said, For God's sake, that's the last thing I need. Pending further orders, General Kilpatrick is to stay put.

As he attempted to leave, young Oakey, who had been a grade-school teacher before the war and hoped to study for the ministry when the war was over, found himself penned in by the troop movements. He became confused in the swamps, and unwittingly rode into the thick of the battle, where General Morgan's embattled units were holding off a major Reb assault. Oakey quickly dismounted and joined the fray. The troops were arrayed in two lines behind the breastworks, the front line kneeling, the back line standing, and to the shouts of the commanders they were volley-firing into the advancing Rebel line. After repeated losses from the withering fire, the Rebs drew back, whereupon the men found themselves assailed from the rear, another brigade of General Carlin's and a supporting reserve brigade under Colonel Fearing having given way. Now the Morgan men jumped over their parapet and took positions on the other side to respond to the flanking attack. But they saw bluecoats among the attackers. For fatal moments they hesitated. Should they be firing on their own men? Oakey recognized the ploy—the same thing had happened with Kilpatrick at Monroe's Corners, Rebs wearing Union blue to create chaos and get them with their guard down. Rebs, they're damn Rebs! he shouted, waving his pistol, and in another minute the works were breached and he was knocked down and leapt upon by one of the attackers in blue.

Oakey was a slightly built fellow who wore glasses. These flew off his face as his head was repeatedly banged into the ground with two heavy wet hands clopping his ears. The Reb was huge.

Oakey's right hand, which held his pistol, was pressed flat by the weight. But intending one final skull-crushing blow, the Reb raised himself high enough so that Oakey had the opportunity to put the pistol in play: he twisted the barrel upward and fired directly into the man's stomach. He fired again and again until the weight slumped upon him no longer moved. With effort he pushed the body away and groped around for his glasses, giving them a cursory swipe on his sleeve and hooking them back where they belonged. He still couldn't see clearly through the mud smears on the glasses but he made no further attempt to clean them. Not seeing much of anything, he felt calmer.

With the battle raging around him, Oakey sat there in the rifle pit catching his breath. His head hurt. His tunic was soaked in blood. He looked at the lifeless hulk lying there and prayed for God's forgiveness. Struggling under the weight of this behemoth, he had felt the fury of a nonhuman intention. It was as if a bear had fallen upon him and was simply acting according to the demands of its animal nature.

How many minutes later he didn't know, a brigade of the Twentieth Corps had moved in to stem the attack and Oakey said to no one in particular, I had a horse here somewhere.

VI

A S THEY'D FOLLOWED AFTER THE ARMY, CALVIN
Harper had come to think of his traveling
companion as an interesting crazy man. He allowed himself this reflection because the balance
of their interests—each needing the other—
made for reasonably stable progress on the road.
He'd been taking pictures as he wanted, and he'd
felt he could continue to take his pictures until
the opportunity arose to disentangle himself.
Until then, it was a matter of maintaining his
dignity and exercising his will without endan-
gering himself. He seemed so far to have done
this successfully. It was not always comfortable
from day to day, but nothing so far had made
him feel that he was in imminent danger.

What was interesting was how the man
wore disguises. He put on something and pretended to be that person. He was like an actor in
the theater where the costume you wear is the

person you are. He had appeared back in Barnwell as a Union soldier though he was a Southern white-trash Reb. Both of them were, the dead friend, too, who had to be dressed as the Reb he really was before Mr. Culp could take the picture. And then after the picture was developed, and Mr. Josiah Culp was dead, he decided to be him, Mr. Culp, in his own suit and coat and hat. Calvin had gone along with all of this with a degree of fascination despite himself. At times, in public, he'd seen this pretend Mr. Culp who knew nothing about photography as more the photographer than the real Mr. Culp. And that was because the man really seemed to believe he was Mr. Culp. All of that was clearly interesting and also clearly mad. For only a madman would have conversations with a picture in his pocket, as that was what had become of his dead friend in his mind, not a body in a grave but a picture in his pocket. And he talked to it almost as much as he talked to Calvin. And so nothing was what it seemed, and all of it was crazy. And that gave Calvin some confidence in his ability to control things. There was some errant spirit in the man that made him maybe not so single-minded a menace as he first appeared.

Now, as they came along on the road to Goldsboro, they stopped for the night at an abandoned farmhouse. Though the sun had set, they could still hear the sounds of battle in the dusk: cannonading carried by the east wind over the fields and rivers.

You see, Calvin, why I said this road? We'd be up to our necks in hellfire, we gone after the other column. That is some damn battle they're having, like they have finally run into an army equal to theirselves.

Some moldy fodder for Bert in the barn, Calvin said. But nothing for us in this pantry. Whoever these people, they been gone awhile. Place is picked clean.

I know my Gen'ral Sherman, Arly said. That is his feint to Raleigh we're hearing. I 'spect it's more'n he bargained for. But anyways he's not there. He's up ahead enjoying hisself thinking of Goldsboro where he means to alight like the eagle on the flagpole.

We're down to the last bag of cornmeal and 'bout a spoonful of lard if I can get this stove to fire up, Calvin said. How you know where he is?

Gen'ral Sherman and me have the same quality of mind, Arly said. I need only think of myself as him and I know what he will do.

And you of such a low rank, Calvin said. Don't seem fair, somehow.

Arly took another swig from Mr. Culp's last jar of sour-mash whiskey. Calvin, he said, were I not pleased with our progress I might take offense at your freeman's talk, but you'd best not try me.

What are you going to do with your photograph of the General? What then?

Why, it will be a recognition on my part of him, and on his part of me. It will be a meeting of the minds. It will not be just an ordinary photo like you have been gathering. This will mark an occasion to make history. This will be a photograph the likes of which the other Mr. Josiah Culp couldn't have dreamed of. I am an inspired soul, which means it will be not just me taking that photo but God as he instructs me.

You and God know the lens to use? The exposure time? How to coat the plates and where to set the camera?

We leave you to attend to those small matters, son. That is the kind of menial work your race is fitted to.

THIS NIGHT ARLY decided to make his bed on the floor in the empty upstairs. The laths showed where pieces of the wall had crumpled away, and he had to find a spot to lay the blankets down where the floorboards weren't broken. There was a rot smell of old wood, and it was colder than downstairs by the stove where Calvin was, but it behoved a man to keep to the natural order of things.

He lay down with his arm around Calvin's box of lenses. This was an extra measure of caution, because Calvin knew that without Arly riding with him as his Mr. Culp he would not live five minutes as an independent nigger businessman in God's own country. Guerrillas still rode and took care of what had to be taken care of. Calvin could hitch up Bert and run away, but without being able to take another photo how could he fancy himself Mr. Culp's chosen boy? It may be the slavery of the future, tying down a free black by his white airs. And I have devised it.

Arly was not aware, in the midst of his thoughts, of having fallen asleep. But when he found himself awake some time had clearly passed. It was not just that the light was different, the moon casting a milky sheen everywhere in the room including on him. No, but the sound. A peculiar whispering chuffing sound, and a clinking, but mostly the sound of human presence you can sense even though no sound was made. He went to the window and looked out on a sight he could hardly believe: it was a whole army on the road passing by at a quick pace, a ghost army it looked like, though real enough in its blocks of companies and the guidons and the occasional officer cantering by. Every mother's son of them leaning forward under their packs and looking at the road. And no one was talking for the effort of making a night march, and if there was a gap the following companies came along at a trot. What is this, Arly thought, these Yankees are going the wrong way! He pulled on his boots and ran downstairs. From a back window he saw they were coming across the fields too, streaming around the house front and back like a river overflowed of its banks. He lamented what he saw—Yankees tromping over these lowlands in the arrogance of their numbers. But then it dawned on him: of course, this is General Sherman returning to the fray back there where our boys have put the scare of God into his other column—damn! Yes, that's what this is about. Well, Gen'ral, 'pears you have made a mistake to have to go backwards like this, who was already practically wining and dining yourself in Goldsboro. Will, Will, I am truly sorry you can't see this, we got an army still raising hell yonder in Bentonville, we are putting the great Sherman to the test, and there's to be many a dead Union boy before it's over.

Then Arly thought he saw the General himself in a cavalry contingent riding past in the field—maybe fifty men on horses, and someone at their head flinging the reins to his left and right who he thought was Sherman, all right, like a mad rider under the moon making for the battle. Arly had seen only that photo of General Sherman, he had never seen him in the flesh, but he was convinced, as the horsemen disappeared over a rise, that it had been Sherman without a doubt. Don't you worry none, Will, he said, smiling there in the dark, it's all right, it's all right. You and me will just go on to Goldsboro while he cleans up his mess back here, and we'll be waiting for him to take his portrait picture, assuming a course no one has kilt him in the meantime.

CALVIN, WRAPPED IN a blanket behind the stove, had heard the entire conversation. Arly went back upstairs, and soon enough he was snoring away. And then after another twenty or thirty minutes the last of the marchers had passed and everything was quiet again, but Calvin could not go back to sleep.

If I was a Rebel soldier given to disguises what would my purpose be? It would be to get out from behind Union lines, to get back to my own to fight again or to get out of the war altogether and go home. But that's not his thinking.

He couldn't have planned to costume himself as Mr. Culp. As we came along he did it as the opportunity arose—it was an idea that had popped into his crazy head. So what was the idea? From all of his constant chatter day after day, it is nothing but to catch up to General Sherman on his march and take a photograph of him. Why? To make his mark in the photography business? That don't seem likely given how little he cares for the art of it. He started out knowing nothing and he knows no more now than he did then.

In this war every man is on one side or another. Even a crazy man. If I am crazy, I am still for the Union. If he is crazy, he is still a white-trash Johnny Reb.

Calvin felt a chill remembering that back in Georgia, at the camp in the pine trees, where General Sherman had his headquarters, Mr. Culp did not need but a minute to persuade the General to pose for his picture who even called his entire staff to pose with him. Mr. Culp had said to Calvin, As a photographer you get to know human nature, and one thing about human nature is that it is the most famous people who think they are not getting enough of the world's attention. So they want their picture taken and put on display, or their portrait painted or books written about them, and no matter how much of this is done it is never enough for some of these people, except maybe for President Abraham Lincoln, who is an exception in this as in just about everything. Because Mr. Culp had taken his picture, too, before leaving Washington, and it had been an effort to get the President to sit down for it, and he wouldn't have, had Mrs. Lincoln not insisted.

By now Calvin was pacing back and forth with the blanket wrapped around him. His train of thought left him terribly unsettled. He had been too forbearing. This madman had sent Mr. Culp to his grave. He had taken that pistol and pointed it at them and stolen Mr. Culp's clothes and his name. And now he is become a madman in a contest in his mind with the General of the Union armies, William T. Sherman, whose picture is to be taken.

But his opportunity, if it comes, will be mine, too. I will tell them of that carte de visite in his pocket that proves him as a Reb before he can do whatever it is he intends, or what he intends by way of carrying out God's intentions. Whatever it is, it must not be allowed. Even if it is just what he says it is. Even if he wants to take a picture of General Sherman because it is just his simple craziness, he must not be allowed to take it. I am the photographer, not him. Making photographs is sacred work. It is fixing time in its moments and making memory for the future, as Mr. Culp has told me. Nobody in history before now has ever been able to do that. There is no higher calling than to make pictures that show you the true world.

Mr. Culp had put him in his will, and now when he got back to Baltimore the studio would say on the window: Culp and Harper, Photographers. It angered Calvin that his camera now could be used for the purposes of someone who didn't know any better, someone like this crazy smart-talking white-trash Reb. Calvin said to himself, If Mr. Josiah Culp and me had come through Barnwell a day earlier, or a day later, we would not have met up with this madman. And Mr. Culp would be alive and we would still be going about our work just as always. Oh Lord, and now this is where I am and there is no way out of it.

Calvin heard the beginnings of a whimper rising in him, but he cleared his throat and squared his shoulders. I've got my side, too, he thought.

VII

TWO DAYS AFTER IT BEGAN, THE BLOODY BAT-
tle at Bentonville was over. Having doubled
back on the Goldsboro road to bolster Slocum's
column, both corps of Howard's right wing
were methodically deployed and the Confederate general, Joseph Johnston, was persuaded the
initiative was no longer his. Finding his forces
outnumbered and fighting furiously just to
maintain position, he prepared to withdraw. In
this he might have been encouraged by the ag-
gressive flanking maneuver of General Joe
Mower, who without orders led a division of his
troops through a swampy woods and threatened to cut off Johnston's means of retreat, a
bridge over the Mill Creek. Sherman learned of
the attack in his field headquarters some distance from the front lines and, fearing that
Mower was overextended, ordered the daring

General to return to Union lines. This weakness Joe Mower has for swamps, Sherman said. Show him a swamp and he wades right in. He's a great fighter, as you'd expect of someone descended from crocodiles.

It was raining heavily the night the Rebel forces pulled back and made their way north. Sherman's army was given no orders to pursue and so it encamped where it was, the soldiers wrapping themselves in their blankets and canvas half-tents and lying down in the mud.

Under the incessant pounding of the rain, the Medical Department continued its work. Led by the moans and cries for help, volunteer details roamed through the woods picking up the wounded, loading them into ambulances and wagons, and distributing them among farmhouses and plantations commandeered for surgeries on the road back to Averasboro. Wrede's surgery was set up in a small Catholic church. A rubber sheet was laid over the altar table. The wounded lay in the aisles or sat slumped in the pews. Candles and smoking torches threw the scene into flaring or waning light. Some of the men had been lying out there unattended for two days. Their wounds were already purulent. The nurses tried to deal with the stench with masks made of bandages.

When men no longer able to withstand the pain of their wounds begged to be shot, and Wrede concurred that the case was hopeless, they were taken out in the darkness and accommodated. The attending priest, an elderly man, had appeared, and he knelt in the last pew near the door and prayed. Later, whenever he saw a man in the throes of death he rushed over to give last rites, not bothering to ask for an affiliation any more than Wrede asked whether the patient was Union or Confederate. The old priest wrung his hands and wept, and by midnight an exhausted Pearl, too, could not stop crying. She finally sank to the ground and sat beside a soldier and held his hand as he breathed his last. She kept holding his hand after he was dead, until Stephen Walsh gently lifted her to her feet and took her to the rectory house, where the boy David and Albion Simms had been put to bed, and the priest's housekeeper showed her to a room and put a blanket over her when she fell asleep.

DAVID HAD BECOME fascinated with Albion Simms and in the morning, once the wagon trains were under way, he sat beside the framework box and listened to the song:

Oh the coo coo
Is a pretty bird
And she wobbles as she flies
But she never sings her coo coo . . .
Oh she never sings her coo coo . . .

Till the fourth day a July, David reminded him.

Till the fourth day of July, Albion said. Are you a good boy?

Yassuh.

Are you a good boy?

Yassuh.

Are you—

I done tole you I is.

What is that in the window?

That not a window, that the sun comin in the wagon.

The sun?

Yassuh.

It's always there.

Not in the night, not if it rainin, David said.

It's always there. See? It's there now, and it's always now. Are you a good boy?

Yassuh.

What did I just say?

Am you a good boy.

Yes. And what do you answer?

Yassuh. Why your hands tied to this bar here?

Are they tied? Untie them.

But they tied.

Yes, untie them. Aren't you a big boy?

Yassuh.

I don't like my hands tied. I am in misery. What did I say I am?

You in misery.

I am. Yes. David, what is your name?

You done said it, the boy giggled.

What?

David.

Is that your name?

You done said it yousel'!

Are my hands untied yet?

Naw. This a big knot goes round an over an under.

Around and around?

Yassuh.

Oh, the coo coo is a pretty bird . . . I'll show you a trick. What will I show you?

A trick. There, that your right hand now. What kind of trick?

Watch, Albion Simms said, smiling. And raising his free hand he touched with his forefinger the spike embedded in his skull. What's this?

It the iron stuck in your haid. Do it hurt?

No. Watch this, Albion said, and lightly tapped the spike with his index finger.

That no trick, David said.

Roll the drums, Albion said. Slowly he extended his arm. Are you watching?

I is.

With the heel of his hand Albion drove the spike into his brain.

THREE DAYS AFTER the battle at Bentonville the sun was shining and Sherman's troops were encamped and recovering in the hills and pine groves around Goldsboro. The junction had been made with Schofield's thirty-thousand-man army, as planned, and with uniforms and supplies and mail due imminently from the coast by railroad, and the entire Georgia and Carolinas campaigns having gone just as Sherman had designed them, he should have been somewhat satisfied with his situation. But he couldn't get it out of his mind that the Reb General Joe Johnston had caught him by surprise. Yes, in the face of the numerically overwhelming force finally deployed against him Johnston had retired from the field, and, yes, the books would record Bentonville a Union victory. But Sherman had let his columns diverge to the extent that Johnston was able to bring his entire army against Slocum's column, isolated back there, and hard pressed to defend itself. Sherman, encamped a dozen miles away, had to be awakened in the middle of the night to be told what had happened. It had required that backbreaking night march with Howard's wing to secure the lines and force Johnston to give up the fight. And hundreds of Union men had died and a thousand more were wounded.

Colonel Teack intuited from the General's moods, by turns brooding or agitated, that it was exactly this line of thought that was eating away at him. Yesterday morning Sherman and his staff had stood on parade in the Goldsboro town square as his bedraggled troops came in from Bentonville. There was no hailing Uncle Billy this time, and the salutes were indifferent at best. The men were hungry and exhausted, and so worn with months of marches and skirmishes and battles that there was nothing left of them but sinew and muscle. They were angry as only exhausted men can be. The clothes on their backs were not to be dignified as rags, and their shoeless feet were bloodied and swollen. There were no drummer boys to keep the pace. There was no pace. Look at them, Sherman said to Teack as they sat their horses in review. Have you ever seen a finer army than this? They have given me everything I've asked for and then some. When this damned war is over, I would have them march down Pennsylvania Avenue in just this disreputable state, so that the people can see what it takes to fight a war, how it strips away everything inconsequential from a man and leaves a hardened fighter with guts of iron and the stout heart of a hero.

Teack believed that Sherman had made more than one mistake in the past week. It is not unusual for the loyal adjutant to entertain the thought that his tactical skills are a cut above his superior's. To the degree that Colonel Teack worshipped his General and stood ready to die for him, he nevertheless knew that he, Teack, would not have pulled General Mower back from that flanking movement in the swamps. Johnston was virtually pinned and about to be deprived of his one avenue of retreat, the bridge at Mill Creek. Instead of ordering Mower's division to fall back, Sherman should have sent in massive support. Johnston would have lost his army, and that would have been the end of all opposition in the Carolinas.

It was uncanny that almost at the same moment Teack was thinking these thoughts, Sherman began speaking of the matter. They were dining well in the mansion of an obliging tobacco merchant who had retired to a farm he

owned, leaving everything under his roof—
including his servants and his pantry, cellar, and
humidor—for the use of the occupation. What
would you have done in my place, Teack? Was I
wrong to pull Mower back? Was it a mistake? I
thought his position was vulnerable. I suppose
I could have backed him up. But in any event it
would have been bloody. Johnston would have
fought to the last man. He's the best they have,
Joe Johnston. He's better than Lee. They pulled
him off back at Atlanta and gave his command
to that stupid Frenchman Beauregard. That was
our good fortune, let me tell you. Johnston
wouldn't have defended the cities as Beauregard
did. How stupid and ineffective. Augusta,
Charleston. And never an army united enough
to do anything to stop me. Johnston would have
used the land, as a good soldier would. He'd
have held us at every river, at every crossing, at
every hill and swamp and given ground only for
our precious blood in return. We would be
where we are now, but with more losses to show
for it. By the time Johnston took over again he
had only dribs and drabs to work with. But he
pulled them together into an army and put
them in the right place, and for a moment he
had me. So send in Mower? I still say no. I saved
lives. What can Johnston do now against this
ninety-thousand-man army? I saved lives, and

not just our own. Father Abraham wants those Southern boys alive so they can go back to their farms and put some food on their tables. And I? I will simply march on, as I have, with men now so honed to hardship and battle that they are almost superhuman. This war is over, Teack, whatever any miserable little band of skirmishers think they can do about it. We have won, and everyone knows it. The South is mine, and Joe Johnston knew it the day I came marching down the lowlands from Atlanta.

Teack was relieved that he was not required to say anything.

Sherman looked bad—tired, green around the gills. He had a cigar going constantly and drank more than he ate. When he wasn't running on at the mouth, rehashing the same issues compulsively, or raving about his rank and file, he exhausted himself with details that ordinarily would be left to his subordinates. He dressed down the chief mail agent when the mails did not come up from the coast on time. He examined samples of the new uniforms and shoes ordered for his men, actually feeling the materials and hefting the boots like a customer at the haberdasher's while the embarrassed Quartermaster General Meigs looked on. He ordered inspections and canceled them, he called for a parade and rescinded the order even as the men were gathering. These men deserve their rest and we'll give it them, he told Teack. At the same time, he was anxious to get on with it, and the sense of a dissolution of purpose and the loss of his spirit-army that he had felt in every city, with the troops encamped and wandering about drinking more than was good for them, assailed him now. He wanted to be on the march, he wanted the ranks to fall in, he did not like city governance and dealing endlessly with whining civilians, and to simulate the good, hard earth in a tent under a tall pine tree he threw his blankets on the floor of his bedroom and slept by the hearth under a pup tent set up for him by Sergeant Moses Brown.

Teack conferred with Brown. Fatten him up a bit, Sergeant, and get him into a hot bath. He's overworked and overtired. The stoic Brown nodded. He had also watered the decanters of the General's wine. He didn't need to be told what his General needed.

Sherman felt better busying himself with a reorganization of his army. Now that he had Schofield's troops, he planned a three-column march so that no one column would ever find itself without immediate support. The central column corps would be under Schofield. He had Slocum and Howard, of course, for his flanking-wing commanders. And General Joe

Mower, Teack noted, had now been promoted to command of the Twentieth Corps under Slocum. Three columns, Teack, ninety thousand strong. If I were Johnston I would throw down my arms and run like hell. This is a trident I've made here, three sharp prongs to draw blood. Teack said, The trident was Poseidon's weapon, General. The god of the sea. Well, Sherman said, there's been enough damn rain these last months to turn me into a Poseidon.

The morning he learned that Willie Hardee, the sixteen-year-old son of the Confederate General Hardee, had died fighting at Bentonville, Sherman retired to his rooms and wept. Apparently Willie Hardee had pleaded with his father to join the fray though he was not officially under arms. Sherman sat down to compose a letter to Hardee, whose division, according to the latest intelligence, was encamped at Smithfield with Johnston's forces. And now, General, he wrote, we have both lost our sons of the same name. Though my Willie was too young to ride, it was the war that killed him just as surely as the war has killed yours. How unnatural is this age when, in violation of God's grand stratagem, the young are unbodied of their souls before the old. In Ecclesiastes it is said (as I blunder to remember it), "As some leaves fall and others grow in their place, so too with the generations of flesh and blood, one dies and another is born." I can imagine you wishing in your grief that God had spared your Willie and taken you instead, for that is what I wished—I mean, when I lost my Willie. I curse our inverted time, when so many thousands of us, fathers and mothers, have given our children to this damned war of the insurrection. I look forward to the day this nation is again united and the natural order is restored and our generations die once again appropriate to their God-given ranks. At that time, my dear General, I hope we may meet and commiserate as fellow soldiers and survivors. Desiring that you accept my sincere condolences. I am, sir, your humble obedient servant William Tecumseh Sherman, Major General.

STILL RESTLESS, SHERMAN decided there was nothing for it but to make a quick trip up to Virginia to meet General Grant. He called his wing and corps commanders together to advise them of this and to propose the order of march when he should return. They were met in a large conference room on the ground floor of the state courthouse. Outside, the trees in the town square were in early leaf. Sherman's maps were spread out on a walnut table that had been polished to a shine. The sun shone through the

floor-to-ceiling windows, and the generals, but
for Kilpatrick, were cleaned up for the occasion
in their midnight-blue dress tunics, the buttons
gleaming. It was almost grand. Sherman sighed.
He himself, he knew, was no sartorial model,
but, really, Kilpatrick was an egregious slob,
with his stained jacket, his beard stubble, the
dried manure on his boots, and damn it, the
man did have a kind of hump, but why couldn't
he stand straighter as befit his rank?

With his pointer, Sherman illustrated his
thinking as his generals hovered over the table.
Heretofore we have marched into their cities
and towns. We have torn up their railroads, destroyed their armories and manufactories, deprived them of their currency, helped ourselves
to their cotton. Now the situation is changed.
We want just to destroy Joe Johnston's army.
We met him last week on his terms, now we
want to meet him on ours. Conceivably Lee can
choose to pull out of Virginia and make a junction with Johnston down here. Yes, though he
might break his heart by doing so, he could do
that by traveling light, divested of wagon trains,
coming through here, and here, Sherman said,
moving the pointer southwest from Richmond.
He should. He commands a tired worn-out
army, his desertion rates increasing by the day.

Grant will cut the last link to Danville, and what then can Lee do but stand and fight till he dies of attrition? So even with Grant on his tail a march to North Carolina is his best move, and I wish he'd make it, because with my ninety thousand I don't even need the Army of the Potomac. We can end the war right here, and the honor is all ours.

At this, the generals turned to one another with grins and expressions of approbation. An exultant flush rose upon some faces.

But my guess, Sherman said, is that Lee will do the gallant stupid thing and hold his position. So what does that mean for us? Johnston has, at most, thirty-five thousand troops. If we could handle his and Lee's combined, what then is so difficult about Joe Johnston alone? Well, I'll tell you. The man is a master of retreat. You remember how deft he was at Atlanta. He understands retreat as the powerful military move it is. We will hope he defends Raleigh, but if not, if he runs, our task complicates. He runs, turns vindictive, scatters his troops in western North Carolina, Tennessee, he fights a guerrilla war and it can go on for years. Years, gentlemen. Knowing as well as we the art of foraging, and with a civilian population prepared, however secretly, to furnish him with what he needs—no, this is the last thing we want him to do. We've got to turn his flanks, box him in, and if he doesn't surrender grind him to dust.

General Kilpatrick's attention at this moment was diverted by the two young black women coming into the room with silver platters of cups of coffee and decanters of brandy. They were handsome young things, smiling like the free girls they were—free to smile, free to do anything their hearts pleased.

General? Sherman said.

Yessir, Kilpatrick said in a hoarse voice. He almost snapped to attention.

I asked you if you are shoeing up your cavalry.

Absolutely, General. The mounts will be fresh shod and ready to ride.

Because I will depend on you to seal off the roads west, and hold there until my columns come round, Sherman said.

THE CONFERENCE OVER, the generals relaxed, enjoying one another's company and sipping their coffee from tiny china cups with all the elegance they could muster. The sun shone into the room like the promise of final victory. Every one of them had reason to feel competitive, as officers inevitably do in military bureaucracies, but the long campaign behind them and what they knew so well of it—the terrain they had trod, the rivers crossed, the obstacles surmounted, the organization they maintained, each in his own realm but in the grand cooperative adventure of a noble cause—made them companionable and appreciative of one another's qualities. The daring swamp-wading Mower, when not in battle, was soft-spoken and diffident. Slocum, in firm command of the left wing, had the droopy eyelids and prim, calculating mind of an actuary. Howard, of the right wing, was a truly paternal presence, a large thoughtful man, given to talking of his family and inquiring with genuine interest of the families of the others. And, moving among them, in a better mood than he had been in for days, Sherman laughed and joked, and felt their admiration as he expressed, in slantwise remarks, grunts, and nods, his appreciation of them.

This is an important part of leadership, noted Colonel Teack, who was in attendance and standing by one of the windows. Knowing when to be human, knowing how, without embarrassing yourself or your men, to represent your faith in them. So that, when the time comes, if necessary, they will die for you.

In the midst of these reflections, Teack happened to glance out the window. One of those

U.S. photography outfits had pulled up in the street and a man in a long coat and derby was standing with his hands on his hips and looking up at him. Sherman, passing by Teack and lighting a cigar, caught sight of the fellow down in the street and, understanding instantly the opportunity this afforded, turned to the room. Gentlemen, he said, the world is calling. Let us go and get our picture took. We'll sit for it out there in the sun, with the flag of these United States flying above the city of Goldsboro, so the citizenry will, ever after, know the glorious brotherhood of the Army of the West.

AS THEY HAD approached the courthouse, with the guards standing about, Arly said to Calvin, All right, he is in there, son, and now we are going to make history. I am going to shoot Gen'ral Sherman's picture. But if you do anything to make it harder for me—

Why would I do that? Calvin said.

Because you are a wily free nigger. Tell me, was you ever not free?

No.

More's the pity. 'Cause then you don't know the things that can happen to your kind when they don't do right.

I think I do know.

I hope you do. God has looked down upon this war and in his usual mysterious manner he has put us to the test. He is testing our mettle, burning us out and shooting us down and setting our black folks to thinking they better than they are. But none of that means your Pres'dent Lincoln is going to win his war. All it means is that we are consumed by fire so as we can rise from the ashes, new and reborn. All it means! Amn't I right, Will? Why else would God put you in jail for desertion and me for sleeping on duty except greater and grander things were intended for us out of our disgrace?

ALL TOGETHER THERE were eleven generals. Chairs were brought out and set in the plaza in front of the courthouse steps. One grand armchair for Sherman, four straight-backed chairs for the two generals seated on either side of him. The rest stood in a row behind the chairs. Sherman, of course, directed who should sit and who should stand and where.

As the preparations were being made, a crowd of passersby began to collect. Colonel Teack added to the guard detail and troops, with their arms at the ready, stood between the generals and the street.

A light breeze was blowing and the morning

air was cool. The Colonel was the person to talk to. But how? Calvin needed time. He fussed with the equipment, running back and forth to the wagon to get this or that, whatever he could think of. He kept changing the position of the camera, moving it closer or farther back, slightly to the right or left. He knew that eventually the generals would become impatient. Sherman sat with his legs crossed and his arms folded, assuming the pose he wanted to be recorded for posterity and waiting for the photographers to do their job.

Arly muttered, Any time Calvin, any time at all—it's just all the generals of the Yew-nited States waitin on you. For answer, Calvin dropped the photographic plate he was carrying. It shattered on the ground. Then he had to pick up the pieces and run back to the wagon for another. This caused Arly the same embarrassment as it would have Mr. Culp. He responded by deciding the generals needed instruction on their various poses. He indicated who among the standees should show his profile and who was to face forward. He pulled down the corners of his mouth to indicate that there should be no smiling. How did he know that? Calvin wondered.

Anyway, Calvin thought, if Arly intended to do harm, he would have done so by now. He'd certainly had the chance, being this near to

Sherman. Calvin glanced at the generals posed in their solemnity, with the white columns of the courthouse rising behind them, and he thought it would make a fine historic photo if it were actually going to be taken. But he had done some things. The plate he slipped into the camera was not coated—it would not record the image. To make doubly sure, the lens he screwed into the box was the wrong one for the distance between the camera and the subject. He felt peculiar, subverting his own craft, denying history its rights. But he was determined. Whatever was going to happen, whatever this crazy Reb intended, no picture would be taken by him.

As the generals obeyed his instructions, Arly began to enjoy himself. His coattails flapping, he strode back and forth, yanking Mr. Culp's derby down on his ears and praising the sight before him. This is a moment for the ages, he announced, and the Josiah Culp U.S. Photography Salon is honored to take its picture.

Sherman was becoming impatient now, turning his head to mutter something, scratching his beard, changing which leg to cross over the other. Now, gen'men, Arly said, you know at the time the camera is exposing you cannot move a muscle, lest the photo be spoiled. He seemed only then to notice something not right with General Sherman. Sir, he said, would you consider accustoming yourself to a temporary head brace? For with all this preparation you may become restless in your chair, and without absolute stillness your image will not be clearly drawn. Sherman frowned but nodded in agreement, and Arly sent Calvin back to the wagon for the brace, a calipered bar attached to a stand. Calvin knew that in this morning sunlight, which required only ten seconds of exposure, no head brace was necessary. But this was his opportunity. He stood behind Sherman and affixed it and whispered, hardly able to catch his breath, Sir, that man is not a U.S. photographer. He is a crazy Rebel. And he ran off. Sherman couldn't turn his head. What? he said. What's that the Negro said?

Seeing Arly diverting himself with the camera, Calvin moved quickly to Colonel Teack, who stood in the shade at the side of the terrace. Sir, he said, Mr. Josiah Culp is dead. This man in his clothes is a crazy Rebel soldier.

What are you talking about, Teack said. What Rebel soldier?

The Colonel grabbed him by the shoulder, but at this moment Calvin was stunned to see Arly unscrewing the lens from the box. Did Arly know it was the wrong lens? But how could he? Tearing himself from the Colonel's grasp, Calvin ran toward his camera with a sense that something terribly wrong was being done to it. Arly had ducked his head under the black cloth. His muffled voice was heard. Hold still now, Gen'ral Sherman, the moment of exposure has come! Then Arly's face rose into view contorted to a rapturous expression that Calvin would remember for the rest of his life. Poking through the socket where a lens should have been, and what Calvin did not in time realize, was the barrel of Mr. Culp's pistol. The first shot, like a bolt of heat, tore past Calvin's eyes and blinded him. But he had lunged at the camera, tilting it awry, and the second shot had found Colonel Teack in the chest, knocking him to the ground, though Calvin could not have known it. He was down on his knees, bright lights flashing through his head, and when he put his hand to his eyes they were wet. He didn't know what the wetness was until he found himself swallowing it. All around him men were shouting. He heard running footsteps, he heard Bert the mule braying. On his hands and knees, and with blood coursing down his throat, he felt the sharp point of a bayonet at his back.

AFTER ARLY PULLED the trigger for the second time, jumping out of the way to avoid the toppling camera, he cursed at Calvin, stood back and, as several troopers advanced on him, threw off Mr. Culp's coat and hat and stood waiting for his capture in a neatly buttoned gray tunic taken from Mr. Culp's store of uniforms. He was knocked down with the butt of a rifle, pressed to the ground under someone's boot, and then dragged roughly to his feet, while complaining loudly of the ill treatment: Damn, that ain't right, you near to have broken my shoulder! As he was being hustled away he demanded to be imprisoned with his fellow soldiers of the C.S. of A. This was a honorable act of war, he shouted. I am a soldier!

In the excitement and confusion a guard detail had quickly formed around the eleven generals. Sherman, somewhat shaken, ordered Teack carried back into the conference room. The generals, after determining that Sherman was unhurt, were all asking one another if they were hurt. It turned out none of them were. But they agreed it would be best to go back inside the courthouse and settle themselves with more brandy and coffee. Maybe forget the coffee, Kilpatrick said, loping up the steps. The others followed in dignified fashion, careful to avoid unseemly haste, though one or two looked back at the crowd standing beyond the plaza, lest anyone else was out there pointing a gun. Isn't it odd, one of them said, that accustomed as we are to being under fire we should find this situation unnatural.

Sherman stood on the steps for a moment and looked out at the crowd that had appeared in the street. How did the damn fool get so close? he said to no one in particular.

THE COFFEE CUPS were swept away and the Colonel was laid upon the table with Sherman's own tunic folded up for pillow. Though white with pain, Teack was more concerned about the damage to his uniform. And it seemed to him unfitting that he should lie there in the presence of general officers. He tried to get up. Nonsense, Teack, Sherman said, and pressed him to the table.

Wrede Sartorius was one of three surgeons to arrive. He was immediately deferred to by the others. He offered the Colonel an anesthetic. It was refused. The bullet had cracked a rib but lay shallow enough to be extracted without complication. Bone splinters were removed. Two small bleeding arteries were ligated. Wrede percussed the chest and was satisfied the lung had not collapsed. He sutured and put lint over the wound but did not bandage it. He called for orderlies and a stretcher, and told Colonel Teack that he would be required to rest in a regimental hospital tent.

All the while, the generals had stood watching like students in a medical college. General Sherman kept asking questions—what is this for? why do you do that?—and Wrede kept not answering, which impressed Sherman greatly.

Wrede gave postoperative instructions to his assistant surgeon and left to attend to the black man who still lay outside in the courthouse plaza. Sherman turned to one of his staff and said, Who is that colonel? What's his name? He carries himself like a soldier, unlike most of the Medical Department.

AT DAWN THE next morning Arly Wilcox was executed by firing squad, a ceremonial event complete with mounted officers, a military band, a pine coffin, and a detachment of Confederate prisoners taken at Bentonville who were present for purposes of instruction. Arly, having argued he was a bona fide prisoner of war, had been assured by his amused guards that that was why he was going to be shot rather than hanged. Well, Will, he said to the picture in his pocket, so we're back where we were there in Milledgeville. But leastwise it's the damn Unions doing the executin rather than my own army, which suggests to me God's continued mercy and maybe future recognition of my martyrdom.

Required to dig his own grave, Arly had squared off the sides with the shovel's edge. This gonna be my new home I want it nice, he had said.

CALVIN HAD NOT been executed along with Arly Wilcox because of his injury and because the extent of his complicity was not clear. There was some question as to why a Negro would assist in such an enterprise. Wrede Sartorius was to decide when Calvin Harper would be fit to appear for the administrative hearing that would determine his fate.

But now orders were delivered to Wrede assigning him provisionally to General Sherman's staff. He was to accompany Sherman to the Army of the Potomac headquarters at City Point, Virginia. He could not imagine for what purpose, or how he could be more useful to the army than as a regimental surgeon.

Not knowing the duration of his provisional transfer, he believed it likely that he would be back before the Negro's recovery could be vouchsafed. The nose was broken at the bridge and both corneas had been seared. The blindness might be partial or total. It was too early to tell. He left instructions regarding the patient's care, packed a few things, picked up his field-instrument case, and left without advising his staff where he was going.

Wrede was still angry about the loss of Albion Simms. The brown child should never have been left alone with him. Of course, it is my own fault for having taken on people who have no medical training, he thought. Stephen Walsh and his Miss Jameson are children themselves. They are well meaning, but look what I have lost. When I return, I will send Walsh back to his regiment. The girl will have to fend for herself.

VIII

A LOCOMOTIVE HAD TAKEN THEM TO MORE-head city, and there they boarded a coastal steamer for the overnight trip to City Point. The sea was like glass but Sherman said, What can you do for seasickness? Wrede prescribed tincture of laudanum and Sherman drank it greedily.

Among the things I have to talk to Grant about is this business of executing a Negro, Sherman said. The Southern papers would go to town with that. And I want you to look at Grant when we get there. Tell me if his liver is intact. I hope so. I would prefer he kept drinking—he thinks better when he's drunk. I can tell when his letters are written under the influence—they're precise, to the point, clear, and beautiful to read.

After Sherman fell asleep Wrede stood on the foredeck and looked out to sea. Army life demanded a self-submission that did not come easily to him. Here he was, aboard this steamer with his medical instrument bag for luggage and the obligation to attend a general like some factotum.

It was difficult on this overcast night to see where sea and sky were different. Wrede Sartorius saw, as if reflected, his inherently bleak state of being. He smiled, a man who lived alone, his own mind his only companion. He had been in America for almost twenty years, but he felt no more settled here than he had in Europe. He was contemptuous of the army's Medical Department and no longer saw any reason to share his findings. The war was almost over. He was ready to resign his commission.

GENERAL GRANT'S RESIDENCE was not elaborate but well situated on the bank of the James River, with a view of the harbor. It was a place. It stood still. Sartorius found himself sitting in a tufted parlor chair with his knees together and his hands in his lap while Mrs. Grant sat opposite him and gallantly attempted to deal with his silences. Somewhere along the march, he supposed he had lost the talent for polite conversation. She was a charmingly homely woman, Mrs. Grant, a thoughtful hostess, and he appreciated her effort to entertain him while

her husband and General Sherman were se-
cluded. But she did ask him his advice about
Ulysses, who was having some trouble with his
back. Then she herself admitted to some difficulty breathing when walking up a stairs.

Grant, when he appeared with Sherman,
was almost shockingly unprepossessing—rather
short, stocky, brown beard of a thick texture, a
quiet man clearly not interested in making any
kind of impression, unlike Sherman, who didn't
seem to be able to stop talking. Grant's color
was good, and his eyes only slightly bloodshot.

Wrede was included in the luncheon, an af-
fair of about twelve, mostly Army of the Potomac staff, with Mrs. Grant at one end of the
table and the General at the other. His tunic unbuttoned, Grant sat slumped in his chair, not
eating very much, nor drinking anything but
water. Uley, Mrs. Grant called to him, Dr. Sartorius has a liniment for your back, if you would
consider it. I think that is so very kind of him,
don't you?

After lunch everyone stood up from the
table and Wrede didn't know what to do when
Grant and Sherman walked out of the room and
made to leave the house, but Sherman came
back and beckoned to him, and he joined the
two generals as they strode down to the wharf
and went aboard the **River Queen**, a large white

steamer with an American flag flying at the stern. After the bright light of day, Wrede needed a moment to acclimate himself to the dim light of the aftercabin, where a tall man had risen from his chair to receive them. He had the weak, hopeful smile of the sick, a head of wildly unmanageable hair, he wore a shawl over his shoulders and house slippers, and Wrede Sartorius realized with a shock, this was not the resolute, visionary leader of the country whose portrait photographs were seen everywhere in the Union. This was someone eaten away by life, with eyes pained and a physiognomy almost sepulchral, but nevertheless, still unmistakably, the President of the United States.

After these many months of nomadic life in the Southern lowlands, Wrede could not quite accept his proximity to Abraham Lincoln. The real presence and the mythic office did not converge. The one was here in a small space, the other unlocatable anywhere save in one's own mind. Lincoln's conversation was deferential, too much so. You could not imagine any European leader appearing this self-deprecatory before underlings. The President at moments had about him the quality of an elderly woman, fearful of war and despairing of its ever ending. General Sherman, he said, are you sure your army is in good hands while you're away? Why,

Mr. President, General Schofield is in command while I'm gone who is a most able officer. Yes, Lincoln said, I'm sure he is. But we'll have our little talk and we won't keep you.

Sherman was ready to speak of the war as if it were over. He thought that, for the peacetime regular army, new regiments should not be commissioned but, rather, that existing regiments should be replenished from the ranks. Ah, General Sherman, Lincoln said with a faint smile, so you think we have a future? Sherman, humorless in this situation, replied, General Grant will agree with me that with one more good battle the war will be won. One more battle, said Lincoln. How many would that make, now? I think I have lost count, he said, bowing his head and closing his eyes.

General Grant asked after Mrs. Lincoln, and the President excused himself for a moment to summon her, at which point Grant came over to Sartorius. The President appears to me to have grown older by ten years. What do you have in the nature of a nostrum to brighten him up? Do you have anything? It is hard for all of us, but we are in the field. He can only wait on our news, sitting in Washington without the hell-may-care that comes from a good battle.

Before Wrede could reply, the President returned and announced that Mrs. Lincoln was not feeling well and had asked to be excused. The President's heavy-lidded eyes suddenly widened with an alarmingly self-revealing glance directed at Sartorius. An embarrassed silence ensued.

At this point the President and his generals retired to another cabin. Sartorius paced about and tried not to interpret the sound of their conversation as it drifted through the wall. He did not hear the actual words but the voices—the baritone murmurs of the President, the occasional gruff utterance of Grant, and the louder exclamations of Sherman, who sounded the upstart assuring his elders that he had everything in hand.

Finally the cabin door opened and Sartorius, standing upon their return, was able to see now how tall the President was. His head almost brushed the cabin ceiling. He had enormous hands and large, ungainly feet, and the wrist where his shirtsleeve was pulled back showed curled black hair. The long head was in proportion to the size of the man, but intensifying of his features, so that there was a sort of ugly beauty to him, with his wide mouth, deeply lined at the corners, a prominent nose, long ears, and eyes that seemed any moment about to disappear under his drooping eyelids. Sartorius thought the President's physiognomy could suggest some sort of hereditary condition, a syndrome of overdeveloped extremities and rude features. Premature aging might also be a characteristic. That would explain the terribly careworn appearance, the sorrows of office amplified by the disease.

What is most important, the President was saying, by way of conclusion, is that we not confront them with terms so severe that the war will continue in their hearts. We want the insurgents to regain themselves as Americans.

At this moment Mrs. Lincoln appeared, after all, a stout woman with her hair tightly bound to frame a round face, and eyes filled with undifferentiated suspicion. She seemed barely conscious of the visiting generals, to say nothing of Wrede, but went right to her husband and spoke to him of some later plan for the day as if nobody else were present. Then, frowning in response to some invisible disturbance, she departed as suddenly as she had arrived, the cabin door left open behind her, which Lincoln moved to close.

The generals, who had risen to greet her, could only think to resume their conversation.

Wrede was startled to find the President looming up. The odd exhilaration one felt in being directly addressed by Mr. Lincoln made it almost impossible actually to attend to what he was saying. One had to not look at him in order to listen. General Sherman tells me you are the best he has, the President said. You know, Colonel, this war has been as hard on Mrs. Lincoln as on the longest-serving battle-worn soldier. I do worry about her nerves. I sometimes wish she could have the advantage of the latest medical thinking, the same that is available to any wounded private in our military hospitals.

It was only a few minutes later, as Wrede Sartorius accompanied General Sherman to the steamer waiting for the return voyage, that he was made to understand of what a presidential wish consisted. I'm sorry, Colonel, Sherman said, but you're off the march. You are reassigned to the Surgeon General's office in Washington. You will embark with the President's party.

Sherman made to go aboard but turned back. There can be tragic incongruities in a man's life, he said. And so a great national leader suffers marriage to a disagreeable neurasthenic. They did lose a son. But so did I, so did General Hardee. All our Willies are gone. Yet my wife, Ellen, is steady as a rock. She does not plague me with her fears and suspicions while I attend to the national crisis. I will have your things sent to you. Good luck, Sherman said, and ran up the gangplank.

IN CITY POINT, Sartorius bought some clothes and a bag to put them in and repaired to the **River Queen** for the trip to Washington. He had to accept his situation, there was nothing else for it. Mr. Lincoln may be under an illusion about the quality of care in army hospitals, he thought. If so, it is his only illusion.

I have no nostrums—none. I have a few herbs, and potions, and a saw to cut off limbs.

He could not stop thinking of the President. Something of his feeling was turning to awe. In retrospect, Mr. Lincoln's humility, which Wrede had descried as weakness, now seemed to have been like a favor to his guests, that they would not see the darkling plain where he dwelled. Perhaps his agony was where his public and private beings converged. Wrede lingered on the dock. The moral capacity of the President made it difficult to be in his company. To explain how bad he looked, the public care on his brow, you would have to account for more than an inherited syndrome. A proper diagnosis was not in the realm of science. His affliction might, after all, be the wounds of the war he'd gathered into himself, the amassed miseries of this torn-apart country made incarnate.

Wrede, who had attended every kind of battle death, could not recall having ever before felt this sad for another human being. He stood on the dock, not wanting to go on board. Life seemed to him terribly ominous at this moment.

IX

WHEN THE LOCOMOTIVES SCREECHED INTO the Goldsboro junction railroad yards, the earsplitting sounds were heard as a fanfare. Lines formed before the commands were given. Soon the soldiers were showing one another their sparkling new blue tunics and trousers. They marveled at the repeater rifles that came out of the crates oiled and gleaming. They clumped around delightedly in their thick-soled boots. Their rags and worn shoes were everywhere consigned to little celebratory fires. The bandsmen had new skins for their drums, new reeds for their clarinets, and the Quartermaster General was everywhere praised as the finest officer in the army. Mail had arrived, too, and allotments from the paymaster, and with the weeks of camp rest, and the refitting, and the mail from home, and their pay in their pockets, the ninety thousand men who moved out of

Goldsboro punctually on April 10th were re-
freshed, replenished, and ready to end the war.

Unwinding from its encampments, the
army slowly extended itself in a forty-mile-wide
swath along the Neuse River, and on roads that
cut through rich acres of young green corn.
Down the line to the lumbering wagon trains
came the news that Lee had been driven from
Petersburg and Richmond. That would account
for the cheers that Stephen and Pearl had heard
floating back to them over the hills. Now the intent of the march was simplicity itself. There
would be no great wheel to the northeast and
Richmond. It was on to Raleigh and the Reb
army of General Johnston.

Stephen and Pearl were too unsettled to
share the prevailing mood. When Dr. Sartorius
had not returned, another colonel from the
Medical Department had merged the surgery
with his own. Stephen having no credential as
an army nurse, was ordered to return to his orig-
inal regiment. Pearl being a civilian volunteer,
was told she was not needed and to go home,
wherever that was supposed to be. Pearl was
frightened, but Stephen said to sit tight, and so
they had ignored the orders. Stephen knew
about the army as she did not. He knew that,
given the turmoil of the refitting of the troops
and the administrative reorganization General

Sherman had implemented, there would be enough confusion for them to wait things out and find a place for themselves in the march. This was particularly necessary, because Calvin Harper was in their charge. When a detail from the Medical Department removed the two ambulances and one supply wagon assigned to Sartorius, Stephen had asked the lieutenant in command what to do about the black man standing there with his eyes bandaged. He's all yours, son, the lieutenant said. That was hardly enough to relax their vigil. Another lieutenant, or captain or general, might come by with a different idea. Of course Calvin had told them the whole story. Pearl nearly wept that this man who so loved taking picture photos might never see again. Dr. Sartorius had said that was possible. And not an hour passed when Calvin Harper didn't lift up the bottom of his bandage to find out if his eyes were any better. I can see light, is all. Not anything but light. The boy David watched him closely, and it was his own idea to hold Calvin's hand so that he could move about without hurting himself.

While it was true that Calvin Harper had warned General Sherman and, more coherently, Colonel Teack, that the man behind the camera was a Rebel soldier, he knew the top general of the army, with everything he had to do, would never be bothered to depose, and that the Colonel, with a wound of his own, was unlikely to be a sympathetic witness. My only chance, Calvin said to them, is that I am a Negro and with everything else going on they will forget about such small potatoes. That's my only chance.

Stephen thought that was probably right. It was a multitude, this army, and its war was winding down fast in a way that loosened military discipline. The generals, in anticipation, had built themselves a new bureaucracy in hopes of controlling things. The right wing was now the Army of the Tennessee, the left the Army of Georgia, and that new column from the coast was the Army of Ohio. What did it all mean? There were corps, divisions, brigades, detachments, now battle flagged and distinguished from one another for administrative purposes that escaped the ordinary foot soldier plodding along under the sun. Stephen didn't even know if his old regiment was still the 102nd New York. You could go for miles without seeing an end to the procession of troops and horses and wagons. An eagle aloft in the April winds high over the landscape would only see something iridescently blue and side-winding that looked like the floodplain of a river. Stephen proposed to float on this the Josiah Culp U.S. Photography wagon and hope that as he sat up on the driver's box his fresh blue uniform would be all the credential needed.

The only problem was Bert.

THEY HAD TAKEN a place toward the rear of the wagon train, so many miles behind the advance corps that they couldn't hear the usual sound of skirmishing as the Rebel cavalry pecked away and fell back and pecked away. There was only the April breeze and the creak of the wagons and the steady clopping of the hoofs on the hard dirt road. But Bert the mule did not like walking directly behind one wagon and in front of another. He kept balking and holding things up behind him. He kept trying to get out of the procession and into the cornfields. When cavalry galloped by too close alongside the road, Bert raised his head and showed his teeth and brayed.

This mule of yours, Stephen called back to the wagon tent. He is not enjoying the trip.

That's Bert for you, Calvin said. He always did have a mind of his own. He is like an old friend to me. You let me talk to him a minute and see what I can do.

That is not a good idea, Stephen said. I think you'd better stay under wraps there.

A while later, they came to a stream where the bridge was blown and the engineers had had to put down their pontoons. The current was swift and the pontoons sashayed a bit, and Bert, not liking the hollow sound of his own hoofs, almost directed himself and the Josiah Culp U.S. Photography contingent into the water.

Stephen got him across but immediately took the wagon out of the line and stood with Bert under a pine tree.

Pearl hopped down from the wagon. What we going to do?

We'll wait. They'll have their led horses and mules coming along. We'll trade this creature for an army mule.

Who would want him?

Then I'll try to cadge one however I can.

You need to buy it, Pearl said. No one make you a gift of a good army mule.

They looked at each other. Stephen had not gone to collect his pay. It was the sure way to end up back in his regiment.

Pearl took her knotted handkerchief with the double eagle out of her pocket.

No, listen, Stephen said. You gave away the other one.

Don't matter. Calvin, she called, where you say you live?

Baltimore, came the reply.

We gettin a new mule, Calvin. This one of yours won't ever see Baltimore.

There was a long silence. O.K., Calvin said.

BOBBY BRASIL, WITH the advance in the town of Smithfield, found himself under fire from Rebs. Muzzle flashes came from warehouses and second-story windows. One Reb was firing from the bell tower of a church. Brasil turned a corner and down the street saw a barricade and ducked back just in time. A shell burst right where he'd been, and when the smoke cleared the street was cratered. He'd been made a sergeant for having outlived two predecessors. His platoon were upstate farm boys. They crouched down in the shelter of an alley in complete bewilderment. War was supposed to be fought from dirt pits and behind trees, across rivers, and in swamps. Not down streets. Not from building to building. You yokels are lucky, he assured them. Bobby J. Brasil has been a street fighter since the day he first walked. He is a terror of the Five Points, and the scourge of Centre Street. It's about time this war became civilized.

Leading his men down the alley, he brought them into an area of trash yards and outhouses. They climbed over wood fences, broke open the back door of an empty hardware store, and came out the front door, having turned the barricade. They flung themselves down on the porch and commenced firing. Before the Rebs knew what was happening they were shot down, a good half dozen of them, including the two artillerymen manning the Parrot gun. The barricade taken, Brasil and his men received the salutes of cavalrymen riding past.

By the time they had advanced to the town square, bluecoats were pouring in from all directions. Smithfield was taken. The men gave a cheer, and after twenty minutes of milling about they fell in again to continue the march.

AT THE WEST end of town the Rebs had burned the bridge across the Neuse River. The march was halted, and the men sat down on the hillside. The upstate yokels smoked their pipes, and Brasil lay with his hands behind his head and stared at the sky while the engineers brought up their pontoons. Brasil was beginning to enjoy his command even if it was this hapless bunch of nine Dutchmen as he suffered now. This truth might have embarrassed him even a month ago, but he had to acknowledge that he had become a good soldier. From nowhere, it seemed, he had developed a sense of responsibility. His idea of army life was no longer entirely personal, no

longer just a matter of looking out for himself in
any and all situations. He chuckled, thinking
what his da' would say or his uncles, the Brasils
being a family of pure spitting copperheads. But
an army was an interesting thing and he was beginning to take pride in it, as if it in some way
belonged to him, or he to it. He thought he
could do well enough running a company or
even a regiment. He knew that only West Point-
ers became generals, but there was a lot more to
an army than its generals.

When the bridge was across, the marchers
continued down the road to Raleigh. They
passed burned-out farmhouses, crops that had
been trampled. Children barefoot and half
dressed, with their thumbs in their mouths,
stared at the soldiers from porch shacks. In the
fields well back from the road was the occasional
plantation, shuttered and with no sign of life.
All along the march, black people came down to
the road to walk along with the troops and
dance and shout and praise God.

Brasil realized that he was happy. He felt accomplished—never before in life had his rebel-
lious nature rewarded him with that feeling.

An early camp was made in the meadows
about ten miles east of Raleigh. The rifles were
stacked, the tents pegged, and cook fires started.
Some of the men went down to the river to cool

their feet. Brasil was sitting before his pup tent thinking he might do the same when he heard a noise that he couldn't identify. It definitely wasn't gunfire, it was a harsh but smallish sound, like wind blowing through a window that was opened a crack. But then he did hear muskets going off, and he grabbed his rifle and stood up because it was louder now, and he could hear voices shouting, and some of the sound was almost in distinct shrieks, and it was getting closer, coming from the east back toward Smithfield where most of the army still sat. All the troops in his company were on their feet. Some came running up from the river, and everyone was asking everyone else what in hell was going on. And then they heard horns blowing, the regimental band tubas humphing and the trumpets pealing, and it was nothing like music, everything was going crazy, those were tin cups beating against tin plates, and it seemed everyone in the army knew what had happened except Bobby Brasil, until a cavalry officer came riding through, waving his hat, rearing his horse, circling, and yelling Hazoo! like a maniac, and then a couple more just like him, completely lacking in the dignity of their rank, Brasil thought, until he heard the actual words, or put them together from all the yelps and hats flying into the air, and idiot soldiers dancing with one another, and it was now become like a great hoarse male chorus echoing over the hills, with muskets shooting into the sky like firecrackers and the whole Army of the West in voice sounding the ground up through his feet like a cathedral organ in deep basso tones as if it was even God joining in celebrating the surrender. Because that's what it was: Lee had surrendered, and it was over, the damn war was over! The roar was enough to scare the birds out of the trees, it was enough to scare the rabbits into their holes, the foxes into their dens, and the Rebs into their cups. Brasil sank to the ground in the cross-legged Indian fashion and put his hands over his ears so he could hear himself thanking God for letting him survive. *I thank you, God, for allowing this city lad to survive*, he prayed, and, yes, he was joyful, of course, and someone came along and picked him up off the ground and soon he was yelping and dancing around with the rest of them, and joining his company commander, who was serving drinks out of his tent, and he lifted his tin cup to Father Abraham and again to Uncle Billy Sherman and again to the Grand Army of the Republic, while thinking under his grin that it was just his luck for the war to end when he had finally found something for himself that he could believe in.

—

SHERMAN'S SPECIAL FIELD Order announcing that General Lee had surrendered his entire army to General Grant on the 9th instant, at Appomattox Court House, Virginia, did not mean that there wasn't still work to be done. It remained to be seen if Joe Johnston would scatter his forces and bring on a protracted campaign—an endless march, as it were, to make this of Georgia and the Carolinas a mere prelude, with more and more of the country to be ravaged and left desolate. Glory to God and our country, Sherman had said in his message to the troops, and all honor to our comrades in arms. But he ordered Kilpatrick's cavalry to advance on Raleigh, and planned a southerly course for his infantry corps to prevent Johnston's run in that direction. While still in Smithfield, he received a trepidatious civilian delegation entrained from Raleigh to ask for the protection of their city. They were four shaken city fathers who had had to endure the brute obstructionism of Kilpatrick before he let them through. It was left to Sherman to comfort them and assure them that, as the war was all but over, the occupation of their city would be peaceful and the civil government would continue to discharge its duties. What the deuce is the matter with Kilpatrick? Sherman said afterward to his adjutant, Major Dayton. You'd think Kil doesn't want the war to end. But he laughed and rubbed his hands. And if the city fathers come out under a white flag, can Joe Johnston be far behind?

ON APRIL 13TH, Sherman entered Raleigh and, moving into the Governor's Mansion, wrote orders for column movements toward Asheville via Salisbury and Charlotte. Then he sat back and waited. Sure enough, the next day he received via Kilpatrick, encamped twenty-five miles to the west, a letter from General Johnston delivered under a flag of truce. Johnston wanted to discuss a cessation of hostilities. Sherman asked Moses Brown for a schooner of brandy, lit a cigar, and dictated a reply to Major Dayton that gave him what he later said was the most pleasurable letter-writing experience of his life.

The agreement was to suspend all military movements, the armies to remain in place, while the two generals met on the road between the Union advance at Durham and the Confederate rear at Hillsboro. Sherman undertook to spiff up for the occasion, brushing himself off and allowing Moses Brown to polish his boots and supply him with a fresh shirt. On April 17th, at eight o'clock in the morning, as he was about to board his private train to Durham, the telegraph operator ran down from his office above the depot with a wire from Secretary Stanton, in Washington. It was still nothing but dots and dashes, but if the General held the train for a few minutes he could have it in English.

Sherman paced back and forth in the waiting room, his elation waning with every passing moment. He hadn't liked the look on the operator's face. By the time the telegram was handed to him, his mood had darkened into a presentiment. I somehow knew, he later wrote his wife. Stanton was always the bearer of bad tidings.

President Lincoln had been murdered. An assassin had come up behind him in his box at the theater and fired a pistol ball into his brain. Secretary of State Seward had been badly injured in a separate attack. The conspirators were of unknown number, and presumably General Grant and himself were also designated for assassination. I beseech you, Stanton wrote, to be more heedful than Mr. Lincoln of such knowledge.

Sherman folded the pages and slipped them into his pocket. Too late, Stanton, he thought. They've already made their attempt on me. They missed. Better if they hadn't. Better if they had missed the President and gotten Sherman.

—

THE TELEGRAPH OPERATOR was still standing there. Sherman said, Has anyone seen this besides yourself? No, sir, the man said. On no account, said Sherman, are you to speak of this or allude to it or even look as if you knew of its contents—to anyone, do you understand? I do, yes, the operator said. You are a resident of this city, are you not? If the word gets out before I get back, if the army learns of it, the consequences to this city are not to be imagined. I understand, General, the operator said. You don't have to draw a picture.

At Durham Station Sherman was met by Kilpatrick, given a horse, and with a platoon of cavalry in escort, and following a single rider with a white flag, he proceeded down the road toward Hillsboro. It had rained the night before and the fields were fresh-smelling and the roadside grass was dappled with raindrops that shone and sparkled in the sun. Lilacs were in bloom, and the scent of pine trees proposed a land cleansed of blood and war. Sherman saw approaching down the road a mirror image of his own party, the two white flags bobbing toward each other. And there was Joe Johnston, lifting his hat, and so I will as well.

The two generals sat alone in a small farmhouse while their officers remained outside and the owner retreated to his barn, assuring his anxious wife and their four small children that someday their house would be a museum and tourists would flock in to see where the end of the war was negotiated.

Johnston, an older man with a silver-white mustache and goatee and an impeccably fitted smart gray uniform, was clearly shocked when Sherman handed him the telegram. Beads of sweat appeared on his forehead. Surely, he muttered, you do not charge this heinous crime to the Confederate government. Never to you, sir, Sherman said, nor to General Lee. But of Jefferson Davis, and men of that stripe, I would not say as much. This is a disgrace to the age, Johnston said. I have always recognized in President Lincoln a man of compassion and forbearance. That if the war ended badly for us, he would mete out terms that were just and charitable.

The two generals sat for a while in silence. This makes everything so much more difficult for you, Johnston said. For both of us, Sherman replied. At that moment he recognized in Joe Johnston the West Point training that he felt as well brimming in himself, and that had been in him all along after these many years in the army without his having given it a thought. The way the man sat a chair, his diction, the gravity of bearing instilled only in those whose responsibilities will be of a general officer—all of it harked back to the lectures, the precision marching, the courses in tactics, the studies of foreign wars, and the memorization of Homeric verses. Suddenly, Sherman felt a great sympathy for his enemy, this wily old bird with the small bright eyes and a nose like a grosbeak's. There was a bond of recognition here, they were of the same school. They were both damned fine soldiers. He felt more trusting of this general, an enemy, than he was of his superiors in Washington—Stanton, Andrew Johnson the presumed new president, the whole cabal of Washington politicians who aroused in him, at best, a wariness of their intentions.

Now that Lee has surrendered, Sherman said with as much gentleness as he could muster, you can do the same with honor and propriety. The other course is not feasible, is it? You do not have that much left with which to oppose my army.

Johnston passed his hand over his eyes. Yes, he said, to continue would be not war but murder.

They were still to get down to business. But Sherman was exultant, full of the generosity of the victor. He took up the late President's charity and forbearance as if it had been deeded in a will. He'd always said that as relentless as he had to be in war, he would be that assiduous a friend when the South laid down its arms. And so, little by little, during this conversation and the ones that followed, he would be not quite aware, in his exhilaration, of giving more to Johnston than Grant had given to Lee. The agreement hashed out would be angrily rescinded in Washington, and Grant himself would have to come to North Carolina to put things right. Now, however, Sherman was made only rapt by the negotiations. The issues were many. What other Southern armies deployed in Alabama, Louisiana, and Texas could be included in Johnston's surrender? What weapons would officers and men be allowed to keep? What warranties were required for the restoration of citizenship? What would be the legal property rights of the surrendering insurgents? What rations could be offered the Confederate veterans so that they would not ravage the countryside on their way home? And Jefferson Davis and his cabinet? Would they be given amnesty?

And so the war had come down to words. It was fought now in terminology across a table. It was contested in sentences. Entrenchments and assaults, drum taps and bugle calls, marches, ambushes, burnings, and pitched battles were transmogrified into nouns and verbs. It is all turned very quiet, Sherman said to Johnston, who, not quite understanding, lifted his head to listen.

No cannonball or canister but has become the language here spoken, the words written down, Sherman thought. Language is war by other means.

ONLY AFTERWARD, IN the late night, as Sherman sat by the hearth in the billet provided him, did he feel a peculiar envy for Joe Johnston and the South he represented. How unsettling. In one hand Sherman held his cigar, in the other his schooner of brandy. He stared into the fire. There was this about the end of a war, that once the cheering was over, you were of two minds. Yes, your cause was just. Yes, you could drink your flagon of pride. But victory was a shadowed, ambiguous thing. I will go on wondering about my actions. Whereas General Johnston and his colleagues of the unjust cause, now embittered and awash in defeat, will have sublimed to a righteously aggrieved state that would empower them for a century.

AFTER INFORMING HIS generals of the death of the President, and ordering certain precautionary measures, Sherman let the word out in a Special Field Order to the troops: The general commanding announces with pain and sorrow that on the evening of the 14th instant, at the theater in Washington City, his Excellency the

President of the United States, Mr. Lincoln, was assassinated by one who uttered the state motto of Virginia. As he had anticipated, a great cry of grief and anger arose in their camps. Soon thousands of men, undirected, and raging in their disorder, not an army now but in the technical state of an uprising, advanced on Raleigh with the intent of burning it to the ground. They found themselves a rabble confronted by the lines of the Fifteenth Corps under General John Logan, the streets blocked with artillery, and the rows of bayonets of their own comrades fixed and pointing at them. Logan himself, riding a great stallion, roamed in front of the lines. Again and again, he ordered the men to return to their camps. He was not killed in Raleigh, Logan shouted. Our President was not murdered by anyone living in this city. No one here did this, return now to camp! Turn around, turn around, I say!

As quickly as the mass mind had changed from jubilation at Lee's surrender to grief and a roaring anger, it now dissolved almost as quickly into a muttering and shamed calm, as the men slowly dispersed and turned back. The situation still tense, Sherman had guards posted about the camps and patrolling the streets of the city.

—

WHEN HE REACHED Washington, Wrede Sartorius had reported to the Surgeon General's office and was assigned to the U.S. Army General Hospital. Installed in his own operating room and ward, with an assistant surgeon and a staff of army nurses, he was soon engaged in the same work he'd performed as a regimental surgeon in the field. Here, though, a greater number of the crises were postoperative, where additional surgery had to be performed in the cutting away of gangrenous tissue, or the removal of limbs that had failed of resection. And proportionately more of the patients, veterans of Grant's Army of the Potomac, were suffering miasmatic disorders, eruptive fevers, or degenerative social diseases than he had seen in Sherman's army.

For almost two weeks Sartorius did not hear a word from the White House, and he was rather relieved. Then, in the early evening of April 14th, he received a visit from a White House aide: Would Colonel Sartorius join the President and Mrs. Lincoln at the theater this evening. That very afternoon there had been an influx of patients transferred from one of Grant's field hospitals. These were men wounded, sadly, in the last skirmishes with Lee's army. Many of them had been ill served in the field hospitals and Sartorius, overwhelmed with work, and standing before the aide in his rubber apron smeared with blood, declined the invitation. The aide, a young lieutenant, confided that several people had already turned the President down, including the Grants, Secretary Stanton and his wife, and two or three other couples. I'm sorry, Sartorius said. Perhaps because it is Good Friday, the aide said as he left.

Later that night, while Sartorius was still at work, word came that the President had been shot. Sartorius and another doctor on duty quickly found a hansom and rushed to the scene. The President had been removed to a house across the street from the theater. He was lying diagonally across a bed that was too short for him, in a small bedroom and with several doctors, including the Surgeon General, already in attendance. One flickering gas lamp was all the light. Sartorius pushed his way in somewhat rudely and knelt to examine the wound, a small hole behind the left ear. Mrs. Lincoln sat at the side of the bed, holding the President's hands and weeping. A hand reached past Sartorius and lifted away a blood clot, not the first, that had formed at the wound. This and the mistaken application of brandy to the President's lips, causing him almost to choke, and the placing of hot-water bottles at his feet, and the keeping of charts recording his vital signs, were all that these many doctors in attendance were able to do.

The President's shirt had been removed. As Wrede knelt there, he observed spasmodic pectoral contractions causing pronation of the forearms, a cessation of breath, and then a forcible expiration immediately after. One pupil was concised to a pinpoint, the other widely dilated. Wrede stood and was suddenly enraged at the numbers of doctors in the small room. The President's breathing was becoming more labored. Mrs. Lincoln, hearing the rasp, screamed, Oh Abe, Abe, and she fell across the bed. Wrede said loudly to the hushed assemblage, He is finished, he will not last the hour. Your medicine is useless. You should all get out. Leave him alone—he does not need an audience for his death. And, unhearing of the shocked responses of his colleagues, Wrede pushed his way past them down the hall to the front door, and strode off down the street. He had no idea where he was going. The night air was wet, the gas lamps flaring and dimming in the fog.

WHEN COLONEL TEACK learned of the death of the President, he decided it could be nothing less than a conspiracy if both Mr. Lincoln and General Sherman were in the same brief time tracked for assassination. The Reb had not been interrogated before he was put before a firing squad, and that was another mistake of the General's. You find out everything you can when something like that happens. You want to know if it's just some Rebel maniac or if there are orders behind him. It had been a shrewd thing, his coming in as a certified photographer.

Teack got up out of his bed, and though still in pain, and with a late-developing weakness in one of his arms, he met with the captain of the provost guard and ordered the darkie who worked for the photographer to be brought before him.

We don't know where the darkie is, the provost captain said. We never had our hands on him. He was given to Medical.

Why?

His own man shot him, sir. The doctor has to release him before we can put him before a board.

Well, find the doctor!

I wish we could. Colonel Sartorius is gone. His surgery is reassigned.

I don't like this, Teack said. I don't like this at all. The darkie has to be somewhere. And they had a damn wagon—where's that at?

Sir, in all the confusion—

He said something to me, he knew what

was happening, Colonel Teack said. I'll find him. You say he's wounded. How far could he have gotten? I'll ride out myself if I have to.

AS THE NEGOTIATIONS went on, with General Grant now quietly arrived in Raleigh to redraft the too generous terms Sherman had written up—there was nothing, for example, requiring the Rebs to abide by Emancipation—it was apparent that the truce might expire before an agreement could be hammered out, and so the troops of both sides drifted into a peace of their own making. Nobody wanted to march back into the South, and the Confederate rank and file had long since been aware that their cause was lost. Discipline became slack, and in some of the camps between Raleigh and Durham Station the combatants actually began to fraternize, ragged Reb soldiers drifting in, unarmed, and sitting about the campfires with their Union counterparts. Rations were meager in the Johnston army and the Reb boys were hungry, and many of the Union soldiers shared their dinners. It was possible also for blue and gray to talk about the battles they had fought as something they had done together, something shared.

Stephen Walsh saw all this as advantageous to the plan he and Pearl and Calvin had worked out. In preparation for their trip north, he'd become something of a forager, riding the new mule bareback every day the miles into the advance camps and drawing rations, as if entitled, from the various commissary tents. Nobody asked questions, such was the mass state of mind as it was slowly losing its military pinnings. The warm weather helped, too. Desertion was casual and out in the open on the Confederate side, where the boys were not that far from home. There was a constant trickle of them along the roads. Some Unions, too, in anticipation of a glorious, triumphal march in the nation's capital, had taken it upon themselves quietly to begin the trek there, the word having gotten out which corps were to be so honored and which were to stay to garrison what was now called the Department of North Carolina. All of this seemed to be almost complicit with the ordinary daily routines of parade and drill, even the field officers yawning at the habitual duties. There was, overall, a lassitude creeping up from the bottom ranks—though it had not yet reached the level of the general officers or their staffs, where the planning continued as if the war would, and the back-and-forth between the ungrateful sentiments of Washington and the put-upon feelings of Sherman loyalists were a source of tension not unlike that of actual combat.

Over several days Stephen was able to bring back to the wagon sacks of cornmeal, rice, coffee, dried peas, boxes of hardtack, cans of sorghum, and packs of salt pork, but also the trash he found on the road that he thought would be useful—discarded tent sides, a shovel, eating utensils, blankets, and even an old Springfield rifle that he found half buried in a ditch.

It was Pearl who had one evening seen an officer she recognized from when she was traveling as General Sherman's drummer boy. That was that tall colonel of his, cantering his horse along the wagon train as if looking for something. So they were now being especially careful. The half-tents were tied to hang over the wagon sides so that the Josiah Culp sign could not be seen. Stephen took a position toward the back end of the wagon train in sight of the Negro refugees camped there. It was not as big a community as once followed the march, but it was large enough for Calvin Harper to get lost in.

Each morning Pearl in her nurse's uniform went to Calvin and washed and redressed his eyes with the salve Dr. Sartorius had prescribed. He was hunkering down with a group of women and children who attended to every move Pearl made. The first day or two the women held themselves aloof from the white lady but they were finally impressed by her daily visit and the care with which she was treating Calvin Harper. She brought rations, too, for them to share, and they thanked her kindly.

And how are y'all this morning, Pearl would say, and everyone would affirm their well-being. And, Calvin, how you farin? Calvin, blinking in the light with the bandage off, would say, I think a little better thank you, Miss Pearl.

The only thing Pearl didn't like was that little David had chosen to stay with Calvin. The two were inseparable. For reasons she didn't analyze, she was put out by the boy's having attached himself in this way, though she supposed it was good there were other children here for him to play with. Well, David, she said one morning, I see you got you some friends. Yes'm, David said. Not yes'm, Pearl scolded, not yes'm, David. Just yes. Say it. And when he did, slightly puzzled, she said, And from now on that's what you say to answer a question. Not yes'm or no'm but yes or no—two clear words like that, you hear? Yes'm, David replied, and everyone laughed, even Pearl. She was embarrassed that she had suddenly flared up so.

STEPHEN WAS GOING about the preparations so patiently, in his fashion, that Pearl thought they would never be on their way. But he was refitting the struts that held up the canvas over the wagon bed and making the canvas taut, so that there would be more room inside for everything and everyone, and so that it would look like a well-maintained means of travel. For Calvin thought en route they could take pictures again and make a little money that way.

He can't see to make a picture, Pearl said as she watched Stephen work.

He can teach us, if it comes to that. Everything it needs is here. All his trays and plates and chemicals. The camera is nicked a bit, is all.

Calvin says it was our Colonel-doctor who stowed it back in the wagon when he treated him out by the statehouse steps. He was kind underneath, wasn't he? Though he never said much. Do this, hold that. But we did. And then he leaves without sayin a word. He just sets off.

Reassignment, Stephen said.

Yes, reassignment, but what does that mean 'cept he's gone. I felt safe with him, didn't you?

You are safe with me, Stephen said, and that was the end of that conversation. She knew how much he looked up to the doctor. But it wasn't something he cared to talk about.

PEARL WAS SILENT for a while. She was listening to the birds in the field. She watched the redwing blackbirds skimming along the furrows, lighting on the bushes.

That David, she said. He don't care for me no more. It's Calvin he likes. Takes him by the hand everywhere, won't leave his side. Don't a child need mothering?

Stephen jumped down from the wagon bed. Calvin is a Negro.

I'm a Negro!

Stephen shook his head. No, Pearl, with skin as white as a carnation, not in that boy's eyes.

He touched her face and brushed the tears. Nothing stays the same, he said. Not David, not Sartorius, not the army on the march, not the land it trods, not the living, and not even the dead. It's always now, Stephen said with a sad smile for poor Albion Simms.

AND THEN A few days later it was time to leave. Stephen came riding back from Raleigh. The end of the war was official and Generals Grant and Sherman were reviewing the troops. Pearl could hear the band music faintly even at this distance. They will be occupied for a while with the peace, Stephen said. He took off his tunic and cap and put on a plain jacket he had found in Mr. Josiah Culp's costume pile.

They turned out of the road, and Stephen directed the mule to the campsite of the black folks and they picked up Calvin and the boy, and said their goodbyes. We will have at least a day's start, Stephen said to Pearl. We are going due east, back through Goldsboro and to the coast. They will march the straight line to Richmond and Washington. We will be out of their way, and they out of ours.

SHERMAN, STANDING BESIDE Grant on a platform with the American flag, felt the presence of the man. Grant was shorter than he was, but perhaps sturdier on his feet for that. He seemed to see something in the parade marchers of the Seventeenth Corps that made you look to see what it was. And they were Sherman's men!

He had secret thoughts, Grant, you always felt that about him. Such private feelings of presumed depth that an ordinary mortal could only aspire to. Sherman had a respect for Grant akin to worship, but there was that assured thing about the man, that his private mind harbored no ill intent. He had no guile and no self-interest in this war, and that's what was so unsettling.

The men seemed to know of this goodness

as well, of this steady state of the man's mind, and they marched by with a serious face, and even somewhat less proud than usual of their shabby grooming and dusty uniforms. What rose up from their ranks was awe.

And the terms of surrender after Grant had arrived to define them were simplicity itself. All acts of war by soldiers under Johnston's command were to cease. All arms to be delivered to ordnance officers of the U.S. Army. Rolls to be entered of officers and men, and each one to obligate himself in writing not to take up arms against the Government of the United States. Side arms of officers and their private horses and baggage to be retained by them. Their written obligations done, all officers and men permitted to return to their homes. And Johnston and he had signed it, and with that penmanship the four-year war was over.

My not having rested my own perhaps overreaching negotiations with those clear, simple points has got me into trouble, given my leg to that political dog Stanton, who has published intimations that by my generosity to the Southies I may have been intending myself to overthrow the United States government with my army. Such is the thanks I get for my lifelong service to this republic. And now everything of the past four years has come down to a parade, as it will in Washington. We have been but marching to a politician's parade.

Before I go up there, I want to find a cool grove of pine trees one more time. Sherman's Special Field Order to himself: You are to go into the forest and pitch your tent, and light your fire and cook your dinner and go to sleep on the hard ground under the stars and wake at dawn with the silly birds in time to hear reveille. Then you may journey to Washington and stand for the parade.

Though this march is done, and well accomplished, I think of it now, God help me, with longing—not for its blood and death but for the bestowal of meaning to the very ground trod upon, how it made every field and swamp and river and road into something of moral consequence, whereas now, as the march dissolves so does the meaning, the army strewing itself into the isolated intentions of diffuse private life, and the terrain thereby left blank and also diffuse, and ineffable, a thing once again, and victoriously, without reason, and, whether diurnally lit and darkened, or sere or fruitful, or raging or calm, completely insensible and without any purpose of its own.

And why is Grant so solemn today upon our great achievement, except he knows this unmeaning inhuman planet will need our warring imprint to give it value, and that our civil war, the devastating manufacture of the bones of our sons, is but a war after a war, a war before a war.

ON THE WAY, there was a discussion about the army mule, who as yet had no name. Calvin was loath to name him Bert. This one clopping along smartly is no Bert, Calvin said. He does what you ask. He has no character. Now, Bert he was smart. He wanted the good life for a mule, which was not necessarily what you wanted. He thought for himself, and if he did what you asked you knew it was by his leave or that he was going along for his own purposes.

Well, if we give this young one the name, Stephen said, maybe it will be inspiration for him, something to live up to. Bert the Second.

I hope not before we reach Baltimore, Calvin said.

They were making good time without trying to. The road was dry and beaten down hard by those thousands of army feet. At midday they turned off the road and went down the gentle slope of an untilled field, and found there a clear slow-moving stream, where the water divided on the rocks and boulders and met itself again in a determined way, like something with a mind. There was good shade under an oak tree, and Pearl put down a blanket for the midday meal of hardtack and salt pork and water from their canteens.

I am happy to be going home, Calvin said. He lifted the bandage over his eyes and said, You know, I really can see a little now—it is very much like a photograph beginning to come out in the developing tray. I see you in a grainy way, Miss Pearl. I see you, Corporal Walsh. And you, David, he said to the boy nestled in his lap, you are the easiest to see. He laughed.

Pearl took off her shoes and lay back in the grass and stretched. I feel free like never before, she said.

Calvin said, Culp and Harper, U.S. Army Photographers, has here in this wagon a precious store of army pictures. Mr. Josiah Culp and me, we were on the road for a good year. The pictures will bring in money besides being valuable in themselves for their history. And I am sure I will be busy taking portraits and carte de visites of the returning soldiers who will want one more picture of themselves in uniform before they take it off. I hope to make a good living. You are all welcome to join with me, he said after a moment. There could be enough for all of us.

Pearl had sat up. Stephen looked at her and cleared his throat, about to say something, but

Calvin had pressed on. You have saved my life, he said. Your doctor was the one who used this wagon for an ambulance to take me back to his surgery. He saved my camera and Mr. Culp's store of photos, and all I told him was my name and that I had tried to stop the shooting. And all of you have saved my life. I know you mean to go to New York City. But that is a long way from Baltimore and Baltimore is a long way from here, so maybe you would think again. Or maybe stay awhile with us, earn some money enough to ride the train up to New York and not worry about fodder for it.

Who is us? Pearl said.

Well, David and me and Jessie. She will love this boy.

David got up now and went to where the mule was grazing and patted its neck. Pearl watched him. Something on the ground caught his attention and he squatted down to look at it and then, with a twig, poke at it.

Jessie is your wife?

I am not the marrying kind. Jessie's my sister. She is a maiden lady who has no children of her own. But she sews up quilts that she sells, and teaches the Sunday school in our church. The children love Jessie.

CALVIN AND THE BOY both napped after lunch, and Pearl and Stephen walked downstream and found some stepping-stones to a big, wide rock in the center, and there they sat, Pearl with her skirt hiked up to her knees and her feet in the water.

Truth is, she said to Stephen, once I take that letter to the Lieutenant Clarke's mama and daddy at the Number 12 Washing-ton Square I will come out their door, and which way I go, the left or to the right, or down this street or down that street, it don't really matter 'cause I won't know where I am or what I want to do with my free life.

You will come with me, Stephen said.

And if I be white until I have my black baby? Then what will you do?

I will be its father, if I am its father.

She looked at him, startled, until she saw the grin on his face. Naturally you are its father—who else would I have for a husband? Pearl said. You bein silly now—this a serious matter.

I have the three hundred dollars in the bank from my enlistment, Stephen said. I have thought about this. I want to read the law.

And what will I do?

You will go to the public school and catch up quick as a flash with your mind. And later will go to medical college.

You work that out for me?

I saw you in the surgery. You are a natural at doctoring. Don't tell me you never thought of it.

I did until I 'membered I'm a nigger girl. You have a passel of plans for your three hundred dollars.

If they don't let girls in medical college you will be the first, because I will argue the case in court. Pearl looked at him and shook her head. All at once her tears began to flow. Stephen Walsh could bear it no longer. He wrapped her in his arms and kissed her on the lips and on the cheeks and on the eyes. Pearl was kissing him back and crying at the same time. They held each other.

If you want to take David with us, that is all right with me, Stephen whispered. He kissed her ear.

It different up there?

No.

You a crazy man, Stephen. You a soldier from the war but you don't know the fearful life.

I think I do, he said, Irish as I am.

They sat quietly, looking at the water. Birds flew past them, following the path of the stream.

If I live white, how free am I?

Freer than the other.

Free everywhere 'cept in my heart. Is that freer than my mama Nancy Wilkins?

You will have to let the world catch up to you.

When's that?

It may take some time.

She stood, and brushed her skirt. No, she said. He should go with Calvin and Jessie. Calvin didn't bother to ask, but that's the best thing for the chile. And we will write each other letters soon as he learns reading and writing.

LATER, BACK ON the road, the shadows began to lengthen as the afternoon wore on. The green of the land grew softer, and the road, in a slow descent, passed into a valley. And then there was a dark, thick grove of pine where some of the war had passed through. A boot lay in the pine needles, and the shreds of a discolored uniform. Behind a fallen log, a small pile of cartridge shells. There was still a scent of gunfire in the trees, and they were glad to come out into the sun again.

Acknowledgments

—

The author's heartfelt thanks to:

Daniel F. Roses, M.D., F.A.C.S.

Jules Leonard Whitehill Professor of Surgery

and Oncology

New York University Medical Center

Joseph T. Glatthar

Alan Stephenson Distinguished Professor of History

University of North Carolina at Chapel Hill

Marc K. Siegel, M.D.

Associate Professor

New York University School of Medicine

and

Kate Medina

Executive Editor

Random House

About the Author

E. L. DOCTOROW's work has been published in thirty languages. His novels include **City of God, Welcome to Hard Times, The Book of Daniel, Ragtime, Loon Lake, Lives of the Poets, World's Fair, Billy Bathgate,** and **The Waterworks.** Among his honors are the National Book Award, two National Book Critics Circle awards, the PEN/Faulkner Award, the Edith Wharton Citation for Fiction, the William Dean Howells Medal of the American Academy of Arts and Letters, and the presidentially conferred National Humanities Medal. He lives in New York.